Praise for *Godshot*

Long-listed for the 2020 Center for Fiction First Novel Prize

"[A] spirited debut."
—*The New York Times*

"Surreal . . . *Godshot* culminates in a dizzying depiction of childbirth—a true holy rite that instantly reveals the falseness of the rest."
—SAM SACKS, *The Wall Street Journal*

"[A] haunting debut . . . Bieker smartly writes through the lens of a teenager on the cusp of understanding the often fraught relationship between religion and sexuality . . . It's a timely and disturbing portrait of how easily men can take advantage of vulnerable women—and the consequences sink in more deeply with each page."
—ANNABEL GUTTERMAN, *Time*

"Drawn in brilliant, bizarre detail—baptism in warm soda, wisdom from romance novels—Lacey's twin crises of faith and femininity tangle powerfully. Fiercely written and endlessly readable, a novel like this is a godsend."
—MARY SOLLOSI, *Entertainment Weekly*

"You do not have to survive a cult or even have left a toxic environment to relate to Lacey May—*Godshot* is about the ways all women are under the patriarchy's thumb."
—DELFINA V. BARBIERO, *USA Today* (3 out of 4 stars)

"A nefarious religious cult right out of Gilead, a phone sex line, and a beautifully-rendered mother-daughter relationship—if you're not intrigued already, maybe there's no salvation for you. Think Maria Semple's *Where'd You Go Bernadette* meets Emma Cline's *The Girls*."

—*O, the Oprah Magazine*

"[A] breathtaking debut." —KEELY WEISS, *Harper's Bazaar*

"Godshot, from debut author Chelsea Bieker, is an unnerving tour de force. Exploring the gritty, confounding ways innocence—especially girlhood—clash with spirituality, family, love, and gender." —LAUREN PUCKETT, *Elle*

"*Godshot* is dark, suspenseful, and surprisingly funny."

—KATHERINE BARRETTE, *Cosmopolitan*

"Depicting the ravages of economic disaster and the cruelty desperate people will accept in return for promises of a better life, *Godshot* is about patriarchy, extremist religion and their result, misogyny and sexual violence. And yet, despite being distressing at times, the book leaves room for light and a twisted sort of humor—even as Peaches spirals into darkness."

—CHRIS BARTON, *Los Angeles Times*

"Bieker has written a debut that joins Emma Cline's *The Girls* and R.O. Kwon's *The Incendiaries* in exploring the uneasy intersection of repressive religious belief and burgeoning sexuality, but Bieker's exploration of the way that poverty and environmental ravishment also add to the subjugation of the female body adds more rich layers to this narrative . . . A dark, deft first novel about the trauma and resilience of both people and the land they inhabit."

—*Kirkus Reviews* (starred review)

"Bieker's debut novel is a vivid and cutting exploration of unconditional female love. It observes how mothers shape daughters, biological or otherwise, and how daughters must ultimately learn to mother themselves. Young readers will admire Lacy May's resilience, moxie, and ability to survive in a world she did not choose."

—*Booklist* (starred review)

"Lacey May's is an irresistible voice, part gullible believer, part whip-smart independent spirit who surprises at every turn."

—*Library Journal* (starred review)

"*Godshot* is a monumental exploration of faith, family and what it means to be a woman in a strange, cruel, wondrous world . . . Bieker has pulled off a stunning debut, revealing a deep-rooted talent that will, no doubt, bear more fruit." —*Shelf Awareness* (starred review)

"Stunning . . . In the rendering of loss, which occurs over and over in the body and the narrative, *Godshot* shines. It also glimmers in its hypnotic prose, in its use of humor and color and sensual detail and its unflinching portrayal of the ways people hurt each other, and how they show up for each other . . . *Godshot* brims with hope, even a deep sense of love and forgiveness. It beams through the edges as we root for Lacey in her tenacious search . . . *Godshot* is an utterly readable novel."

—SARAH NEILSON, *The Seattle Times*

"Bieker has a knack for coruscatingly describing humans at their most vulnerable . . . This multilayered debut is filled with moments that are starkly grim and intensely moving. Bieker proves her mettle as a writer in how she expresses, through her characters, the whole gamut of emotions from selfless love to bottomless grief. Ultimately, this story illustrates the resilience and strength required to be a woman in an unforgiving man's world."

—RABEEA SALEEM, *Chicago Review of Books*

"A spectacular novel . . . What follows is a gritty, gripping tale of girlhood, spirituality, and how salvation comes from the unlikeliest of place." —*Esquire*

"Glittery in an unexpected way." —*Glamour*

"It's a harrowing but elegantly wrought exploration of trauma and autonomy." —ARIANNA REBOLINI, *BuzzFeed*

"*Godshot* is a piercing debut novel filled with devastating imagery (sticky baptisms performed with soda instead of water) and a girl named Lacey May Herd who is brought up to believe that suffering brings you closer to God. When Lacey May is forced to live with her grandmother after her troubled mother abandons her, she must reckon with the pastor's grand plan for Peaches and the damaging ways we choose to satisfy our thirsts." —MARIS KRIEZMAN, *Vulture*

"A deliciously twisted California gothic tale . . . Bieker's writing is compelling and propulsive, illuminating the darkest corners of the sunniest state." —KRISTIN IVERSON, *Refinery29*

"*Godshot* distills the darkness, light, and wild courage that are so entwined and necessary in the process of becoming yourself. This coming of age story masterfully balances the particular obstacles that Lacey must face: an absent mother, a manipulative and domineering religious leader, the blind devotion of her peers, and lastly, her own gleaming will and desperation to do right by the land that she loves." —JULIA HASS, *Literary Hub*

"It's a literary masterpiece."

—ELIZABETH ENTENMAN, *HelloGiggles*

"A gothic phantasmagoria, Bieker's book explores the ways in which cultish devotion in times of ecological catastrophe can seemingly push groups of people towards a social apocalypse—a novel eerily pertinent in 2020." —*The Millions*, One of the Most Anticipated Books of the Year

"*Godshot* is a dazzling, darkly funny debut from a writer whose charm, wit, and blistering intelligence will scorch your heart. With unsentimental compassion and unprecedented style, Bieker steeps this brutal, harrowing story in hope. The prose shimmers and swerves—so full of gritty truths and resplendent beauty, I drenched every page in highlighter."

—KIMBERLY KING PARSONS, author of *Black Light*

"*Godshot* is wise, tough, electrifying, beautiful—every raw detail sings true. Chelsea Bieker writes about pain and resilience like nobody else." —LENI ZUMAS, author of *Red Clocks*

"Chelsea Bieker's *Godshot* is an absolute masterpiece. A truly epic journey through girlhood, divinity, and the blood that binds and divides us, it is a feminist magnum opus of this, or any, time. Bieker is a pitch-perfect ventriloquist of extraordinary talent and ferocity. Imagine if Annie Proulx wrote something like *White Oleander* crossed with *Geek Love* or *Cruddy*, and then add cults, God, motherhood, girlhood, class, deserts, witches, the divinity of women . . . Terrifying, resplendent, and profoundly moving, this book will leave you changed." —T KIRA MADDEN, author of *Long Live the Tribe of Fatherless Girls*

"I cried as I finished reading *Godshot*. It's a novel of rebirth: baptism and heartbreak, daughterhood and motherhood. Lacey May is a yearning, whip-smart, brokenhearted believer, and I miss her now that the novel has ended. Chelsea Bieker has written a wholly real and beautifully written coming-of-age tale that is sure to be an instant classic." —LINDSAY HUNTER, author of *Eat Only When You're Hungry*

"*Godshot* is the kind of book you find yourself thinking about incessantly. By turns desolate and rich, Chelsea Bieker's novel lets a parched tongue find relief in its pages. It is a book about the kind of salvation we can find in other people, but also about the miracle of finding that kind of all-consuming love inside ourselves. It is tenderness and trauma. It is violence. It's sorting through the mess, looking for answers. Bieker is a dynamo, and *Godshot* is a beautiful blow to the heart." —KRISTEN ARNETT, author of *Mostly Dead Things*

*To Willy —
what an honor to
Read your work,
Thank you!*

GODSHOT

A Novel

—

Chelsea Bieker

Chelsea Bieker

CATAPULT
NEW YORK

For
Harper, Finn, and Brenon,
forever

Copyright © 2020 by Chelsea Bieker
First hardcover edition: 2020
First paperback edition: 2021

Hardcover ISBN: 978-1-948226-48-6
Paperback ISBN: 978-1-64622-055-7

Cover design by Nicole Caputo
Book design by Wah-Ming Chang

Library of Congress Control Number: 2019946561

Printed in the United States of America
10 9 8 7 6 5 4 3 2 1

Remember this, for it is as true as true gets:
Your body is not a lemon.

INA MAY GASKIN

GODSHOT

Chapter 1

To have an assignment, Pastor Vern said, you had to be a woman of blood. You had to be a man of deep voice and Adam's apple. And you should never reveal your assignment to another soul, for assignments were a holy bargaining between you and your pastor and God Himself. To speak of them directly would be to mar God's voice, turn the supernatural human, and ruin it. So not even my own mother could tell me what her assignment was that unseasonably warm winter, wouldn't tell me months into it when spring lifted up more dry heat around us, and everything twisted and changed forever.

I longed to know where she went when she left our apartment each morning, returning in the evening flushed, a bit more peeled back each time. I imagined her proselytizing to the vagrants sleeping on rags in the fields at the edge of town, combing the women's mud-baked hair, holding their hands and exorcising evil from their hearts. I imagined her floating above our beloved town of Peaches, dropping God glitter over us like an angel, summoning the rain to cure our droughted fields. I imagined all these things with a burn of jealousy, for I had not received my woman's blessing yet, the rush of blood between my legs that would signify me as useful. I'd just turned fourteen but was still a board-chested child in the eyes of God and Pastor Vern, and so I prayed day and night for the blood to come to me in a river, to flood the bed I shared with my mother. Then I would be ready. I could have an assignment too.

THAT SPRING PASTOR VERN decided we were due for a congregation-wide revival. We filled an abandoned bathtub behind the church with liters of Check Mate Cola and one by one he held us under just long enough for the lungs to burn, for fearful desperation to set in, and we came up gasping and sticky, his face the first face we saw, a God to us. Our tongues darted to catch the sugar drops falling from our brows. How we cheered as the sugar dried on our skin under the ruthless burn of the sun. There was no wasting water, and so the soda would do. It was such a small sacrifice, to use soda instead of water, that I almost mistook it for a thrill.

After the baptisms, he lined us up. He paced like a mad daddy. The valley floor had sunk thirteen inches over the last year alone, and where, Pastor Vern asked, did we think we were going?

Of course we already knew. Hell was always waiting.

He said in order to save the land we so loved we would need to step over the lines of our comfort. To open our arms, span them wide, and risk being shot down by God. He fell straight as a post onto his back to demonstrate. I spread my arms, my mother next to me, other mothers beyond her and their girls. The boys and the men were there too but it's the girls I noticed most, girls like me, ready. I thought we looked tough lined up like that, like soldiers, the hay-dead field our battleground, that vast open plain of beige nothingness surrounding. I remembered what had once been here, a land so fertile you could throw the pit of a peach after eating the sweet flesh from it and underfoot would sprout up an orchard, how we had walked lightly over the dirt, electric with the possibility of

small seeds creating bounty, lettuces and kales shimmering opu-
lent, where before there had been only earth.

But now all was dry, and the steady stream of infidels we might
recruit was dwindling. No one wanted to have the rodeo here anymore. No one wanted to hold an agriculture convention where
there was no agriculture. And without new believers how would we
ever offer Pastor Vern's message to the world? How could anyone
trust the faith of God's own chosen people if they could not restore
their land?

Pastor Vern stood up and looked straight at me. There might
have been crows in the sky circling. There might have been a child's
cough or an old man's sniffle or sneeze from all that dust, or the
scraping shift of bare feet in the hot dirt. I thought maybe Vern
would look at everyone this way, and maybe he did but I couldn't
see anything beyond the way he was looking at me, like he knew
me through and through, eyes saddened by my natural-born sin yet
still hopeful. There was no sound but for my own blood rushing in
my ears. I felt a wave of desire rise up in me—I could have jumped
into his arms. He looked looked looked and finally he made a gun
of his hand and pointed it at my face. Pulled the trigger.

REBAPTIZED OR NOT, the next day brown water still ran from
our taps, but praise, it turned clear by the time we counted to ten.
It was dawn and I perched on the bathroom counter in one of my
mother's camisoles, a silky black thing that felt glamorous but she
liked to remind me it was one hundred percent polyester, not silk.
I wore too-small underwear she picked up from Goodwill that
were clearly meant for a little boy, a penis hole and yellow tractors.
I didn't complain. She wore nothing, mowed over by the heat, and
leaned toward the mirror, smoothed cream foundation over her

sweaty skin even though it would slide off before she walked out the door.

"Holy holy, praise almighty," she sang. "Our King is here, He is here. Hell is hot. Don't drink the water. Stand and feel the fear."

I was past the point of desiring sleep at this hour. What I desired most was time with her. I handed her the mascara and she craned her head back and opened her mouth as she raked black ink through her lashes, smudged raspberry glow into the hollows of her cheeks. I eyed her body, the thicket of light brown hair between her legs. She told me she never nursed me a day in her life and that's why her breasts were still buoyed up on their own instead of sinking down in flaps of sadness. She was very concerned that one day they would give up so she gave them little pep talks—come on, girls, don't fail me now. Ready steady.

I loved watching her. My mother was the sun in a dark room.

"Can I try?" I asked, hungry to look like her, to do my makeup like her, or better yet, to have her lean close and do it for me.

But her eyes settled on my crotch.

"Lacey May," she whispered.

She swiped a finger across my thigh and then held it to the light. We both saw it—the red smear.

I looked down at myself. It was as if something deep inside me had cracked open and now wanted out. I jumped off the counter and pulled her to me, but her arms stayed by her sides.

"Looks like you're ready for a real spiritual assignment now," she said into my hair.

"Like yours?" I asked.

She pulled away sharply, but then softened. "He'll have something special just for you."

I felt a surge of new self tingle within me. I didn't like the way my mother's face flickered when she saw my first blood, I could read her so well, I could tell something troubled her, but it seemed selfish of her when now I was finally a woman. Surely the rebaptism had sparked this flow, and I smiled with that warm believer's glow of confidence that came from answered prayers. I primed my eyes toward destiny. I would have an assignment and Pastor Vern would bring the rain at the right time and the town trusted him and loved him and all God's people would be tended and the crops would persevere, amen.

I pulled the camisole over my head, kicked off the bloody boy unders, and stepped into the shower. "Can I?" I asked her, hand hovering over the faucet.

She shrugged in a way I knew to mean yes.

The water rained brown on my skin, almost like blood, I thought, as it streamed down my thighs, wasted its way down the drain. Then clear and clean, the smell of metal. *Hard water*, everyone called it. My mother liked to complain it made our hair dull but what could dull me now? I was electric. I was thinking in glitter and gold. Thinking, with my hands raised in praise right there in the shower, of Vern's original miracle, the way he'd cured the town of drought years before when I was just seven years old. His dying daddy had ushered him in as a replacement, the new pastor of Gifts of the Spirit church. Vern had confused everyone at first with his proclamations of the supernatural and foresight, his golden robes and long blond hair curled in ringlets, sprayed to a starch. No one in town had seen him in over ten years—he'd been on mission trips around the world, it was said, casting God into the hearts of infidels. The top of his head was shaved clean in what he called a Spirit Hole, so that God could reach him without hair in the way.

"I'll bring the rain," he'd told everyone on his first day. And even though Peaches was in desperation times—several farmers, including my own grampa Jackie, had killed themselves over the shame of their barren crops, drank bottles of pesticide and lay down for the long sleep—and even though there were threats to turn off the water for good and condemn the whole place to death, the doubters in the congregation had gawked at Vern with little faith. For they did not yet know the most important thing about working the land, and that was that the land was not theirs to work, but God's.

Of the Herd women, only my grandma Cherry attended church at that time, grasping at faith after the death of Grampa Jackie. She had stood in the fields to see Vern command God's attention. He had knelt in the dry burrs and thrown up his hands. Cherry had seen the clean sky turn back like a page, gray eating blue, rolling into a great thunderclap. She felt the first drops on her hot skin, and then it was crashing rain for days. When it flooded the streets, when the old Peaches canal overflowed, when the news reported the rain had only fallen in the bounds of our little county—population 1,008, barely 3.2 square miles in size—there was no avoiding the truth. Vern had shown our town what God could do. He'd summoned something from nothing and no one was the same after that.

The next Sunday, rain still falling, my mother and I had lined up with everyone else to touch the new pastor's robes. To listen to that magical voice that had brought the rains. And who was my mother then?

She was a day late and a dollar short, a water bottle of gin in her purse, in the glove box, a waitressing job at the Grape Tray, and one lousy boyfriend after another who sat potbellied and spread-legged in our kitchen, yellowed fingers ashing cigarettes into empty chili cans.

And me?

I was only her bastard daughter, unsaved and seven years old, daddyless and dirt-kneed, whole mind a sin plain, my fingers pocketing gumdrops from the candy store, eyes watching cartoons of coyotes dropping anvils on heads. Someone I can hardly remember. But thank the good God, I learned that day, the past was of no matter. The rain soaked my sundress and Vern blessed us out of that life and into another.

I STEPPED OUT of the shower and let the heat of the apartment dry me. My mother was still at the bathroom mirror, head flipped upside down, filling the bathroom with hair spray. Some might think a good religious woman must be plain and clean-faced, but at Gifts of the Spirit it was fine for a woman to prepare her body and adorn herself in God's light. The brighter the shine, the easier His angels could spot us. Vern wanted the women pretty because everything Godsaved was beautiful. He wanted the women pretty maybe, I wondered sometimes but did not say, to attract infidels to the church, to dangle a prize to be awarded on the other side of conversion. Nevertheless, it was something of evil to make a man stumble.

Whenever the sermons turned to the matter of stumbling, I pictured men with black holes for eyes, walking but falling, arms reaching out, hands landing upon women's bodies unawares. Under a trance they were, and whose fault was it?

Women, God created beauty.

Women, lead men not into temptation.

But what was my mother to do with her beauty? She couldn't pray it away. It came up from inside her. It was not just the arrangement of eyes and nose and mouth. It was something unnameable

that could not be achieved with makeup or manipulation of hair-
style. She had a gap between her front teeth that she considered
an imperfection, but it was what threw her beauty over the edge.
It was what drove her men crazy. I knew Vern was captivated by
the way she looked, considered it to be God's gift. I had to agree. It
was a gift. I imagined no one had what she had for miles and miles,
though we hadn't left Peaches since becoming saved, so there was
no way of making sure.

Under my towel I reached between my legs and pressed a finger just inside. I wondered where the blood was coming from exactly. I wanted my mother to sense my question and tell me all I
would need to know, really fawn over me. But she handed me a pad
wrapped in thin pink plastic, no ceremony at all. "Maybe keep this
between us for a little while."

A chill came over me in the still heat of the bathroom, and
though I'd never come down with a prophecy before, the prickle
that spread from the top of my head to my fingertips felt close to a
kind of warning.

"But Mom."

"Just wait until the next one. It's not that long to wait."

I brushed past her and into our bedroom. I left the door open
so I could see her finish getting ready. What was it I loved about
watching her so? It wasn't as if I saw myself in her, some future
promise. Though I had her honeyed hair down my back, her freckles and water-blue eyes, I carried the blunt nose and jutting chin of
my father, a truck driver out of Needles, my mother had told me,
someone who left before I could remember, she liked to say.

I knew it wasn't true. I had memories like floaters in an eye,
there one moment, gone the next: his arms throwing my mother's
thin body into a deep dumpster one day, and plates crashing against

walls overhead on others. His boots as he kicked her. The sound of a person spitting on another person is a particular shame.

She never mentioned any of that but was quick to recall his one short leg, the way he had mixed up letters when he tried to read and how he took one look at me and said I wasn't his.

I put the pad into my underwear and angels did not sing. Out the window all was the same, dead grass and paint-peeling apartments. I got back into our bed, the double we'd shared since we were saved and no men came for visits anymore. It was a bent metal frame propping up a mattress that sagged in the middle, a feature I loved because it caused my mother and me to roll into each other in the night, waking each morning with our backs warmed and stuck together. I tried to pray but nothing came. I didn't want to disobey my mother but I sensed that obeying her by not telling Pastor Vern about the blood might mean something much worse.

She stood in the doorway now. "I am your mother," she said. A reminder not to me, but to herself.

Chapter 2

I waited for the click of the door, the jangle of keys, the sound of our broke-down Rabbit sputtering and fading down the road. I put on one of my mother's dresses, floaty and white, one that made her look like a dream of man. Cocked a sun hat low on my brow.

Gifts of the Spirit church was a one-mile walk from our apartment complex. The Lakes, it was called, though there was not a single lake around, or any body of water for that matter. After Vern's first miracle things were better for a time. The rain returned and the winters cooled and deepened and fog settled over us when it was supposed to and the grasses shone each morning with dew. The spring skies released heavy downpours and it seemed each time we got itchy again, worried again, just a little prayer could shift the clouds, Vern's goodness enough to earn the land's potential. But slowly as the years passed, Peaches crept back to the dry. Vern couldn't do it alone forever. He was only one man atoning for all our sin, he said. He needed our sacrifice now.

For now the reservoirs and canals were empty basins, home to deflated soccer balls and broken glass bottles and the skeletons of birds that I imagined had died in flight, too hot and thirsty to go on. I passed where the row crops and orchards used to be, now a flat brown stretch, vegetation nowhere. Then came Old Canal Road, our main street, where every year there was a raisin parade to celebrate our bounty. Men in huge raisin costumes pumped their white-gloved hands, their chunky gold cross necklaces moving in the sun as they danced to praise pop, gleefully handing out foil-wrapped tri-tip sandwiches on seeded buns from Mike's Meat Market. I had heard talk that this year there wouldn't be a parade because who wanted to rejoice over a failed harvest? But we of Gifts knew better. As long as Vern was around there was always something to celebrate. Always reason to hold out. *Don't quit before the miracle*, we liked to say to one another, easy as a greeting.

If my dead grampa Jackie had just held on a few more months all those years ago, he too could have found Vern. He could have stood in the middle of his fields, mouth opened to the falling water, and been converted. I didn't like to think of Grampa Jackie in hell, so I tried not to. I tried to work out a way perhaps he had slipped into heaven instead, but it was true he had a filthy mouth and a hankering for single malt, and Grandma Cherry said sometimes he'd pretend she was a ghost and withhold words and love from her for weeks on end until she started to wonder if she had really died and truly was a ghost. But still he had the best eyebrows, a severe arch to them that made him seem playful, and he treated me the same as my boy cousin Lyle and let me get my hands dirty. Grampa Jackie made it so I understood the love of the land, the love of grapes lying perfect on trays plumping in the Godkissed sun.

This, he would say, looking out over his vineyard. Press my hand to soil. *This* is the perfect climate for raisins.

So even now, drought upon us again like disease, I believed Peaches was the most blessed town there ever was, capable of providing the world's food, Godkissed and set apart. Everyone I passed, nearly everyone I knew, was sovereign to Vern and if they weren't they could be spotted with ease, trudging through town, heads dipped lower than a snake's belly in a wagon rut. Like Quince at the Pac N' Save, who never came to church on Sundays and we all tried to save her but she stuck her middle finger in our faces. She had taken to wearing a pentagram necklace and black lipstick for theatrics but I didn't sense any true evil coming from her, just stupidity, which could be worked with. A few teachers at the junior high and high schools who drove in from Fresno would not disclose their religious whereabouts to us no matter how we pressed, which is of course how we knew they were bound for damnation. We left small Bibles on their desks and never followed prompts, but wrote papers about God and created collages of the Second Coming when Vern would meld with God's golden beam. We painted beautiful portrayals of our pastor kneeling in rain-drenched vineyards that only a heartless person could look away from without provocation. We would get to them eventually and when we did they would shriek with gratitude.

But the most unholy sin of sins in Peaches was the Diviners: A Lady on the Line. It was a phone sex business housed in a leaning red Victorian mansion filled with pale witches no one ever saw come or go. They were the unreachables, rumored to have snakes for hair, eyes of fire, and poisoned nethers that could strike a fool man dead. Most days I forgot about them. Nothing in my mind could compute how someone could have sex over the phone, practically speaking, and I held my breath if I ever passed near the house, which wasn't often, because it stood exactly on the opposite end of town as the church, where the canal went on and became Fresno, another county entirely.

BY THE TIME I arrived at Gifts of the Spirit, my mother's dress was wet against my back. The pad in my briefs felt heavy and I wanted it off. A thicker heat swept over me. There had never been air-conditioning, never even a swamp cooler. If God brought the heat we were meant to be hot.

In the emptiness, the space seemed smaller. By some impossible magic the whole Body fit here every Sunday. In the center of the groaning floor the tired wood drooped and made the church a shallow bowl. There was a fine layer of God glitter permanently on it like a varnish for there was no need to sweep away a physical wonder of the spirit. The pews were built by the hands of men when Vern's father was a young pastor. The ceiling was high with rafters surrounding it, and a single stained-glass window loomed behind the pulpit, featuring a pack of fearful flying cherubs. The light filtered orange through the stained glass and below it, on the wall, hung a portrait of Jesus with a bloody and beaten face, a reminder of the horrors He'd gone through. Next to it was a portrait of Vern in imitation of Jesus, his own face woeful, smeared with what I assumed was fake blood and makeup, but it looked so real I didn't know for sure. Vern wanted us to be reminded that our sin hurt our pastor in the same way it had hurt Jesus and God—likely more.

Vern was always here throughout the week, preparing sermons in his small office in the loft like a full-time job, sometimes rehearsing them on the stage, I'd been told, but had never seen myself. We weren't to disrupt him unless it was an emergency, and now here, the confidence I had felt on my walk over faltered. I could still leave, I considered. I could go back home, maybe talk it over with my mother again when she returned from her assignment, when she would be a little tired, heat-beaten to a sweetness and willing to agree to anything to stop my badgering. I stepped back toward the doorway.

But then a voice from above. "You have something for me,"

Vern said from the top of the stairwell, a blue shiny cape fastened around his neck. His hair shone and his cheeks were covered in gold sparkling God glitter. It was a sign he had been with the Father transcribing a message. I'd interrupted.

He held his arms out and his face broke into a smile. I felt myself exhale. I ran up the narrow stairs and he folded me into a hug. I thought for the slightest moment I smelled cigarette smoke on his cape, but he would never smoke. He was above humanly desires, he told us, and smoking was just a way to fill a God-sized hole. "I knew I'd have a visitor today," he said, ushering me into the small office. My worry fell away then. Nothing was better than aligning with one of Vern's messages from God.

The wall behind his wooden desk was covered in crosses but no crucifix. Christ didn't stay on the cross, he always told us, just as Vern himself also would not have tolerated hanging there, bleeding out. Vern likened himself to Jesus often, saw himself as an equal or even a superior to Him, so we didn't really worship Jesus because Vern was also God's chosen son, just in current times. Every so often when the need was great, God would decide on a son, and Vern was it now, and Jesus was like Vern's retired spirit brother, and was mostly left out of things. "Let Him rest," Vern had told us from the first sermon I had ever heard him preach. "He is tired, but I am powerful."

We sat across from each other and he looked at his hands, eyes closed. I could see the shaved Spirit Hole on top of his head, the little spiky regrowth. I closed my eyes, too, and imagined my assignment. I secretly hoped it would be something people could see me doing. I wanted to be stationed somewhere, in the Pac N' Save maybe, bringing people to faith in the soap aisle. I would summon the God glitter and even Quince would not be able to resist my good news.

I looked up and Vern was staring at me, face a calm pool. I realized I mostly saw him in motion, whirring across the stage of the church. But here, in the silence, so up close to him, he could have passed for one of my mother's men, sort of ruddy-faced, a bit dark under the eyes. He had blackheads on his nose and I felt my breath catch a little. I wondered why he didn't get rid of them, or ask God to. Then I felt ridiculous for my vain fixations. Vern was dealing with more important things than blackheads. "What brings you?" he said.

I had wanted him to pull the truth from me on his own so I could remain innocent—not having betrayed my mother, and not having betrayed him. But I knew in a true faith there was no such thing as both, so I chose.

I pulled out a piece of bloodied toilet paper I'd carried with me in my purse. I set it on the desk between us. Here was the proof, and it would talk for me. I could even get creative and tell my mother that Vern saw me walking through town, blood on the back of her white dress.

He pressed the stained toilet paper between his fingers, lifted it close to his eye. I prepared for him to jump up from his seat, maybe enclose me in another hug. But he straightened his shoulders. Let the red paper flutter to the floor. "This could have come from anything," he said. He picked up a pencil and began to write something in his sermon notes as if I wasn't even there.

I scooted back in the chair. I just had to get through this part and then I could have my assignment. But how did he want me to do it? I pulled my mother's dress up a little. I started to raise a foot to his desk.

"Please." He tapped my foot with the pencil and I put it down. "We've been waiting on your blood for a while now. Forgive me for taking this seriously."

The way he was talking tripped me up. Was he implying I wasn't taking it seriously? Nothing could be more serious to me. It was like he was scolding and praising at the same time, and suddenly the office felt too hot, too small.

I thought of my mother, how I'd been annoyed with her but perhaps I'd missed something. Now it was too late.

"My mother didn't want me to tell you." These words came from my mouth easily.

He leaned back in his chair, let his head fall to one side. This was the soft Vern, the hugging sort, back again. "You're lucky coming to me so early in your life. Your mother sinned for a long time and I've washed the marks of her sin but I can still see the scars."

My mother never liked to talk about how she was before her transformation. After my father left, her drinking had taken her over like flames through a house. I remembered feeling scared for us sometimes, when she drove down the road swerving and braking late. When she would close herself in our room for days, silent, and I'd sleep on the couch watching television late into the night, *M.A.S.H.* and *I Love Lucy*. For a while she'd had a boyfriend who didn't wear pants around our apartment and I could see his flesh poking out from under his T-shirts. His eyes were always bleary, and he gave me sapphire earrings one night while my mother was passed out. He had pulled me close to him so he could put them on me, only to find I didn't have pierced ears.

He bent me over his lap that night. He pierced them with the dull poke of the earrings themselves while I called out for my mother and she never came. What a pretty little girl I was, he said, when it was over. And now, looking at Pastor Vern, my heart surged with affection thinking of that time, for it was he who had delivered us out of it.

The conditions of deliverance were these: one, that my mother never drink again; two, that she remain chaste, a bride to the church. Vern had held her to his chest and my mother got starry-eyed. Yearning for something good, she agreed.

"So what do I do?" I asked him now. He put his hand on top of mine, and in a rush, the pounding heat, the sweat on my skin, seemed to cool like a broken fever.

"Each member of the Body needs to be in a place of trust with their fellow brother. The men of this church have been appointed to lead. It's the holy structure . . ." He released my hand and wiped his nose, which had begun to drip. "Hay fever," he said. "No trees blooming, no grass, but still, allergies."

I wanted to ask why God hadn't healed his allergies but he kept talking. "I'll ask that you trust this structure with every piece of yourself."

But my mother wasn't just waiting around and trusting. She was going somewhere every day like a job.

"Everyone's assignment will look different," Vern went on. "Each person has their own gifts within God's army." He leaned forward and kissed my forehead with dry lips. I smelled the sun on his skin, intoxicating. Tears welled in my eyes. This wasn't what I'd expected. I'd wanted to leave with a notebook full of instructions.

"How is your mother?" he asked.

I couldn't tell him that along with spring's arrival, beers had appeared in strange places around the apartment, in the back of the nightstand drawer, behind our collection of canned beans. That she kept them in brown paper bags, drank several each evening standing before our sliding glass window looking out at the parking lot filled with half-broke-down Fifth Avenues and Novas. That her eyes had changed from ambitious to roving. Toward what I still didn't know.

"Blessed," I said. He smiled wide and I saw a shine of silver fillings in his molars. The devil came over me and I imagined his silent wife, Derndra, kissing his mouth, reaching her tongue back during her wifely demonstration and touching those hidden gems.

"Don't overdo it in this heat," he said, but I was used to the heat by now, the heat that never set on us, that only maintained through the night, beckoning me from sleep, the damp sheet kicked off onto the floor.

ON MY WALK home through the dead fields, I thought of my mother in the hot breeze of afternoon when I was five years old, just before the beginning of that first bad drought. A patch of watermelons had sprouted up in the small square of dirt under the second-story stairs of our apartment and she was on her hands and knees marveling at their strong vines, the big green leaves and the basketball-sized melons. She patted them and laughed. She brought me close so I could see.

"I threw seeds down here forever ago," she said. "Who knew all this time they were growing right up?"

The melons were bright and healthy. They were beautiful and ripe. How had we not seen them before?

She talked all night about them. The sapphire-earrings boyfriend grew more and more agitated with her adoration of something that wasn't him. He didn't like her when she was up. "Acting like you've never seen a fuckin' watermelon before," he said. He slurped Bud Light all night. My mother was oblivious to his growing anger. I wished she would just shut up. I knew what happened when she kept on pushing his buttons, but she didn't seem to have that awareness, not then, not ever. She couldn't believe the watermelons were there and she was taking it as a good sign. She didn't want us to eat one just yet. She called Grampa Jackie, who had been predicting the coming drought, could taste it in the air and had taken on a low demeanor of dread. She laughed like we'd been struck by great fortune, tried to cheer him. "You always said the land was a gift, Daddy," she said. "It still is!" She didn't drink that night and Sapphire Earrings slammed out of the apartment and didn't return until early morning, when he shoved me out of my mother's bed and onto the floor and took my place.

When my mother woke up, we raced out to check on the melons, to pet and encourage them, but someone had smashed them all. Ripped them from their vines and thrown them against the sidewalk. Their pink insides reeked a sickening perfume. She let me miss school and we sat on the steps while she drank brandy out of one of my old plastic baby bottles, waiting for the killer to return to the scene.

But the killer was in the apartment. It was clear as day that Sapphire Earrings was responsible, but she didn't seem to understand that at all.

"I'm sad sometimes," she'd said to me as the sun had left us.

How I'd wanted to fix it for her. How I wanted the world to be good enough so she wouldn't have to feel its rough edges. If someone could just see her when she was at her best, the way she was in the morning back then, getting ready for the day, dancing and singing, the soft dander of her cheek. The way her neck looked when she tilted it back in the car and sang "Great American Cowboy" along with the Sons of the San Joaquin. I didn't know what to say to fix it, to make her eyes go clear, to make her steps sure and straight, her breath her own without the bite of alcohol on it. "I'm hungry," I said instead, and she sighed, went back inside, and got drunk enough for the sadness to reset itself to happiness, only to go back to sadness again.

MY MOTHER RETURNED home that evening with a small cake to celebrate. A reward, probably, for keeping my first blood as our secret, though she didn't say that. I lay in the bed we shared, feigning cramps though all I really felt was a small ache in my lower back that radiated into my hips. I could have gone to school with the thick pad in my underwear and been fine, but I had wanted to be alone all day with my sinful lies, the impure vision I'd had of Vern, pray for forgiveness, and wait for my mother.

"Meet sugar, your new best friend."

She opened the packaged coconut cake, forked off a hunk and brought it to my lips. I swallowed the stale piece nearly whole. I hated coconut, would have preferred chocolate, but I didn't tell her that. It felt near to the time she forgot my sixth birthday. The next day, when she'd remembered, she had gone to the Wine Baron and filled a brown bag with lemon Laffy Taffy, a random candy I had never shown affection for. I smiled then too.

"It hurts."

"Get used to it," she said. "Women have a long history of suffering."

She lay next to me. Sighed. I smelled the familiar yeast and it turned my stomach. "Do you know there are people in this world who put gingerroot up their heinies?" she asked. "For fun?"

"Mom."

"It's called figging," she said, matter of fact.

I could barely admit this to myself, but sometimes I was thrilled by her new crass talk. It made me feel alive in an unknown way, but I shouldn't have been surprised by this. That was the design of sin: to be the most attractive thing in the room.

She got up, walked to the kitchen. I heard a can open.

"Most people call a woman's holy place a vagina," she said, "but the vagina's the part up *in* there, and what they're meaning is the vulva. So really just saying pussy brings it all together." She drank so deeply I could hear her gulp from the bedroom. There was the sound of a second can cracking open. "Now that you're a woman you ought to know."

Pussy. Pussy. The word sparked and hissed. I should have asked her what was giving her such strange thoughts, but instead I asked her about the beers, and if she'd been praying over them. Surely she hadn't been taking these sinful thoughts to her weekly women's Bible study. But as soon as I thought this, I realized I wasn't even sure if she was still going.

She looked at the can in her hand. Shrugged. "Sure," she said. "And I woke up to another hot and thirsty day all the same."

VERN SEPARATED THE girls by blood. Girls who had it and were under the marrying age of eighteen were ready for the true mission, and were set apart. Not yet knitted to an earthly husband, able to offer the church a singular focus, these girls were special, and now I was one of them. I understood that being in this group normally meant a deeper study of the Bible alongside Vern's wife, Derndra, or perhaps hours of door-to-door proselytizing and rigorous chastity. By the time a girl was eighteen, marriage seemed the most exciting endeavor there could be in a life, if only because of the possibility of newness, possibility of pleasure, even pain. But drought times were different, and the girls of blood would be particularly useful now, Vern had said, though none of us knew what that meant, exactly.

I felt lucky to have gotten my blood at such a perfect time, when it would matter most. I suppose I had strange dreams of glory, that the things I would do as a useful woman would be preserved somewhere, that they would make some difference to dirt and seed and stalk. We were bloody, but around the church we were known simply as the Bible study girls.

Denay and Taffy were my best friends and had already had their bloods for months, walking the church with prim proud smiles, full of use. Now I was in the club. I put my hand between my legs and held myself, looking for the calm it usually brought. My mother's sleeping back rose and fell next to me. The smell of beer hung around us like a net. I remembered how before she'd been saved, when we were poor, very poor, she'd drink anything—Listerine, lemon extract, cough syrup she'd steal from Cherry's cabinets, the Pac. The beer at least was a drink meant for drinking.

"Tell me where beer is in the Bible, Lacey May," she'd said a few months ago after she started drinking again, when I had held the phone and threatened to call Grandma Cherry and report her sin.

"You don't want to make that call, little girl," she'd said. "You want your mama around, and you know it."

She was right, and now the secret had roped around us, including me in its grip, sickening me from sun up to down. I was trapped. I felt a little crazed by it.

MY FIRST BLOOD dried up within days. I missed the alarm of color waiting for me on the toilet paper when I wiped. On the way to church, I saw someone had plastered signs all down Old Canal Road—SAVE PEACHES! BRING WATER HERE NOW!

Over another sign—PRAY FOR PEACHES!—someone had written, It's Global Warming Fools!

"What's global warming?" I asked my mother as she peeled into a parking spot, creating a cloud of dirt around the Rabbit.

"I've heard of that a few times too," she replied. "Maybe we should be a little more curious."

But I knew I wouldn't mention it again, and my mother would never bring it up. Curiosity was the first rung on the ladder down to hell.

WE FILED INTO the pew next to Grandma Cherry, who liked to sit smack in the middle of the church to feel the highest holy vibration. It had been nearly a week since I'd told Pastor Vern the news of my blood, and I'd relaxed a bit, stopped looking for signs that my mother could sense the betrayal. She was distracted anyhow, concerned with outfits. Today she wore new clear plastic high heels with stars floating in them. A white dress that buttoned all the way down the front and pressed her cleavage up. It was tight and gave the impression that at any moment the buttons could give way, that private places of rose-smelling skin, shimmery and lotioned, could spring forth and be free. The dress and the shoes were not secondhand. Lately she had been ordering things from catalogues that featured women on the front with huge boobs and tiny tank tops held together barely by strings, wearing shorts so short it appeared their butts were eating them. She had been making out checks and signing them fancy, a star dotting the *i* in Louise. I had asked her where the extra money had come from and she said, "Doing God's work all day doesn't mean you have to be poor. Don't you see what I'm wearing?" She had held out her arms so I could admire her new green halter top. "Green attracts abundance," she explained.

Today her legs were slick with tanner and sweat. Lips red and her blond hair thrown to one side. Her wrists were a jangle of beaded bracelets, and Cherry eyed them. Cherry herself was the opposite of my mother, wearing a boring and faded black shift that was tight over her barrel of a middle, her chicken-skinny arms and legs sticking out of it, no grace. Her long white hair was in a single braid down her back. She reached over and snapped one of the bracelets. "Awful flashy, aren't we?"

"God loves a sparkler," my mother said. I'd noticed she'd taken to talking down into her chest to mask her breath. I rested my hand on the bracelets, lightly touching them. She could make anything look special and stylish. Something about the angles of her body and the way they held things up.

I scanned the pews as they filled. Everyone generally sat with family before breaking off into smaller groups. Vern liked to be sure we were all in the same place at the same time once a week. It built community, he said. I could see the women drooling at my mother's new clothes as they walked by, jealous and hoping what she wore would find its way to the Goodwill bins sooner than later, where most everyone got everything. Nearly all the women wore worn simple dresses that came down past their knees but we were free to wear what we wanted within reason. I wasn't sure my mother's new clothes were within reason, but I was proud of her. She was working hard in her assignment and God was rewarding her. Having a beautiful mother was both a jewel in my crown and a curse. Beauty attracted the wrong sorts of things and people all the time. Her beauty was safe and enjoyable only as long as it was confined to the church.

Vern took to the pulpit, his eyes pulled down in woe. Sometimes he would weep openly under the weight of God's unending love and it would cause us to weep along with him, blissed out from the cleansing sting of tears on cheek. After the weeping we would sing while Vern twirled around the church like a dervish, his glimmering robes a flame behind him.

Sometimes he read from the scroll of Fears and Reasons, things we should and shouldn't do that week, advice brought on by his Saturday night visions. *Don't patron the Ag One, there's a demon in the basement. Venture to Tent City and pray over the infidels in groups of five. The burger at the Grape Tray is ripe with listeria, AVOID.*

But he didn't pull out the scroll today. "I have an announcement to make," he said. Looked at me. "Lacey May Herd, please stand."

I felt myself rise slowly, as if lifted by an invisible string. I kept my eyes on him. Everyone turned and stared, and my legs went soft. I chewed my thumbnail like a baby, not wanting to look at my mother. I knew she was staring at me, mouth open, betrayed. I smelled her beer. It was like another person in the room.

"Lacey May was anointed with her woman's blood," he said. He began to clap. Everyone joined in. "She's the last of my expected, a true blessing. This will rocket our intentions to the next level. God fulfills!"

The boys' club, scattered around the church, stood and cheered louder than the rest. They were fourteen years and over, unmarried, the future godly men and leaders of the church. One boy let out a whoop and lassoed his arm in the air. To have a room cheer for you and only you is a strange treasure. It felt like everyone liked me more than I had ever known and I was unwrapping their affection for the first time like a gift.

A burst of gold God glitter drifted down slowly upon us from the heavens, coating our sweaty shoulders in the finest gleam. We dropped our kneelers to pray but my mother stayed still. I thought once she saw how wonderful everything was, she would join in. She would see it was good I had gone ahead and told him. But no. The second Vern said *Amen* she pulled me out of the church in a rush to the car, buckled my seat belt for me like she never had when I was a child. She steered the Rabbit with her knees.

"Heat makes people crazy." She pressed the accelerator. The Rabbit choked and tried its best to be fast. "I guess that must be why you went ahead and told him. Went and did the one thing I said not to do."

She blew a stop sign and then another.

"Didn't you see how happy everyone was?" I said, small and low.

"I was suffocating in that church."

"Forgive her, God in Vern."

"They were hot in there, too," she said.

"Don't be mad at me."

"I used to think I was going to be a movie star," she said. "It's like I've forgotten that part of me for years and lately it's coming over me, banging my head like a bag of bricks. All the things I never did. But you know what? I can still do those things. I ain't dead."

It was like she wanted to wreck the car. We careened into the parking lot of the Wine Baron, tires squealing. "It's hard sometimes when God doesn't answer your prayers."

"You mean the rain?"

She put the Rabbit in park, squinted like she was just remembering where we were. I could tell her mind was switching to a different track.

"You think it's possible to fall in love with someone you've never met?" she asked. She looked me in the eyes. She really wanted to know. I had wanted to talk about me for a second, my blood and what it might mean. I even liked that she was mad at me, that I had her attention. But now her voice was dreamy again, back in her otherworld.

"No," I said sharply.

Her shoulders drooped and she let out a big tired sigh. "Hmm," she said. "You're probably right." She seemed disappointed by me, by my lack of creativity, of fun.

"Well," I said. "Maybe." I thought of God then. I had fallen in love with Him, hadn't I? We had certainly never met in the traditional sense. "Maybe you can."

I knew nothing of love.

She perked up and smiled at this admission, but then her eyes attached to a man who was idling on his motorcycle next to the Rabbit. He was tall and covered in leather, a ruddy bush that curled over his top lip. He wore dark glasses. My mother got out of the Rabbit and slammed the door, cocked her hip into the mean sun. The man's jacket said *Valley Fine* on it. He was just her type.

"Want some fairy dust?" he said, and she stepped up close to him like they were familiar, threw her leg over his seat, wrapped her arms around his waist.

"Just the ride."

He revved the engine. She looked at me blankly, not a worry in the world as they rolled away.

I ran inside the Wine Baron. From the back came Bob, an Indian man with a thickness of white hair and a tunic that buttoned to his neck. He was a nice man. He must have considered us regulars by now, I realized.

"My mom's on a motorcycle," I said.

"Television," he said, offering the word like a consolation prize, gesturing to the small screen mounted above the Slurpee machine that no longer housed Slurpee.

I took a palm-sized green Bible, small enough to fit in a pocket, so convenient, from my purse and set it on the counter. "You open to Vern's work in your life, sir?" I said.

He looked at the Bible but didn't touch it. "Mom likes beer" was all he said.

"I wish you would pretend to be out of stock when she comes."

He slid a pack of watermelon gum across the counter. "I can give you candy and that's all I can do. Don't ask me for cigarettes."

What would it be like if Bob were my father? I could spend my days working at the Wine Baron, saving all the patrons who came in for their fix. We could fill the bottles of whiskey with food coloring water and my mother could be in love and we could bring Bob to Vern and Vern would convince Bob to make her not drink anymore. I wanted to ask if he was married, but then I saw myself through his eyes and knew he would not want a daughter like me, grease-haired and begging for help in a quickie mart, a wife driving drunk through town, getting on trashy men's motorcycles for no reason.

"You should get rid of those dirties you got back there," I said. I pointed to the adult entertainment aisle where I'd accidentally lifted the yellow plastic cover off one of the magazines the week before and not understood, not entirely, what I'd seen. All the flesh pressed together sent a shock through me, the slick shaved skin, the faces of the women painted and hard.

"I sell what people want," he said. "And everyone wants that."

I left Bob to tend his cigarettes and waited for what felt like hours outside the Wine Baron. I spat on the ground between my feet. I wondered if I'd have to walk home. If the motorcycle man would be with her when they finally showed up and, if so, if he'd never leave. What would he need from me? I was older now and the thought scared me.

But then she came: my mother, like a mirage, back from the ride, her voice high-pitched, carefree, a performance for the man. She looked revived, cheeks red, clutching him like they'd known each other for years. "You have to do it, Lacey! It's amazing."

"Better make room on that motorcycle for God," I said.

The man said, "Come on, little country girl, when you gonna get to ride a hog like this again?" There was a laugh in his eyes but I knew the quick underside of it would be a violent hand.

"Feel this motor!" my mother squealed like the dumbest person alive.

I looked at her. "Tell me where you go," I said. "Or I'll tell everyone you've been sinning."

She smiled. "You don't know what I've been dealing with, little girl."

"Take me with you, then."

The man grunted, bored. He needed my mother's attention. "She's got baggage," I said to him.

"Come on, Lacey, be nice," she said sweetly, but the man guided her roughly off the bike by her arm and pulled out of the parking lot. I knew we'd never see him again.

On the drive home I wanted her to say it was all a joke, that she wasn't pulling us into that same hole we'd lived in before our conversion. But she didn't, and I felt us falling and falling and fear filled me, for I knew the hole we were going down would be darker than ever now that we'd been living in the light.

Chapter 3

The next Sunday my mother was drunksick. She lay in bed and writhed around like the possessed. I pressed a cross to her forehead for healing. I said, God, please God.

She swatted the cross away. "That doesn't work."

I pulled back, stunned, for we'd seen it work countless times. Seen Vern pull sickness from the mouths of children, seen old Wendall Meeker, a Vietnam vet with no cartilage in his knee and a bad heart, hobble in and lie before Vern, and Vern had restored the knee, and Wendall walked out of there with the strength of a boy, his memory wiped clean of the war that ailed him each night like the cruelest hammering. His sure steps were proof alone to me, but my mother acted like she'd never seen such enchantment.

I guided her to the bathtub where she vomited yellow into the water. I took a cup and poured some of the filth over her head. "Be baptized!" My voice echoed in the tiny room. She covered her ears. I pulled her up by the underarms and I dried her and dressed her. "We never miss church," I said.

"I made you into a fool," she slurred.

I grabbed the keys and guided her out the door.

She vomited into a dead stick bush outside that used to bloom poisonous white flowers in the spring and each spring my mother would tell me as if for the first time of the boy who cooked a hot dog on a branch from a plant just like that one and how he had dropped dead after eating it.

In the parking lot, she considered the Rabbit, her body tilting to find balance. Finally she walked around to the passenger side and got in. "You drive," she said, challenging me, thinking probably that I'd back down.

But no. In the name of Vern I jerked us down Old Canal Road, braking and jolting, my mother giggling, sunglasses over her makeupless eyes, unknown bruises up her bare legs, offering me no direction on how to operate a vehicle. Part of me wanted to laugh, too, just pull over and die of laughter, let this whole sadness kill me.

I led her into the pew and we sat next to Grandma Cherry. She looked at my mother and then at me and shook her head.

"Summer flu?" she asked. She poked my mother's leg. "Smells like a tavern after a fight."

My heart pounded. I knew in this moment that it was a mistake to have come at all, but if we didn't show up Vern or an elder would surely have come looking. I had imagined them finding her sick in bed, casing our apartment, deciding we were unfit believers. They might throw us out of the church and then what would be the point of living at all?

The Body pressed into pews, avoiding the nails that poked up from the old wooden seats. I looked at the pulpit and hoped my cousin Lyle, two years my senior and recently well blessed with spirit speak, would come in soon to distract Cherry from my mother, who was sinking down in her seat, spineless, head to one side.

I was never to have ill feelings toward the church and I never had. But a small voice within me kept nudging. My mother had only begun this downhill slide since she'd taken her assignment. I had almost thought to follow her some days to see what she was doing, but the Rabbit seemed to speed away from me so fast. I didn't want to imagine her assignment was somehow pulling her away from the church, but I couldn't shake the feeling that Vern had given her something she clearly couldn't handle.

"Happy Easter, ladies," an older man named Gentry Roo said as he found his seat.

Happy Easter. I looked around and realized every girl except me wore white frills and that every woman except my mother wore a white floor-length canvas dress, and the men wore their sequined capes of many colors. Vern had said the capes were delivered by angels, so everyone who laid eyes upon the men of the church would be pulled into belief, the capes so hypnotic. Like many traditions of the church, I couldn't remember when exactly the capes arrived for the men, only that they did. Cherry wore black for she was widowed, and my mother and I were in jean dresses smudged with dirt. On my mother's feet was an unmatched pair of flip-flops.

Lyle walked in and came straight for Cherry and kissed her on the cheek, but his eyes were on my mother and me. I tried to nudge her so she'd sit up, look alive, but her legs splayed apart instead. He sat between Aunt Pearl, my mother's older sister, and Uncle Perd, her husband. Pearl shook her head at my mother and faced forward. "Lordy be," she said.

Vern stood at the front wearing a special gold robe of sequins over loose-slung jean overalls with holes worn in the knees from frequent prayer. He raised his arms, his curls gleaming under the new bright spotlight they'd just installed. His feet were bare, the tops of them sun-browned. I knew if I were to kneel and kiss them I would see he had penned a little black cross on each toenail. Music filtered in from the line of ten stereos all set to play the same CD at the same time, a ghostly refrain of screaming bagpipes.

"He is Risen," Vern said now, jumping a little bit off the ground. The Body bellowed back, "He is Risen indeed!"

I hoisted my mother up for the singing but she shook me off and leaned against the back of the pew in front of her, her butt on full display to the Stam family, who sat behind us. Wiley, the father, stared openly, his tongue hanging out like a dog's in the desert, while his wife shoved the hymnal before him. Their daughter, Sharon, was my age, a fellow Bible study girl, and she looked at my mother side-eyed and amused. She had never expressly seemed to want to be my friend—her eyes struck me as judgmental and joking, the way whenever I said anything, Bible verse or prayer request, she sort of covered her mouth in a private laugh, but what she was laughing at exactly, I never knew. Her pig-faced brother, Laramie, stood still, mouth unmoving, his fat fists clenched at all times ready for a fight. I met Sharon's eyes and she crossed them and her mother nudged her. I was so embarrassed by my mother I could have happily never looked at her again.

At the center of the stage, Vern knelt on one knee and held up a hand to catch the spirit. "Yes!" he shouted. "I've heard what's been said about Peaches. Oh, I've heard. That Peaches's soil is no good. That Peaches might as well be shut down, but I'll tell you, this is not God's plan. God will restore Peaches's soil and Peaches's sky. He will bring the bounty up from the ground, He will bring forth water from thin air. This is the holiest uprising that Peaches . . ." He paused, his face screwed up, reeling in the message. "No. That the *world* will ever know!"

My mother and Cherry liked to say Vern could have been a televangelist star with his bravado, the way he could really make you feel something when nothing else was happening to make you feel that thing. That was spirituality, my mother explained once when

I asked her why sometimes I wanted to cry just because Vern was, even if I hadn't been paying that much attention to what he was saying. Why when the Body stood up and swayed in song, did my body do the same almost on its own? These were the mysteries of faith. And one of the tenets of faith was accepting that mystery, living in it day after day, and liking it.

I loved when Vern spoke his goodness like he did now, but I was distracted by my mother, who was drawing lazy pictures of the moon cycle on the back of her hand with a silver pen she'd taken to keeping in her pocket. She had been on about the moon lately, about planets in retrograde and our sign compatibility. It seemed like a new religion to her. *Two Aries in one house*, she'd said to me the week before, holding her hand to her heart like she was delivering some real bad news. *War of fires.*

I glanced at Lyle. If I was jealous of my mother's assignment, however wary I might have been, I was doubly jealous of Lyle's. He was Vern's newest favorite, staying late after sermons, walking and nodding behind him up the stairs to Vern's tiny office, so smugly a part of the boy's club, so secretive and full of giftings.

I reached over Pearl's lap and poked Lyle. I hissed, "Vern gave me an assignment."

He shushed me. "The dead Jesus is about to come on out of the cave tomb."

Lyle was right, Vern was gearing up toward telling the most exciting part, when Jesus ascended into a white cloud and the apostles stared on in utter reverence.

The Body began to mutter, prayers laced in the tongues of the gifted. Most in the church were gifted in the way of spirit speak, and though she was silent that day, usually my mother's tongues were like a high and soft whisper, while Cherry's were raspier and hurried, a mean staccato. I bowed my head and waited to be over-taken with a language beyond my understanding. I hummed aloud with my eyes open and nothing came. I wanted it to be over, for the time to come when someone would take the stage and read the Bible aloud while Vern rested, curled up to the side of the pulpit on what I knew to be a sleeping pad for a large dog, but in this church it was his spiritual resting dock.

The prayers died down and I opened my Bible and waited for the reading, for Vern's final blessing, for the praise pop to come on the boom boxes so he could run up and down the aisles, cape trailing him, high-fiving us all with firm, almost painful slaps. But then came the voice of a man with a slow drawl I didn't recognize.

"Where's she?" the voice said. "Where's my beauty queen?" The church snapped silent and craned necks to see who would interrupt the commencement of Vern's sermon.

"Louise, you here?" the man shouted. My mother's name. I looked at her but she had folded in half, her head between her knees. "Oh God," she groaned.

For a moment in my fearful heart I wondered if this was my father back for us at last. I stretched to see him again but the man's turquoise cowboy hat shaded him, made him faceless, and he wore a dark suede button-up shirt tucked into white flared dungarees. I thought of the man on the motorcycle, was this him? But it wasn't. This man before me appeared almost unhuman somehow, his limbs too long and bending strangely like they'd been loosely screwed onto his broad body by someone with all thumbs.

Vern didn't flinch. He swept back to where the man stood and asked if he'd like to be baptized.

The Turquoise Cowboy stepped within spitting range of our pastor. "Here I am a nice man, an entrepreneur to be sure, and my Lou says, I can't love you in real life, honey, until my pastor approves."

"If you're here to be saved," Vern said flatly, "we don't have water in our tub, but God knows our intention."

The Turquoise Cowboy cocked his head to one side. "What are you, jealous or something?" he said, and took a lazy, openhanded swing at Vern's face that sent him flat on his back. The Body rushed to our good pastor, helping him back to his feet. My mother bolted up and ran toward the men. Stopped before them, frozen. I knew she didn't know what to do.

The Turquoise Cowboy kept his thumbs hitched in his belt loops and a collection of long rabbit teeth emerged from behind his lips. He was happy to see my mother like a man viewing his prize sow before slaughter.

She looked from him to Vern. She seemed to have sobered quite a bit and now was plain scared. She could see the storm she'd brought on, the familiar calamity from the beforelife, when my mother said all number of things to men and meant or remembered only half of them.

"Baby," the Turquoise Cowboy said. "I'm here to make you a star."

Everyone looked around at one another, at Vern. Some whispered. A woman behind me said, "Well, some folks just out looking for the devil."

Vern smoothed his curls. He walked my mother by the arm to the front stage. My mind raced to configure how my mother had even come in contact with the Turquoise Cowboy at all. He certainly wasn't of Peaches.

"You know that man?" Cherry hissed into my ear.

It occurred to me then that over the past few months I had

done something very bad. I had looked away from all my mother had been showing me when I'd needed to look.

The men of the Body assembled around the cowboy like a mob. Vern gripped the back of my mother's neck and raised his hand to heaven. He was inviting the Father down and a puff of gold God glitter drifted from above and settled on our sweatslick skin.

"Church," Vern said. "It seems that one of our own has strayed."

My mother looked at her feet. I thought rapid silent prayers, a series of helps.

"First she tried to keep her own daughter's first blood from me, holding up our plan for rain," he said. "Now this, coming to church mowed down by the devil's elixir, a man of sin clamoring behind."

"I've only been doing my assignment duty," my mother started. "Employed by the Diviners: A Lady on the Line."

The Body gasped. My praying mind stopped dead. This was much worse than I could have imagined. I thought of that leaning red house, the force field of evil surrounding it. And my mother had actually gone in. This fact struck me down, how I'd slept next to her in the same bed and never once imagined that's where she'd spent her day. But it all made sense. Those sinful women must have cast something wrong deep inside her, led her away from God and back to the drink, to this cowboy. Fury burned in me toward women I'd never met in my life.

"I spoke sensual wordings, but my heart was with our Papa God," my mother said. "I was bringing men to holiness one phone call at a time and bearing witness to the working ladies." She looked at the cowboy, her eyes open and watery, like he could be of some help.

"I should have known you were never really purified enough to stand against evil without becoming it," Vern said.

"Whore!" screamed Shirl, an old woman who often rolled around in the front, honking and croaking in her spirit speak during worship. She spat into the aisle.

"I did everything you asked," my mother said to Vern. She squared to him and I saw another sort of communication occur, something wrapped and hidden from the rest of us, the end of it just beginning to unfurl.

Vern smiled. "But you didn't," he said.

It seemed my mother had something else to say but it was stuck inside her. Vern led her off the stage but she turned, shook him off. "Wait," she said. Her eyes locked with mine. "Try to understand. I was testifying. I let God lead me to the right scripture. They trusted me and told me their sorrows. It soothed them. I've converted at least nine souls, most of them local infidels. You may not want me in this church no more, but I'm not bad. I tried, and on the way I fell in love."

Vern was stung and it was a spectacle to see him this way, thrown off, befuddled by anyone, least of all a woman. "Love," he repeated, the word gagging him.

My mother pulled her arm from his grasp. "Lacey," she said. "Ask Lacey. She'll tell you I've been sober. I haven't touched a drop since conversion. Tell them, my girl." Her eyes begged.

I didn't understand how it had come down to this. What could my voice matter in her sea of obvious transgression? Anyone in a five-foot radius could smell the booze on her breath. If I lied now I could be banished too. If I lied now I might not be useful anymore. That thought was terrifying to me then.

"I don't know," I said.

"Lacey," Vern said. "Tell your church family just how your mother has sinned."

"Let's go," my mother said to me. "Let's get out of here. Come on. This is over. This is all over."

I stepped toward her but then my body stopped. I saw a flash of what I knew our life would be. I saw the Turquoise Cowboy just like all the others. I saw her skinny body passed out at odd angles across the bed, the shrunken world of her hangovers that could last all day when nothing else could go on around her, each sound too assaulting, even my quiet voice too mean. The way she would refuse me simple things, drives to school, bread from the store, until I was red-eyed from staying up all night either wondering where she was or wishing she would leave again. The frightful way she would look at me like she was reaching out from a black hole, trying to drag me down into it. Nothing was over. It was only just beginning.

"She's been drinking," I said.

"Well," Vern said, turning to my mother. "Your drinking alone is grounds for banishment, not to mention the love you're in."

A small sob escaped from my mouth. "Wait," I said. But it was too late.

The Body became a flurry of movement. The men screamed for exorcism, arms to the sky. Someone grabbed me and held me up over his head, repeating that he was *saving the daughter*, and the women formed a circle around Cherry, sputtered in their protective ways. I saw only a glimmer of my mother's long hair before she disappeared through the side door without me. I looked for the Turquoise Cowboy but he was gone, too. I primed my heart to my mother and sent her messages: *I'm coming. I'm sorry.* What a big misunderstanding, I thought. That's all it was. A misunderstanding.

Chapter 4

My mother gone and gone, I spent the night at Cherry's. She dragged a dusty mattress made for a baby in from the shed to the craft room. She handed me a thin sheet and kicked back her crates of sewing supplies and cookbooks then puttered down the hallway to remote control her way to heaven with her beloved televangelists. I curled into a ball on the mattress and decided there was no reason to ever leave that room. I counted flowers on the peeling wallpaper. I listened for cawing crows out the window. I dreamed in feverscapes, my betraying words a haunt running through me. *She's been drinking, she's been drinking.*

BY MY SECOND motherless day, Cherry took to bringing food and leaving it on the dresser and then standing over me with a heavy iron cross, poking me with it like I was some mystery, a possibly dangerous animal. *God in Vern*, she'd pray. *Rid us of your devil.* At night she'd toss chocolate sandwich cookies into the dark and they'd land on my face and across my body. I'd eat them slowly and feel sorry for myself. I understood clearly then how shut-ins were born.

AFTER A WEEK, Cherry finally softened toward me, lowered her round body and squatted on the edge of the tiny mattress. She patted my back. "Maybe it's time you get out of this room and face the music."

"I'll come out when she comes back."

"My own momma passed on when I was eighteen years old," she said. Her eyes sort of drifted above me and settled on a crack in the wall. Her mother had been a busybody of a woman, Cherry explained, and one day she took to her bed, covered herself in blankets. Cherry knew something was the matter, for truly her mother never did rest like the lazy. They checked on her every hour, and she was sweating and shaking in fever. Finally she called them in and pulled back her blankets, and her skin was covered in sores a-fester and she said, "The mortification has set in."

My mother had never mentioned any of this.

"We didn't know what she was on about, the mortification, but she died the next week."

Cherry clapped her hands once, like *that was that.* Her eyes bore into me. "You know what I did after she was no more?"

"What?"

"I put her out of my mind. I knew no amount of slothing around was gonna bring her back. A girl can be fine without a mother."

But my body told me this wasn't true for me and it wasn't true for Cherry either. She had missed her mother desperately and still did or else she wouldn't have told me the story.

Young Cherry, a woman I'd seen in photos, trim and wind-kissed, that long hair always in tufts around her face and down her back, her sharp nose and pointed chin. Cherry was unpossessed by beauty, yet arresting, hard to look away from. I imagined her a girl looking at her mother's sores, the fear she must have felt, and I pulled myself out of the craft room by afternoon, and Cherry saw that it was good.

"Praise be to the Lord of honey and milk! She's back and I see the life of the church still in her!" she proclaimed into the phone. "Yessum. Okay. Well, I suppose." She hung up. "Vern said he'll see us when God tells him the time is right. Until then, pray."

"He's not coming over?" I asked.

"Lucky you weren't thrown out with the bathwater of your mother, keeping her dirty shames all to yourself," she said, hard suddenly. Like it was difficult to imagine how my mother and I were of her family tree at all. My mother's face was not capable of getting this hard, I didn't think. "Sin's a disease like anything else. Sit in a barbershop long enough, you're gonna get a haircut."

Like everything in Peaches there seemed to be Before Vern and After, and this went for Cherry too. The Cherry of my early life was not prone to such hardening, was soft toward my mother, was understanding of her foibles because at that time there was no Vern to steer her straight, there was no light. She would listen to my mother go on and on about all her cruddy men and she'd lean over the kitchen counter and nod and pat my mother's hands. Hand me sweet after sweet so they could go on talking.

You think it's possible to fall in love without meeting the person? my mother had asked me. Maybe, I'd told her. Maybe you can.

It felt bad to have Cherry's boxes strewn around my head as I slept, the haphazard shadows of the clutter looming against the wall at night, so I tried to move her things into the closet to make more room. For what I didn't know. All my belongings were at the Lakes just where I'd left them. I'd been wearing the same jean dress I'd worn the day my mother left, the denim thick and stiff from my sweat.

The closet was its own spectacle, and in it I unearthed clear plastic tub after plastic tub of what looked like still and stiff stuffed animals that smelled of urine. I brushed a finger against a squirrel's tail and it felt so real I pulled my hand back. It even had sharp little teeth. Under the squirrel were dozens of mice with long wormy tails and fear-struck eyes. Where had these come from, I wondered. I'd never seen anything like them sold in Peaches. I shivered and closed the lid and moved on to a duct-taped brown box. *ROMANCE* was written on the outside in black marker. I ripped it open and inside must have been forty compact paperbacks, looping cursive titles down each spine. I opened one to the middle and the first sentence I saw was *he palmed her breast.* I recoiled as if from a hot flame, tossed the book to the ground, kept my eyes on it like it was a striking snake. I called for Cherry. I pointed to the tawdry cover with skin spilling from corset and demanded who was reading such sin. She pressed her lips and said, "Wouldn't crack a math book, but those your mother loved."

I looked at them wary but I felt a strong pulling current coming from them.

"You was just a little thing, but you remember how it was before Vern, just living life to live, no meaning whatsoever."

I figured she was going to take the books away, burn them in the yard. Call the church and report them. But she shuffled back down the hall. "Anyhow," she called. "Don't touch them animals in there. Them's my specials."

I looked back to the crates of stuffed animals, imagined them writhing inside, chewing one another's little tails clear off. I heard Cherry turn the TV up in the living room. The books called to me. "God," I said aloud. "Why are you testing me this way?"

I put my hand on one of the books and felt a warmth. Felt, maybe, my mother. I was powerless. I took to reading the entire collection straight away.

EARLY THE NEXT morning Cherry woke me by thwacking something against the floor by my head. I looked up to see a deep brown oiled cane in her hand, curved at the top and veined.

"What is that?" I said, poking the cane. I'd never seen her use it before.

"Made from the finest of bull penises," she said. "Steal of a price, you would not believe."

I turned away from it and groaned into my hands. Every waking was another reminder my life was real. Why wake up if all that was waiting for me was a cane made from a penis?

She handed me a metal scraper and a spray bottle full of bleach. "Time to clean the flies."

CLEANING THE FLIES meant getting down on my hands and knees to scrape the brown fly larvae from the corners of the walls where, she showed me, they were piled and ready for the hatch. Under the refrigerator, around the baseboards, in the grooves of the windowsills, where she had a theory they were getting in. Wriggling maggots appeared from the brown and those needed to be smashed one by one, or if a group of them was discovered I was to warm soda until it was hot and thick and burn them alive. The already birthed flies swarmed the house in immense clouds. If I was still but a minute, three would land on me. And they were lazy. I could kill them easily but it didn't matter. They appeared by the second. That morning I kept an eye peeled for baby flies thinking it might grant me some compassion toward them, to witness their helplessness, but they seemed to be born immediately adult sized and by noon I killed them one after another without remorse, stiff bodies crumbing the warped wood floors.

"When did this get so bad?" I asked.

"I hate to say it," she said. "But it was about the time you arrived."

I waited for her to laugh, or take it back, but she was serious as disease.

"No more cows in the fields for them to land on," I said.

"Blessed land," she said. Sadness pulled at her face. The land was like a person we missed. "Now make a plate of bologna sandwiches and come have lunch with your Cherry."

She sat on the pink floral couch and patted the seat next to her. I made the sandwiches on white stale bread. The mayonnaise was on its last day. When I sat she flopped her head down on my lap, closed her eyes, and opened her mouth. "Feed me."

I took a bite.

"Feed. Me." She grabbed my wrist and brought it to her mouth and snatched a hank of bologna from between the bread. In between bites she whined on and on about what she called her wasted life. I watched her old teeth chew, the mayonnaise collecting around her gums. She told me how years before when she'd quit her job at the Pac N' Save as the bakery manager, no one believed the reason, that she truly had dislocated her pubis, but she had, and not a soul cared not even her own grandchildren, not even me. Lyle was a boy of vigor on his way to something, of course, so she could excuse his not noticing easier than she could mine; me, who was headed nowhere but in circles.

I remembered Cherry working there, how my mother and I would pop in and Cherry would slide a free cake our way, or a cookie. *The secret is just a spat of spittle*, she'd say, and wink. I'd never taken her serious but after this I could picture her spitting into the batter easy. Those days seemed far from me now. I thought of Vern's sermon when things had begun sliding back toward drought, just before he'd announced his idea of assignments. How he'd said that if we had a true faith we would not travel outside of Peaches for supplies. We would have belief enough that God would provide. I didn't know what that really meant then, but now I knew we were a long ways from eating fresh-baked goods at the Pac.

"How do you dislocate a pubis?" I asked. She chomped the last bite of the sammy out of my hand.

"See, all I get is doubt." She got up and started toward the door. "I've become a certain way living alone out here," she said, kicking open the screen. "Goldie Goldie Goldie! Goldie Goldie Goldie!"

Goldie was her cat. It hadn't been seen by a human eye for the better part of five years. I myself had seen Goldie's remains on the side of the road not a mile from the house the very day Cherry had mentioned Goldie hadn't come in for lunch. My mother had shaken her head when I pointed out the smear of orange fur. We resolved not to tell Cherry about it, but I thought maybe it wasn't so bad. Maybe Goldie was happier dead. I remembered when she'd had kittens and became depressed and didn't mother, but settled her plumpness over their bodies and smothered them. Cherry thought they were nursing and told me to go have a feel of a baby cat and I was already holding the tiny kitten in my hand when I realized it was not moving, not breathing. The feeling of a dead thing in the hand is unmistakable. On reflex I tossed the body to the ground and it hit the floor with a thud. On the way home, after I had stopped crying, my mother said it wasn't at all strange that the cat had done that, how Goldie was too young to have all those babies, just a baby herself.

"Help me call now," Cherry told me, so I stood next to her.

Her hand trembled, gripping the cane. Her voice shook as she projected it as far as she could.

"Goldie!" I called with her. "Goldie, come on home!"

But Goldie didn't come on home. The dead don't come back.

THAT NIGHT I sweated until my hair was wet and I dreamed of fat black flies in my sweet tea, in my mouth.

I LEARNED BY my second week at Cherry's that I had to guard my own pleasures when I could, before I was sentenced to fly duty or any number of other Cherry-care chores she wanted me to perform on her—waxing the fuzz that grew on her legs, tweezing the corkscrews that sprouted on her chin, combing and plaiting her long hair while I sang whatever hymn she was craving. Quality time, she called it.

THAT MORNING I settled into my new favorite pleasure. I snuck a romance called *Cowboys and Angels*, about a poor feed-store-worker girl and a traveling bank robber turned lovers, into Cherry's bathroom and I stripped naked. I sat on the toilet and read until my legs ached, wayward from gazing into worlds where men held women in soft caresses, where they were hard with muscle but their insides were made of sweet taffy. The men voiced their love feelings loud. The women dipped their heads back, necks arced and pale. They loved the love and it showered them. They returned from the love cleaner than before and wore it like aura, a pastel rainbow above soft curls. The books described women feeling a pulse come over them, a great wash of heat and light. The women would touch themselves sometimes imagining their

lovers. I breathed hard. I could not look away. If this was sin it had
me in its grasp.

Pussy, pussy, I could still hear my mother say, and here was
the word all the time. *Pussy pulse, wet pussy, slippery puss, hot pussy,*
even *gorgeous pussy.* I myself had only ever felt the special pulsing
accidentally—in a bumpy car ride, climbing the rope at gym class—
but now I was finding I could feel it when I read if I moved just
right. And when I moved just right I was in nowhereland, not here
at Cherry's, not even in Peaches. I only wished the feeling would
last longer, that divine forgetting.

I had my hand working overtime when Cherry thunked around
on the other side of the door, cursing the day. "Blasted devil's ways!"
she shouted. I held still. "Time for consequence!" The doorknob
rattled. I threw my sundress over my head, kicked the romance behind the toilet. I knew she was going to take the pleasures from me.
She'd beat me until I'd never read another romance again.

But she wasn't on about the romances. She was on about clearing out my mother's things from our apartment.

"I'm not going," I said.

"All right then. We'll just burn it all."

I DIDN'T LIKE going places with Cherry because she didn't have
a car, she had a magenta hearse, and not just any. It was the hearse
that had held Grampa Jackie's coffin and within that, his body,
and she loved it and sang to it and still wiped it down with one
of his old shirts most every day. After his service, she had insisted
on riding along with the driver, who was young and quiet and she
distrusted him immediately based on the dopey way he held his
face, his slight underbite. Halfway to the fields where Grampa was
to be buried, Cherry demanded the driver stop, and she pushed

him out and threw a wad of bills at him before she sped off. We saw it happen, my mother and I, for we had been driving behind the big pink thing, my mother nervously laughing about how much Grampa would have hated it. The driver collected the bills off the ground and began a solemn walk back in the direction he came. For weeks we waited for him to return and collect the hearse but he never did and no one ever called. "Country magic," Cherry said, an explanation for why the hearse was suddenly hers. Soon she would understand there was no such thing as magic. Only God's giving and taking away.

"Get in," Cherry said to me now, opening the pink passenger door. "Ain't no ghosties gonna bite you, just your dead grandpa in here feeling like a damned fool to have gone bellied up."

"You think he regrets killing himself?" I said.

She winced, but then recovered. "Missing out on your mother pulling this, maybe he made the right call."

THE LAKES, APARTMENT 204. Little green Bibles littered the mat where the Body had shown their concern, a deep red cross drawn on the door. *WHOREWITCH* under that.

Perd and Pearl and Lyle got out of Perd's dirty work truck, *Perd's Valley Pest* emblazoned along the side. "We're here with bells on," Perd said, and took a long greedy drink from the liter bottle of Mountain Dew that was, in varying degrees of fullness, his constant companion. None of them had come by to see me since my mother left, and I expected they might hug me now, or say something kind, like people should when someone has died. But nothing.

Pearl braced her legs apart and raised two hands toward us and closed her eyes. "God in Vern, do not let Louise's sin that has rubbed off on her daughter rub off on us. Keep us pure and purer in our devotion to you." She opened one eye. "Had to put my armor on, you understand."

Cherry fumbled with the lock and Lyle came close to me and said, "What's it like living at Cherry's?"

I paused. Did I want to tell him the truth? How my fingertips bled from scraping the larvae and my nails had worn down to stumps and my eyes burned from the bleach and I missed my mother in each place on my body, that my neck had stiffened and knotted, that all my sadness was stored in those knots and if I pressed a finger into the largest most painful one, tears arrived behind my eyes as if on command?

"Not what I expected," I said to him instead. But he was already pushing his way inside.

INSIDE, THE APARTMENT was how I left it, upturned, the carpet covered in rice cake crumbs and candy wrappers that seemed to have never not been there. I looked for a note, a phone number, a sign in case I missed something in the flurry of searching moments the day I'd come back to the apartment and realized she was gone, but there was nothing. I stood in the doorway as they threw things into garbage bags with not a lick of grace. Perd muttered to himself about how it was his one day off and tossed my mother's toothbrush in with a box full of opened Ajax containers and stained washrags, and then put her sprays and lotions in after that. My mother had always turned her nose up at Perd and Pearl, making fun of his nearly incomprehensible valley drawl and the way Pearl was plainer than soda crackers in looks and mind. Pearl and my mother seemed at quiet odds with each other, my mother the one others took to with quickness. It was true that people wanted to look at a beautiful thing.

"Let's just pay one more month of rent," I said to the room. "What will she think of us getting rid of her stuff like she's dead?" I tried to sidle up to Pearl, my mother's own blood sister, after all.

"You think she's off making sure this guy's gonna be a good daddy for you?" Pearl said. "If I were you I'd be praying double-time."

Guilt covered me. I hadn't been praying. For the first time since Vern had claimed me saved, I was at a loss for words when I knelt before the baby mattress at night and closed my eyes. And I knew that each minute I spent with my romances was a minute I was not spending with God. I hung my mother's pageant sashes around my neck. I'd never seen her in pageants. They were her other life before me. I'd never considered she could have a life apart from me, but here I was in it.

"Can't imagine a child living in this filth," Pearl said, shaking her head. "No wonder she wouldn't have us over. I'd have left myself just to get away from the mess."

It was filthy. My mother stopped cleaning after she'd taken up assignment and we lived amid our trash. I only saw it clearly then, though, the blond hairs balled up in the corners of each room, the trash overflowing out of the kitchen to the living room, the brown of the toilet bowl. The dishes in the sink and how once they were dirty they were dead to us. We just didn't use that dish anymore. Now, though, a smell had taken hold, my mother's iceberg lettuce rotting on the countertop, the decay of stuck macaroni and cheese in a dish, cans left open and waiting for nothing. It was strange, I could not remember eating with my mother, only the image of her leaning over the sink, picking at things. Never cooking, just opening cans and handing them to me. Once she said to be careful not to cut myself on the sharp raw tin and it felt like a kind of care. I loved Spam and sardines and could imagine that she was cooking up delicacies, but now seeing the piles of cans on the floor I felt embarrassed for us.

CHERRY SMOKED A pink berry-scented Sweet Dream cigarette in the corner, muttering to herself. The smell of the Sweet Dreams covered the rot a bit, but meant a probable headache for me. Cherry told me I just had to get used to them and had offered me one in the living room a few nights before when I was sullen and it was agitating her. I smoked it and coughed and got a headache so bad I asked all night for God to take me in my sleep. I imagined telling Lyle about the cigarette to make him jealous or shocked, but something told me that it was like the dirty apartment, another thing to hide.

"Vern's right," Pearl said. "First thing to go is your obedience, then the church, then your community, then your ever-loving mind. And them witch women. That's another story."

Them witch women. I tried again to imagine who they were, how they'd poisoned my mother with their ways. It was clear something had happened to her working there. Something they said maybe, that slowly pulled her from faith. From me. Something that pushed her to start drinking again, and when the opportunity came, to run and not look back. It seemed likely that all of this was their fault, a curse we were under.

"You're lucky you've got us around to keep guiding you," Pearl said low. "Lyle said just the other day he was going to start coming by to help you in your Bible studies and whatever else."

I looked at Lyle in the kitchen dumping my mother's collection of colorful plastic forks and knives into a bag. He'd never shown me any attention before. The extent of our contact was rolling our eyes in solidarity when Cherry loaded stale years-old raisins into her special meat loaf for Sunday dinner. Pick them out and mouth *gross*.

As they worked, I pulled things from boxes, making my case for why they should stay out. I tried to create a pile of necessities for when my mother came back but Cherry put the pile in a garbage bag when I wasn't looking and added it to the others. I touched my things on my small shelf by the bed. The costume jewelry she'd given me, my angel figurines. Who needed any of it now? I tossed it all in a garbage bag and then went into the tiny bathroom and took out my romance. I was deep into the story about the two fugitive lovers, how the whole time the reader knew that the woman had it out for the man, that she was the smarter one, and was biding her time. They did have romantics, though, for sometimes she gave in to her woman's needs and the necessity of satisfaction.

Women's needs had never been mentioned in the church, never mentioned by anyone that I could remember, and I lapped up any sign of them by instinct like a long-starved wolf. My mother had held this same book before me, but why hadn't she ever told me she'd read it when she was my age? It felt like something I should know about her. All the things she'd never told me waited just under the surface of this world like untouched land mines.

Lyle came in and shut the door behind him. In the small bathroom there was really only space for one person, unless it was my mother and me, who got ready side by side in our synchronized routine. The bathroom never felt small with us in it, but with Lyle here it was crowded and my knees nearly pressed against his stomach. I curled them up to my chest. This close, he seemed taller. Thin, but arms long with rivets of muscle, his shoulders stooped a little, the last evidence of his boyness. His sandy hair swooped over his forehead. He brushed it out of his face and then I saw myself. Yes, there were my same eyes. My high freckled cheeks and pointed canine teeth.

I turned the sink faucet on and let brown-tinged water cover my dirty toes.

"Takes a gallon of water to grow one almond," Lyle said, turning off the tap.

"Pearl says you're gonna teach me the Bible. You don't think I know the Bible by now? Been at church long as you."

"We're concerned over the quality of your belief," Lyle said. "GOTS ain't just any church, you know. You can find a church anywhere. Vern's church is different."

I wondered if Vern had put him up to this, if he still cared for me and hadn't forgotten my use.

Lyle turned the tap back on and looked at me. It seemed like a permission to waste water, to be bad. His hand grazed my leg. Drips of sweat clung to his earlobes. He cupped my shoulder and I could feel a low tremor run through him to me. "Lacey," he said. "This is what family's for."

When all was loaded into Perd's truck we drove together to the Peach Pit Mini Storage and Cherry went in to do the paperwork. She charged back to the car after a few minutes.

"I'm not shelling out forty-five a month to store a bunch of crap," Cherry said. "She's your sister, Pearl. Maybe you could contribute something here."

"Mama, this isn't my fault," Pearl said in a high baby whine.

Cherry turned to Perd and said, "To Tent City, then."

Tent City wasn't really a dump, but a name for the town homeless encampment, though it was well known that you could take your garbage there, your broken dishwasher, your kicked-in armoire, and someone would find use for it. The homeless of Tent

City were in Peaches proper, but they were not of Peaches. They were a Fresno problem that had leaked over. Everyone called it Tent City on account of the makeshift tents everywhere, and the town knew to wear thick-soled shoes because of the needles. I asked my mother what the needles were doing there, why there were so many, and she said the needles were to inject the devil right into you, and that was just what some folks wanted. We were always trying to convert the people out here because they were desperate for any kind of saving, but now it was deserted aside from a few sleeping lumps, shaded by cardboard boxes. It seemed most had left for greener pastures.

It was a familiar place to me, but somehow I had never noticed that from Tent City you could see the red Diviner house in the far-off distance where Peaches ended and turned into Fresno County.

Cherry watched me and lit another Sweet Dream. Clucked her tongue. "Don't even think about it."

THE DRIVE HOME in Perd's truck was quiet. I was happy for it. I felt if I spoke I would cry and I didn't want to offer that up to any of them. Before I got out of the truck Lyle leaned over and handed me a plastic bag with something light in it. "Thought you might want it." He smiled gently, like he understood that my mother and I were not monsters.

I waited until I was safe in Cherry's bathroom with the door locked before I opened it. My mother's yellow bikini. Lyle had saved it for me. I smelled it. Chlorine, something salty, a little mold. The elastic had lost its strength, but she still loved it. The high waist of the bottom covered her belly button, the one part of her that wasn't perfect. My fault. I had pushed it out when I was in her stomach, she said. Made it ugly. The top had wires that crammed her boobs together, made two half moons of flesh rise up toward her collarbones.

Before Vern she had always talked about taking me to the sea, to let me hear the ocean. It wasn't even that far away, she told me. A few hours' drive. She'd been there once with Cherry and Grampa Jackie and Pearl when she was a child. She had kept it close to her, the memory of eating hot clam chowder under the smudge of overcast sky, how they had all shared one bread bowl because they didn't want to spend money and how my mother wanted a kite like the other kids but buried her toes in the sand and looked out over the crashing blue instead and was still content. She said she had seen her whole imagination right there in that water, glimmering out toward the endless horizon line. Once she became a believer, she said, she realized what she had seen was God.

Chapter 5

Loneliness. That's what this feeling was, the wiry crawl under my skin telling me something was about to go very wrong all the time, making me jump at the slightest noise, imagining the Turquoise Cowboy's car out front, him giving my mother thirty seconds to find me and if she didn't he would take her away forever and it would be my fault, so stupid I was, busy daydreaming. I was on high alert even in sleep, my body an electric wire waiting for the contact of another, but no one ever came. Who can say, until it is gone, how much you will miss the warm body that sleeps next to you?

IN THE SHED I hid from fly duty. I looked around at Grampa Jackie's things, hammers of every size, tin boxes full of nuts and bolts. A chain saw leaned in the corner, a shotgun hung high on the wall. My second blood had colored my underwear in the night and I folded one of Grampa's old hankies into a pad and put it in the bikini bottom. I had my current romance and some of my mother's things from the apartment I had jammed into my pockets. With her deodorant and a few of the crystals she'd amassed during her assignment work, I set up a little altar and tried to pray for her return. I touched the crystals lightly for I feared they harbored dark spirits, but they were too beautiful to be truly afraid of.

I knelt and whispered *mercy, mercy* to God, and when neither He nor my mother appeared, a wish came over me that my mother was dead. It seemed I was on a course of evil, thinking like that, but I wondered if it would be better somehow. Having a mother gone by a Godstricken force rather than a perfectly alive mother who simply chose another life. But while I wanted my hatred of her to cover me, to harden my skin to scales and become me, the opposite happened. I only loved her more.

As I walked back from the shed to the house, I saw old Officer Geary sitting with Cherry on the porch, drinking sweet tea, long white braid down his back and a white suede Stetson on his head.

I hid just along the side of the house and listened. Geary tapped at a clipboard.

"It's a formality," he said to Cherry. "Her mother ain't here to sign her off to you, but if anyone came around poking, they ain't gonna know that. Looks close enough to her signature, don't it? Just says in the case of her absence you're the guardian. You decide what the what is. You know."

"Mmhmm," Cherry said. I heard the scratch of pen on paper.

Officer Geary was a sort of half-retired sheriff who occasionally tried to keep Peaches matters under control so the Fresno police didn't have to come out. He was a good GOTS believer and said his main job was policing for sin. I had never been on the wrong side of it so I'd never cared, but had seen him thwack the legs of the shoplifting infidel boys behind the Pac with a long rod. Heard him call a waitress my mother used to work with a bitch when she gave him his bill and hadn't comped it. I'd seen the stares he'd given my mother any chance he'd gotten, the way he liked to pull her in for a long long hug each and every time he saw her as if they were lost lovers reunited after shipwreck.

"I don't like the way it makes the church look," he said. "Some strange man just showing up for her, clearly not even from here. It's all people can talk about. Just how'd she get herself in a mess like that?"

"We was without Vern for a long time. And now who's paying the price? Cherry is."

"Well, Cherry, we need Lacey here to stay in line. To listen to the brethren."

I stepped up onto the sagging porch. "Sir, I'll inform you my mother is coming back."

"Hush up, child," Cherry said.

Child. I hated that word. Nothing could feel further from the truth. "I'm no child," I said under my breath.

"Speak up now," Cherry said. "If you're going to be a smart aleck, give it to us loud and clear."

My heart fluttered. I felt my legs brace. "I'm a woman," I said. It rang out high and false, my voice not my own.

"A woman?" Geary said. "Well, I should hope so."

"Blood and all," Cherry said, half smiling.

"We'll see just how useful you'll prove to be," Geary said. He stood and got close to me. If he tried to hug me like he'd done my mother I'd sock him in the gut. He took Cherry's hand and gave it a kiss. She blushed. "Good day, ladies."

After he drove off Cherry lit a vanilla Sweet Dream. Clutched the bull penis cane.

"Don't you care where she is?" I said to Cherry. "She's your daughter. We should make a missing person's report." I knew that this was standard protocol from watching *America's Most Wanted* as a young child, one of my favorite shows before I was saved.

She put the Sweet Dream between her teeth and held her hand to the sky, clenched her eyes for a vision. "She's still breathing out there. I wouldn't get my knickers in a twist yet."

I HADN'T BEEN out in public since my mother had left, but now my loneliness pulled me to the Wine Baron. As I got closer, I saw it was dark inside, the shelves empty. Bob was nowhere. Even the little TV in the corner was gone. A piece of paper was taped to the door: *Runned out of here in the name of GOD!* It was signed *Gifts of the Spirit* and the handwriting was clumsy and rushed. The note was a tag, some kind of claim, perhaps an assignment complete, I thought. Maybe they had tried to convert him and he refused. But where had Bob gone? It frightened me that he could be here one day and then every trace of him wiped clear.

Gone the liquor and the naughties. Gone my mother, too. I walked back toward the main strip and sat on a bench in front of the Ag One hardware store, which was still open, a few old farmer men milling about inside. On the bench sweat poured under my dress. I kept my nose in my Bible but inside the Bible was a romance. I didn't want to talk to anyone exactly but I wanted them to talk to me. I thought perhaps my mother had been in town all along, moving from store to store in a trance, looking for me and all the while I'd been sequestered away at Cherry's. I wanted a strange angel to come sit next to me and put her arms around me. I wanted God then in physical form. I wanted His body with me and over me and around me. Instead I looked up and there was Lyle.

"Caught you," he said, snatching the romance from the thin tissue pages of the Bible. He held it up away from me, opened it, and read. "Dolores reached around and pulled Simeon to her by the throat. She kissed him long and hard until the rock of him strained his jeans." He threw it on the bench next to me like it was stupid but I saw his cheeks flush.

"They were my mother's," I said. "I was just reading them to see if I could find any clues."

"The main clue here is that your mother had a natural disposition toward sin."

I thought of Lyle's mother, Pearl, how she sipped wine from a mug all day and was probably just as bad as my mother, but managed to hide it better.

"Thanks for the bathing suit," I said.

Lyle smiled and looked at his feet. I wondered if he'd had a crush on my mother. It didn't seem strange to me if he did. I assumed most men had a baseline crush on her, something that was just a fact because of how she looked, something that wasn't really a choice for them.

"Well, see ya around," I said.

"See ya at church," he corrected.

"Vern say it was time for me to come back?" I asked.

He nodded. "God is good, all the time."

I RAN BACK to Cherry's. I couldn't wait to tell her I'd been summoned, but I stopped short in the doorway. There she was, tummy down on the floor of the living room, surrounded by the stuffed rodents I'd seen in the craft room closet. She was making them talk to one another, chirping and clicking like a young child playing dollies. They were in various states of fine dress, corduroy pinafores around little mouse bodies, tiny hats and bibs on baby rats, and leather slippers on an old man possum. Their tails were stiff and curled, their chins raised in thought. One wore glasses. I got a sarsaparilla from the fridge and watched as Cherry got off the floor and entered into some sort of exercise regimen. She sat on her stool spread-legged, toes planted, two of the mice in her hands like tiny barbells. She pivoted half circles, strengthening calves, did biceps curls with the mice, rewarding them with a pecking kiss each time she lifted. Out came the petroleum jelly, and she glossed her forearms with it, between her fingers, landscaping cuticles. Then she did her neck. Pulled on the skin and said *gobble gobble* softly to herself.

"Gotta keep the body tight for any sort of spiritual rapture," she said, winded, when she finally noticed me staring. "These guys keep me company."

I knelt down and touched one of the hard-bodied animals. "They're so real."

She clicked the remote. "My babies' commercial comes on every five minutes, just have you a wait."

Sure enough, an older magician-looking man in a suit of green velveteen appeared on the small TV screen showing off the stiff animals on his palm, a squirrel duct-taped to his shoulder. "Don't ever be alone," he said. "Adopt a companion today!" He held out an empty palm and suddenly a tuft of fur with a face appeared in it, a twinkle in its eye. Cherry ogled the screen like a gambler.

I saw why she was entertained by the man—he was entrancing and different—but total amazement overcame me the next day when I stood by Cherry as the green velveteen man himself unloaded her new order on the front porch. His suit, upon close examination, was not two separate pieces but a onesie.

Cherry invited him in for a feast of pastries, but he declined. She practically pulled him by the arm, and he stopped her.

"Ma'am," he said. "I'm not getting paid to be foolish."

His rejection made her testy and so a few hours later she placed an even larger order, what she called on the phone an *emergency*.

But to Cherry's dismay, when the emergency order came a few days later, it wasn't the older magician man, but a scrawny someone wearing the green velveteen, but his long skinniness didn't suit it, didn't fill it out proper, and instead of evoking otherworldliness I saw it for what it was: a Christmas elf suit from the Dollar Disco. He tossed the package of mice on the porch with no ceremony at all. The box nearly landed on my toe. Cherry said, "Where's Eugene?"

He turned. "My uncle's setting up to retire. All's you get today is me. I can paint your lawn if you want me to, though. That's my very own business." He pointed to his sky-blue truck, where he had handwritten in thick black marker, *Central Cali Valley Lawn Painting*. Under the words, a smiling orange garden snake poked its head up from a lush patch of grass.

Cherry snorted and pushed the boxes toward the door with her cane. "Painting lawns. Boy, I don't know what you're on about."

"One hundred dollars for bright green grass. Grass that looks like nature but better. Grass that looks like there wasn't ever no drought. I'm telling you, God couldn't even make grass this nice. The only thing that'll ruin it is rain, and rain ain't gonna happen."

"You wouldn't know God if he bit your ass and called you Sally," Cherry said, and shuffled inside.

The man shrugged, looked at me. "Crazy bat," he said, and winked.

Never pay mind to a man who winks, my mother always said, even though hadn't all of her beat-down boyfriends been winkers? The man spat on our dead blond weeds and walked slowly back to his truck, twirling keys on one finger. He got in and reached his arm out the window, patted the outside of the door like *giddy up*. I watched him from the porch squinting against the sun. He wasn't like any man I knew from church, that was for sure. I looked down and saw one of the packages had a different address, for a Haggard Wayne down in Kerman. I picked up the box. "Hey!" I yelled. He took his sunglasses off. I started to skip but then walked instead with no rush, the package against my hip. I was some other girl walking then, jaw clenched. I realized only when I was almost to the truck that I was wearing the yellow bikini and nothing else. No matter. I stood, holding the box just out of his reach.

"Well, hello, savior," he said to me.

"You're not from Peaches," I said.

He scanned me toes to tits. "And you aren't from Peaches either, little girl, or you would have said *ain't* just now."

"I'm no hillbilly," I said.

"No hills around here." He pretended to scan the distant flatness. "Me, I'm from Popcorn, Indiana, population forty-two—well, forty-one now that I'm gone, unless one of them broads had another kid, as broads will do. Just landed here a few months back, ready to start anew, and lawn painting is where the money is. You wait and see, I'm gonna have every house in Peaches back to a state of glory."

It was like the world had contracted and opened back up new and distorted. He didn't scare me even though up so close I realized that he was older than I'd first noticed. I didn't feel my throat get tight like I usually did when a man talked to me. Perhaps I had entered the place where the Diviner house was, where my romances existed, and now, I thought, where I was a body who stood talking casual-like to strange men in trucks.

"You a believer of God?" I asked.

"My name's Stringy." He reached his hand out to me and I gripped it hard. He winced and pretended I'd hurt him. I giggled in a way that would have embarrassed me to high heaven had I heard it come from my mother, but here I was laughing just like her, as natural as sin. He pulled me close to the truck and snatched the package like a trick.

I waited for him to ask my name, but he didn't.

He peeled out lifting a hurricane of dust around me. *Lacey May Herd*, I should have told him. *Pleased to meet you.* I watched him drive away as the dirt settled on my mother's bikini, and I felt something strange happen inside me, or perhaps it was in the atmosphere— like the air I had always breathed had shifted into something unfamiliar. That by breathing it, I was now an unfamiliar kind of girl.

I THOUGHT OF that lawn painter the rest of the day and into the night and by next morning I saw he'd been thinking of me too. Cherry's grass was a neon green wash, loud and alive with color. I could hardly look at it directly, it was so bright.

Cherry thought the green grass was a sign from God and not a sign of admiration from the lawn painter. She called me into the bathroom, her home waxing kit hot and ready, and wanted me to get at her pits. She wanted someone to photograph her on the lawn, arms raised in praise, and send it to a newspaper somewhere far away. She wanted the headline to read: *Most blessed believer receives sign of rain to come!*

I waxed one pit but the stink of her, the layers of unwashed skin and sweat, got to me. I walked out onto the porch to stare at my grass in peace but there was Lyle sitting on the rocker holding a Bible.

"Let's go somewhere Cherry won't interrupt," he said.

I thought of Cherry, sweating and waiting for me to service her, and I nodded toward the shed. Lyle pushed the door open and set his Bible down on Grampa's workbench. One of his knees was bloody—from playing pickup baseball in the rock dirt fields behind the church, he said, and his white shirt was now yellowed and ripped. I was wearing the bikini again, a new skin, my breasts indecipherable under the bag of the unfilled cups. I moved the strap to the side to see the pale flesh under it and peeled a shred of burned skin off my shoulder. I had no idea how I looked to anyone else. I was accustomed to people focusing on my mother's appearance out loud, telling her she was beautiful, affirming what she knew as fact. My body felt like a new thing to me without her next to it.

I sat on the workbench. Put my hand on his Bible. It was tattered with notes and folded pages. "God's testing me," I said.

Lyle looked sad. He understood my grief maybe, or was trying to. It was more than I could say for anyone else. "Vern said something interesting the other day," he said. He paused. He shook his head. "No, I can't tell you."

I clasped his arm. I could smell Perd's deodorant, metallic and peppery. "I'm a woman," I told him, confident this time, my voice steady.

"Something's going to take this town over, and it's bigger than all of us combined. It might take time for everyone to get it, to really understand it, but once they do, the gifts will know no bounds."

"What could be more powerful than when Vern brought the rain?"

"It'll be bigger than that. But people are afraid of power when it comes down to it."

"I'm not afraid," I said, wishing it were true.

Then Lyle hugged me. I was stiff at first but then I softened into it. We stood there like that, and the skin of my stomach brushed against the hot button on his Levi's. I didn't know what to do with my feet so I left them their natural way, toes turned in.

When he kissed me on the forehead I held very still.

It was nothing, I decided later in the craft room, sleep nowhere to be found. But for a reason I wasn't sure of, this nothing seemed like something to keep to myself, so I did.

Chapter 6

Sunday morning rushed me like a pack of wild-eating dogs, and Grandma Cherry tried to do me a kindness. She brought out one of my mother's pageant dresses, laid it across the bed, and patted it like a prize.

It was an off-the-shoulder tangerine organza gown with sheer sleeves, points that looped onto the middle fingers, tight through the bodice and poufed at the hips. It was the dress my mother had worn when she'd won the Miss Peaches Supreme pageant when she was just a few years older than me. She had qualified to Miss California but by then was craving cinnamon rolls and pork rinds, performing, against her hopes and dreams, the ordinary burden of pregnancy.

"It's perfect for your first day back," Cherry said. "A real showstopper."

I didn't want to stand out today. I wanted to blend into the walls, to reappear so slowly no one would remember I had ever gone. But I saw she was sincere and I felt seriously if I didn't wear the dress I would pay for all eternity. More fly duty. More coddling her and feeding her bologna sandwiches while she crooned melancholy. The dress hit midcalf, a strange length for such a gown, like my mother had caught a wild hare and chopped off the bottom to run through the crops. Maybe she did, I thought. But she had never told me such fabulous stories.

In the church parking lot Cherry looked into the sun. "Land burning right up on account of your mother."

But I stopped hearing her, because there it was: my mother's car, sitting where she'd left it.

The tires had been slashed and the body of the Rabbit laid down dead in the dirt. Red and black crosses had been painted on the hood, the windows were smashed in, and I wanted to reach through the shards to grab at her hairbrush on the seat. I remembered the way she used to drive through town in the months before she left, a plastic cup full of iced beer that she liked to pretend was soda between her knees, how she'd bring the coldness to her forehead and say she would die of the heat and at that time I didn't think a person could die from heat but now I was beginning to think different.

The Bible study girls rushed over, putting their fingertips lightly upon my arms like I could be anything, a girl, a mirage. I saw Denay glancing behind us to see everyone watching. Her smile shone brighter with an audience. "You're back from the shadow of your whore mother's sin!"

Taffy tilted her head up weakly at me, like we'd never met before. I wanted to reach out and shake her, but they guided me from the car and toward Vern. When he saw me he hugged himself.

"Welcome back, dear one," he said. "We've been preparing for your return."

My heart filled my throat. Daughter to father, my body pulled itself close to him and I pressed my head to his chest. I felt there must be endless truth and wisdom with which he could cover me. He would say something about my mother that would bring it all into clearness. Part of me wondered if my mother would be brought back into the light by me simply standing in our kingdom, returning to me with the same dark magic that had made her disappear. But my mind flashed then to the sin I had steeped myself in since she'd been gone, and shame vibrated within me. Of course I'd need to convince Vern of my worth again, all the tawdry books I'd been reading, all my spooling doubt. "Bless me," I said.

He put a hand on my head and breathed in. "Faith wavering, full of sinful wondering."

I felt his body shift away from me. His head craned to the side and his gaze fell to the next member. I stood still. "Can you bless her return?" I asked.

"She was banished," he said through a locked smile, waving to the Body. The crowd pushed me and our connection was broken.

"Sorry for your loss," said one of the choir women. She wore a large wooden cross around her neck, her eyes bugged out and her smile was sloped from a stroke she'd had a few years before. She came in close to my ear. "My own mother died when I was a girl. I was never the same."

"My mother's not dead."

"My mother never found Vern," she went on. "I can feel her soul burning in here." She placed a hand on her chest. "It's not heartburn, either. It's my mother's soul."

"Mother's soul my foot," Cherry said, rolling her eyes as she led me on and into our same pew where we always sat, now without my mother.

Vern walked past us toward the stage. He seemed smaller somehow and his hands were nervous, pulling at his blue cape. His curls were stale, frizz flying from them as if he'd just woken up. I closed my eyes and opened them again, wondering if I was seeing things.

"Church," Vern said. A smile broke over his face. His hands went up to summon the Lord and a burst of gold God glitter rained down upon us. "I had a vision last night. God told me it was finally time to tell you the next unfolding of our plan to save Peaches from destitution. See, I knew I couldn't do it alone. I knew I would need each of you to remain steadfast in your assignments. And I knew, like any great leader, that I would need a solid group of young men to be a power force among us. A new brethren to pull us through this trying time."

Lyle emerged from the back of the church and down the center aisle holding a foot-long bejeweled wooden cross out in front of him. The rest of the boy's club followed in their robes of shiny red. Under the robes I knew most wore dungarees or coveralls, white holey shirts with high-hitched jeans, but the robes covered all that and made them into other men. They moved in unison like a marching band, forming a tight line on the stage, matching pinned lips. Their presence all together like that was unnerving.

Vern put his hands on Lyle's shoulders and more glitter floated down from the ceiling. Cherry stuck her tongue out to catch some. I looked into the rafters and thought for a moment I caught a glimpse of Trinity Prism, Vern's teenage daughter, with her hand thrust out. But it couldn't be.

"These young men are humble servants," Vern said. "Obedient and watchful, keeping their sisters and fellow men on God's track. They will bring GOTS into a new age with new rules and new ways. Are you all ready?"

New sounded wonderful. New sounded different. And different was what any of us wanted. We wanted to be the Raisin Capital of the World like we were before, but now we wanted even more. I remembered the Sun-Maid men inspecting Grampa Jackie's vines, shaking his hand and signing money promises to paper. I'm sure he was rich, but farmer rich is different. He and Cherry still reused paper towels, spread their jam finely. Now we wanted life to be as gold as God glitter.

It seemed there would be no mention of my mother during the sermon, or me, and I relaxed a bit. I let my eyes blur over the cherub in the stained glass, wondered where my mother was at this moment. She was in new places with people I had never met. I liked to imagine she had begged the Turquoise Cowboy to wait for me, but they were too reckless. My mother could be that way but usually she would remember I existed at some point. Maybe as they'd driven away she imagined she was taking a vacation.

I started to think of all the exotic places she might be, the things she was wearing, but Cherry nudged me out of my fantasy. Lyle was standing before me, hand out. "Be baptized again," he said. I took his hand and let him lead me to the stage. Baptism was always a relief to me. A way to start over. In the past when there was water it was a way to pretend I was swimming, but there was no bathtub filled with water now. Not even soda today. There was nothing but Lyle and me.

He produced a small lighter from his robe and held it up so the Body could see. It was the same kind Sapphire Earrings bought every time he went to the Wine Baron to get his cigarettes. Because of him our apartment had one in every drawer, fallen from the pockets of his jeans left on the floor. I saw Lyle's hand shake.

He brought the lighter to the bottom of my mother's organza dress and made a flame. Nothing happened. I gathered the hem up in my arms.

"What are you doing?" I said to him.

"Trust me," he said.

I looked to Vern, who was sitting cross-legged on his dog bed at the far side of the stage. He wanted Lyle to perform a wonder. I thought of the time Vern had brought in a rattlesnake to handle and when he opened the cage it slithered away down the aisle and disappeared, never to be seen again. I could still hear the sound the rattler made.

"Lacey," Vern said, reprimanding me with just my name.

I wanted to do the right thing. I looked to Cherry, who would surely call it, come to the stage to get me. Perhaps this was a test of her devotion to me as her granddaughter. All possibilities swam in my head other than what was suddenly happening, a flame licking my leg and the organza blooming with fire.

The flame crawled up the dress bodice and I screamed. I threw myself on the ground and beat the fire with my hands. The Body cheered. Am I hurt? I wondered. My panic had numbed me. Then I was wet. Brown liquid came from above.

I patted the dress, its once-floaty skirt a brown mush now, ruined. The Bible study girls gathered around, hugging me and praising God. I felt rays of joy and heaven being sent toward me, and my face contorted of its own volition into what felt like a crazed smile. It sent the Body into spirit song and my skin tingled with their light. "Home," Vern said, standing over me. Home. The Body wanted me, I could see. I was so highly prized. I had never been called to the stage before for such a demonstration. I had always been in the crowd, watching on as people transformed in loud dramatic displays. At one time my mother would have been proud of me up here like this, but now I imagined her embarrassed by me, above us all, a luxurious movie star, probably in at least one commercial at this point. I wished both things could be true, our faith and my mother's wandering, but they could not. I pushed my mother away.

"Go ahead and heal her burn," Vern said to Lyle.

I looked down at my exposed thigh where there was a red mark, but it was a scrape that had already been there and no longer hurt. Lyle covered it with his hand and said a low garbled prayer. Vern announced me healed.

"Do you feel foolish for your doubt?" Vern asked, reaching down to help me up. I nodded, looking into his eyes. We all knew he could read us so clearly, he could pull truth from any of us with a glance. I looked away. I did feel foolish. But over what, I was still trying to understand.

Chapter 7

Mother here, Mother gone. Lyle the old way, Lyle the new way.

I SAT ACROSS from him in the shed and tried to concentrate on my Bible though I was hungry and thirsty. *I will repay you for the years the locusts have eaten—the great locust and the young locust, the other locusts and the locust swarm—my great army that I sent among you.*

"Why bother sending the army on us if He's only going to repay us in the end?" I said.

Lyle looked up as if I'd shaken him from a deep fog. There was something especially restless about him today. "You can thank your sister Eve," he said. "We could all be living in paradise if it wasn't for her." He looked around the shed. "Where's that Cherry?"

"Probably stroking her mice, looking out over that nice green grass."

He smiled. I figured he was thinking about the lawn. Maybe he'd ask how it came to be, and I could tell him about the strange lawn painter just to feel my voice consider the whole encounter out loud. I wouldn't tell him that I felt proud of that green grass like I had earned it somehow, or that the image of the man's tattooed arm hanging from his truck window had caused a rush to where the bikini bottom pressed, a clear slick left on the fabric like evidence.

"I think you're ready, Lacey," Lyle said, and for a moment I thought he meant ready to speak of the lawn painter.

"I've been thinking day and night how to tell you," he said. "But I finally decided it's not something I can explain with words." A red flush cropped up on the skin of his neck and I realized he wasn't restless, he was nervous. I had never seen him quite this way, but suddenly it was as obvious as the heat. He was here to tell me my mother had been found dead somewhere. Surely there would be no right words to tell a girl her mother was dead, surely a person would look as nervous as this.

"Lie down" is what he said, but I was busy thinking, *she's dead, she's dead.* In my mother's romances the characters always asked if the person was sitting down for bad news. How the town sheriff would arrive at the door to report a gone and loved soldier and the woman would faint into his arms. *Let's get you lying down,* the sheriff would say.

He got me lying down. My body tingled all over. I waited for the news to crush me. The light shifted under the door, the light shifted over the skylight Grampa Jackie had put in years before.

Lyle swung a leg over me and sat across my hips and his face was kindly but his knees worked to pin me down. "Vern says I have a perfect holiness inside me and it's time I give it to you."

"How did it happen?" I said, stupid heart still set on my mother.

"Are you faithful?" he asked.

And before I could answer, Lyle's lips landed on mine hard and dry. He pulled back and paused, waited for me to do something, I think, but I didn't do anything. My first kiss was over. I hadn't known it could happen like this, happen to me.

I tried to sit up but he held me down again.

"It's fine," he said as he unzipped his pants. Flesh and fur sprang out. It reminded me of one of Cherry's squirrels for a moment, my mind a flurry of familiar objects trying to make sense of this new one before me, this eye-scalding thing I was never supposed to see but was now so close to I could smell. It was risen, pressed to his stomach. The tip was wet. "Don't worry," he said as he pulled my bikini to the side. He paused for a moment. "It's my assignment, too." He sounded almost sorry.

I remembered my mother telling me that sex hurt the first time, that it was a pinch, a sharp pain and sometimes there was blood. I felt nothing as he pushed inside me. Good, I thought. Then this must not be sex.

I turned my head to the side and watched my hand shift on the blanket as he moved over me. I stretched it out and touched the back of my fingers to the dirt floor. Part of me was off the blanket. My hand was doing what it wanted. I made a fist then released, fist then release. I floated around and saw Lyle from the ceiling, saw him speed up, heard his breath run fast and then stop. Run again, and then he collapsed on top of me like he'd been hit from behind in a car crash.

"Done," he said into my neck. No kisses now. No looking at me now. He leaned on my hair as he got up, pulling it. He zipped, combed his fingers through his own smooth hair, the same color as mine. I saw a coat of shame wrap around him. He rushed to collect his things.

"This is just for us to know," he said, as he walked out. "At least for now."

My assignment, my assignment. All this wondering, when my assignment was just lying down. Something anyone could have done. Something people did all the time. I couldn't help but think I'd been tricked. That maybe I had dreamed it, or perhaps I was being tested. All the prayers I'd prayed to be useful to my church, all that was needed was this. What would become of Lyle's holiness now that he had given it to me? I pictured a glimmering gem coming out of him and passing into my place, going up up up inside me, making my faith perfect, too.

As the light in the shed shifted dim, I got up and paced as if there was something to be done. A thick drool of clearish white dripped down my thigh. I squatted over the quilt and watched it fall out of me. There was no gem. This was sticky and in the heat it smelled like the bleach I used to kill the fly larvae. I screamed into my hand.

Where did women go when this happened?

Chapter 8

The body always knows.

I ran the land and felt the valley consume me, push me far, far down Old Canal Road. Barefooted in the bikini, hair blazing out behind me, my hips sharp in the night air. *The valley floor sank thirteen inches this past year . . . pulling water from underground aquifer ducts . . . the ground is deflating like a leaky air mattress.* The newscaster called the cause of the sinking *subsidence*. Vern called it wrath.

The Stam family came roaring up the road behind me, then slowed. Wiley rolled his window down, a toothpick hanging from his bottom lip. "Hey, girl," he said, his eyes consuming me. He didn't offer a ride or anything useful. In fact, his presence seemed solely to make me uncomfortable or to prompt me to offer him something, of which I had nothing to offer. I nodded in return. Sharon sat in the backseat next to her brother, staring at me openmouthed, like she could read what had just happened. But they could not look at me and know. My body had enclosed what happened somewhere inside.

My feet ached but it didn't matter. What did matter now? I wondered. Either I had acted in complete faith and would be well blessed and forever a bounty would cover the land, hearty kale and globes of citrus, the grapes of faith, jobs would return, the raisin parade would fill the streets, and we'd live in God's paradise once more. Or I had committed an unspeakable sin. Both would change everything.

"Go with God," Wiley said. Then they rolled past. I looked down into the cracked and collapsing canal. I remembered when it rushed with water, when each summer it was common for a local child to get swept under and never come back up, the temptation of a cool blue swim too much to resist. Their bodies were always found pressed to the bars of a drain, but still I imagined the fragments of their bones lining the floor of the canal like fallen bark.

Another stream of cars approached and I sat on the edge of the canal. I could not imagine it full of water anymore. Now it struck me more as a tunnel. I eased myself in but it was deeper than I thought and I landed hard on my knees and my wind knocked out. I waited for my breath to calm and an excitement filled me. A secret passage had revealed itself. I ran into it, hand brushing the dry dirt walls. Headlights streamed above me but I was unseen now.

When I reached my estimation of where I'd need to turn off, I carved a foot hitch with a rock and climbed out. I liked to feel my body work this way, my hands dirty and fighting, my muscles electric. With each pump of my running legs, I felt myself wake up. I sprinted down the unmarked turnoff that led to only one place. We never came down this road, but I was in a new world now. The sky thick and black over me, star show ablaze. The Diviners' house loomed ahead, its slight slant, and the full-bellied moon glared over it like a spotlight.

When I got close to the house I sat in the dirt to catch my breath. I looked between my legs and a different woman's blood had surged onto the yellow fabric. I heard my mother tell me the story of when she had fallen in love at fourteen during an unusually damp lightning summer with a Mexican boy who worked Grampa

Jackie's fields. He and his father barely spoke English and they had come across the border under the floorboard of a van. This was when there was enough work in Peaches to attract migrant workers by the hundreds. Now no one was stupid enough to come here and expect anything. My mother said the boy was tired a lot, worried a lot. Wanted a lot. He hated the valley, she'd said, stirring instant mashed potatoes in the foam cup they came in. I was ten years old and too young to realize she was showing me her heart. She said he wanted to live in some snowy place he'd seen on TV and that she'd told him she'd go with him.

When he left after the harvest she had cried for weeks. She thought he would come back with his father the next summer but he didn't. I hadn't asked her if he had pushed himself into her on a dirt ground and how her body felt and if love had covered her or fear, or something of the two.

I stepped closer to the house and a glare of motion lights bathed me. From a megaphone: "Who's there?" I jumped back out of the light. "If you're here to deface our property think again. We're trained in archery."

Archery! The thought of these seductive slinking women holding bows and arrows in their lingerie struck me as absurd. But of course the house was like nothing else in Peaches. It might have been mistaken for some fine historic Victorian museum if not for the sinister lean, the paint peeling off in large strips. No one in Peaches, believer or not, wanted anything to do with it. The graffiti was beginning to fade but I knew it had appeared after my mother's banishment. I wondered if the women inside were scared. What did they think of this church that hated them? The cleaning spray smell hung on me. I stepped into the light and knocked on the door. "I'm here about my mother," I heard myself say.

For a while there was nothing, a silent negotiation taking place between me and them, of whether or not to make this contact real. They decided yes, and so did I because I had not moved. A dead bolt from the other side undid and the creaking door opened.

I first saw a slightly swaying crystal chandelier hanging in the entryway, wallpaper of black lace. My eyes adjusted and I stepped inside. Under my bare and filthy feet was a huge smooth cowhide, white with black spots. Polished hardwood ran into a long hallway, and creamy crushed velvet the color of sliced beets blanketed the stairs. Buttons adorned puffy satin chairs in rich mustard yellows and emeralds. I could see a long white leather fainting couch in a back parlor. Framed above it was a black-and-white portrait of a nude woman, her long silvery hair falling over her face. She was turned so only one breast could be seen and her legs were firm with muscle and her waist cut in as if carved with a knife. The halls were silent, the door to each room closed.

In the corner was not a lingerie-clad archer, but a girl about my age wearing a black tank top and black shorts, black lipstick, and a white lace ribbon tied in a dolly bow around her neck. Her eyes were rimmed in burgundy pencil and her skin was pale as chicken fat. Her hair was not a mass of writhing serpents but lank and long and black. She flicked open a switchblade. "Can I help you?"

Seeing her, a real person before me and not the imagined women the church spoke about—their skyscraper heels and racy negligees, garish rouge and ratted hair—I wondered what else we could have gotten wrong. "I'm looking to find out"—my voice cracked—"what you all said to Louise Herd to make her go off and leave." I cleared my throat. It seemed I had acted in some nightmare jolt of energy. I hardly remembered how I'd arrived here at all.

The girl closed the blade but kept it in her hand. "No one can force anyone else to do anything. I'm sure you know that."

But I didn't. I'd seen Vern force all number of beliefs and actions over us, and I'd seen, in response, obedience.

"Daisy'll be off her call soon," the girl said. "You can wait in the hall. I'd love to chat but I've got a history paper to write."

I must have looked at her strangely because she said, "Not everyone goes to Peaches Valley High. Not everyone's a member of the holy roller army."

A moon-cycle chart hung behind her and I recognized the formation of circles and crescents from my mother drawing it on the back of her hand like a habit. She had been taken by the moon before she vanished, saying things like *Tonight is a beaver moon, prepare for new awareness, a super blood wolf moon, opposite of the sun, but ruled by the sun,* and I'd look out at it with her, loving how low the moon hung in the valley skyscape, nothing for miles to compete with its grandness. Even the polluted smog that settled over us became romantic, a mysterious mist, and she'd close her eyes and bask in its particular light. *Wolf moon, blue moon. God created the moon,* she said. *Lacey's moon.*

I moved up the velvet stairs before the girl could change her mind. On the landing there were three doors. I pressed my ear to the first one and heard murmuring. A low moan and then a high-pitched *yes yes yes.* I walked farther. I felt an urge to pray, but stopped. I was too self-conscious in front of God in this place.

Then a voice filtered out of another room, its door open only a crack, sticker gems spelling out *Daisy* on the wood.

"Don't send me a fur coat," I heard the deep voice say. "I'll never wear it in this desert. No, I won't give you my address; now now, you know I can't do that. Of course, hon, now put that hard rooster right in my mouth just how you want."

I watched her through the crack. A telephone was perched between her shoulder and her ear. She was topless and rubbing oils from brown glass bottles into her neck and cheeks in forceful upward motions. The candlelight illuminated what seemed to be scars covering one side of her face, pink raised streaks across her chest like ribbons. Her breasts were rounder at the bottoms, her nipples more assertive than my mother's, pointing sidewise and brown. Her stomach was smooth like fine-spread frosting on a cake and her white hair was pulled into a bun and secured with long obsidian chopsticks.

"Your balls are as soft as a little bird," she said into the phone. "No birds? You don't like birds, okay, writing that down, forgive me, never again."

I could have watched her all night. Was this what my mother did when she was here, sit at a wooden vanity, topless on the phone talking like this? Daisy's voice seemed to command something. It wasn't what she said exactly, but how she said it, as if there were chamber after chamber of secret meaning behind each word and only she held the particular knowledge of what anything meant. The recipient was along for her ride, not the other way around.

Now in the mirror, Daisy's eyes met mine. A smile crept across her lips. I felt embarrassed for her nakedness but she didn't make a move to cover herself. "Okay, I'm going to give you one big squeeze and I want you to blast all over my tits, yeah, or my face, baby," she said, still looking at me. A laugh lit up her eyes. "My beautiful, perfect, gorgeous face." She knew her face wasn't beautiful, not in the way the man was picturing it, and the joke belonged to her.

I turned and put my back against the hallway wall. The image of her speaking this way on the phone. Why was it so entrancing? It was sin, but still I wanted to keep looking. Her voice was a poem.

She poked her head out the door and pulled me into the room, closing it behind us. She threw on a black sheer silk kimono. "I sensed you coming," she said. "I swear I can see the future since he burned me. Gave me some magic powers, I'd like to think."

"Who's he?" I asked.

"Oh," she said, surprised. "Your mother really wasn't much of a gossip. Well, it's a long story, I won't bore you with it."

"My mother never told me anything about you. Or this place. It was her secret assignment."

"I pictured you older-looking," she said, appraising me. "But you have her face. You walk the same way, too, like you're not sure where you're going."

"My grandma Cherry says I have the face of a truck driver."

"I'll let you in on a secret," Daisy said. "You're going to be really pretty someday, and she can't stand it. Don't you have any intuition, kid, or do you just believe what people tell you about your own self?"

She watched as I looked at the jagged raw-cut pink and jade crystals lining her desk, like the ones my mother had taken to collecting. "Let the crystal pick you."

"I don't believe in that stuff," I said.

She twirled a clear oblong wand between her fingers. Held it up. "Selenite. Keeps the bad away."

She tried to hand it to me but I stepped back. "It's because of you and this place she started drinking again. She never would have if it wasn't for you."

Daisy sat on her pink velvet chair. A fan blew a few wispy bleached hairs around her face. One of her eyes was white all the way through, and I saw clearly then that the portrait in the entryway was of her. "Your mother's got that emptiness inside her and she's gonna fill it with something. Drink, church, men. Always switching seats on the *Titanic*."

"No one else will help me."

"What happened here?" Daisy said, pointing at my crotch. I looked down and saw there was more blood than I thought. Saw that my life was so different than it was just a month ago when my mother was still teetering on the edge of disaster but still here at least. We still completed our days together, some idea of the future ahead. Now the future was this and I hated it. Blood had smudged onto my thighs. The yellow bikini didn't hide it at all.

"People underestimate young girls but they never should," she said when I didn't answer. "I look at my own daughter—you saw her there downstairs—and I realize I don't know her experience at all. She doesn't tell me a thing. And why should she? If I'd have told my mother what I was up to at her age she'd have taken me outside and shot me."

"My mother has no idea what she's done to me."

She took a light pink kimono off a hook near her vanity and draped it over my shoulders. I felt immediately comforted by its feel, its vanilla scent. "Is this one hundred percent polyester?" I asked.

Daisy scoffed. It was not. Silk at last, I thought, fingering its fineness.

"Your mother's not in good standing with me, either, I guess we have something in common." Daisy drank from a tall thin glass bottle. Water. My desire pulled at me. "Broke my number one rule. She let one of these fools convince her he was gonna make her a real star. I told her they all like to promise that. If I had a cent for every man who heard my honey-whipped-cream voice and told me I could make it on the screen I'd be rich."

"So you know where she is?"

Daisy took her hair out of its bun and respun it in one motion, tying it in a knot. "Well. I know the phone number of the caller who stopped calling so much the day your mama went bye-bye, and that's all."

"The Turquoise Cowboy," I said.

"But giving it to you would be far against our confidentiality clause. We're a clean business above all else."

"Please," I said.

She pulled me closer by the belt of the kimono. "Tell me why you came here barefoot and bleeding."

I shook my head.

"If I had to guess I'd say you've been with a man," she said. "Or a man's been with you."

I felt myself about to cry, just like I hadn't wanted to. Crying was an exhausting pursuit and I'd done so much of it by now. I'd proven its worthlessness.

She took my hand. She squeezed. "Whatever's happened to you can either make you beautiful, or it will ruin you forever. You decide."

I pulled my hand back. "I'm not beautiful."

"I don't mean beautiful like you're thinking. I mean *beautiful*. I mean, deep and changed. Affected. Wise. When you see a woman like that, you know. She's beautiful because of her undoing. Beautiful because she rebirthed herself from ashes."

"Are you a woman like that?"

She smiled, looked at her call log, penciled something in. "My own mother was a traveling psychic and had no clairvoyant talent whatsoever. You can imagine how deranged she was. But if she had left me I would have walked through high desert and low river just to drag her back to me by the hair."

She pressed her fingers into the thick scars on her cheek. Lifted the bottle to take another drink, but stopped short. "You want something, you gotta ask for it. Staring like a sad pup won't get you anyplace." She tilted the water toward me. Everything in me wanted to reach out and take it. I didn't move. Finally she gave up and took a drink, set the bottle down. "It's time for you to go."

But I didn't want to go. I wanted always to be under her gaze. I was spellbound then, thinking if I stayed near this woman she would lead me to my mother.

"Let me work here," I said. As soon as it came out my body registered it as desire, awful and wild. "I'll clean for you, or I can help with the front desk. Whatever you want." *And I can find out where my mother is*, I thought but didn't say. My eyes twitched around the room, looking for a call log maybe, some envelope of answers.

"I have enough help," she said. But I saw her crack a little. The house was not full of women as I'd imagined, phones ringing off the hook. It felt a little deserted, even.

"I'm a woman," I said. "I can take calls. I can do anything a woman can do."

"You're a woman?"

"Of course. I bleed. I know what there is to know."

I remembered my mother small-talking about weird sexual positions and fetishes and how at the time it had made my face burn, but not now, after what had happened to me. Now things were only things. Words only words. I thought I saw Daisy's expression soften.

"What about all my mother's clients?" I went on. "You must

need someone to replace her. And I can sound like her. Sure. I can be her no problem." I threw my head back like my mother did in the mirror, opened my eyes halfway, and peered at Daisy with what felt like my mother's gaze. How strange it was to become her, but there was something natural about it, as if she had lived within me all along and had just woken up.

"The reason I started doing this work in the first place," Daisy said, "is because men on the phone can't beat you around. They can't touch you at all if you're looking to not be touched. And here's the secret. It's not really about sex. It's about connection. I like to think of myself as more of a therapist than a therapist. These men can't say this stuff to their therapist. This is the last house on the block in terms of total authenticity."

She handed me a card. DAISY DARNELLE, it read. AIN'T NO-THING FINER THAN A CALL WITH A DIVINER.

"All that to say, it's not as easy as you think."

I picked up her bottle of water and finished it. I told her I'd be back the next day, and the day after, waiting for her to say yes.

Chapter 9

But the next day arrived and it was time for Bible study.

DENAY LIVED IN a small tract home in a grouping that was built when I was a baby in the hope that Peaches could grow into something bigger. Farming families moved in and so did Fresno families who had no idea where their produce came from at all, but wanted a taste of that country life, somewhere to have chickens in their backyard, a small horse for birthday parties. The homes here all looked the same, all a beige stucco style with high pillars standing guard in front of unimpressive front doors with broken screens that didn't quite fit the frames. *Tuscany can be yours!* the faded sign read out front. Now Denay's father was barely making it as a checker at the Pac, his raisin days long gone. But they wouldn't leave. Being of Vern's church was its own vocation.

The door opened. Denay's eyelids were shellacked in heavy gold glitter. Her boobs stuck out and I could tell she was wearing two bras. "Listen," she said, blocking my entry. "I'd rather if we just didn't mention your mom at all. I'm on a real good track right now with God and I can't have you bringing any weirdness in here."

"I have an assignment," I said.

"My daddy says there's two kinds of assignments," Denay said, leaning in close. "Important ones that actually mean something, and ones that are just to keep folks busy."

"What sort did you get?" I asked.

She moved aside to let me in, eyeing me. I flopped down on the big pleather sectional that took up most of their living room. A big-screen TV was cockeyed on the wall and a blanket featuring a huge lifelike embroidery of Vern's face her mother had made was strewn across a recliner that matched the couch. I used to be jealous of Denay's big house and all their nice things but today everything looked wrong next to my memory of the red house. Denay's mother's collection of unused Bath and Body Works candles, her apron that hung in the kitchen that said WINE O'CLOCK, the worn gray carpeting—it all seemed fake and cheap and stupid. I had touched velvets, I had seen the gleam of hardwood floors, cowhide rug underfoot.

"Don't tempt me, Lacey May. Jesus." Denay smoothed the Vern blanket. I thought she might wrap herself in it even in this heat to show off her dedication, but she didn't. She sat next to me.

I wanted to tell her I felt like I was going crazy in this heat and was she? Was she? Had anyone laid over her and how did it make her feel?

Taffy walked in, no knocking like she lived here, wearing a cropped top and white jean shorts. She was petite, and I could put my chin on top of her head if I wanted. Her blond hair was thin and wispy as a baby's.

"We were talking about assignments," Denay said. She cast a look to Taffy and I knew they had discussed more than they were saying now. Taffy smiled. Leaned back in the recliner right on top of the blanket.

"My mother would still be here if it wasn't for her assignment," I said.

"I hope you're not blaming Vern," Denay said.

"Hers was probably the hardest, biggest assignment there was," I said.

"If that even was her assignment," Denay said. "Some folks think she just went crazy and started working there all on her own. Can't stop a true-born whore, some might say."

My mind flickered to my mother's world. *Ain't nothin' finer . . .*

"Do like me and don't question every little thing to death," Taffy said. "Just focus on your assignment and it'll all work out." She patted her flat stomach. "I'm hungry. Your mom make anything? No food around my house. My daddy said it's depression times. I was like, I ain't depressed. Make me a frozen pizza."

A stand-up fan wobbled in the corner of the room but it was no match for the heat of Peaches pressing into us from outside. I sucked sweat from my upper lip and missed the way I used to be with Denay and Taffy before the drought, how the only land we were concerned with was the plains and hills of our bodies. Denay would pull us into her small bedroom and perform a sort of puberty roll call: we took down our pants and stood leg to leg to leg looking at one another and ourselves, how I had hardly any garden growing, how Denay was the clear winner with a thick brown hedge, and how Taffy had long blondish fur collecting like the underchin of a kitten. We never spoke of it out loud, the way we would examine and appraise and then pull our pants back up or smooth skirts back down, fasten bra hooks and close the sights up inside our minds for next time when we would compare again.

"My mom said I'm not allowed to give anything away," Denay said. "Just think about how skinny you'll get and be blessed."

Bottles of water lined the wall in the kitchen. I wondered if I could steal one without her noticing.

"We had those before everything," Denay said, watching me. "Don't even think about taking one."

I peeled my sweaty thighs off the sectional and went to the bathroom down the hall, past the mural of decorations Denay's mother crafted by hand, painted wood planks that said, *In this house we do forgiveness* and *We will serve Vern.* I sat on the toilet and tried to look at myself. Did I look different? It didn't seem so. I ached. I always expected sex would happen years from now, with my husband, a man I loved. A man I had seen from across the church, maybe someone new to town but rich in faith. But not my own cousin. I wanted it to have been the exact right thing but then why wasn't God granting me His peace?

Then my mother was in my mind, but this time we were with Sapphire Earrings on the side of the road where his car had broken down. He was taking us to Mexico, where he could buy "drugs, so many drugs," but we barely made it an hour outside of Peaches and my mother and I wandered the aisles of an air-conditioned Long's while we waited for a tow and I saw a postcard that said, *The greatest happiness you can have is knowing that you do not necessarily require happiness.* "William Saroyan," my mother read over my shoulder. She smacked her gum. "Didn't know what he was talking about."

But this idea had stuck to me for some reason and I thought of it again now. Perhaps the chase of happiness was only a trap to pull us further from God. I wasn't happy in this life but what did that matter when faced with eternity? This was the big question. Was anything really worth an eternity apart from our church family?

I walked out to Denay and Taffy. Seeing them huddled together on the couch, I had the sensation that I was watching my own life go on without me. I wasn't quite here with them like I had been before. I was different now. The feeling felt repulsive in a way, but under that was something else. I didn't let myself dwell on it. I joined them and we read aloud to one another from our Bibles and I went back to being a good member of the Body, Daisy in the rearview. And I knew people on the outside of the church wouldn't understand how I could stay instead of leave, withstand instead of run. I would say those people have never been under the hand of a bad thing so bad it can start to seem good.

Chapter 10

Cherry dragged me to the Pac N' Save so I could watch her hand over her very own money for the groceries that fattened me. "You could use a lesson in gratitude," she'd said that morning. "I want you to watch an old lady pinch her pennies and see how much you like them greasy canned pigs feet after that."

The Pac N' Save could no longer afford to stock bottled water or fresh produce and all that littered the aisles were canned goods and the occasional bag of corn chips. They could not afford to keep the freezers running, so gone were the TV dinners, the syrupy half-melted popsicles. It looked like the whole place was an empty warehouse temporarily being used for a food drive. *Buying the water of another town is like a slap in the face to God!* Vern had said to us. *To me.* I felt his eyes on us all around.

She filled her cart with canned whatever. Whatever was there was fine enough for us, she kept muttering. Canned whole chicken, canned scorpion, three cans of fish mouths.

"You aren't gonna eat any of these," I said. I remembered the square meals she used to cook for Sunday lunch, hot piles of mashed potatoes, asparagus in olive oil, roast so soft it melted from bone. I threw a canned cheeseburger on the pile and my stomach clenched in craving for the real thing.

"These is famine-of-Egypt times," she said. "I'll eat you if you don't watch out."

I walked ahead of her and scanned the town bulletin board. Ads for babysitters and dog walkers and an old depressing faded ad for toddler swim classes. What I wouldn't give to wade in a pool. Grampa Jackie used to complain about Fresno, how almost every house had not only a pool but a sprinkler system that sprayed water over clean-cut front yards rich with grass that nary a child ever played on, and sometimes the sprinkler would be broken and the water would just be spraying the concrete, flooding the street, and no one stopped it. No one caught the water in buckets and worshipped it, but let it dry on the asphalt under the unrelenting sun. Sick, he would say, as if he were talking about murder.

When we turned down the next aisle there was old Gentry Roo standing with an empty basket in one arm, his other arm outstretched as if reaching for something. He was frozen, it seemed, his eyes fixed on the nothing or everything that lay before him. Long legs in his pale cornflower jeans, torn at the knees and hitched high on his hips, a checkered cotton shirt buttoned up to his chin, the sleeves cut off leaving a raw hem, an amethyst bolo tie around his neck. He was hatless today, and his white hair was yellowed in places, combed over a sun-beaten scalp. His lips were creamy in the corners. Thirst was an easy ailment to spot.

"I'm caught in the devil's grasp," he said finally. He still didn't look at us directly. "A little help?"

Cherry went to him and placed her hand on his arm and his head fell. Sweat hung in teardrops from his earlobes like little diamonds. Grampa Jackie would have been about the same age, I figured.

"Now. Gentry," Cherry said. She put a hand to his forehead. "Think you might just need a drink of water?"

"I haven't been drinking any," he said. "Just like I was told."

I handed Cherry a pop-tab can of peaches in syrup and she pulled the top off and handed it to him. He drank the can steadily until the juice was gone and then we watched him eat the slippery peaches one by one, his tongue slow like a thick fish. "My, oh, my," he said. "I've seen the light."

"We best be on now," Cherry said.

"Wait," he said. He lurched forward and pushed his hand against my forehead. His palm was cold against me. He closed his eyes and the lids fluttered. "She's been chosen," he said.

Cherry scrambled up close to him. Laid hands to his arm to catch the foresight that had become him. "Anything about me?"

"This one," he said. "Chosen."

I stepped back and his eyes shot open, such pale blue circles. "Don't be a fool," he said to me, so clear and clipped, nothing like his slow take-your-time voice. It reminded me of a parrot. *Don't be a fool, Don't be a fool.*

Cherry was annoyed and pulled me out by the wrist, leaving our canned goods behind. She arranged dirty towels over the scalding leather seats of the hearse and plopped down. "He could have told us something we didn't know, like how many more days of this. Or maybe what color my Mercedes-Benz is in heaven. How high I can pump that air-conditioning."

I buckled up but I felt shaken and a little angry. I wished God would tell me what to do himself, not through the mouth of a man.

"Once we're in heaven all this will be worth it," she said. "I'm going to have one of those leather purses with the LVs all over it and a mansion with a swan swimming in a swan pool in the backyard."

"Will you swim with the swan?"

Cherry snorted. "The swan is for looks. It's to tell people, I'm so rich I got a pool just for a swan." She drummed the steering wheel. Silence folded over us for a short time and the hot air of the car began to make me tired. She yawned. "Sometimes I don't want to go home," she said. "When I was a kid I used to imagine I was in a coma and I was just dreaming all the things around me, that my real family was standing over my body in a hospital bed saying, *Cherry, Cherry, wake up!* That's a weird thing for a kid to be thinking, ain't it?"

"I don't think it's too weird," I said.

She put her hand in mine and held it. "The closest to a real family I ever felt was after Vern came here and gathered us all up. Made us care about one another. Before him I was just drifting along." My instinct was to pull away but I grasped on to her anyhow.

"He wants the best for each of us, I do believe that," she went on. "It's a relief, ain't it? Knowing someone's got your life in his hands."

I looked at her wrinkled, sun-painted face. Her face like this, soft and sad, always did remind me of my mother's.

TIME HAD PASSED in an odd way after my mother left, fast yet slow, day running into night creating the feeling of one continuous day that never really ended or began. I needed her I needed her. It was not even the fantasy that things had been great when she was around, because that didn't matter. I needed her body next to mine to remind me of my own. I don't know why I loved her the way I did, in this aching way that could not be explained, other than she was my mother. There was no reason beyond that.

The temperature never cooled, never offered relief, and then somehow it was mid-August, time for school to start again. I waited outside the gate that bordered the classroom trailers until the last moment before I had to go in. A huge SUV sailed into the parking lot like a boat, a pop song about undeniable California girls blaring from the speakers.

The cheer girls got out one by one, their knee-length blue skirts rolled at the waist so their periwinkle undies could be seen. I was surprised they were coming back to Peaches Valley High at all. It wouldn't last long, I knew. But it seemed the drought hadn't touched them, still probably having cookouts with Costco hot dogs and jugs of corn syrup limeade, showering at their granny's house in the right county. Their legs long, muscles cut in a line down their thighs. Ribbons perched high on their heads. Some of them were part-time believers, but they didn't come to our church. They liked to say our church wasn't actually Christian at all, didn't follow the true words of the Bible, didn't believe in grace, and didn't know the real Jesus, like he was just a nice casual guy we were refusing to meet. *Cult*, they called us, their sterling silver crosses swinging around their necks.

But Vern liked to remind us that they didn't know that true belief meant giving your whole self away and that anything short of that was just a hobby. They wore their faith like a loose sash they could put on and take off when the moment struck them. Some went to the Journey, a big warehouse church in Fresno County, and attended Rage every Friday night, where a Christian rock band did worship and couples made out behind the building while the cool young pastor played video games with the boys. It sounded both useless and intriguing, a place where it seemed no one had to earn God's approval and where salvation was handed out like a participation ribbon.

"Spacey Lacey," Farley Sampson said. She was the head cheerleader and a Rage girl. She loved God in the way you might love chocolate sundaes. "Meet any spirit fairies in the sky this summer?"

"An eternity's a long time," I said. "Are you prepared?"

She rolled her eyes. Took out a bottle of Crystal Geyser water from her backpack and drank it slowly. Her tiny silver cross necklace glinted in the sun. I wanted her to pull me into her SUV and haul me out of Peaches then, lead me to a simple life where the drought was something you heard about on the news but didn't connect to your actual life. The rest of the squad crowded around her, pressing powder from black MAC compacts into sweaty foreheads, smearing their lips in sparkly Oh Baby gloss.

"Can I try that powder?" I said. I knew it was nice makeup, much more expensive than anything in my mother's makeup bag. But they had already forgotten about me, huddled together. I was invisible.

I scanned the parking lot for Denay or Taffy, but they weren't there. I walked to the edge of the gate where Laramie Stam's red truck tore down the road, Lyle and some of the boys' club standing up in the bed, puff-chested like ship guides. Lyle wore rolled-up jean overalls with a black torn shirt underneath, new white cowboy boots, and his hair was combed back in a smooth wave, his teeth a wet shine. He looked more alive than ever. More vibrant. I hated that he reminded me of the photograph of my mother that hung in Cherry's entryway, her arms out as if about to take flight, the flat stretch of land behind her, all teeth and pulled-back eyes. Like her, Lyle smiled up at the sky and reached his arms out, captain of the world. Family was a strange idea, how it connected us by appearance, locking us to one another through similar noses, cheekbones, smirks. I hated that Lyle looked like my mother.

The truck breezed past me. I opened my mouth and tasted dust. They parked in the last row and Lyle jumped out. He clapped Laramie on the back and then he turned. Came toward me.

He had taken a cool distance from me since the shed. He'd been busy, so busy, with Vern. I hadn't seen him up close since it happened, and my body responded: I held my breath. I pulled my dress down. My legs clenched together and my jaw was a trap.

"Coming in?" he said.

"I need Vern to tell me himself that what we did was right," I said.

"Did you think your whole life would remain the same forever?"

"I wish I could just go in there and be normal and not have to think about the drought or any of this," I said. "Like Farley Sampson. I wish I could be her. No cares at all."

"You think stooping as low as an infidel is gonna bring anything good? You wouldn't dig through a trash can to get to a steak at the bottom, would you?"

He brushed past me, entwining his pinky with mine before he went, just for a split second, so fast I couldn't be sure it had happened.

I looked at the school one more time and a nervous laugh came out of me. I just wouldn't go. I'd always gone but now I wouldn't. I took backward steps away, waited for someone to run out and grab me but there was no one. The world didn't operate on the rules I'd once thought it did.

I RAN ALONG the fence until it ended and I paused to catch my breath. A car idled next to me. It was Pearl.

"Geary came by and asked why I didn't take you in, as if it's expected for the sister of the sinner to make everything right. I'll have you know, missy, I've got a lot on my plate. I'm working overtime at the post and I've got Lyle as my very own son, lighting matches and invoking the Holy Ghost in his own room all the night."

Pearl seemed a strange apparition then, a version of my mother, but not my mother. A cellular twin of a kind, but the traits were scrambled on Pearl and not of comfort to me. She told me to get in.

She smelled of heavy chemical perfume and wore pearl earrings, her trademark, what a surprise. I smelled her wine seeping from her skin, the bitter twang of noble rot, cinnamon Altoids working to cover. I could turn her in right now, couldn't I? Why wasn't she afraid of meeting the same end as my mother? She turned down her Amy Grant CD.

"Your mother used to skip all the time. She'd hitchhike into Fresno and do God knows what. Once she ended up out at Motel Drive calling me from a pay phone. She thought there was a real audition for a teen dream soap out there. That's what kind of girl she was. A dummy."

Motel Drive, I hardly remembered ever passing it, the low-ceilinged row of motels, the flickering neon signs. Women leaning over the railings, leaning into car windows. *One hour rates*, the sign said, and I'd wondered who needed a hotel for just one hour, but I didn't ask my mother, and she kept her eyes on the road. Now I knew all that could happen in an hour.

"I ought to take you straight to Vern and have him give you a nice long kiss and taste all that sinner's wine," I said.

She turned and looked me up and down.

"How you gonna shut me up?"

She tugged at the hem of my mother's sundress. "I can see your holy grail right through this fabric. Guess you wouldn't mind some new clothes," she said, steering the car toward the Dolly Do clothing boutique. It was situated in the one strip of shops in Peaches, between the Peaches and Cream Malt Shop and the Ag One.

Inside, old Ms. Crenshaw sat like a bony hawk at the counter patting cold cream into her cheeks with her eyes closed. "Sinner's delight," she cawed. She peered over the counter. "Here for some self-respect?" She clicked her tongue at Pearl. "The things girls wear today. Just like they don't care about the fine bodies God done give 'em. Like they want every man to turn into a dog and start sniffin' up their cooters. In my day we wore gingham up to our eyelids and the boys wished they could have a look." She pecked her face in closer to me. "But they couldn't. And that's why they wanted to marry us."

I looked around at the broad-shouldered clothing. My mother never shopped here. She called it the Sad Lady store. I put on a beaded necklace and a pair of sunglasses and looked in the mirror. Behind me Pearl held up a rail-stripe coverall, large and straight in its dimensions with buttons from the crotch up to its collared neck. It looked like a jail suit. "This is perfect for every day and'll keep you of singular mind."

"Keep the wrong boys away," Ms. Crenshaw said, nodding.

"Tell me," I said to Ms. Crenshaw, holding the suit up against my form. "Why you never married if you wore so much gingham?"

Ms. Crenshaw pursed her lips. "Some's called into singleness. Your mama was clearly meant to be one of them, but I guess she couldn't hold down such a commitment."

I gripped the rail-stripe canvas. I decided I would cut the sleeves off and the legs off and tie a jump rope around the middle like a sunsuit. "I love this," I said to Pearl. "I want it."

"That was fast," Pearl said. "Your mother would have taken hours and tried everything on before deciding. She would have twirled around the store waiting for compliments. Maybe there is some hope in you."

"My mother," I said, looking at Ms. Crenshaw, "wouldn't have touched this place with a ten-foot pole."

I imagined turning and telling them both what Lyle had done. But I stopped. I wouldn't be a fool. To tell them about Lyle would only be telling them about myself.

VERN LIVED WITH his wife, Derndra, and their daughter, Trinity Prism, in a white stone house on the edge of church property. On each stone of the house was a Bible verse written in thin-point marker giving the effect of marbled stone from far away. They were not home as far as I could tell; no activity outside in the dead field surrounding the house, no rustle of a window curtain. But their car was in the driveway, a tan sedan stamped with personalized bumper stickers: *Remember who brought the rains* and *If you were on trial for following Vern, would there be enough evidence to convict you?* The hood was covered in silver glitter with a black cross painted on it, flashy.

Trinity Prism and Derndra could rarely be seen about town, the two of them claiming allergies to the sun. If they came out you could find them with white parasols spinning over their shoulders, covered in floor-length dresses, tattered and thin like they'd been cut angrily from sheets. Their eyes seemed to have a pinkish hue to them, hay fever perhaps, and once my mother had commented that they reminded her of twitching white rabbits. *You don't ever want to be compared to a rabbit, trust me.*

Trinity Prism didn't speak to the Body much, but moved in a whispering orbit around her mother, and they both wore pinched faces like someone was slapping them but they had decided to endure it. Trinity was not one of the Bible study girls. Instead she was set apart as what Vern called his angel helper, a role that would live and die with her alone. It seemed to me the pastor's daughter should be involved in all number of church activities, but it wasn't so.

I knocked on the door but nothing. I edged around to the back-yard and unhooked the side gate. Nothing there either but then my eyes adjusted. What I saw, I didn't know. My eye had forgotten how to take in a verdant green, the healthy leaf of a plant thriving under morning sun. But before me stood a lush vine in the middle of an otherwise barren backyard, clearly alive, and on it, heaving pale green muscats. I was panting, I realized, looking at them. The perfection of their roundness. How they might feel in my palm, the burst of juice down my chin at first bite. I could pick a bunch and run. I could fill a basket and take them home to Cherry and she might let me off fly duty for at least a week. I remembered Grampa Jackie bent over in his rows, the way he delicately laid the thick bunches on paper trays, like each one was a newborn child. If he could see this now.

Halfway to the vine I heard the sliding glass door open but I kept my pace.

"Each day I come out and say a prayer for it," Vern said, walking toward me. "I ask God to keep it alive and He does." I knelt at the vine and he stood over me. Being near it was intoxicating. "Now imagine if every believer in Peaches had my level of faith. Imagine how much more green we might see."

I felt my hands tremble. The sight of the vine was almost too glorious to bear, it almost looked fake. "I doubted you," I said.

The confession poured out, my shame laid bare—shame for feeling afraid of what Lyle and I had done. I'd perverted it, I saw now. Vern, our dear pastor, God's chosen son and confidant. I wanted to eat of the grapes so badly. I reached out to grab one but he grasped my wrist. Then he softened, knelt next to me. The knees of his white jeans became brown. He reached forward and plucked a grape from its stem and popped it in his mouth. He put one to my lips, and I bit through it with my front teeth, the wetness on my tongue, the long lost dance of fruit sugar.

"You know, for a time I would see you and your mother together and think how alike you were. But now I see you different. I see you as a woman of your own. A smart woman."

"She was smart," I said.

"Was she? She didn't stay obedient. She didn't stay around here for you. But you know who has? Me. Your church family. We're here for you."

He pulled another grape from a stem and put it in my mouth, held his finger to my bottom lip. "Eat and be well."

I closed my eyes. These were nothing like the soggy purple imports that used to litter the Pac N' Save. This was the taste of life.

"I'm worried what I've done is bad," I heard myself say.

He sighed. He put his chin in his hand like a boy waiting for ice cream. I wondered what he was like before God began using him. "It's hard leading the people, you know," he said. He looked at me and it seemed he wanted to tell me something then. I leaned closer. His eyes were soft, tired. But then he straightened.

"Our humanness, our meager shames and fears. They are nothing in the face of His glory."

"I miss her so much," I said. He wiped tears from my cheeks. He pulled me to his chest. I tried to listen for his heart but there was only stillness.

"You've already done the right thing. Keep on now." He pushed me away from him, gentle but firm, and the kind repose was gone. I saw Derndra's rabbit face watching from behind the glass door.

I trembled all the way home. I understood Cherry then, how you could witness a miracle and how it could change the way you saw everything forevermore. Perhaps this was what it would have

been like to see those first rains fall over the land, as shocking as
that brilliant vine against all the dead. My mind brought me back
to the red house every other thought, but I could fight against that.
It was just a temptation common as any.

WHEN I GOT back to Cherry's, I wanted to tell her of my reali-
zation, I wanted to celebrate and dance, the grape juice still on my
tongue. But Cherry wasn't out on the porch looking at her grass. It
was Stringy, the lawn painter from Popcorn, Indiana, sweating on
her rocker, a box of stone chinchillas under one arm. "No one answered, so I figured I'd wait," he said. "See how you liked my little
present." He looked out over the lawn, which was still a neon shout.

I went inside and brought him out a cup of warm soda. His
lopsided smile was simple. There was nothing behind it, I decided.

"I love it," I said.

I could still feel Vern's finger on my lip, the salt of his skin
mixed with the sweet of the grapes, but I liked hearing Stringy talk.
On and on he went about nothing, his cares so small. I liked how
he looked at me, like I amused him, like he'd never known a girl in
all his life.

"Let me get your number," he said. "I'll take you out sometime."

I told him I didn't have a phone but he said that everyone had
a phone. I held my hands out, empty. I told him how Cherry didn't
like the house line tied up in case she wanted to play Telephone
Testimony, calling up randoms from the phone book and trying to
convert them through an even lecture of terror and love. He nodded like he understood and then made a remark about how I wasn't
wearing the bikini today.

"You're not in the green elf suit," I said back. Instead he was
freshly shaven, a few spots of dried blood on his cheek where a

razor had sheared the heads off pimples. His eyes were wrinkled around the corners, but his body was all boy, skinny in his black T-shirt and black sagged shorts, white socks pulled up midcalf. He didn't dress like a country boy, like the boys of Peaches with their faded jean cutoffs, soiled white shirts that came from a ten-pack. His shirt said *Blink 182* and had a picture of a harshly pretty nurse who I strongly suspected wasn't really a nurse pulling a blue glove over her tattooed arm. I wondered if this was the type of woman Stringy wanted to be with, someone with angles of makeup drawn on, breasts pushed up until they kissed. I couldn't help but feel that she had taken whatever sexiness I might have had and canceled it out with her own.

"You found God?" It came from my mouth like the deepest routine.

He looked me up and down, side-smiling. "I found you." Then he told me he'd be back in an hour. I went inside and imagined I'd never see him again, but then after hardly any time at all there he was on the other side of the screen holding up a bright blue bag. "I activated it for you and everything."

I pulled out a box and inside was a small silver phone with rubber number buttons and a little square screen. I thought of the sapphire earrings from my mother's old boyfriend, how after he had pushed the posts through my skin they had rusted and made my swollen ears bleed red and yellow pus. I would take them out at night so he wouldn't know and I'd put them back in in the morning, eyes watering. How he looked at me and pushed my hair back each time he saw me to make sure I was wearing them. The gift had come with a high price.

I handed the phone back to Stringy. "It's too nice."

But he set it on the ground before my feet and walked back

to his truck, arms up. Said that maybe it was okay for me to take something nice.

LYLE DID IT to me five times. Always in the shed, me on my back. Each time he came to it like a chore, or sports practice of some kind that he was only half interested in, his eyes resigned, his face flushed and exhausted with effort.

I marked them in my notebook where I had once listed my mother's beers. I tried to make little notes alongside each one—*did not hurt as much, was faster this time*—but then I stopped bothering. They all became sewn together in my memory as the first time it had happened. The other details fell away, aside from the fact that by that fifth time I was completely rid of myself and made new into a girl with a stone for a stomach, a jittery wire running through my veins. I felt nothing from Lyle, not a tingle or hint of pleasure as it happened. I left my body like I had trained myself to do, and I became better and better at it. I prayed during the time, I didn't despair. I thought of telephones ringing, my mother on the other end. I pictured Vern's kind eyes and I tasted the grapes, juice on my lips.

I was fine and things would be well but my eyes grew black with insomnia and I peeled the skin from around my nails and had taken to eating it.

"Are we going to get married?" I asked Lyle after that fifth time. For I still didn't know what it was all for. A unification of the Body, perhaps, some pact or bonding secret, but what it would provide the land, or the church, was hazy and out of focus. This muddled goal was what bothered me most.

In all my not knowing, I decided it must be something that would eventually occur within me, like Lyle had hinted at. Some heart change, some transfer of power that would give me a higher order of gifting. I knew through my romances that real sex caused a quickening of the love pulse, made you moan in pleasure. Made your body swell and burst.

He pulled his shirt over his head. The shed walls seemed to pour heat on us. Grampa Jackie's old rodeo posters had peeled and died, their pictures gone, just browned paper now. It was midday and the sun sat meanly overhead, finding its way in through the slits in the ceiling. Sweat had dripped from Lyle's forehead onto my chest and mixed with my own. I needed cool water to cleanse me. I dabbed at the sweat but stopped. What if we were to be married? I had better get used to his sweat. I tried to picture myself in a white dress, saying *Are you sure?* to God, hoping that maybe everyone could forget we were cousins after all. That fact embarrassed me. I supposed I could learn to love Lyle. It would happen with time, with God's help, all things were possible. Weren't they? But Lyle shook me from my daydream.

"Our work is done. You aren't the only one I'm making holy with my seed. I have a quiver full of arrows."

A tightening ran through my ribs. I braced both hands on the floor.

"Vern said you're a full-moon bleeder," he went on. "Now we've done all there is to do and we've done it at the right time. There's gonna be rewards beyond our wildest dreams. Rain like you wouldn't believe. Get your umbrella ready, Lacey May."

I reached up and my hand gripped the neck of his shirt. "Who else?"

"Are you jealous? Of your own cousin? That's just sad."

"You've been with more than just me? Is this a big joke?" Blood throbbed in my ears. I felt ordinary then, utterly unspecial. I had thought myself supremely chosen, but now I wasn't the only one. "I'll tell Cherry what you've done."

"You mean what *we've* done."

Full-moon bleeder. I remembered how Vern had lifted my bloody tissue to his nose. How my mother had told me to wait. Not to go. And I'd disobeyed her immediately.

"By the time everything is revealed," he said. "You, too, will believe in the white light that came upon you in the dark, in your bed while you were alone in prayer."

Chapter 11

Days and days and days of heat. I tried to remember what a chill felt like to the skin, but I could not. *No sun like this anywhere else in the world . . .*

August left us and by mid-September my mother had still not called. This was no vacation she was on. My meager fantasies about what this was were no longer holding up. This was abandonment.

Stew-brown water sludged from the faucet and we gave up on trying at all. Our toilets were useless bowls, and Cherry instructed as I dug a basin in the backyard and we propped a rusted lawn chair over it and cut a hole out of the seat. There was talk that someone would deliver barrels of rationed water each week but when I asked Cherry where they were, she said it wasn't the will of God that we would allow some infidel from the next unholy town to bring in our blessing on four wheels. We'd rather be a believing town, waterless, but believing.

But it was hard to keep believing when the stench of the filthy Body during church services was enough to send us girls outside to vomit in the dead grass. As it splashed on my feet I wondered how it was that no men seemed to need to throw up from the smell. Denay leaned against the wall hunched over and groaning while Taffy petted her and dry heaved, a worse punishment, pain with no release. Sharon retched and moaned and her vomit came out in thick globs like oatmeal.

"I can't take it anymore," she said. "I'm gonna crawl out of this town and hope a truck runs me down or picks me up. I don't even care which."

"My mom said it ain't that bad," said Maisie Lynn, a beanpole of a girl with a frizz of black hair. "I told her to take a hike and she slapped me."

I wondered who exactly had been with Lyle. I couldn't help but picture Taffy with him. I was sick again in the dirt.

"Maybe we're coming down with a possession," I said. I sat against the building. I felt emptied out.

Denay scoffed. "As if demons would dare approach us. Do you know how important we are to this church?"

Maybe he'd been with her, I considered. I wondered if he got to choose. I wondered how any of this had happened.

"Shut up, Denay," Sharon said.

"You're all weak in faith," Denay said. "The time is now. This is the trial, when it really counts to God." She wiped her mouth on her bare arm. Her brown waves fell over her face and she looked pretty, the sun filtering through her hair from behind, but there was something energetically off about her, something that could not be explained, but felt. "Anyone can be a believer when times are easy, and God knows that." I wanted to know where her confidence came from. She walked back into the church, leaving us all there like cows at trough.

AT CHERRY'S AFTER church, the nausea kept on as I lay on the kitchen floor and cleaned the fly larvae.

"This doesn't make any difference," I snapped, scraping the black patches of eggs that had reappeared overnight. I flicked a squirming flesh-colored maggot off my hand.

Cherry stomped around with the bull penis cane, swatting the flies out of the air. I could hear their bodies hit the floor, fat and slow. That morning I'd woken up to a layer of them on my face, my neck, rubbing their little stick arms together like they were trying to start a fire.

"You ever make my mom do this when she was young?" I asked. "Or was she too valuable to you? Too pretty to break a nail?"

"She was supposed to win Miss California," Cherry said. "We even sent her pictures to *Playboy* magazine. That was before we were believers of the highest order, of course, Vern forgive me, but they wrote her back. They said *almost*. We'd like to see more emphasis on the breasts. Oh, we did her hair up in a beehive and had her half naked at the stove cooking. She chanted, *Eggs eggs eggs. Bacon bacon bacon.* It gave it a realness."

I remembered the pictures perfectly, how before our conversion my mother had tacked them up in our bedroom with pushpins, a collage of her face and body, along with Polaroids she had taken of herself pouting and shellacked with body glitter. In one she was bent over in a thong, hands on her breasts and a whistle between her teeth. In another she was kissing a woman for show, both their eyes looking at the camera, tongues out and searching. My mother had come home with this woman after meeting her at the DMV. They had become very best friends in the waiting area. The woman drank Welch's grape juice all day from a big plastic bag with a spigot she carried around in her purse and the whites of her eyes were tinged purple from it. She had a slew of children that seemed to be naked and breastfeeding all day, pulling her tit out at their whimsy and drinking from it like a hose—standing up and bending over, all kinds of gymnastics. I was entranced with them feeding from her in this way and stared openly until finally she asked if I wanted some. I was six years old and proud to be a big first grader. "That's for babies," I said, as her son who was my same age gulped from her nipple. "Oh yeah?" she said. She pulled the breast out of his mouth and squirted me in the face. The milk landed on my lips, some reached my tongue, and I froze. It was warm. I think I had expected that grape juice would come out of her, but no, it was dairy, sugar sweet. She cawed with laughter and slapped her knee. "Your face!" she kept squealing. "What, you never drank your mama's titty before?" She stuffed her breasts back into her bikini top. I looked at her kids and felt sorry for them. They probably felt sorry for me.

"What are you daydreaming about, you little weirdo?" Cherry asked. Her demeanor had shifted. She was suspicious of me now. She lit a raspberry Sweet Dream and blew smoke into my hair. "Wondering where that mama of yours is? I know I am. 'Bout time she came back to relieve me from housing the ungrateful."

My fingers ached. *Ungrateful.* How I wanted away from Cherry with such a deep desperation. How I'd do anything to get my mother back, to get out of there.

"Where you think that cowboy took her?" she asked.

"I know how to find out," I said.

Cherry tossed her head back. "Oh boy, she's all full of ideas."

I didn't really know, but I wanted Cherry to imagine me strong, smarter than her, smarter than she ever knew me to be. My mind raced with what to say.

"Come on now," she chided. "Tell your Cherry your secrets."

I closed my eyes. At first there was nothing, but then I saw it. The red house. The red house held all the answers. I let myself feel it fully. But I didn't want Cherry to come with me. They would take one look at her and slam the door. She would ruin everything.

"You don't want to know," I said.

She cocked her head to the side, trying to figure me out. Clicked her tongue. I wondered if she was thinking of that red house too, and knew that it would have to be me and me alone to go there. Get what we needed. She turned away and put the Sweet Dream out in her full ashtray. She nodded at the wall. "Don't tell your old Cherry the sin of your heart."

I wouldn't, I decided. I wouldn't tell anyone.

BY THE TIME I arrived at the red house it was nearly dusk, not another soul for miles that I could see. The fields caught the last of the sun and shimmered back an odd orange. The smell of manure was gone. Most of the livestock had been shipped out but a few of the very sickly ones starved and died and their carcasses lay in the fields, sharp bones poking skywise. I remembered how before the drought, Lyle had been involved in Future Farmers of America, how he'd raised up a pig named Twanda in their backyard and how he loved the pig like a pet. It wore a red bandana around its neck and sniffed the dirt like a pup. He took her to competitions and showboated her around a tent in his Wrangler's and Grampa Jackie's tan suede cowboy hat. But then they slaughtered her and had us over for a pork feast and we all ate Twanda, and I remember watching Lyle, the pig grease glossing his lips, wondering how he'd done it, killed the thing he loved. Of course I'd been around it my whole life, the raising and the killing. I'd watched animal blood spill from hanging gut, splashing on the butcher's boots. I'd smelled the metal of death, that was survival, that was country living. But I'd never known a boy to love a pig like that and then eat it.

I knocked on the door. Waited. No megaphone this time. It swung open and the girl was before me, earphones around her neck. Black coal smudged her cheek and fingers. Her eyes were rimmed in green eyeliner and her lips a ghost white. There was a notebook behind her on the desk where she'd been sketching a picture of a horse skeleton.

"My mother and I took bets on if you'd come back," she said. "I said never and she said absolutely. Guess she does know how to read people."

The smell in the house was deep and sweet, streams of smoke coming from long wands of wood cradled by porcelain dishes on the desk. A ceiling fan whirred above and the air was artificially cool like I hadn't felt in so long. "Daisy here?"

"Hasn't left since we moved in three years ago."

"How is that possible?" I asked.

The girl looked at me blank. "How is anything possible?"

A laugh shot out of me and it startled her, but then she laughed too. How was anything possible? Yet so many things were. Suddenly I felt tired.

Daisy came down the stairs, her black kimono trailing behind. She wore an emerald velvet long-sleeved leotard under it and knee-high black leather boots. The heat outside was nothing to her. It didn't exist. Her scars were covered in a thick pancake of foundation, her cheekbones artfully contoured with bronzer. If I squinted it was almost like seeing her without the burns entirely but for her white iris. There was not a lick of dirt anywhere on her.

"You've met Florin, my daughter," Daisy said. She put her hand on Florin's shoulder. "She feels she has a tragic life but I tell her it will only make her less simple, which of course is a good thing. No one wants to be simple."

"I'm here," I said.

Daisy nodded like she knew all about it, like she knew I had lain with a man unmarried, that I had read the pornography of the romances and craved them and I had touched myself so many times I couldn't count. That I had lied to my mother about my first blood and now here I was, one sin leading to the next like a knotted rope I'd hang myself with when I reached the end of it.

I would do anything to find my mother. I was here and I'd do anything.

The phone rang. Florin looked at the caller ID. "It's Forne," she said. "Tractor supply guy out of Sanger. He likes to feel adored and then he likes you to detail how you'd tie him up and put him in the trunk of his own car and drive him around town past his wife's salon and past his kid's soccer practice. Then you untie him and tell him everything's going to be okay while he weeps like a willow. That's basically it. Then you pretend you have some insider knowledge of his wife coming up the drive and he'll hang up on you in the world's biggest rush."

"What's the matter with him?" I asked.

"Nothing," Daisy said. "We all have fantasies. We're just happy these men can unload the lifetime of shit they've been fed their whole lives and be vulnerable while keeping to themselves."

"Otherwise they get out of hand," Florin added.

They talked about men like they were dumb dogs that needed to be herded around but were still big and strong so you had to be careful with them. My mother always hated dogs—she said don't ever trust someone with a dog who thinks it won't eat their throat if it's hungry.

"So it's a deal," I said. "I work and you give me the number."

"I guess we'll see how you do," Daisy said.

"What else do I need to know?"

"Well, how's your imagination?" She knocked on my head. "You read books?"

Did I ever. I nodded.

"You'll be fine, then."

INSIDE MY MOTHER'S call room the air hung with her presence as if she'd only just stepped out moments before. I smelled her rosewater, saw her hairs clinging to the back of the chair. On her desk, a framed picture of the two of us. It was taken the year before outside the church. We wore matching dresses on an Easter Sunday when I couldn't have imagined what was to come.

"She was a beauty you don't see every day, I have to say," Daisy said.

I set the frame on its face and put my mother's headset on. Looked to Daisy, who was wringing her hands. Did she want to stop me? Her own daughter didn't seem to take calls. But I wasn't her daughter. "You're in control here," she said. "Not them. One of the few places in the world that's true, far as I know."

I nodded, eyes on my knees. She backed away from me and stood in the doorway. I was in it now, fallen from ship into wild swelling seas. I would be different after the call just as I was different after Lyle, just as I was different after each of my mother's boyfriends had swept our lives into their own and spat us back out. I thought of Vern's sermons of purity, how the worst thing a girl could do was hand her godly husband a flower with all the petals plucked off. How each time you were touched it stripped you of something vital, of your very worth. I saw myself a trim stalk, colorless in the sun. I didn't understand how women could be reduced to those petals. No, it didn't seem right. But who could know what the real truth was? At one time the petal talk had seemed like the most logical, surest way to live I'd ever heard. A safe system of dividing girls good from bad. Something about that simplicity had felt good at the time. Order where before there had been none. Rules to keep a girl whole.

I looked to Daisy. "Stay with me," I said to her, and she nodded at the red blinking call button. I could have gotten up and walked away. I could have saved what was left of my flower, but instead I clicked that red flashing button my mother's own finger had pushed many times. I'm doing this for you, I thought. This is who you've made me into.

"Hello, darling," I said, imitating her slow talk she liked to use on men. "Sunny on the line."

Forne was silent at first, then there was rustling like a squirrel in a sack. "I'm already in the plastic bag for you, Mistress."

"Good job," I said, perhaps a little too enthusiastically.

The rustling stopped. "Am I in a safe place?" he asked slowly. I imagined his eyes darting from side to side.

I deepened my voice again. "Of course you are." I thought to my romances, the steamiest scenes. It seemed often the men in them wanted to be belittled, made to feel like bad children. "But I see the bag isn't tight enough. You have a hard time doing it right."

He gasped. "I'm sorry, I know you like the bag extra tight. It's tight now."

This went on, me trying to describe how I would get his body into the trunk of his car, *a Dodge Stratus*, he had whispered when I struggled to come up with convincing details—"key in the ignition, now, here we go, in the Dodge Stratus." I pretended to drive him all around neighborhoods of humiliation while he imagined himself secure in his plastic bag, bumping into the sides of the trunk when

I went too fast. I wondered if he cared about my body or what I was really doing on the other side of the line. This wasn't sex to me. This was stage play. Something about it felt easy. I felt similar to when I read the romances—I was on another planet. I was happy? Daisy slipped out and I was alone.

"My foot is uncomfortable. I *hate* this," he said.

"Do you want to do something else?" I asked.

He was silent.

"Oh," I said, back in character. "Well, that's what you deserve for being bad."

"Tell me what I did," he said.

"You didn't read your Bible."

"I'm sorry," he whined.

"You probably can't even read."

"I can't, I can't," he moaned. "I'm so stupid."

I spent time detailing how stupid he was. He told me about bad grades he'd received in school, his mean father, and how his mother liked to openly say he wasn't very bright but was good with his hands. I felt sorry for the things he'd endured, so I had to imagine myself talking to my stupid father, the man with one short leg, in order to be mean enough. I pictured him and really let loose. I accused Forne of being a chicken shit, something my mother liked to call my father when she spoke of him, and I made fun of him freely in the way I would never have been able to do to anyone in real life. I was an actress in a movie. I was no longer Lacey. What a relief.

"What's that?" I said. "Is that your wife coming up the drive?"

He moaned a little and I heard more rustling. I wondered where he actually was in his house. The closet floor maybe, the bathroom with the door locked. He clearly was not in the trunk of his car. That would be too risky. His breath got ragged and then he let out a little whoop like he'd just gone down an exhilarating slide. It felt like an adult game where we were both present but each having an entirely different experience. The whole thing was tolerable, fun even. He hung up and it was over.

I came out to the front desk, where Daisy was perched and Florin was typing.

"Well?" Florin said.

"Was it supposed to be hard?" I said, but I felt my hands shaking. A weird high had taken me over like I'd gotten away with something.

"You did pretty good," Daisy said, ascending the stairs. "Give me a week. Prove you're serious."

I waited for Florin to direct me somehow, but instead she went to the bathroom. I heard her through the door talking quickly into her cell phone to one of her friends, not concerned with me at all. I felt tricked. I had worked and expected the Turquoise Cowboy's number in return. I looked at the leather-bound call log on the desk where Florin had been sitting moments ago. I put my hand on it. I felt that a clue to my mother's whereabouts was bound to be inside.

"It's hard, isn't it?" Daisy said, suddenly, somehow, back at the foot of the stairs. "To finally find what we're searching for?"

"I like it here," I said. The truth.

"You don't really want that number," Daisy said. "You don't really want to know about the life she chose."

I took my hand off the call log. I remembered once finding my mother's journal and reading the notes she'd made of our days. *Lacey is whiny today, getting on my last nerve. I hope it's a stage. He hit me again last night after she was asleep. Told me I was the worst names in the book. Sometimes I look at Lacey and I think I won't be around to see her grow up. I don't know why I think that but I just can't see it. I don't know why I can't ever feel good.*

"Steer clear of men like him and you'll do just fine," Daisy said. "I learned my lesson but some women never do. If you come back here let it be because you want to, not because you want anything to do with that disgusting man. She was weak to him, and why be around weakness if you don't have to?"

I wanted to please her, to show her I could be satisfied in this new life without my mother, agree with Daisy's logic of good and bad. That I was above all that had happened. I settled into the fainting couch and pretended to doodle on some of Florin's paper. I waited until I heard Daisy's door click shut from upstairs. I was not above anything.

It wasn't hard to find my mother's name on the call log, or to see the name written next to it multiple times a day every day—*Rick Walden Rick Walden Rick Walden*—until he had come through the phone and taken her.

THAT NIGHT I slept the deepest I had in months, my heart quiet, my mind a dreamless scape.

When morning came, I dialed the Turquoise Cowboy's number—or Rick Walden's number, actually, a name so simple it seemed it couldn't possibly be right—on the go-phone. I remembered how Vern spoke of faith, how faith lived not in the mind, contrary to what everyone thought. It lived in the body. It was an action. You had to throw yourself into action without thinking. Thinking could come later, *would* come later, as a divine happening if you just put the body in motion. I rocked back and forth on the mattress. I needed to pee but everything could wait. I pressed the call button. It rang and rang. Finally a rasp of a woman answered.

"Rick's Angels," she said. "How can I direct your pleasure?"

"I'll need to speak to Louise Herd, please and thank you," I said in a deep voice.

The woman paused. "You talking about Little Lou?"

"Sure," I said. "That's the one."

The line was quiet, then I heard breathing.

"Hello," a voice said on the other end. It sounded strange. I realized I never talked to my mother on the phone much. She had always been right there.

"Where are you?" I said.

A long pause, so long I feared she'd hung up on me.

"You're different," she said finally. I detected a hint of the slanted drunk voice I hated. The voice that told me she wasn't there anymore.

I felt a lump threaten my throat. "I'm sorry." How I'd wanted to say those words to her. "I'm sorry for not standing up for you."

I had imagined spending the first ten minutes of the call telling her she was forgiven, listening as she cried and begged for me to love her again. But she hadn't even told me she missed me. That she was sorry, too. That the whole thing was wrong, but could be fixed. I wanted her to fear losing me, tell me with desperation that I was hers. But I hadn't ever needed to squirm away from her grasp. It seemed her hands never held me tight enough.

"You are my mother," I said. A reminder.

I heard her light a cigarette. "You couldn't say one nice word about me to that church. And now that I'm here, well, I can see you wouldn't like it."

I saw Lyle's body then, I felt the gummy way the white stuff he put in me stuck to my skin, the way it never seemed to properly wash off. The blood on her bikini, my hand off the blanket, in the dirt.

"I just want to be with you."

She was quiet. Sighed. "He thinks television is the way for me. He said I'm television pretty, not movie pretty."

My stomach bubbled. I felt a flu coming on, maybe something I had eaten turned evil. Or like I'd begun to suspect, my motherloss was so real it was becoming a sickness inside me. I dry heaved. I looked around as if there could be a cold glass of water somewhere. I drank some warm Kool-Aid Cherry had mixed with soda and it burned all the way down. "If you could see me," I said to my mother. "You would come back."

"Rick already warned me my own family would be the least supportive," she said. "He didn't want any of you interrupting my process of becoming a star. In fact, if he comes back I'll have to go. Doesn't like us on the phone."

I said, "Mom, I have to tell you something." But then I thought: What was the something? Was it Lyle or was it that I lay down under him? Was it the Diviners or was it me becoming a phone girl? I couldn't bring myself to say any of it aloud.

"Now you can have birthday parties at Cherry's if you want. You don't have to be ashamed of our apartment anymore," she said. "You're practically an adult. I raised you up and now you're grown."

I had never asked for a birthday party. I had never complained of our small apartment, the fact that of course I would never have a friend spend the night because there was not room in the bed we shared and there were not those fruit snacks with the sweet oozing goo in the centers that every kid seemed to have in their lunches, and I had never cared about my birthday because I cared more for Jesus's birthday. I had never burdened her with my childish woes because her burdens took up the whole room. I felt angry she was using them against me now, the things I had never asked for. I heard a door slam, a man's barking voice in the background. The line went dead. I rolled over and threw up in a tin bowl.

THE NEXT DAY Daisy eyed me, tapped a pen against her lip. "You don't look good," she said.

"My boobs hurt," I said. "The skin feels like it's going to burst open. And I'm so tired all the time."

Daisy could see the motherloss on me like disease now. My darkened nipples, how my nearly flat chest had become full so fast, little red squiggly lines appearing all over the straining skin. I thought maybe my heart was swelling to burst, pushing its way out from all places.

"You have a boyfriend?" Daisy asked.

I didn't answer. A boyfriend had nothing to do with this.

"She's asking if you've had sex in real life," Florin said. "Did you wrap it up or not?"

TEN MINUTES LATER I was outside the Pac with Florin, sitting in her car. I lowered down in my seat, afraid someone from the Body would see me with her. She lit a small joint and blew smoke out the window. It always seemed funny to see people smoking here. The air was so bad as it was—the valley was a bowl for other cities' smog and pollution to fill, wiping away any trace of the Sierra Nevada mountain ranges that spread all around. The tagline for the valley was that we were the "Gateway to Yosemite" but I had no idea what that meant in any practical sense. If you cannot see mountains, are they even there? All I knew was that the haze sat heavy in the lungs.

"My mom said you're some kind of puritan or something," she said.

Florin said it like there was something to be ashamed of. Like she was so far above me. I wondered if she would have been converted too if she had seen Vern bring the rain, or if there was something about her that would have never been convinced. "We're doing really important work," I said. "We want to save all the sinners and live in paradise on earth with lots of rain to bring the crops."

"You know what a diviner is?" Florin said. "A water witch? A douser?"

I shook my head no. "They take a Y-shaped rod and they find water underground. Farmers relied on them in old times."

"Is that why Daisy named the hotline Diviners?"

"We come from generation after generation of water-finding women," she said. "Women who could step on the soil and really feel its intention. You all are concerned about water coming from the sky, but there could be water under us right now, untapped."

I told her how we just wanted Peaches to be the raisin queen she once was, for things to go back to normal. Florin listened and nodded and then said she didn't care, that the second she stepped foot into this place she knew she would leave it. She stubbed the joint out in the center console and I breathed the interesting smoke.

"You're probably pregnant," she said, getting out of the car. "But you know that already."

I knew about pale blues. How one day I'd live in a bright, light house painted in those blues. Water would flow from our faucets clear and cool. The vines out my windows would be green and lush and of another place. I knew sharp and sudden that if given the choice I would never have stayed here in Peaches. I was only waiting. Deep down, waiting for the day my mother said we could leave.

———

WHEN WE GOT back to the red house Florin and Daisy crouched next to me as I peed on the stick. They held my hands during the five minutes of wait and no one prayed. They rubbed my back as I threw up in the toilet when the stick said yes.

Chapter 12

Why did women have to suffer so? Why was the bringing forth of another human such painstaking work? I had only just found out about my condition but inside I was stripped bare and replaced. I was already someone who understood I was no longer myself but a vessel in service to another. I would never again know a breath that was only mine. There was sadness in that, a feeling of dread. Perhaps this feeling came with all pregnancies, no matter how planned and wonderful, just a symptom of astonishment, the transformation occurring. I never expected it would feel so dark, this blessing.

I DRESSED FOR church, mother's sundress, the breezy blue one she liked so well it was fraying at the neckline. She had found it at the Goodwill, pulled it from a pile like a treasure, called across the place to where I was elbows deep in a bin trying to find clothes for a naked doll, that the dress was linen! Linen, my mother explained on the drive home, was what rich people liked to wear on vacation. Liz Claiborne! she squealed. I supposed she got these ideas from magazines, from her life before I was born. Of course the dress was perfect on her, of course it was the color of her eyes.

I wondered if she missed the dress, if she ever thought of

coming to get it. The dress fit me nicely now, and I felt relieved that I would still look the same at a glance. Anyhow, most people never looked at anyone else with any clarity, one eye forever turned toward themselves. They wouldn't care to notice my face had filled out a little, my breasts bigger and the small protrusion of my stomach. After all, I hadn't noticed myself until I'd had reason to go looking. I pulled the linen tight against the paunch in the mirror. Now it curved outward and I couldn't suck it back in flat.

At school last year our class almost had someone come from Fresno to talk to us about sex, someone who was rumored to bring condoms and strangle bananas with them, but enough GOTS parents raised a fuss. Instead we had a twenty-five-year-old woman in a pressed white frock give a speech about abstinence. The way her cheeks reddened when she peered out at all of us and said she was a virgin. Cleared her throat. Said it again. *Virgin.* The GOTS parents lining the room like security broke into applause. It had made perfect sense to me then that since she was not married she would be a virgin. But now her words seemed unlikely. How could she have made it twenty-five years without someone taking it from her?

My eyes burned with tears but none fell. Who was inside me? It could be anyone, I thought. My mind swam with ways out. I was only a body containing another body. But no one had seen the body within me yet, no one knew, so did it have to exist? I was scared. I didn't want to imagine it in there, becoming. My mother had said being pregnant was like an alien takeover. She hated it. The way I had stretched and rolled inside her. She said she imagined snakes fighting in there, and that sometimes all she could do was sleep to keep herself from thinking too hard about it. The fact that soon someone would need need need her. She said the thought of a baby repulsed her, all the crying in the night, all the foolish wanting.

But was being needed a bad thing? My disease of loneliness wondered if a baby might be just the cure. For I could not yet fathom all this baby would mean or do to me, but one thing was now certain: I was no longer alone, and never would be again.

I straightened my shoulders. I tilted my chin up. In the wake of my own mother leaving I had transformed into a mother myself, a bizarre trick. Would I be able to mother myself now? Would I no longer need her if I *was* her?

AT CHURCH VERN wore a robe of pewter. There was a somberness about him, a heft in his usually perked shoulders. But his hair had been freshly curled, the ringlets cinched up closer to his collarbones than usual, and the spray holding them was flecked with glitter. The top of his head was freshly shaved, slick oiled skin and a tiny piece of toilet paper where he must have nicked himself, and he looked dewy as if he'd been freshly scrubbed. The boys' club sat on the stage as if awaiting a ceremony and Vern asked the Bible study girls to come forward.

Denay shot up first. She walked to the front and stood with her palms up before the boys. Slowly the rest of the girls came forward and then I followed too. We stood in a line and faced the boys' club. They kept their gaze affixed to us, their expressions placid.

"These are the tireless servants, commanded by God to bring forth amazing miracles. To unite us like never before. Cast out your doubt and let us pray over them."

The Body stretched their fingers toward us. I looked out over the sea of hands and at their faces. Most were eyes-closed, pleased as pigs. But a few stared up at us, brows cross, faces of worry. We were children, weren't we? And what had children been told to do in such secret? I met Sharon's gaze. She was deep eggplant under the eyes and a bruise wrapped around her neck. My hand fell to my stomach. She looked away and stared at her brother. His jaw clenched. To my side Denay smiled and hummed to herself, bounced on her toes.

"Bless these young women and men of God. Allow them to show you our divine dedication, our willingness to submit to you, to raise up a true unfaltering army."

The boys' club kept their hands pressed to their sides. How easy this was for them. How vital and strong they all looked there, untarnished, while us girls stood with our pale and plumping faces, sick and wrung out, weaponless. "Do not doubt them, church. Only doubt your own limitations of mind."

These boys, my body told me, were all dangerous.

AFTER CHURCH VERN brought us up into his office. We crowded in the small space. Crosses no longer hung on the wall behind his desk, but instead a large sheet of butcher paper covered in incomprehensible scrawl had been sloppily taped up. The thick black marker seemed to make an outline of a quickly drawn-up plan in another language, and the sight of it made fear thicken in my stomach. I had always thought Vern to be organized, calculating, and thoughtful. Not in a rush. Not prone to bad handwriting. I narrowed my eyes at it and suddenly my name came into view, the names of a few of the other girls.

The boys knelt close to him, the girls stood shoulder to shoulder against the wall. My skin itched and I scratched red lines down my arms.

"My special children," he said. "How blessed you are. But now

I need to know just how blessed. Who here of the young ladies has not gotten their woman's promise lately? Who among you is heavy with a quivering?"

We girls were quiet for a time until Denay stepped forward. "I," she said. She curtsied to Vern like she was about to commit a beautiful dance.

"Of course." He smiled at her. "Now who else?" I wanted to step forward like Denay, be so blindly happy like her, but something held me back. I would just listen now. I wouldn't make a move.

"Meekness is valued, ladies, I understand your hesitance. And that's good, actually, because you won't be telling anyone about this for a while. For now this is a secret between you and God and your pastor. Think of it as a precious flower pressed in the middle of your Bible, drying. You wouldn't want to take it out too soon."

A secret. He'd had a secret with my mother, too.

I caught his eye for a moment and detected something in his gaze that wasn't quite there when I had first brought him my blood. I saw then we had all changed into something else and it felt like stepping off a ledge into open air, the moment frozen before the fall. I thought what I saw in him was passion, dedication. I wanted to see those things, of course. I wanted not to look at him then, and think he was crazed, but that word, *crazed*, came to me, swam up by instinct, and I pushed it down. Wait for something else, I thought. Wait for proof, as if my own body wasn't proof enough.

The girls nodded their heads yes. I tried to meet Sharon's eye but she stared at her hands clasped white in front of her.

"In the coming months your bodies will bloom forward and there will be a time of celebration. Be filled with gratitude, ladies. You've been Godshot."

———

As we filed out of his office, Vern tapped my shoulder to stay behind. His eyes were red. Allergies again? I wondered. Or was he exhausted, staying up all night? He seemed thinner, his veins protruding down his neck, the tops of his hands.

"Why so modest, Lacey May?" he said. He gathered papers in a stack on his desk and then spread them out again absentmindedly.

"Just being obedient."

"I thought you wanted to be recognized for your faith."

I didn't recall ever saying this to him aloud. It was something he must have seen in me. Perhaps something that was obvious to everyone and I'd never realized. I kept my eyes on my feet. I didn't want him to read me, to know I'd visited the red house. I worried I wore it like a scent. I worried if he asked me anything directly, I would not be able to lie.

"Why this way?" I said. "Why does God want us all pregnant?"

He winced when I said *pregnant*, like the word was lewd. He probably would have preferred *blessed*. He flattened his lips. "I asked myself the same thing when He first showed me," he said. "I thought, this is too complicated. This might even be impossible. But then I kept seeing it so clearly. You follow something like that, Lacey May. Something He shows you that clear. It's not a suggestion. It's an order."

"My mother wouldn't want this for me," I said, my voice barely above a whisper.

"Your mother." Vern laughed. "Of course she wouldn't. Oh, she had all kinds of ideas before her demise. All her own ideas."

I was pulled away from him then, though we were still in that cramped office, though I could still smell the sweat of him, the coffee breath. I was with my mother, trying to imagine what her ideas had even been. Why they hadn't included me at all.

"I don't think they were her ideas. I think they were yours, and then they were the beers' and then they were that man's from the phone. I think she learned to ignore her own ideas a long time ago."

"That can be good for a woman," he mused. "As long as you keep your eyes right here." He pointed to himself.

"Thank you," I said, and the words nearly stuck in my throat. "May I go?"

OUTSIDE THE CHURCH, Lyle kicked a soccer ball back and forth with Laramie. I intercepted the ball and drop-kicked it far into the field. Go fetch, I thought as Lyle motioned for Laramie to get it.

"You could have spared me," I said when Laramie was out of earshot. Lyle jogged closer to me.

"It's not yours, Lacey. Relax."

"What do you mean, not mine? It's in my body," I said.

He leaned in so I could feel his breath on my ear. "Listen. It might not rain," he said. "We're all hoping it does, but a church like ours has to be prepared. Vern thinks if we ever need to leave it will be hard to keep the Body together. He wants us all united for if that day comes."

He spoke so serenely, with so much confidence, as if he'd memorized a script. He did not register at all how empty his words sounded in the face of what he was saying—that somehow the baby inside me was not really my own—I could tell. He pulled a Big Hunk candy bar from his back pocket. Opened it with his teeth and took a huge bite. He smacked and chewed the sticky nougat loudly, a fleck of peanut resting on his lip.

"How could you have done this to me?" I said.

He held his hand up like *hold on* while he finished chewing as if he were having a conversation about baseball.

"Children unite the Body," he said. "Children ensure another generation of soldiers. Parentless children who are tended to and cared for by everyone, who belong to the church itself, are the most useful gems." He lifted the candy bar to take another bite and I smacked it out of his hand. It hit the dirt.

He took a deep breath. Picked it up. "This is my last one of these, Lacey, and the Pac won't be getting any more shipments."

I imagined someone else rocking my baby and then passing her on to someone else who would feed her, and then to someone else who would teach her the word and then to Vern to make her into a Bible study girl and all the while I would watch her and want to show her I was her one true mother but her eyes would meet mine and she would already be gone. She would not know me. I would not be able to bear such a loss. I wondered how my mother was able to, how she was able to breathe at all, without me. But perhaps she wasn't, perhaps she was distraught with longing, and this made me feel even worse. It was easier to imagine her heartless.

"Look," he said. "I'm obeying what I've been told. What else can I do?"

I felt so stupid. I wanted to claw my way back through time.

"Say something, Lace. Come on. Don't be like this. It just makes everything so much harder. These are celebration times and here you are being difficult."

My mother had been difficult, too.

"Take care of yourself," Lyle said, pressing his hand to my stomach. "You're carrying church property."

WHAT I NEEDED was time, I decided, looking up at the ceiling of the craft room. Time to pause, to make the baby mine until everything was sorted. It seemed my possessive worry over the seed within me was innate, though I'd never babysat a child in my life, though I'd never spent much time with children at all. It was as if another woman in me had been awakened, who would do anything to ensure that what had happened to me would not happen to this child.

I had less than one hundred dollars from my work so far on the phone lines. It might be enough for a bus ticket, but what was a bus ticket? Something I must have heard about on TV at some point, or some common thing from the beforelife, because no buses rolled through Peaches. Believers had no business on buses when there was so much to be done here. It was only a theory and not something I could grasp on to.

I skimmed my mother's romance novels for answers: Engorged lips, long neck, wide hands, hot skin, in love, lust thrust push hold squeeze kiss ripple turn I want everything about you I'm in love I like you he put his shaft inside her and she was never the same all night all day I missed him I loved him I had to you made me. I flipped to the back of each book. As I read the endings I realized that almost all of them had something in common.

A white dress, something borrowed something blue, rice sailing through the air, kiss the bride, until death do us part.

Marriage. Marriage was always the final scene. Only then did opposing armies back down, threats cease, and villains retreat. It was something that could not be disputed. It righted the wrongs of the past. A marriage was the period at the end of the sentence when everything else was fallible. A boyfriend meant nothing in the books. A boyfriend was trash, however attractive, that would one day have to be taken out. And in the eyes of God a marriage meant a cemented union that no one could come between. A marriage to a man would take me out of my marriage to the church.

A marriage was what I needed.

Something buzzed near the mattress. The phone from Stringy. I had nearly forgotten about it.

Good night princess, the message read.

My heart pounded. He wasn't of the church, he wasn't my age. And if he were my husband, the father of this child and not Lyle, then the child would not be a holy property anymore. I would not be Godshot. The child would just be a common shame, the result of sin with an infidel, a couple who were uncareful but who were doing their best to make things right.

I texted back, *Thinking of you*. Like everything was normal. Like I wasn't about to ruin him.

Chapter 13

In the brash heat of November, smoke filled the valley from wildfires north and wildfires south, settling over us like a warning. I listened to the news saying the town of Paradise was burning, that people had died in their cars trying to escape. A man who had abandoned his burning car said he ran past countless people frozen behind their wheels in gridlocked traffic. He knew they would all die. It sounded horrifying but I couldn't fathom another town aside from Peaches in any clearness. All the same, the smoke from the death towns filled my chest until it ached. The only thing that would clear it was rain.

"God's smiting them," Cherry said, shaking her head as if Peaches was better off somehow. But I saw the tremble of her hands. I knew we were thinking the same thing.

We were next.

ONE NIGHT AFTER a long shift at the red house, I came home to Taffy waiting on Cherry's porch. She stood quickly when she saw me. She looked me up and down. "The world is all over you," she said. "I can practically smell it."

"You're smelling smoke," I said.

She peeled a long strip of skin from her cuticle and it bled hot red. "I just want to know if you've been blessed."

"Who can say what a true blessing is?"

"Did you not speak up because you are or because you aren't?" I stood still. I could tell she was ready to brim over. She heaved a sob. "Tell me you weren't blessed either. Tell me I'm not the only one."

I looked at her little child's face. Her flat chest and her clear clean skin. "You've never received your blood, have you?"

"God hates me."

"What do you think's going to happen to all these church babies?" I said.

She put her face in her hands. "Of course Denay went right ahead and got shot like it was so easy. Got her blood in a fine red stream. I saw it in the toilet, all that glory."

"I'd count yourself lucky," I said.

"Lacey, if you're saying that, you're not in Vern's lane, that's for sure. If you're shot it's not fair. It's not fair at all!"

I felt anger looking at this old best friend. Someone I had once cared about, thought of as a sister. "Maybe you just haven't been obedient enough," I said. I couldn't stop myself. "Maybe you're just not worthy."

I WENT TO the red house every day, keeping my secrets deep within me like a good GOTS girl, but I felt the river of my sin widening, felt myself up to my neck. I would need the money now from the phone calls with a baby coming, I told myself, and I craved the comforting way Daisy looked at me. The way she knew of the child I carried and the way she let me try on her lipsticks and wiped the dirt from my face and fed me glasses of water from the jugs she had delivered. The water was reason enough to go. I thought I would die without her water.

The town seemed to thin even more, moving trucks in infidels' driveways. Quitters is what Cherry called them. What remained was the Body and our assignments: proselytizing, deeper commitments to prayer, keen eyes tuned to spot anyone set to step out. Obedience would bring rain, a fact as true as the sun. But I had figured out by now that only the young unmarried girls like myself were making a real sacrifice. It was only us, the girls of new blood who shifted around town, heads down veiled in mystery. I asked Cherry what her assignment was and she pretended to load a shotgun and pointed it at me. "You," she'd said. "Kapow."

I sat in church on Sundays, eyes on my knees. I wanted to blend into the pew. I was trying to put together a puzzle that would never fit because I'd always be missing the most important piece.

I wrote my mother a letter I could not send because I didn't have her address. I wrote, *I miss you.* I wrote, *You leaving was the first bad thing to happen to me.*

The trouble was that I was transforming in two directions—seemingly into my faith role in the church, silent and Godshot, and equally somehow into a phone sex operator, shameless and in command of the hand that pressed that blinking answer button.

I PAINTED MY nails black at my mother's call desk, swiveled in her chair. I tried out some stretches and gave up. Everything made me out of breath now. A call blinked through. It would be Forne at this time, ready for more plastic bag adventuring. I answered the phone and he seemed down. I could tell immediately. Voices give everything away when you really listen, the lilt and register of a voice tells you all you need to know about how to be, what to say.

"I feel a heaviness around you, honey," I said to him. I pretended I was Daisy. She always talked to her callers like they were some mix of child and man, son and lover. "How can Sunny help your heartache?"

He sighed. "How are you?" he said.

"Oh, I'm really nice, all dolled up. I know how you like it—"

He cut me off. "No, how are you? You the person."

I paused. This was weird and went against our rules. This was how my mother got lured in, went off script, and ended up a stolen woman.

"No," I said. "I know what you're doing and I'm not here for any of it. You got a hard-on I can help you with or you're feeling real curious over a gal you haven't ever met? One or the other, and only one road leads to us staying on this call."

Maybe this was part of it. He wanted me to talk down to him some more. It felt good to talk to him this way, get my anger out.

"My wife found out about the calls," he said. "She saw my credit card statement. She normally doesn't look at anything like that, but she did."

"I'm hanging up now." I didn't have any interest in his problems, truly. They annoyed me. It felt like he wanted me to lift weights with my mind to solve them. "Sorry about your shattered dreams."

"Wait," he said. "My wife wasn't mad at me. She didn't care, actually. She acted like she knew. She said what she was mad about was me spending our money on calls while bitching to her about going to the expensive hairdresser, the one that uses the organic dyes."

"Does something in your brain think I care? I don't."

"It just got me thinking about you. I really like talking to you. You know the real me."

I dropped the singsong southern accent. "Sunny isn't even my real name. You don't know anything about me. Don't be a fool."

"I just don't know why there have to be these walls between us.

I want to know what you like to read, what you watch on TV. If we went to a diner, what you gonna order? Chicken fried steak, or some kind of fancy salad with crunchies on top?"

"You've lost it," I said. "I have to go now."

"I'm sick," he said.

"You are, I'd say so, yes."

"Like I'm dying, I think."

I stopped. I took a deep breath. Maybe he was lying but maybe he wasn't.

"Well, what's wrong with you?" I said.

"That's why I want to know about you. Here I am, a man with not much time and I just want to hear about how you're doing."

"I'm fine."

"Fine is never fine."

"What are you, a counselor?" But as soon as I said it, I wondered if maybe he could help me. Would he be able to find my mother?

"I'm not trying to make you uncomfortable."

"You want to help me?" I said. "I've got a missing persons case on my hands."

"Okay, sure."

"Her name is Louise Herd," I started, but then I heard that plastic rustling on the other end. "Hey, what are you doing?"

Forne moaned a little. "I'm here."

Goddamnit. He was messing with me. The rustling got faster and faster and then he let out a pitiful little squeal.

"Never call here again," I said.

"Baby," he said. "I want to come pick you up in my hot rod and take you away from there. I'm serious about that."

I slammed down the phone. My cheeks burned. I felt so stupid. This was my mother's mistake. She had let feelings come her way over the phone and it had cracked open her heart. I hated to admit that for a second I saw it all before me. How easy it would be to tell him where I was and just see if he came, and if he came, how easy it would be to get in that car and have him drive me on out to another life, trust him and let him help me. The prospect of another life was mysterious and blank. Who knew what horrors would fill it, but I knew they would be different horrors, and somehow that sounded like a risk I could be stupid enough to take.

After Forne, I sat with my head down on my mother's desk imagining that each second passing was really just hurtling me closer to my inevitable death. I would quit the phone lines. Every call I took was just making me dumber and dumber, no closer to my mother. I went downstairs. I told Florin never to connect me with Forne again.

"He's your best caller," she said. "Anything that went wrong on the call I guarantee had more to do with you than it did with him."

"Just don't connect him to me. I'm done, actually. I quit."

She smacked her gum. Looked at her phone lighting up. "You sure? Got a new one here. Don't you need the money?"

I did need the money. Of course I did.

"Just be cool," she said. "Take a breath and let it go. These are just voices. They don't mean anything unless you let them."

I stood there thinking. She picked it up. "Welcome to your fantasy, where nothing's finer than a call with a Diviner." She looked at me, motioned for me to get upstairs. I didn't want to leave the red house, not really. I went and picked up.

The man cleared his throat and a tingle ran through me. *Something different*, my body alerted.

"Hello, darling," I said. "Have we had the pleasure of speaking before?"

"Honey on a muffin," the man said. The low and long voice was familiar and different all the same. Where had I heard it?

"Well, you're cute," I said. My pulse raced. Florin had forgotten to tell me his name. He might not tip now if I couldn't come up with his name, give him a real personal experience. But I didn't have to say anything. He started in.

"Speak to me, are you lonely?" he said. My mind ran and ran. The voice was familiar but who was it? I saw the answer up ahead of me, just out of reach. I closed my eyes, tried to steady my breath. I looked at the photograph of my mother but she provided no answer in her closed-mouth smile.

"I'm lonely," I said. "Does that make you happy?" I'd meant to say *horny*, but *happy* came out.

"It makes me real sad, honey," he said. "Makes me wonder if I could make you less lonely."

"That's what I'm here to do for you," I said.

"Now, I'm listening to you here, and I'm thinking wild thoughts. I'm thinking, this gal's a star," he said. "Tell me, what does your pretty face look like?"

What did my pretty face look like? I didn't know. Instead I saw my mother standing before the edge of a cliff. Falling free, chest open into a pit of fire. *Rick Walden, Rick Walden*, I imagined her chanting as she fell. For it wasn't a regular client. It was him. It was the Turquoise Cowboy calling from a new number, out fishing.

I wondered then if God worked in more mysterious ways than I had ever imagined. If God had sent me a direct line right to her. *Here you go*, I imagined God saying. *What, you thought I forgot about you?* I heard Florin's voice: *Be cool.*

"How's the weather where you are?" I said. I pressed my ear

into the receiver. Would I be able to hear my mother in the background? Would she sense it was me?

"Weather's always fine in heaven," he said.

"You got rain?"

"We got wind and sleet and just the other day I drove through a flash flood and nearly hit a stag. Lightning every which way. You looking for that kind of excitement, dolly?"

"You got a lady with you in that flood?" I tried to imagine my mother in the passenger seat while crashes of water fell on top of the car. Maybe it scared her, all that water. Maybe she yelped like she did when she rode the mechanical bull at the annual Peaches rodeo, her eyes scanning the crowd of tight-jeaned cowboys leaning around, bottle necks between calloused fingers, her radar sniffing out the most troubled one to take home. Did she think in the flood that she had traded bad for bad? That this new cowboy was still a cowboy like any other?

"You're my lady now," he said. If I was a foolish girl, I'd be prone to believe a voice like his. But I was no fool. I was no girl. And I was not my mother.

"What are you wearing?" I asked. It seemed a comical question, for it relied on the idea that the cowboy's clothes were hiding a sexiness that could and should be slowly revealed, but when I tried to envision him naked I saw something akin to two broomsticks for legs, a tin garbage can for a middle.

"Are you touching yourself?" he asked me.

My hands were on the desk like they usually were. I never touched myself during the calls. I wondered if my mother had, if she had let herself feel it. I rested a hand on my thigh. "Sure," I said.

"Now picture me," he said. "Right on top of you. You can barely breathe and I'm the only one who can save you."

I saw the tin can squishing me. My ears burned. My hand inched closer to my underwear line. I wanted to understand her. How this had worked on her. I wanted to be a woman who would do the things she had done just for a second to know what it felt like to throw myself overboard. My breath caught. A roll of nausea overtook me and I snapped out of it.

"Why don't you give me your address?" I said. "I'll come for a visit. It'll be real nice. Enough of this phone stuff, what do you say?"

He was quiet. He cleared his throat and his tone shifted abruptly into something less smooth, less kind. "I like to come get my women. I'm old-fashioned that way. A real gentleman."

"I like me a gentleman," I said. I pulled back. "Now let's talk again real soon."

"You think about me," he said, like he was giving me home-work. "And think about how you want this life of yours to go. You like jewelry? You like lace panties? They all like that shit, why ask? You'll be living in a pile of diamonds, high-heeled shoes of every color. Glamour."

"You know me so well, honey."

I hung up and his account charged thirty dollars. I ran down the stairs and stood before Florin at her desk. "That was Rick. Rick Rick, like my mom's Rick."

"Oh shit," she said. "We had him blocked. Must have called on a new number. They do that sometimes."

"I might be able to get information about her."

"Daisy's not going to like this," she said.

"Just give me a chance with him." I ate a bite of brown banana from the sad fruit bowl on her desk. "Please don't tell her," I added, as she shoved her stuff into her backpack. A book slipped out. *Cults Then and Now.*

"Fine," she said. "But don't blame me when this all goes wrong."

"What's that?" I said, eyes on the book.

"A little light reading." She snapped it up.

"I know what you think of me. You think I'm real dumb. You think everyone in Peaches is dumber than dirt."

"I don't think you're dumb, that's the thing. I'm trying to figure you out. I'm trying to understand how everyone in this place believes what that psychotic man says."

"He was everything to us," I said. "You couldn't understand."

"I could. I understand exactly how you could fall in love like that. I've done it myself."

She was different then, on the verge of revealing herself to me. I wanted it desperately.

"What do you mean?" I said quiet, careful not to break the spell.

"You ask Daisy sometime about who made all our money when she was depressed after her attack. Before we came here we lived in a shithole apartment in Fresno and she thought she was a witch. Spent all her time making potions in our bathtub. She was mad she was ugly and burned. Couldn't see straight without her beauty back then. Daisy's not a bad person, but she only knows one trade."

"Phones?" I asked weakly.

She laughed. "Phones came later. Phones were my idea after I couldn't take the in-person anymore." Something closed within her. She was done with story time.

"Rick paid your mom twice as much as any other caller," she said. "And with your mom's beauty she could have done a lot better than him, but I could tell she didn't know her worth." She sat down at the computer and clicked around a bit.

"Are you still mad at Daisy for what she made you do?" I asked.

"Sure," Florin said. "But she's all I have. And she's sorry. She's sorrier than sorry. I know that deep down. She's better than some. I have a theory that I did something pretty awful but not too awful in a past life, and my months working was my punishment. Now I've paid up and it's smooth sailing from here on out."

"I wonder what I did in a past life," I said.

Florin narrowed her eyes at me. "Probably same as me. Like nothing too, too terrible. You didn't kill someone or something. But you probably fucked up pretty bad."

"I don't know if I believe in all that," I said.

"Well, believe in this," she said, looking at her computer. I came up behind her and saw she had typed in "fourteen and pregnant." A slew of videos had come up. She clicked one, and a girl my age in a dim room rambled in a chirpy voice, hugged her huge stomach with skinny arms, and did "belly shots" where she pointed the camera on her midsection and swished her hands over the tight fabric of her tank. She sucked a pacifier and called her own mother a cunt, casually without malice, as if she was letting us know her mother was named Amy. She changed the diaper of a teddy bear and said, "Of course I'm ready to be a mom," fiddling with the Velcro straps.

The comments below the video made my breath stop. *Rot in a trashcan bitch*, said one. It reminded me of the way my mother's men spoke to her sometimes, such biting murderous things. These comments were angry, but angry at what, was hard to say. It seemed they were angry at Dezi for existing. Some comments had only to do with her appearance—*ugly ass butterface*—which should have been irrelevant, but was not, and never is.

Dezi confidently reported she wanted three babies by the time she was eighteen. "I always wanted to be a mama. And now I am." She concluded the video by detailing pregnancy dreams, one in particular a sex situation involving Billy Joel.

"Who's Billy Joel?" I asked Florin, and she groaned. "No hope for you at all."

I felt better after watching. At least I still had sense about me. At the very least, I wasn't sucking a pacifier while applying butt cream to a teddy bear. This was a truth no one could dispute.

Daisy came down the velvet stairs, her arms open like she was about to accept an award. "Hello, preggo! Gonna keep it or what?" she sang.

"Of course I'm going to keep it," I said.

"It's early enough to get rid of it if you wanted," Florin said, her eyes down. I thought of the billboard GOTS had sponsored near the freeway on-ramp by the church featuring a scared-looking punked-out pregnant teenager with a thought bubble coming from her worried face saying: *My mom's going to kill me!* Another thought bubble stemmed from her belly, where a pencil-drawn fetus floated. From its mouth: *My mom really IS going to KILL me.* We had all had a vote in picking the billboard we wanted. It had created quite a gleeful stir, all the choices in the catalogue. How we'd gathered to watch it be put up and cheered, and I never once considered there were plenty of women in the crowd who had lived lives before Vern. Who may have experienced just the thing we condemned so openly.

"You can choose what happens to your body, you know," Daisy said. I looked at her scars and the paleness of her flesh. Years without the direct touch of an outside wind, years without walking even to the edge of the road to get the mail. She was wrong. You couldn't choose what happened to your body. Between the two of us, that was clear enough.

"It's already a baby in my mind," I said. But that wasn't really the reason I knew I would keep it.

"You've gone and got emotional. Women are so prone to that, aren't we? The second I found out I was pregnant with Florin I cried my eyes out in terror but that same day I bought the cutest little onesie at the Baby Depot. Carried it around in my purse like a nut."

I wanted to tell them about Lyle then, and how Vern thought these babies would prove our worthiness to God, how they would restore the kingdom and rain would fall like gold. But I liked being with them in their space, having them think I was just an uncareful teenager, a commonplace idiot like Dezi. If they knew everything they might not want to be near me, and I couldn't deal with that.

"I have a man anyhow," I said. "Father of the baby wants to be around."

"Oh?" she said, her eyebrows raised. "And who's this?"

"He's a famous lawn painter. He's also in a band."

They exchanged a glance between them, one that made me feel small and strange, like they were one thing and I was another.

"Think what you want," I said. "It's my body, just like you said."

What I didn't say was that the real reason I wouldn't get rid of the baby was because I had begun to think myself a mother, even if it was foolish, and I would do all I could to not be a leaver. I would do anything if it meant I would not become like my mother, even if it was hard. Even if it killed me.

AFTER MY SHIFT I walked out to the road and crouched in the canal. I couldn't wait any longer on my plan. I had to get a marriage going now before any more cells multiplied. Before I started showing for real. I texted Stringy. *Pick me up? At the south end of the canal?* I pressed SEND. God, if you don't want this to happen, then create a storm to stop it. Don't let him answer. Reveal another way.

But the roar of the Central Valley Cali Lawn Painting truck came down the road a few minutes later and I pulled myself up. Stringy slowed down next to me but didn't stop all the way. He opened the door from the inside and I ran and grabbed his hand and he pulled me in like we were escapees, bank robbers, villains.

He had a wad of Big Red chewing gum in his mouth and he handed the pack to me. The inside of the truck smelled like cigarettes. The gum burned and made my mouth water, made me want to grind my teeth together.

"We're going somewhere we can be free and easy," he said. "Young and in love." He laughed loud and open, eyes on the road.

Love. There was that word that had gotten my mother in so much trouble. Love. I pressed my back into the seat and the truck crossed me over an invisible line toward free and easy. I may as well have waved goodbye to God right then.

He drank from a can of Four Loko between his knees and winked. "At night, Tent City parties hard."

"I thought it was just a dump."

"It's so much more than that, honey."

We pulled off the main road down a small side lane until it opened to a clearing with a dozen lifted trucks with huge CEN-CAL stickers on their back windows. The trucks formed a circle around the mob of his friends, thick-necked angry-looking men in a uniform of facial sores and tight black shirts that said TAP OUT and AFFLICTION and black star tattoos racing up the muscled meat of their arms. He put his arm around me as we walked up to them. Their names were Jason or Jay. One was just called Dog. One was Big Country. Dog handed us two full red cups. "You've never been drunk before," Stringy said, like he was reading my fortune.

But he was wrong. Sapphire Earrings had let me sip his beers. We would sit on the couch watching *Married . . . with Children* together some nights and he would pass me the can without looking at me and I would drink a long spell and pass it back. This would go on for some time. I would feel light and lighter with each sip and then I would sleep sleep sleep. I didn't tell Stringy about it. Couldn't tell Stringy it wasn't right for a woman with child to be drinking anyhow. There wasn't supposed to be a baby—not yet, at least.

He put the cup up to my lips. "I've heard God himself loved a nice glass of red," he said, and a little of the drink seeped into my mouth. I remembered as a girl my mother called rum and Cokes *Cuba libres*, struggling with the words, slurring them. *Croo-bra lee-bray*. It embarrassed me when she said it. I knew somehow she was saying it all wrong. I had sipped some out of her glass once when she wasn't looking and had never found that taste again in anything, until now.

"Cuba libre," I said, and Stringy looked at me funny.

"Broads like to be so fancy, don't they? It's 'bout the cheapest rum you can find and warm cola. Don't get too excited."

One of the Jasons looked me all over. "Sorta hot," he appraised. Clapped Stringy on the back and handed him a small baggy.

They all had their radios tuned to the same song, and it blasted out of their car speakers, about California and knowing how to party. I saw now that there was a group of girls too, standing together smoking cigarettes, wearing cut-off denim skirts over bruised orange legs. Fresno girls. One wore fur boots that came up over her knees and a skirt so short and so low-waisted it looked like a belt. Her pink thong strings were pulled up on her bare hips and she snapped them with long sharp nails. I was repelled by them but I also wanted to be with them, standing in their circle, knowing their thoughts. Maybe I could. I touched the Liz Claiborne linen of my mother's dress. No, I heard her say. You're different.

Still, I wished I had made Daisy curl my hair, put eyeliner on me, wipe the grime from my skin with one of her cool lavender cloths. My stomach was a little paunch forward, safe and invisible under the dress.

"I don't want to see you smoking with those hags," Stringy said. "I've fucked most of those chicks and they're all going to be hoarse-throated cancer cases by the time they're forty, and baby, we're better than that."

He lit a cigarette.

"Most of them?" I took another sip from my cup without thinking.

He looked at the group of five women and nodded. "I think so. Not a one was my girlfriend except maybe that black-haired one but she's a liar."

Dog came up and pulled Stringy over, started pointing to the rims on his truck. I felt nervous standing alone. I took another small sip from the red cup, just wanting something to do with my hands. I felt it trickle down my throat. In the dark here it seemed that what happened with Lyle could have never really happened. Here I was with my boyfriend at a party. I remembered my mother had told me once she'd had a beer a day when she was pregnant with me and that I turned out fine. She said it like she was proud, as if she'd cheated a system, but I knew that one beer meant at least three. I took another sip and my stomach churned but then settled into the burn. I could see why people drank, being here. How else were they supposed to make it through the night? This was how my mother had mustered the courage to leave me. All the beers she drank had given her permission. I looked at the group of girls and walked over to them.

"Hi, little sister," a bleached blonde with a lip ring said. It sounded like she was sucking a mouthful of hard candies, but soon I realized it was just her voice.

I thought about how I'd been instructed by Vern to witness to strangers, *always say your name nice and clear . . .* I took another sip of the liquid and it wasn't strong anymore. In fact it tasted no stronger than the cola we used for baptisms. I wondered if God had extracted the rum from it to save me. A wobbliness occupied my legs and my hands tingled. I didn't hate the way it felt. "I'm Lacey May Herd."

"Come on closer. We ain't gonna do nothing to you," she said.

"God protects me and I recoil from sin as if from a hot flame."

The blonde looked at her friends and shrugged. Fanned her face with her hand. Even at night, sun nowhere, the heat was heavy upon us. It seemed to come up from the earth. "God ain't nowhere around here," she said.

I took another sip, syrupy sweet. Someone turned the music up even louder. I had to sort of yell, "Have you all found God?"

"Oh, she's one of *them* girls," an extremely orange one said. "You know, what are they called? The Gotsers or whatever? My mom said you all are on that voodoo magic. You ain't no kind of church. Just act like one to rope 'em in."

"Do you take long showers?" I asked the orange one.

"Huh?" she said.

"You're wasting water," I said. "Don't you care about the drought?"

"The what?" she said.

The black-haired one spoke. "What're you trying to do, bring Stringy to Jesus? 'Cause Jesus don't want him."

They all doubled over laughing.

I drank a little more. I liked how the action of bringing the cup to my lips could stand in for speaking. The black-haired girl shook her head. "Stringy used to be a methed-out skinhead wannabe. I'd be careful, little girl. The only reason he's not anymore is 'cause his ass went to jail. You want a jailbird boyfriend?"

"I can baptize you right here," I heard myself say. I was on auto-pilot then. I wanted to be asking about Stringy, maybe even asking about their lives, what they did to make money so I could get some new ideas. But the Vern girl in me just kept talking.

"What's wrong with this bitch?" one of them said.

"You don't even know him," I said. "He's from Popcorn, Indiana."

They all burst out laughing.

"He's born and raised in the dankest part of the 'No. His mama's a hooker at Motel Drive," the dark-haired one said. "And." She walked closer to me. She smelled like cheap berry lotion and BO. I wanted to ask why her mother had never told her perfume didn't cover up stink, that it only makes it worse. I wondered if maybe she was motherless, too, like me, grasping at clues on how to be and failing. "He's old. Real old."

I took a deep breath. "He warned me you were a liar."

The drink seemed to loosen something in me, but at the same time it was taking something critical away.

I went to find Stringy, amused at the sight of my own feet walking zigzags, but then I was picked up from behind and lifted in the air.

God? I wondered. Was I flying up and out of here?

Arms set me down in the bed of a truck and the music swallowed me, rap so fast I couldn't hear the words, but the beat ran up my legs. I felt only the presence of a man's body behind me, a thicker man than Stringy. With the music so loud I thought perhaps the man behind me was irrelevant. This was a party. I started to dance. Maybe my mother was dancing, wherever she was, to music like this, taking her clothes off while the men stared at her, and I moved like never before. I felt my own hands run up my body and I pictured my mother my mother my mother. This is what she deserved. To have a daughter drunk at a party dancing in front of all these people to the music of sin.

The man pulled my ass back into the wide low trunk of his body, and my feet came off the truck bed sometimes, and the dancing was a little painful. I started feeling dizzy, up high, and I wondered what would happen if I fell off, would it kill the baby? The baby. There was a baby inside me and I was dancing like a fool. I squatted down and tried to focus on the space between my feet, make the world go still. Hands tried to pull me back to standing and I looked behind me to see a portly guy, shirtless, two sets of tiny footprints tattooed on his chest. Were these the footprints of his children? It seemed appalling. "I'm gonna barf," I yelled at him, and he backed off, turned and jumped off the truck onto the ground, started grinding up behind some other girl like a dog in heat.

I lowered myself to the ground and looked wildly for Stringy. I sat in the dirt when I couldn't find him. The Cuba libre came back up and I vomited between my knees and then he was walking toward me. I said, "Why did you leave me?" And he said, "Well, you're drunk. You like it?"

Did I like it? Did I like my swimming head, my body taken

away from me? I never wanted to feel like this, exactly like this, ever again. "No," I said. "It's bad."

"You're a good girl, Lacey May."

He left me there on the ground. Went to be with his friends. Maybe he said to take a little nap. I don't remember. But I felt like I didn't have a choice, that my body would take the nap for me, and it must have done so, because when I woke up I was alone there between the trucks and the music was still raging like not a second had passed, but this time Stringy was nowhere, and fear ran through me. My head ached but I could see again. What had I done? I was supposed to make him want me. The whole point of seeing him at all was to make him my husband, and I was failing. I got up and looked around. My small purse with the cell phone was there beside me and I clutched it.

I walked the circle of trucks over and over in a loop looking for him. Finally he came out of one of them, eyes bloodshot, and gripped my arm like we'd both been lost for days without food or water or sense. He sniffed and wiped at his nose. It felt like we were the lone survivors of something.

We got into his lawn-painting truck and he turned up the radio, some kind of punk band whining. He peeled away from Tent City and he tried to get the truck to go one hundred down Old Canal Road, but the wheel got shaky at ninety. I wondered if he was mad at me and was just taking me home. We approached the Pac N' Save. "Turn in there," I said. He pulled into the deserted parking lot and stopped the truck at the outer edge of it. "I'm all jazzed up," he said, sniffing, jerking his head around.

"Do you like me?" I asked. It was now or never.

"The lawn painting's getting big," he said. "I can afford you a steak dinner once a month if you want."

"Sounds like you've got things figured out."

He let out a big sigh and clicked the radio off. "I've been want-ing me a new girlfriend," he said. "But I had to get rid of the old one first. I'm a gentleman and those things take time, if you need to know what was taking so long."

"You broke up with her for me?" I asked.

"She was heading off to some school to teach her how to tattoo eyebrows on chicks. I was sick of hearing her talk about it."

I worked my eyes up his body in the light of the streetlamps. He was tattooed most everywhere. Skulls, winding smoke, a mermaid. A raised and fresh outline of the state of California, a star in the valley over a woman with her hands between her legs, breasts bare, head tilted back. The tattoos continued up his arms and under the sleeves, a collage coming up his neck. *Only God Can Judge Me* neck-laced his chest. I imagined Vern scoffing at that one.

My mother might admire something in Stringy, his sure large hands on the wheel of the car, the way he smelled like cinnamon more than cigarettes and his clean small teeth. I liked the way he looked at me like he'd known me well for a very long time. She would comment on the tattoos. Run her finger lightly across one to flatter.

"You've got to have a clear view on your hopes and dreams to make it in life," he told me.

"To make it where? To the big dirt nap?" I asked. Some of the alcohol was still swimming in my blood.

"To, you know. Your goals. To feel good about the life you've lived."

"My goal was heaven, but now I'm not so sure I'll ever make it."

"My mama went through a religious stint," he said. "She took me to a Buddhist temple, and a Catholic mass, and a hippie convention in the desert where she walked around topless with paint all over her and ate acid."

"Which did she choose?"

"None," he said. "She died in a car crash when I was twelve before she ever really got right with any of them. She was on her way, in fact, to a Mormon church when she was taken. I stayed home sick that day."

"Wait, she's dead?" I asked. The Fresno girls hadn't mentioned that.

It was as if the smoke cleared out for just that moment, the stars blinked a blinding silver. It was my own wound before me.

"My mother left me," I said. "She didn't even die, she just chose to leave. I wish she would have just died."

"You don't mean that," he said, taking my hand in his. "As long as she's alive there's hope."

He was listening to me, really listening. I felt like he understood the truest part of me. I wanted to confess it all to him, my face buried in his chest. But no. I tried to picture a happy place. I saw a beach scene from an old postcard of my mother's, the ocean ruffled white with waves, the people prostrate on towels. I smiled to lighten things. He wouldn't want to have sex with me if I was sobbing about my mother. But I couldn't help myself. The beach scene faded. "How long until you felt okay without her?"

"You always ask yourself if there was something about you that made it happen."

"Like, something you could have done to stop it?" I asked.

"No. Like I was bad and I caused it somehow. I don't know. You don't need to hear my sad song."

Watching him talk I felt heat expand within me. He was a person like I'd never met. A person wise and worldly. There in the car his skinniness turned sleek, his old acne scars became pleasantly rugged, and the grease black of his hair reminded me of the Elvis poster Cherry had framed over her bed. *Blue suede shoes.* I liked the way he seemed to like things, his bands and his tattoos, his truck and his friends. He had a whole mysterious life. This would work. I was carried away and I didn't even try to fight it.

I brought his hand up my mother's dress, all the way up to the little cups of her bra. My *bosom.* I was a woman from the romance novels now. It was never this way with Lyle.

He buried his face in my neck and in one motion pulled the lever on the side of my seat so the back went flat. He'd obviously perfected the move many times over. I didn't care. I kissed him and kissed him. This was my first kiss, I decided. His mouth was dry as sawdust. His fingers moved all over me. I closed my eyes and I was in a clean house with an ivory rug and a clear glass coffee table with one iced glass of water sitting on it and a pool I could see from the sliding glass window and yes, there was a cityscape of lit rectangles beyond that pool and I immersed myself in it and yes. A heat burned under his hand and I focused on the center of it like staring into the sun, and on that coffee table was a slab of undercooked red steak and I bit it and the blood dripped down my chin. Yes. This is what my romances were talking about, this final moment, two breaths connecting into one.

I pressed my head back and in the black of my closed eyes came hot light and a treacherous feeling took me over. I couldn't move. A drum inside me beat and beat.

He finished quickly and then lay on me and I could scarcely breathe. I felt his heart my heart the heart of both our bodies.

"That was my first time," I said, liking the way all this felt. The awayness of it. I liked life for a moment and its strangeness. And

God was either with me or he wasn't. How could a person tell? I was only sure now of the way my lower back had hit the seat like a song.

He looked into my eyes. We were lovers. "That wasn't nobody's first time."

I CREPT BACK into Cherry's, stepped carefully down the hall. I turned on the light of the craft room and there she was lying down on the baby mattress, eyes open. The room reeked of Sweet Dreams and an ashtray was full of the butts next to her.

"Oh my God, what are you doing?" I said. "Scared me half to death."

She sat up. "Vern came looking for you tonight. Said he had a bad feeling about your soul. And what was old Cherry supposed to say? That I didn't know where you were?"

I shuffled around the room not looking at her. I took the dress off and threw on one of Grampa Jackie's old tractor supply shirts. I tried to imagine a story to tell but my mind was scrambled from the night.

"You made me lie to my pastor, Lacey. I've been in here all night thinking I should call him up and tell him the real truth."

"Which is?"

"I raised your mother. I know a thing or two. After she was grown I told myself I'd never stay up all the night waiting on no person again. And now here you are, stepping out."

"I was with Quince. Converting her."

Cherry lit another Sweet Dream. Ran her tongue over her teeth.

"One lie leads to the next, leads to the next."

"Vern isn't going to banish me," I said. "I've got something he wants."

"Let's hope it's something of worth. Something that will work this time." Unlike my mother's assignment, I knew she must have been thinking.

I thought of what the Fresno girls might say. I rolled my eyes like them. "Relax," I said to her, tossing my hair.

Cherry got up and stood close to me. "I don't know what all you've got going on in there," she said, swatting the back of my head. "But you smell like hell rolled in going nowhere fast."

After she left, I lay on the baby mattress unable to sleep. I imagined Vern at the window looking in. I could talk a big game, but I was terrified of him. It seemed my faith rolled in and out now like a tide. Some moments I was void of it completely and then some, like now, I was ashamed, fearful of the truths I had been told for so long. I wanted a lush green world where I could please Vern, go to heaven, have my mother, and keep my child. I wanted a different world. One that did not exist.

Chapter 14

December. The sky grainy, begging for rain. The smoke from the fires had drifted out to the ocean by now but I swore I could still smell it. The local news reported that temperatures in Peaches had reached record highs while in neighboring towns, mere miles away, there were cool downs, tule fog covers, low visibility on the highways. Kerman soil was said to be moist and Fresno itself was chilly enough for a light jacket if you were going to walk down Christmas Tree Lane in the evening, but Peaches remained a desert wasteland. This was further proof that we were being tested, punished even, for something grave. But how could it be, everyone wondered, when the town was made up of such fine believers, when we honored God certainly more than the people of the city? It was by this I knew something beyond human understanding was at work. I couldn't feel God's love for me now, and I couldn't feel His destiny, but something supernatural was boxing us in this eternal summer and it was why I couldn't let go of my faith completely, even if I wanted to, even if it would have been easier. All I had to do was feel the heat bear down, burning an endless dryness into my body. No man could accomplish something like that.

I sat on the floor in front of the television while Cherry sewed exercise clothes for the chinchillas. The news segment showed a fat Santa handing out candy canes to a mass of people. "You ever walked down Christmas Tree Lane?" I asked her.

Cherry grunted. "There's a house there that hands out hot co-coa for free," she said. "All those rich people with the most beautiful lights. That lane is the best thing about Fresno. Only neighbor-hood worth seeing, you ask me."

"I wish I could see it."

"Santa and elves parading around like they're the reason for the season," she said. "All these infidels decorating their houses like chumps over a holiday they don't even believe in. It's Christ's birthday party, for God's sake. Set out a damn cake and light some birthday candles if you need to celebrate so bad."

"Sounds kind of fun," I said, sucking my stomach in. It was pushing out more now, harder to hide. Earlier I'd tried on one of Cherry's old sweaters from the back of the craft room closet and my skin rashed and itched and my sweat poured under it. I had taken it off within minutes. I dreaded when my body would betray me, when there would be no hiding what had happened in that rainless stretch of summer. I'd fixed it, though, with Stringy, and now I needed Cherry on board.

"I've got to tell you something," I said to her.

She turned down the TV. "That's the tone of a bad girly done wrong." Her lips thinned, she closed her eyes. She stayed still to receive God's premonition, lifted a hand to catch it from the air.

"Stand in front of me, now," she said, holding her hand up like an antenna, moving it from side to side, trying for further clarity. "In some trouble?" she asked.

I was quiet.

"Spell it out."

"I'm full with blessing," I said.

"So it wasn't the cleaning making you sick," she said. There was a long pause. "Soon as this illness passes you can get back to it."

I'd expected a beating with the bull penis cane. For her to call me a whore, condemn me and send me to the floor to clean. Threaten to call up Vern.

"It's the lawn painter's," I said.

She sank back in her chair, twirled the tail of a stilled squirrel between her fingers. Its eyes glinted in the low light of the television. "Been word that some other church girlies are full up too. Suppose it's just a coincidence of timing?"

"I don't want to give this baby to the church."

"Who done it to you, really?" she said.

"Vern won't want the baby if it's half infidel."

She looked up at me. I couldn't place her emotion. She was usually angry but she seemed calm. "A grandbaby," she said. "I did always want me one of those." I almost reminded her that *I* was her grandbaby, but I let her feel her feelings.

She stared out the window and I saw her face begin the slow puff toward tears. It was dark, but even if it wasn't, she'd still be gazing over stick brittle fields, barren. A pair of headlights shone in the distance and faded. I didn't know what to do so I knelt before her and put my head in her lap. "He's gonna marry me," I said.

She groaned. "This won't end well. Just remember your old Cherry told you that." But I felt her hand stroke my hair. I knew there was a part of her that understood. It was the woman part.

CHERRY TOOK MY marriage plan and ran with a gusto I hadn't expected. Made me message Stringy right away. He was at the door within the hour, eyes bugged and tired, hands vibrating and clumsy. I had texted him something about a repeat of the Pac parking lot night. I knew he'd be right there. My mother used to say, before she was saved, and then lost again, that men were easy. I could see now that she was right. But looking at him standing there, a familiarity also came over me. The way I felt now was similar to the way I'd felt toward my mother's men, who had always seemed so below her. How she clamored to please them, how everything seemed to hinge on their approval of her. I never understood it. They seemed like bad men to me, the way they talked and spat, their dirty smells, the way they cussed with tense jaws, teeth concealing the shells of sunflower seeds at all hours. How they loved their sunflower seeds. They looked at me too long and too strange like they were piecing together the mystery of what made up a girl. How it was my job to get the Doritos from the kitchen, to bring them another beer, to wear those sapphire earrings and smile while my mother flitted around nervous and unhappy, trying to keep them there, but why? Now I saw Stringy and he was one of those men. He wasn't so different at all and here I was, desperate for him to save me.

"Thought you could make sex with God's precious property and not marry her?" Cherry said.

He looked at the door behind him and Cherry hit her cane against it. "Don't even think about it." Her bathrobe was loose and I could almost see her breasts in their totality. "'Cause from what I can see, Fresno'll bring the law on a full-grown man lying down with a girl child."

"Now, now," he started. He looked at me wary, like I could reach out and sting. He held his hands up, unarmed. "Don't get any ideas. Heard of Three Strikes and You're Out? I already got two."

"The proof," Cherry said, pointing at my stomach, "is right here. So tell me again, would you like to marry my granddaughter and make this right in the eyes of God and the law?"

I stepped close to him. I held his hands and pressed them to my stomach. "We can be a family."

"Cut the softy stuff," Cherry said. "It's this or jail time, boy, which do you prefer? No one here in Peaches is gonna care a thing about it long as you're married up nice under the hand of God."

"Is this real?" he said to me.

"Strip it down, young man," Cherry said. "Time to get saved."

I looked at Cherry. "What are you doing?"

"I was sitting here thinking, now what's in this for me? Then I saw a-clear. 'Bout time this old Cherry brings a new convert to Vern. Imagine the pennies in my heaven jar."

Stringy looked at me. He touched my stomach. "I thought you were eighteen," he said loudly, as if to some hidden recorder.

"I need me a man of sin," I told her. "Not a saved man."

"You don't comply, girly," Cherry snarled in my ear, "and I'll call Vern up right now and tell him the truth easy as pie." She looked him up and down. "Saved or not," she said, "he don't amount to a hill of beans. Vern won't want that baby."

"I'm gonna be a daddy," Stringy said, his own world swirling and blinding him.

I nodded and hugged him and he slowly pulled his shirt off and stripped down to his black boxers.

"You taking those to heaven with you?" Cherry asked, prodding the elastic on his shorts with the cane. "Get naked. We ain't got time to pussyfoot around. Sooner we get the two of you married, the better off that child will be and we can put this whole mess behind us."

She filled the tub with several liters of soda and Stringy got in. Cherry stirred the liquid around him with her cane, speaking in her heavenly tongue. *Click click rhombus a dadadadadad.* Stringy's soft penis bobbed in the brown soda. There were tears pooling in his closed eyes. His body began to shiver, spirit moving.

"Out demons!" Cherry screamed, and she banged the cupboards with the cane so the room shook. I sat on the toilet and peeled my cuticles until they bled. I didn't know anything about him at all. Maybe he had been in a gang. Maybe those girls at Tent City were right to warn me.

"This is Stringy, and he comes to you today to be baptized into Gifts of the Spirit, may he heed your heavenly command and discard his ways of sin," Cherry said. "Do you accept our Papa God into your heart for all of your days and submit to the hand of the church?"

I leaned in and watched him. This was always the best part. Transformation was a physical thing, I'd seen it before and I wondered if it would still be possible to my new critical eye. But here it was: Stringy looked tormented. He writhed around and pulled at his own skin like it was a suit he wanted to take off. Then there was a stillness. Moonlight shone in through the small window and made everything glow. Cherry looked at me. "He breathing?" she said, just as Stringy sat up gasping and choking for air. "I saw God!" he screamed. His eyes were electric and his neck veins bulged. "He said he was my own daddy! I never had a daddy and now I do!"

We cloaked him in a Virginia Slims beach towel and walked him naked to the front yard, where I stood next to him under a falling-down archway that used to have flowers growing over the top of it when Grampa was alive, and Cherry brought out my mother's old *Children's Illustrated Bible* and I held Stringy's sticky hands. With his eyes still closed, she married us before God, and we said, *I do.*

He fell asleep on the baby mattress, his body a small ball.

Now it was his bed, too, Cherry said, for we were made one in front of God.

I lay next to him and poked him awake. "You really see God?" I asked.

He grunted. "I'm hungover as fuck. I didn't see no God."

I crept to the bathroom and lay in the sticky tub and read. When I read it seemed time could stop. It seemed perhaps my life was just another book I was in and it was anyone's guess what the real life was. Was Stringy saved or not? It wouldn't matter, I decided. Either way we had defied Vern's plan. He didn't want us to be families, and somehow I'd convinced everyone that was what we were. I read some more. Nothing could soothe me this very way but books. Thirst crawled up my spine and I drank brown drips from the tap, mouth pressed into the metal spigot that tasted like pennies. It was hot in the bathroom, hot forever. Was it cold where my mother was, where her new man Rick was? What was December in Reno?

Cherry appeared in the doorway. She had put on a mauve lace gown, something I'd never seen, and a matching coverlet. Her snarled feet were jammed into mauve satin heels. "Wore this when Pearl was wed," she said, shy.

"Wish my mother could have seen me married," I said.

Her long white hair was back and secured with a golden brooch. "Want to dance?"

We swayed in the living room to no music, Cherry leading. "This is what happens after infidels get married," she explained. "Dancing and presents." We both knew this wasn't true for GOTS weddings, though. GOTS weddings were clerical, businesslike, and holy. If anything, there was weeping. If anything, the bride looked morose in her new responsibility and the groom looked hungry for it to be over, for consummation, which took place in a white tent in the field behind the church with the Body holding hands in a circle just outside the canvas. Children were not welcome for this part, but I imagined you could hear everything. I imagined it was something to just get through. After the couple was finished they would come out and the groom would hold up the sheet with its spots of virgin blood and everyone would lapse into spirit song, writhe on the ground in glorious jubilee. I would not be welcome to marry Stringy in the church this way now, I knew, or anyone for that matter.

I put my head on her shoulder, the old Cherry.

"What's going to happen now?" I asked. It was a small voice that came from me, one I was not proud of but one I couldn't stop. I wanted the pity of a mother. I wanted the love of one, and what was the difference between pity and love?

THE HOUSE FELL silent, Cherry in bed, Stringy a-snore. I crept out and walked in the deep valley quiet, looked for the stars in the smog. I took the go-phone and I called Rick's Angels. I wanted to tell my mother. The phone rang and rang.

"Is Little Lou there?" I asked.

"Our girls don't take no personal calls," the man said. The Turquoise Cowboy.

I lifted my voice so he wouldn't recognize it from the hotline. "Can I write to her?"

"She don't want to hear from no one in Peaches," he said. "She said, 'Don't connect me to no one from there. That's in my past.' I have to respect a lady's wishes."

"This is her daughter."

"She don't have a daughter," he said.

Chapter 15

Being married offered no special treatment at Cherry's. I still had to entertain all her grooming needs at her whim, had fly duty, had to call for Goldie. Stringy was an annoying person to live with, up all throughout the night, building his business, he said, staring into the glow of his phone even though I had mentioned it kept me awake, mentioned it might be bad for the baby. He was too exhausted to really rouse from a lying-down position most of the time. The moment I decided maybe I hated him was when I watched him put olives on each finger and smile to himself as he ate them off. But on Sundays it didn't matter that he was tired in the morning—not a morning person, he liked to say. Tired or not, Cherry told him, Sundays were for church. *And it's one, two, three strikes you're out!* she'd taken to singing around the house. He listened to her more than he did me, almost as if he'd been longing for a mommy to boss him around. He shaved his face clean and put on his favorite black shirt. "What do you think?" he asked her. I stood watching them, invisible. "Don't take off those sunglasses," she told him. "In your case, it's better to keep some mystery."

I WALKED INTO church with Stringy on my arm, head held high. Cherry trailed him like a handler, muttering, *He's taken, he's taken,* when we would pass people, but she didn't mean romantically. She meant spiritually—she'd taken him, so don't bother trying to get a feather in your cap of heaven. She gawked around hoping someone would cause a fuss over it all. We scooted into our pew and I could feel the eyes on his tattoos, the ones that managed to crawl their way out from his clothing. His knuckles: *EWMN*. What does that mean? I'd asked him a few nights before, lying on the baby mattress, him trying to play footsie and me shifting away from him. *Evil, Wicked, Mean, Nasty,* he'd said. I'd waited to see if he would explain. When he didn't, I said, "You're not those things." I meant it like an insult. He'd shrugged. He barely understood himself, I could see.

A few people looked up at us from their Bibles, side-eyed and fearful. We had all become weird other versions of ourselves in the drought. The Body was nervous, thirsty. Dying, probably, from a diet of straight soda.

Denay came in with her parents, wearing a dress made from a sheet, stapled at the shoulders. Her face was full and round, her cheeks a rush of pink.

"What's this?" she said to me, eyes on the lanky man at my side. I had noticed that Stringy hunched his shoulders when he was uncomfortable, and he did that now, sort of turned into me. Pushed the sunglasses higher on his nose.

"My husband," I told her. "Father of my growing babe." I patted my stomach under my tight white tank top. "Here to make things right."

She looked me up and down slowly. "And he's the true daddy under the eyes of God?" She leaned into me over the back of the pew, a light embrace. She whispered, "And you expect anyone to believe that?"

"More believable than a white light in the middle of the night."
Denay laughed. "Not around here."

Vern emerged from the back. The boys were on folding chairs on the stage, Lyle in the center. Vern turned a few times, letting his blue robe fan out from him like he was about to perform a magic trick.

"Vibe's all wrong," Stringy said, sinking low in his seat, his eyes narrowed on Vern. He shivered a bit and crossed and uncrossed his legs.

"He's saved this town once and he'll do it again," Cherry snapped.

"Church," Vern addressed. "The work you've been doing is transforming us. I see it in the air. I can feel your intensity. Who's hard into their assignments?"

The Body shouted, raising their open hands. It seemed in the past months the numbers had been pruned—only half the pews were filled now.

Stringy leaned forward, long fingers drumming his knees, suddenly interested. I imagined both of my worlds combining. What if Stringy was truly converted that night in the bathtub, what if we became a real family today at church?

"Any announcements from the Body?" Vern said.

Cherry stood and pulled me and Stringy up by our hands. "Married! These two, I married them myself under God's holy watch after converting his damned soul! Add another to the army!"

She smiled wide, expecting a cheer to rise but only blank stares blinked back at her.

"We're having a baby," I said as loud as I could.

The Body murmured low, looked around. A young mother pulled her toddler daughter into her skirt and glued her eyes to the top of the girl's sweet head. Lyle stood up in a bolt and then sat down. His cheeks flamed.

But Vern was unruffled. He placed his hands together as if in prayer and bowed at us. I was holding my breath, waiting for something, but he went into the rest of the sermon, a blur of terror, locust-eaten plants and flooded valleys and parched lands like ours where the people died on their long walks to watering holes. That could be us, he kept saying. Is that what we wanted?

"I need to know who I can trust," he said. "Who can I look at and be sure?"

The Body stretched their hands forward. *Me. Me.*

"I should be able to hand each of you a shotgun and tell you to shoot your own self in the skull and you should do it without a moment's hesitation. You should feel that certain that I am your leader."

Cherry hooted and clapped. "Shoot me, Pastor Vern!" she cried.

I thought back to the early fall when all of us girls had vomited like a team against the church, the smells overpowering us. I felt a skittish relief to have removed myself from that group. To be able to watch them now from afar. But next to that relief, a familiar voice of doubt crept in, wondering if I was giving up the best thing that had ever happened to me. Was this how it felt to give up religion? For the rest of your life feeling good good good but always scanning the shadows for an archer, always wondering late at night before sleep if you had squandered your eternity.

How could you not?

Something drifted before my eyes and I snatched it. A white puffy feather. Another, then another. I looked around as they fell over everyone and silence became us. The Body raised their arms. Children twirled under them. It was like what I imagined snow could be. I looked at Stringy and he stared up, his mouth open. I couldn't tell where they were coming from. I didn't see Trinity Prism anywhere in the rafters. She couldn't be throwing these feathers anyhow. They were coming from everywhere, thin air, impossible. I smiled. I couldn't help it.

Vern gazed upward, laughed as they stuck to his sweaty skin. "But for you who fear my name, the Son of Righteousness will rise with healing in His wings!" he cried. "I am here now! God among you in human form! Let your doubts be cast aside."

Stringy held his palms out and the feathers collected in them. Cherry was weeping now. I looked back up and I couldn't see the ceiling anymore. I was in a white cloud. I didn't notice for a long time that Stringy was no longer next to me.

When the last feathers had fallen my face was damp and my skin tingled. Nothing had ever been more beautiful. How quiet we'd stood under the feathers. The thing about signs is that they are up to each person in how they will be believed. I felt then that God was with me again. He was smiling down on my plan, all I'd done.

AFTER THE SERVICE, Stringy leaned against the hearse, smelling of smoke, wired to the hilt. "Mizz Cherry," he said. "You saw this man pull rain from the sky?"

"I ain't the only one."

"Hard to believe," Stringy said.

I thought of the grapes in Vern's yard, how no one would believe me if I told them that here in this barren valley I'd eaten of bulbous aching fruit.

Vern came out, smiling wide and shaking hands with the last trickle of the Body, the hangers-on who so desperately wanted to be touched by him. "That headache's nearly gone!" old Mrs. Jenkins said, clutching Vern's shoulder. "Praise!"

He waited until every last person had left and then walked toward us.

"Newly saved, and now wed," Vern said to Stringy. With his sunglasses on Stringy didn't look as old as normal and I was glad. Vern reached out and placed a hand on my belly and I stepped back.

"Jumpy," he said. "But you were so eager inside, for everyone to know."

"Don't forget we've got a new recruit," Cherry said, her lips pulled back so I could see the gray of her gums where they met the teeth.

"Young man, are you certain you've married an honest bride?" Vern smiled, seemed lightly amused by us.

Stringy kicked a toe into the dirt and in a flash I saw him as a nervous young boy, no tattoos to cover him. Under the unforgiving sun I could see where his real hair color, a soft mouse dander, was growing out from under the thick inky dye.

"I'm just doing right by her," he said. "What's it to you?"

"It's everything to me," Vern said. "Lacey is a big part of Gifts. Or didn't she tell you?"

"Well, we best be going," Cherry said. "And I'll get through to this one. You know infidels, the saving doesn't always come easy, but he's in the door, I'd say."

"You are faithful, Cherry. I know you won't do me wrong," Vern said to her.

Stringy walked backward, eyes on Vern like a spooked dog until we reached the car. I had the sense we had gotten away with a crime, but were still under surveillance. Vern's approval couldn't be this easy.

"I've seen him before somewhere," Stringy said back at Cherry's.

He was getting ready to go paint a lawn at a location he could not really describe. "You know that feeling when you see something and you feel like you're reliving it. Like you already did those things and saw those people?"

"Yeah," I said. "I've had that before."

"Déjà vu," Stringy said.

"No it ain't," Cherry cut in. "That's God."

I WENT IN for a Sunday shift at the red house so I could drink water. It seemed others were being steadfast in their waterless ways, Cherry included, and their skin had turned a sheen the color of the soda of their choice—oranges, blues, purples, greens. Teeth were rotting, brown and weak. Cherry had lost one of her molars and bellyached about how sore her mouth was all the time. I worried for my own and had taken to brushing at Daisy's using her natural organic toothpaste.

The Turquoise Cowboy called right after I got there. "I've got a mansion with a boat," he said. He didn't even say hi. "I've got two cars. One of them works and one's for parts. I've got satin bed-sheets and silk drapes. I've got girls of each color, all shapes and sizes. Sometimes I line them up and take their picture all together."

He was very drunk. This would be my chance if there ever was one. I shifted at my mother's desk. Did she like a drunk man? I imagined it was a relief to have everyone as drunk as you.

"Come be with me, princess," he said. There it was again: *princess*. Why did grown men want a princess? Something about it seemed creepy. "Once you see the place. Oh, man! It's like angels walking around all the day, the finest delicacies. Crab cakes and them chicken biscuit crackers. Tuna melts."

"What do I have to do once I'm there?" I said. My voice had

faltered, gone high. Maybe he'd tell me what my mother spent her days doing. I had a dark feeling it had nothing to do with getting famous.

"Number one, you have to work," he said. "Lifestyle doesn't come for free. You have to want people to recognize you on the street and ask after your name signed on their receipts. You have to really show them why they like it. You want that kind of life?"

I knew this was the part when my mother had told him, *Come get me, I'm ready.* She had told him where she was exactly, where to find her. She'd told him so much about her, maybe, that she hadn't even had to say the word *come*, she'd only had to croon sweetly to him and he couldn't be held off. I knew she had been surprised that day in the church when he'd called her name, but not too surprised. If I knew my mother, I would say there had always been a clock ticking within her, waiting for another man to change everything. I was the fool to imagine she had changed.

"I want to get out of this town," I said. "Ain't nothing for me here. Nothing for a star. I need you."

He paused. "Now, I said I'll come get you. But I need to be sure you're ready. I ain't making that drive for nothing."

Perhaps I would only get my way if I threatened a man with a man, someone he would listen to. He wasn't listening to me.

"Give me your address, baby," I said. "I got a daddy with a shotgun you don't want to mess with. They call him One Shot Joe. You don't want to know why."

"Tell me something first," he said.

"Anything."

"You ain't a part of that no-good church there, that church where that crooked pastor's taking advantage of all them nice ladies?"

"Tell me straight what's on your heart."

"I know a gal from there and she has stories, yes she do, about that man and his ways. Said he had been trying to get her to be his other wife for years and she just couldn't take it no more. She was trying to be a good church girl, but he was making it real hard, making her perform all number of naughties in the name of God. And I ain't got no business in what religion you are; hell, I don't care. But I can't be playing therapist to a broke-down Sally who's been brainwashed to hell and back. I ain't got time."

I thought of how Vern forbade my mother from dating, how he held her so prized, how he blushed under her beauty. But had he wanted her to be his wife? Had he touched her? What had I missed in the haze of my adoration? I hated all the things she'd never told me, but here they were circling like a cast of hawks.

"Can't imagine such a thing," I said.

I had him so close. I could feel it.

"Why don't you get yourself another drink and have a seat," I said. "Imagine I'm massaging you. Picture me real now, working on those strong shoulders."

I heard him slurp through a straw. Oh yes, I knew just what kind he was. He was the gas-station-soda-cup-and-Popov-vodka kind. Nursing it all day, refilling it before it got to the bottom so that by sundown the soda was nothing but a tint in the vodka and he would be the type of drunk that had no memory of itself.

I waited until I heard the straw search around in the ice, the sound of emptiness. Then he burped like a baby. Time for a nap.

"You're better than all these broads here. You're the one for me."

What horrors had he lived through as a child? People didn't usually just become this way, I thought. It was probably not completely fair, whatever had happened to him, and now here he was, his untended wound blasting around the world, wrecking things.

"I been telling you that," I said. "Now what's the address, darling?"

He laughed a little. Sighed. I wrote it down. Alibi Drive.

I WAITED UNTIL Cherry was tied up something deep with her Telephone Testimony and slipped from the house. The hearse purred. The sun was setting, a haze of orange lowering in the smog as I pulled out onto the road. No other cars around, cash on my lap, nearly two hundred dollars. I sped toward the freeway in the hearse, grateful for those driving lessons my mother had given me. I'd outsmarted every man in my way. She would be impressed by this. She would finally see the way things should be.

Old Canal Road hit its dead end, the church to my right, the on-ramp to Golden State Boulevard to my left. I gripped the wheel. This was it. Goodbye, Peaches. Hello, Mother. I accelerated, but moments later had to brake. I thought I was imagining things but no—there was Wiley Stam's body slumped over in the middle of the road, a shotgun resting between his legs. He sprang up to a stand and pointed the shotgun at the hearse. The wet of his open eyes glowed.

He tapped the gun on the hood. "You know, Miss Cherry, ain't no believer coming or going out of Peaches right now. Vern's orders. Ain't safe out there."

He got closer and stuck his head in the window. The smell of beer flooded the car, the same kind my mother liked. Didn't they know it made them weak and prone to foolishness? But of course Wiley, man as he was, wouldn't be banished for it.

"I just need to run a quick errand," I said, fumbling. I didn't even know what that errand could be.

"You think I trust a girl on her own?" His lips were sloppy. "I don't."

"How's Sharon?" I asked him. "You know what's going to happen with your very own girl?"

He planted the gun between his feet in the dirt. "I know everything I need to know."

"What are you going to get out of all this?" I said.

"My vineyards'll grow back," he said. "I'll be making millions. Riches like I've never seen."

I thought of the GLOBAL WARMING FOOLS! sign I'd seen months ago. "You won't be rich."

He held the shotgun up and focused his eyes just over the barrel. "You talk too much."

A gun to the face. It centers you. Focuses you. I thought of how when Lyle was over me in the shed I had made a point not to look at Grampa Jackie's guns on the wall. I didn't like the thoughts they brought to me, imagining my own self pointing one at Lyle. "I'll be going on home now," I said carefully.

He spat in the dirt. "Think that's best."

I reversed away from Wiley. He kept the gun on the hearse until I had turned all the way around and was rolling back toward Cherry's. I cried when I got there, sitting in the hearse with Grampa Jackie's spirit, a sort of gulping frantic sob. I imagined Grampa watching me, patting my back maybe, but I couldn't conjure the words he might use on me now. He could never see my mother in any fullness. How he favored her, how he loved her. Everything, even her worst low-down moments, were just strokes of bad luck to him. Was she a bad mother to me? Yes, I thought. Clearly. But he would not have been able to say that. For she was his baby. And I was no one's. My whole body shook. A gun in the face lets you know in an instant just how badly you want to live. *Everything's fine, little baby.* I sent messages to the person within me. *I won't let anything bad happen to you.*

I got out of the hearse and stood on the porch. Looked out into the black land. Anything could be out there, I thought. I imagined my mother walking toward me from the darkness. I might hear her before I saw her, a cracking branch. Then she would be before me bathed in the glow of the moon. She would look angelic, not real. I would ask her if she had found God where she'd been. If she could take me with her. But then I heard Vern in my mind: *The only way to God is through me.* He had said it time and time again. But something about it didn't feel right anymore. I knew he'd told my mother those same words. Presumably they had meant something different for her. How even before assignments had come about, she'd already had one. To please Vern in an unholy way. Either doing it and feeling shame, or fighting it and becoming exhausted. It was spiritual warfare, what he had done to her, holding her afterlife over her head like a bribe. I felt for her, if what the Cowboy had said on the phone was true.

Chapter 16

The next morning, a knock at the door. Cherry yelled from her bedroom for me to get it. I raced toward it like a loyal dog hoping for its owner to come home. But it wasn't my mother, it was Derndra and Trinity Prism. "Cherry," I called. "Come here." Cherry groaned and shuffled out of her room but sprang to life when she saw the pastor's wife and daughter, ushered them inside with bravado as if we could not be prouder of all that was contained in the house. The flies buzzed in a pack around Cherry's head and refused to go out the open door. They were happy here.

I could tell Derndra had paid special attention to her bangs that morning. They sat high on her forehead in a hard layered stack. Trinity's were the same. I sat on a kitchen chair in a top and underwear, started eating lima beans from a rusted can. The mice were scattered about the living room in action poses from the night before. Derndra held out a large gold envelope. "This is for Lacey May. We think it's best she come, even though she's claimed a husband."

"Of course," Cherry said. She tried to smooth her long hair back, and one of her boobs popped out from her loose robe. Trinity Prism's face went red. Our eyes met. I wanted her to smile, to let on she was a girl too, a girl like me, prone to laugh at the presence of an unexpected tit. But she didn't.

Cherry took the invitation and she kissed it. "All married and a woman but still a member of her church." She started to hum. She looked around the room waiting for us all to join. "This is the day that Vern has made!" she sang out.

We will rejoice and be glad in it, I thought, but I let the silence hang. Eventually Derndra said, "All right." And they turned to leave.

"Blessed are the meek, ain't that the saying?" Cherry said when they were gone, tearing open the envelope. She seemed giddy over the sparkly invitation like I'd been asked on some fine date, like I was in the best of fortunes. I kept thinking of the hearse, what it would feel like to leave this place.

I got up to read over her shoulder: GOTS meeting concerning YOU and the other selected soldiers of God's army: you're invited to an informational gathering regarding your special assignments. Please come alone and in faith. 5 p.m., TONIGHT.

"No sense in me going," I said, but Cherry shook her head.

"At least find out what he has to say. This Stringy, I'm starting to think you got a dud here. Sits around all the day like a born loser. I need me my alone time."

"Tell him to go paint lawns," I said. "Give him work to do."

"Maybe you'll come around, Lacey. Maybe you'll hear the good pastor and decide another way. You never know."

At the Pac, I searched for pregnancy magazines. Instead the tiny green Bibles we gave out to infidels filled the space where the magazines used to be. There were hundreds lined up and the sight of them together in this way sent a terror through me, the same books that used to incite such calm.

Quince stood behind me with her arms crossed. "They did it in the night," she said. "Broke in and replaced every ungodly thing with them Bibles." She waved a hand toward them. "I flipped through. That ain't the Bible. I read the Bible before when I was a little kid and that ain't it. But I ain't moving them. I don't want to know how they might replace me. I watched that rapture movie on the TV. People's silver teeth left on their car seats and all that."

"Of course it's the Bible," I said. "What else could it be?"

"The real Bible don't talk about Vern specific. What are you, a dummy? Vern's name is in this shitty book like a thousand times."

My face burned. I searched for an explanation, something to make the Bibles legitimate. I changed the subject. "You got any pregnancy magazines somewhere in the back?"

She looked around like there was someone watching. "We. Ain't. Got. No. Magazines," she said loud and slow. Then she leaned over and whispered: "I saw them on the security camera. All them teen-age boys like a gang of thieves."

WILEY HAD SAID only believers couldn't leave. Florin and Daisy weren't believers, I reasoned on my way to the red house later that day. They wouldn't be stopped.

All my calls were sad sappy scenarios. Daisy said it had to do with Mercury retrograde, just making everyone off and a bit crazy, but I wasn't sure. It just seemed like my own bad luck, these men wanting me to do so much reassuring of their worth and their kindness. I would have given anything to talk about a penis, some tits.

By the end of the shift, I thought of telling Florin that I'd gotten an address from the Turquoise Cowboy. I wanted to ask if they would take me there to get my mother. The magenta hearse had been a bad idea, but I could be concealed in their car. I stood by Florin's desk, the address sweaty in my palm. But she threw down a stack of books she had checked out from the Fresno County

Library. On the cover of one of them was a baby's face descending from space. *Ina May's Guide to Childbirth*, it said. I forgot the address in my hand. I forgot my mother. I hugged the book to me.

BACK AT CHERRY'S I read and read the books and the thing inside me began to become a real thing, an artichoke-sized being who was gearing up to be able to hear me, be someone I should sing a song to. I learned I had a perineum that could and should be massaged. Some of the information in the books was startling, especially the fuzzy photos of bobbing fetuses and the explanation of birth itself, how the fetus was supposed to *twirl* through the canal and emerge face down and the uterus was doing the work despite the woman and her pain or her fear. One book had three women on the cover dressed in colorless smocks like sad townspeople in Jerusalem during the time of Jesus. It said that a woman could not bother pushing at all and her body would take over and her strong amazing all-powerful uterus would expel the baby. They said red-faced pushing was something invented by impatient white men who had entered the art of birthing in a rush, trying to make money and rob women of the one thing we were physically made to do that had nothing at all to do with them. So they screamed at women to push and push and took away their animal knowledge and then when it didn't go well the woman would give up under the weight of all that naysaying, and the doctor would save the day by cutting the baby out in the nick of time, always in the name of emergency.

I looked deeply into the open caverns of these birthing women—a few of the books showed everything—and at first I could not look at the images directly. I had to squint my eyes and then slowly let them return to focus. The pictures were so powerful it felt like if I didn't pay them the respect they deserved the women in their sweat and toil could come off the page and incinerate me.

One of the books was called *Your Pregnancy Week by Week*. It said, "20 weeks: You might find out the sex this week. Are you dreaming of pink bows or blue trucks?" The truth was I'd dreamed of neither. It seemed I was already a terrible mother.

"Hello," I said aloud to the baby. I said it again and it rang out high and strange.

"Hello yourself," Cherry said in my doorway.

"I'm trying to talk to it," I said. This was the moment for Cherry to offer up some female intelligence about baby growing or birthing or something, anything, of use.

"Time for that church meeting," she said instead. I pictured the inside of her brain as an empty bowl, dead Goldies and Grampas flying around like bats, the church at the center, Vern a sniper, shooting down every critical thought from the sky of her mind. "Get on and go."

AT THE SPECIAL meeting the church was emptied just for us. It felt like a lifetime had passed since I had nearly skipped through town to get to Vern with my new blood, how the church was empty that day too but it seemed to glimmer with possibility, the empty pews waiting for God's people and all we would do. Now the emptiness was matte and gray, dust thick in the air, heat pressing in. It was hard to take a deep breath.

I was the last to arrive by the looks of it. The boys' club sat scattered around the church. I saw Lyle shooting rubber bands at Laramie, carefree. He didn't even look up when I walked in. Denay and Taffy sat legs splayed in the front row with the other girls, obvious baby bumps poking out from tight white tank tops. Denay rubbed her belly with her eyes closed. I sat next to Taffy but then I heard *Psssst*. It was Sharon at the end of the row, sitting a few spaces from the rest. I got up and plopped down next to her. She wore what looked like her father's shirt, huge and billowing over her body, and flip-flops on her dirty feet. Her face was swollen and scrubbed. Her brown hair was a nest on top of her head and she absentmindedly poked around in it every few seconds.

"Time to let the world know we've been knocked up by the white light of God. Can't hide these stomachs any longer." She smirked, whispered, "Well, not you, Miss I-have-a-husband. Wish I'd thought of that."

I was stunned by the way she spoke, so different from the other girls. She reminded me a bit of Florin, but more trapped. I didn't sense much belief within her. I considered that perhaps she had never believed at all.

Vern breezed to the front, an impatient energy about him. He wrung his hands and kept glancing toward the main door. "Girls, your stomachs are growing and growing! Praise be to the one who created us. In your wombs are church babies, of course. Future leaders of our army. Miracles in human form, the greatest offering we can turn over to God. Only then he will bless us with . . . ?"

"Rain," we all said together.

I saw Willow, a skinny quiet girl, open her eyes in shock. She grabbed her tiny potbelly. She hadn't figured it out. This seemed ridiculous to me, but I would probably be like her if Daisy hadn't explained everything.

Vern went down a list. We were to take care of ourselves in terms of spiritual fitness, which would nourish the babies far more than anything we ate or drank. Only God words through the mind.

Only GOTS influence. We must stay steadfast in the face of nay-sayers. Be prepared for the less faithful to doubt our plan. We were to offer nothing to these people. No explanation. No apologies for our faith. If anything we should feel sorry for them.

Lyle kept his face primed at Vern. He wouldn't look at me.

"There's one among us who isn't following," Denay said, pointing in my direction.

"What's to happen to these babies?" I blurted out. I thought of the gloriously smushy-faced infants I'd seen pictures of in my books, how my heart swelled to bursting when I thought of my own baby coming out just like that, nothing but innocent.

Denay's face broke into a smile. I knew she was excited to meet her own baby, too.

"Their sole purpose will be to share the gospel," Vern said. He explained it slowly like I was dull. He came up and squatted before me, put his hand on my knee. It seemed a father's movement, perhaps, after a child has fallen from a bike. But I flinched when he touched me, and he drew his hand back. Stood. "You won't be burdened by the day-to-day care of them at all. Once you turn them over they will become part of the Body. With time it will be like you've never known them as anything more than a face among many. You'll see everyone like that eventually. No more roles. No more labels. It wastes time, valuable time that we could be using to shoot people with spirit."

Denay's smile fell. "What will happen to us?" she asked him.

Vern looked exasperated for a moment, as if there were a text-book on church babies we had not read before class, but he recovered. "You'll do it all again, of course. The common family structure can just fall away. We will be one big family."

"Something like this in the Bible?" asked Taffy meekly.

"Psalm 127, dear." Vern cleared his throat and recited from memory:

> *Children are a heritage from the Lord,*
> *offspring a reward from him.*
> *Like arrows in the hands of a warrior*
> *are children born in one's youth.*
> *Blessed is the man*
> *whose quiver is full of them.*
> *They will not be put to shame*
> *when they contend with their opponents in court.*

The room was still. The verse struck me as beautiful in the way most verses did. My mother had called me sentimental more than once, my eyes threatening tears during the Sunday readings, but now my life was a verse. Now the verse seemed abstract, inapplicable to any of us in a practical sense. I looked at the boys' club. Why did it have to be Lyle? Why couldn't one of these boys have committed the act with me? But I knew why. This way, there could be no real love to distract us. Nothing could turn romantic. We girls would stay in our shame, where we were most pliable. We would hand the babies over, relieved.

"When all this comes to pass, I don't want people thinking I didn't contribute anything here," Lyle whined. He looked to me finally. "Marrying that infidel behind all our backs. When will she pay the price for that little stunt?"

"Lyle, stand down," Vern said. "You're giving her the power to upset you."

Lyle looked at his hands and pushed out deep loud breaths. Vern told the girls we were to go with Derndra, and the boys were welcome to have fellowship out behind the church, where there were snacks and cards for games. Vern had gotten the boys white baseball caps to wear to keep the sun from their eyes. Something useful, I thought. I could have used a cap. The sun was always in my eyes, my nose always in various states of peeling sunburn. But that was the way with boys. Always getting things that made them better—pants with pockets, tools for building—while girls received adornments, things to make us appear better to others.

Derndra appeared from the back of the church and led us up the stairs into Vern's small office, where we could be alone. We crowded together on the floor and she stood above us, presented us each with a large swath of white cloth and a small sewing kit. Then she passed out fun-size bars of Hershey's chocolate.

"I craved chocolate when I was pregnant with Trinity Prism," she said, smile curling her lip. It was more than I'd ever heard before about her personal life. To crave chocolate seemed so human. It made me wonder what else there was.

Trinity Prism remained stoic sitting on a stool behind her mother, set apart from us as usual.

"This cloth will become your Birthing Day dress," Derndra went on. "Everything you do from now until the babies are due is all for the Birthing Day."

"What's going to happen then?" Taffy said. I looked at her belly, oddly high and firm. She saw me and covered it with her hands.

"The thing you might not know about God," Derndra said, "is that He loves a party. He's gonna grant each of you labor and the babies will appear all together as a family. We will let them know they are welcome."

Denay smiled. "God is going to really understand how much we love him. He's going to rain down upon us."

"Whose baby is that?" I asked Denay.

Derndra cut in. "Thank you, Lacey. I was going to get to that. Sometimes God must move as a human to complete His deeds but the specifics are not important. These are God's children come from a blessed quiver. The babies within you are God's and no one else's."

She took out a pair of scissors from her apron pocket. Told us it was time for haircuts. "You're a group now, a special group. There's more chocolate where that came from if you remain obedient."

Denay stood up and Derndra sat her on a stool next to Trinity Prism. "If anyone tries to move, I'll hold you down," Trinity said. I laughed. Skinny pale Trinity, allergic to the sun, would hold us down? Please.

Denay complied perfectly as Derndra cut away hank after hank of her thick long hair. It fell dead to the floor. I couldn't believe it. Denay, who was obsessed with her hair, the smell of it and finding and demolishing split ends. The cut was a jagged chin-length bob with severe baby bangs. It made Denay look like a big crazed toddler.

Derndra tossed a small chocolate square to her like a dog, and she ate it with the quick terror of someone who fears it will be taken away. I thought surely no one else would agree to the cut after seeing Denay, pretty Denay, who had just received the opposite of a makeover. But one by one the Bible study girls got up and sat on the stool. Sharon and I shifted our bodies to the back of the room.

"I won't do it," she whispered to me.

"Me either," I said. I thought maybe we might hold hands in our unity but Sharon didn't seem up for that sort of thing. She bit her nails and cracked her jaw. I watched Denay comb fingers through her new short hair, her eyes gone, her smile wide as she watched the others.

Finally it was just me and Sharon left. I had backed myself

practically under Vern's desk by now. Derndra came close with the scissors. I thought of my hair, how it was like my mother's, a long curtain that was useful, maybe not as useful as a baseball cap, but still something I could hide behind.

"Can't just make it easy, can you?" she said to me.

"No, thank you," I said. "I'll leave it for now."

Trinity in all her frailness became like a wiry bobcat. Pulled me up by the arm and the others descended, clamping me against the wall with unexpected strength. I felt like a butterfly pinned to cork. Derndra cut haphazardly as I cried No No No, and then it was done. The girls came upon Sharon next and I lifted my hands to my hair. Chin-length now, and how ragged the hair looked on the floor mixed with all the other colors and textures, how now we were all the same.

"This isn't the way things used to be," I said, after all was done.

"No," Derndra said, handing me chocolate. "Things are better now."

THE NEXT MORNING I ran to the red house, stopping to breathe, slower now, my belly an indisputable part of me. I kept picturing an artichoke bobbing around inside, with a face and hands, with little listening ears.

"Don't say anything," I snapped at Daisy and Florin on my way in, covering my haircut with my hands. On my mother's desk was a stack of pregnancy magazines from Quince with a Post-it that said, *See, I'm nice.*

I put a hand on my stomach and flipped through them. There was a feature article about a couple who had tried for over five years to get pregnant with something called in vitro fertilization, and they wound up adopting. I could see the kindness in their eyes. I knew they would be good parents. The fine nursery they posed in. The tearful faces as they were united with their adopted daughter. Somehow God had not thought their bodies worthy of a child, but He'd ignited a slew of us Peaches girls with fertility. I didn't know if I was unsettled by this, if it made me feel wrong and ashamed, or if somehow it was proof that us girls really were set apart. *Show off that growing bump!* the next page demanded. *Wow everyone with a bodycon dress!* Under that, a list of embarrassing confessions from "mamas to be." *I peed my pants in the produce aisle! I farted during sex! I barfed in my hands in a restaurant!* These women seemed very carefree about these foibles, though, almost a little proud of them.

All the magazines, I noticed, referred to the reader and any mentioned mother only as *mama*, never as *woman*. Never by name.

One mama confessed that when she walked it felt like her vagina was breaking open. *Vagina's the part up there*, my mother had said. This woman probably meant to say *pussy*.

"I have something special for you downstairs," Daisy said, leaning in the doorway. The late-morning light from the window cast an odd glow on her scars, and while sometimes I forgot about them, other times, like now, they were jarring.

She put a hand to her face like she knew my thoughts. "Sulfuric acid," she said. "Random attack at a beach in Florida." It sounded like a news headline. "Just some man who didn't like that I was sunbathing topless. Didn't like it one bit."

"I'm sorry," I said. It sounded foolish. Anything would have.

"Don't be sorry," she said, backing away from the doorway. "Sorry doesn't fix a thing."

DOWNSTAIRS, THE DECOR in Daisy's back parlor was simple. She liked to say that since her assault, patterns irked her, that she couldn't bear the brightness of a bad fuchsia, the drone of a mustard yellow. Now all needed to be black or white, deep merlots and seafoams, a gentle eye-bath. Her pillows were black and her curtains were black and all of her small stones and crystals and her drawings on the walls of crows and vultures and pigeons were muted, low blues and soothing peach pales, like the inside of a wrist.

Daisy and Florin and a few women I had never seen before sat on the parlor floor on plump cushions circling another woman wearing a sack dress, shapeless, in a kind of fabric I'd never seen before, a thick but soft gauze with delicate metallic threads running through it, the brilliant blues and greens of an imagined seascape. I stepped closer to see it.

"It's handwoven in India on a loom made from a repurposed bicycle," the woman said to my thoughts. She motioned for me to touch it.

I stepped inside their circle and came close to her. She was made of lavender and something unfamiliar, earthy and heavy. I touched the dress. It was a soft finger cushion. "A man dyes the fabrics himself by instinct. It's all very ethically produced." Her breath was tangerines.

"Where did you get it?" I asked, true desire for an object welling in me. My own hand brushed the stiff cotton of the dirty coverall I wore and I cinched Daisy's kimono over it.

"Online," the woman said, like it should be obvious. "You can't find good stuff around here. A bunch of sweatshop shit everywhere you look."

"My grandma Cherry makes a lot of clothes."

"For you?" she asked, looking me up and down, eyes settling on my stomach.

"No," I said. "She has a collection of finely dressed taxidermy."

"I'm not one to judge the hobbies of others," Daisy said. "But this Cherry. Well, she sounds like she deserves to be judged."

The woman took my hand and introduced herself as Hazel. "I'm here to bless your pelvic bowl."

I pictured a bowl of rotting fruit. "The bowl is full," I said. "I'm pregnant."

She nodded with her eyes closed. "And your bowl is medicine."

Hazel introduced the other women as doulas, a word I had never heard before. They had greasy lank hair and flushed clean oiled complexions. Their hands were mannish and worn, bare nails, no jewelry. I sat on a cushion between Daisy and Florin. I'd never seen Daisy so rapt, so excited about something.

"I had Florin research natural birthing and this is what we found!" she said to me, beaming. "A natural birth squad!"

"Birth can be . . . unnatural?" I asked.

"Oh God," Daisy said. "They sucked Florin out of me with a fucking vacuum. I was on so many drugs I couldn't even hold her, and you know that space between your ass and your cunt? They cut it, oh yes they did. I don't want that for you, no sir. They say you'll heal good as new but they lie."

I felt surprised in this moment. Daisy wanted things for me and had considered me in this way, like she might have, well, her daughter. The image of Daisy's cut cunt flashed in my mind, abstract yet horrendous, and I felt relieved this Hazel woman was here with us. Certainly I'd do anything to avoid that fate.

Florin sat straight-backed, her legs curled under her. I tried to catch her gaze but she studied her palms. I wanted her badly as a friend but I worried she didn't see me that way. I liked how she was interested in drawing and math. In nature and the catching of dreams. But I had the sense that Florin had already crossed over into another, unreachable life, just as I had. Maybe we would be too much for each other.

"I'm a midwife and a doula and a woman and a goddess and I love women and I love vulvas and vaginas and cervixes and clitorises, you name it, I love it," Hazel said. "Whatever you think you know about yourself, leave it there at the door. I want you to enter into this experience completely open-minded and ready to receive."

"Are you going to summon God?" I asked her.

"Goddess, praise," she said, holding her hands palm up to the ceiling. "Goddess, praise."

I looked at Daisy to see if she was smirking, but her face was set. She was into it fully.

"You can undress from the waist down or take everything off if you want, when you're ready," Hazel said.

Daisy and Florin got naked easily without hesitation. They had seen each other a thousand times, I was sure. Daisy had a shocking thrush of ink-black pubes in startling contrast to her white hair. Florin was flat chested with tiny pink nipples that were a charm, and unlike her mother, there was nothing covering her, just razor-rashed skin, and I could see the dark of her center, a leaf folded in half, a flower pressed between the pages of a book. The doulas nodded and smiled at us. One made prayer hands and placed them under her chin.

"Can I just watch?" I said.

"Show up for your life, Lacey May," Daisy said. "Same parts."

The room was dim, and I thought about myself naked around other naked women. How we didn't have the same parts. It made me want to be a man, or a woman who loved other women, just to go around exploring all the different combinations of vulvas and nipples and breasts I could find. Maybe men were just as complicated, yet my experience with two of them so far told me they weren't. But with women—didn't it seem there could be endless ways to be with women?

I took my clothes off and closed my eyes. Hazel asked that we envision our bowls, the bird's nest of muscles that made up our pelvic floors. I saw floors and bowls and could not imagine how they were contained within my own body. But once I had thought of my body long enough, a time in the shed came to mind, how after he lay with me, Lyle got dressed and I was still on my back, and I asked him, "Do you think I'm pretty?" And he stood over me and looked for a long time and then said, "Don't be weird. You're my cousin." I had covered myself quickly.

Hazel passed each of us a small mirror. She told us to spend time with ourselves, take a good look around. Open our labia and see what was inside. Examine the all-powerful clitoris, and try to find our cervixes if we were really brave.

"It's like the most beautiful little doughnut you'll ever see," Hazel said. "I'll be coming around with a flashlight to help."

In the mirror I looked at my furrowed brow and burned nose. My face held a slight scowl when I wasn't even angry, I knew. I remembered the time my mother had told me I was no fun. No Fun, she had called me as she tipped back another tall can of beer, when all I had wanted was to have and be fun. I'd decided that when I was a mother I would allow Artichoke the space to be who she really was. I wouldn't make her worry over me to the point that she'd lose her very self.

I tried to soften my face. In the dim light my freckles were sweet and my lips pale and my eyes big. I'd been told I had sad eyes, but when I smiled or squinted they almost disappeared. My nose was a nose and my neck was average, nothing special. My breasts were swollen and hot and puffed up, tender baseballs. I wondered if there was already milk inside, but no. It was still too early according to *Pregnancy Magazine*. My belly seemed huge and different. I used to lie on our bed and eat rainbow cereal from the cavern of my sunken-in stomach. I'd never know that exact body again.

"It's time," Hazel said, switching on ocean wave sounds from her cell phone. "Let's look together."

She sat and urged the mirror down and shone a flashlight into me. "Meet Yoni," she said.

"I've seen it," I said, staring at her face. But it wasn't really true. I'd never looked like this.

"And what did you see?"

"You know, regular stuff."

She nodded. "Let's try again."

"Where's the cervix?" I asked.

"It's not far."

Suddenly I didn't want to see it. I didn't want to meet myself.

Hazel put her hand on my stomach and squared her eyes with mine. "The universe brought us together," she said.

I knew *the universe* was just code for God among people who didn't believe in God, but really truly did believe in God deep down and didn't want the responsibility. And maybe she was right. Maybe God wanted me to have help. People who knew what to do. The idea seemed so delicious. When I felt Hazel's hand on my belly, how I wished it were my mother's. I wondered what my mother would have seen if she could have met herself in this way. I wanted to take her along for this experience somehow, reach my hand out to her cosmically, carry her like a child.

I looked into the mirror. My first thought was *wow*. I felt sad then, for who my mother was, for the girl I'd always been. The one who until this point had never seen.

AFTER WE CHANTED a final yoni blessing, Hazel swaddled us in thick blankets and put pouches of lavender over our eyes and performed what she called a sound bath. I wanted to relax during this part but the whole thing had me jittery. I just knew I didn't want her to leave. Soon sounds filled the room, they seemed to come from everywhere, even from within myself. It was hard to think while hearing them. I opened my eyes to see Hazel stirring nothing in a metal bowl, creating an orchestra.

After she unswaddled us, Hazel told me I could have an appointment with her whenever I wanted. She'd see me for free. I wondered if she would still offer this if she knew the whole truth, that it was my cousin's baby. I didn't say anything.

Daisy stretched her arms up and touched her toes, then studied me as I got dressed. She came close and patted my back. "Florin says you've been talking to Rick. He's not supposed to call here anymore."

I looked at the doulas and Hazel, who were packing up, thankfully not paying attention to us. I hated that Daisy was reminding me of work right now. I didn't want to think of any of it.

"He's money like all the rest," I said.

"Sometimes all the phone would have to do was ring when that man called, and a chill went up my spine, but your mother didn't have any intuition."

Yes, so why didn't you cut her off from him? I wanted to say. Why didn't you do anything?

"People are one way, you think. You watch them every day and you think you know all they're capable of. That's how I felt about your mother. I felt I knew just what she would do in any situation. But that's always wrong. You never really know what any one person will do, or has done." She pressed her fingertips into the mask of scars on her face.

"Do they hurt?" I asked.

She brushed me off. "This is where your life gets fun," she said. "All these trials will bring forth a whole lot of gifts."

"You sound pretty religious sometimes," I said.

She smiled. Held my hand. "Your mother is lucky to have a girl like you."

"She's selfish," I said. "That's all. Disobedient to God and selfish."

Daisy squeezed my hand hard, looked to Florin, who was deep in conversation with Hazel. "I'll tell you the truth. I didn't want to be a mother. Sometimes still I think maybe it was all a big mistake."

"That's awful," I said.

"Is it? Why does it have to be? I loved her anyhow. Even her sharp little fingernails scratching me like a wildcat when she was a baby. The dumb things I loved."

I sighed. I liked imagining them together so many years before, when everything was still unknown, wrapped up in the future.

"But slowly as she got older and older and needed me less it seemed she was becoming a stranger," Daisy went on. "I found I didn't need to smell her head or hold her to my body as much. Whole days could pass and I would have barely seen her. But then out of nowhere I would long for her. I'd reach out to find her and she was gone. A person had replaced her. It gave me wild thoughts. Leaving, starting over. Being a person in the world again not needed so deeply. I suspect most mothers have those moments, those thoughts. But they go away. You catch your breath."

"My mother's didn't go away."

"No, I suppose not."

I wanted to ask her then. *Take me to her now. Take me in your car, let's blow off this life and head down the highway.* I imagined picking my mother up in Florin's fast car, all of us together, women untethered on the road. Men? What men? We didn't need them. We'd forget them all. We'd never see another man as long as we lived and it would be good.

But I didn't ask her. I had begun to feel self-conscious around her when it came to my mother, for I saw how greatly she wanted me to not want her, for me to charge forward into my own strength, somehow above it all.

And a new desire had grown in me: I wanted Daisy to love me the same way she loved Florin. Maybe more.

ON CHRISTMAS SUNDAY there was no tree in the church, no lights. No paper bag and candle luminaries lighting the walkway for fear of fire through the grasslands. We were instructed to wear black, a time of mourning for our town, a time of faithfulness.

Stringy eyed my belly in a strange way and spent more time on his phone. "You know," he said from the couch, "in jail you watch a lot of TV."

"Cool," I said, opening a can of beans. I drank the cloudy juice then pressed the soft pintos against the roof of my mouth, the flavor of nothing.

"I remember one story of this guy baptizing people and all kinds of shit. This little church in middle-of-nowhere New Mexico. Whole thing blew up when someone in the church accused him of having like twenty wives, not taking any of them to the hospital when they were sick. All kinds of weird mind tricks and brainwashing. All them women wore dresses of blue sequins and held hands everywhere they went. Total freaks."

I put the can down. "And?"

"You really think this guy's gonna pull rain from that sky out there?" He pointed to the window and the cloudless and blue-brown sky, the crows swarming against the thick smog backdrop, the sun a strange orange orb.

"He did it once," I said. Because he did. I still could not deny the divinity of that timing, and neither could the rest of the Body. I still could not get that muscat juice out of my mouth.

"He's a fraud. I'm no educated man but it's plain to see you've all been struck blind."

"That doesn't sound anything like our Vern," Cherry said, emerging from the shadowy hallway. "Lacey here can tell you about her and her mama's life before that man brought us into savings."

I hadn't said much to Stringy about the beforelife. The nights spent alone, when I'd wake up in a terror and my mother wasn't next to me. I wouldn't be able to sleep on the couch, longing for our bed. I'd eat jelly beans and watch horse races on the television. How I'd so wanted to be one of those little men on the horses. *I want to be a jockey someday*, I told Sapphire Earrings once, my mother passed out in the room. *You're too big*, he said, mouthful of seeds and chew, spitting into a red plastic cup, little bits of shell in his horrible mustache. But sometimes if I was truly alone, I would jump up and down and scream loud as I could. I wanted the world to know she wasn't there and for someone to change it. In true desperation I'd call Cherry and beg for her to come get me. I'd picture my mother dead somewhere, or just dead in the mind, forgetting me completely. It was true Vern had saved me from all that. It was too hard to explain to Stringy. I had no bruises on my body to show my motherloss, and so to anyone else, did it exist?

"Yeah," Stringy said. "Seems like your mom's doing real good these days. All thanks to that pastor, huh? I'd ask for my money back if I were you."

STRINGY REFUSED TO come to church that day, claiming he was busy with lawn painting. Day to day I didn't notice very many neon lawns, though, and I wondered vaguely what he did with his time if not that. I wondered if he might even have a girlfriend. I wasn't jealous if he did. Maybe he was meeting up with the Jasons at Tent City, letting the seconds of their lives seep away, meaningless.

I stood in the pew next to Cherry and kept my eyes on her cane, on her snarled knuckles. How special I used to feel here at church, my mother at my side, our hands lifted, letting glitter fall on our palms. The blissful smile on my mother's face during worship, dreamed up and away. I had felt so much pride to be hers. Her beauty was blessing enough for both of us.

Vern took to the stage in a silver robe. He pumped himself up with a few jumps, pounded his chest with his fists. This really got the Body excited: *Praise Vern!* But there were fewer shrieks and whoops today. People were sun-whipped and tired.

"How blessed can we be?" Vern asked, as if he didn't notice how small the Body was, how wilted. "That God saw our dedication, saw our steadfast work, and came down in a light and blessed our girls with life. I could hardly believe it myself, but now it's before us. A true and real answer from above."

I thought this was the chance, if ever there would be one. The point where everything might change.

"Come up here, girls!" he said. Cherry nudged me up and gave me a severe look that I knew to mean future punishment if I did not go. We lined up next to him on the stage. Vern jumped into his dog bed for a moment and looked at us and then sprang back up.

"Look at them, everyone! Have you ever seen any miracle like this? Each one of them a testimony!"

The Body looked at us girls, at our stomachs, our haircuts. Little pregnant dollies. They were quiet at first. Eyes on us all together, they really saw.

Finally old Gentry Roo translated for everyone: "Like the blessed virgin," he offered. He raised his arms in a salute toward us.

Aha. Shoulders relaxed. Breaths exhaled. No, I thought. Someone speak out. Someone ask how this happened, really. *Like the blessed virgin*, they murmured. Yes, yes, that was it. The Body raised their hands and a cheer vibrated through the church. The downfall of the Body was that we loved a mystery. Mystery was proof of God. Mystery was not complex, but simple. You never needed to understand it. Acceptance alone would do.

"Let's close our eyes and let this miracle seep into us. If you were worried about Peaches, about the future, lay those worries down." Everyone bowed their heads. I kept my eyes slightly open and watched Vern nod toward the rafters where Trinity Prism stood above us, something primed in her hand. I closed my eyes again. My heart pounded. Seconds later, God glitter became us. I looked at it closely on my arm. It was the same kind Cherry bought from the Dollar Disco for her eyelids, wasn't it? I looked back up to the rafters but no one was there.

AFTER THE SERVICE Denay told me she had seen me driving through town with the witch girl, that I was out of my mind. She wanted me to remember that there was no worse punishment in hell than for the believer who had seen yet chosen blindness.

"Who did that to you?" I asked her. I pointed to her belly.

"I was scared just like everyone else," she hissed. "But I'm obeying. I'm making the best of it. Take my advice. You tell yourself it was God every day, one day you wake up knowing it as truth. That's the way He works."

"Just say it."

"White light bathing my virgin's body," she said. "No man to be found."

The church revealed itself to me then. Creaking wood planks, peeling and hot. Trinity Prism in the rafters, long in the face. The cheap common glitter, no specimen of heaven. Vern in a polyester robe fraying at the edges. I saw everything exactly as it was, dark and dirty, the people covered in filth, farm-beaten and raw, their deadened searching eyes, desperation. And the girls. The girls of blood, all full up like me.

I nodded. Vern was looking at me now, far enough away that he couldn't hear. I wondered if he could read lips. "You don't know who Vern is," I said under my breath.

But Denay stood her ground. Waved and smiled at him. "Neither do you."

Chapter 17

Where gone the town of Peaches, I imagined the country folk muttering, though even in my imaginings no one dared to speak their dismay too loud, lest God hear their grievances and decide to make a bad thing worse. But by now everyone had noticed that for all of Vern's efforts, for all of our assignment work, things were not improving. There were rumors of entire families up and leaving in the night and never coming back, driving into the city to stock up on water bottles, to swim in public pools. It seemed only the most dedicated were following now, mostly staying inside homes praying, but some were struck crazy by the heat, on diets of nothing but canned trash and warm soda. Some could be seen wailing in their front yards, heads shaved and nearly naked, digging at dirt for hidden water. Pacing the one strip of shops, peering in their windows, remembering maybe the ice-cold water that came complimentary with your meal at the Grape Tray. Remembering, maybe, my mother's delicate and straining wrist as she refilled their glasses, how they smiled up at her, how we were happy and together in our raisin-made town. For that was when religion was a ribbon atop a fine existence. When religion made the hard things easier to swallow, when it soothed like a meditation. When it colored death from dark to glory, when every good thing, even a good parking spot, was from Him. I remembered my mother swinging into the lot at the Pac, getting a front-row space, how she'd hold her hand up to cup the grace. *Thanks, God!* she'd say, like God was a good-natured and clever buddy, focused on reserving parking spaces for the faithful.

Yes, religion felt different now, ravaging even, and not only to me. There was something true at stake. A lot of us seemed to know that now.

By February the girls of blood had reached another level of stewardship to the cause, bellies pushing proud out on the street. They claimed in public cry to have been touched by the spirit in the night in a blast of white light. The stories shape-shifted until they became the same story. I kept my mouth shut. I watched them from a distance, always wondering if life would be easier if I just joined in.

Taffy didn't seem to change, but her belly did. Sometimes it was lumpy and low, sometimes it stuck straight out. She waddled like a duck with her arms resting on the bump, proud as pie. Denay led the pack, little women soldiers with the same haircuts, the same matching maternity tent dresses. They put their bellies together and laughed like it was great fun. I watched them with a touch of envy.

For I didn't feel blessed in any way. In fact, I'd never felt worse in my life. The mamas in the magazines seemed to revel in the expanse of their bodies, but no one could articulate for me the particular nausea I carried everywhere I went, the fall-down exhaustion that overtook me upon waking each morning and lasted until I could collapse into bed at night, and why was I out of breath all the time as if I'd just run a mile when all I had done was stand up? My tits hurt my back hurt my feet hurt. I hated all of it. My old self had begun to feel like an oasis, the flat empty stomach, the ease of movement. Would I ever return? And besides all that, I smelled like a barnyard no matter how I tried to wash myself with Daisy's bottled water.

Had I made a mistake? I asked myself every other thought. Now when someone from the Body saw a girl of blood coming down the sidewalk, her belly leading the way, praise was thrown at her. *Glory be! Glory be to the good church girls!*

Not for me, though. For my devotion was up for debate. I received stares now, shakes of the head. Whispers. Was I a chosen girl, or was I just a girl?

It was of no merit to be just a girl.

I BRACED AGAINST it all. I walked in silence, head down. I'd taken to wearing a long blond wig of Daisy's everywhere but at church, a black tunic she'd thrown at me one day because she couldn't stand to look at my belly bursting from the one-piece that Aunt Pearl bought me. I shaded my eyes in her silver cat-eye sunglasses. Aunt Pearl seemed always in a hurry, shuffling around church and town, too busy to pay me mind. She regarded me as if I were only distantly familiar, someone she once knew maybe but couldn't place. I wondered if she knew what her own son had done to me. I wondered if she knew and she couldn't stomach it.

Sharon looked like she'd been dragged by a tractor through the scratch of a cotton field. She wore deep red welt marks on her back where I imagined her father had taken to whipping her. She walked around aimlessly swinging a little Hello Kitty purse, her teeth soft and gray, eyes of yellow.

I was down in the canal on my way to the red house when I saw her walking along swinging that purse, slow and forlorn above me.

"Hey," I said. "Down here."

She squealed in fright. Jumped. "Jesus Christ, Lacey. What are you doing?"

"Just ease down, I'll help you."

She sat on the edge of the canal and then lowered herself in but slipped, landing hard on her knees like I had my first time. "What is this?"

"This way no one can see me from the road. I like it down here."

She looked around squeamishly, taking in the cracked dry canal bed, the bones of the tiny rat rib cage near her foot. "Where do you go?"

I could share the Diviners with her, I thought for a moment. Take her to my other world. But in the land of scarcity there was no room for one more, so I shrugged.

She squinted up at the clear blue above us. "I wouldn't care if this whole place burned," she said. "In Paradise when that happened, a man held his wife in a swimming pool all night while they watched their house burn around them, and then the wife died in front of him."

I shuddered. I hadn't heard that story on the news. "Does dirt burn?" I asked.

She was quiet then and lay on her back. I saw her stomach quiver when she breathed and I wondered if she had been feeling like I was, that something inside was bubbling. I pictured a pot on Cherry's stove boiling over. Perhaps I was boiling from the inside. In any case the sensation was worrisome, like nothing I'd ever felt. If I were in a romantic mood, I'd say it felt like a swarm of butterflies. But I was not feeling romantic.

"You ever feel anything in there?" I said. "Like, movements?"

"Oh yeah," she said. She poked her stomach with one finger

hard like it wasn't a part of her own body. "My mom told me it was just gas."

I nodded. Gas. This wasn't gas. It seemed like Sharon knew it too.

"You weren't touched by God in the night," I said.

She turned her head toward me. "My brother."

Laramie, the beefy red-faced boy who laughed in a dull stutter. I closed my eyes. A part of me had already known.

"My mother told me I was dreaming. Dreaming. She said, 'Sharon, don't let the Devil complicate it.' She baked a cake to celebrate my usefulness." She started to cry. "I'm going to hell, Lacey. They're telling me this is what God wanted but I saw. I had a vision that the whole valley just kept dropping and dropping and I fell through the cracks."

"Do you think Derndra ever tried to stop him?" I asked.

Sharon shook her head. "Her own daughter ain't a part of it. Tells me she isn't too keen on the whole thing."

But I wasn't sure it was so simple. All Derndra kept behind her placid face. She knew everything, didn't she? I'd always thought her a snob, someone who was too holy to talk with the rest of us, someone too perfect. But perhaps she was too scared.

Sharon took a deep breath. Her tears had made pale rivers down her dirty face. "You know I tried to tell the cops after Laramie came at me, and my mom got on the phone and told them I was being dramatic because I hadn't gotten my way. Geary backed them up just like Vern said he would. No one will help us."

"It will be okay," I said, but it came out flat and dead.

"I've been looking into ways of ending it myself," she said. "I figure I can eat enough poison to kill it but not kill me."

"I've never heard of anyone doing that," I said.

"Of course you haven't. Women don't walk around wearing a shirt that says, 'Hey, I ended my own pregnancy!' But it happens. Most of my searches were banned on the school computer but I found one where this girl ate rat poison and it worked."

Everything in me knew this was a bad idea, dangerous, but I didn't say anything. Sharon seemed happy when she talked about it, and I knew she would never really do it anyhow. I'd let her go on imagining whatever she needed to get by.

THE NEXT MORNING brought Officer Geary to Cherry's porch, sweating under his black Stetson. I stepped out of the house and closed the screen behind me. I didn't want him in the house. I didn't want to have to offer him things, wait on him.

"Short on manners, not asking a gentleman inside," he said.

I stood my ground and pointed to Cherry's narrow wooden bench with the one wobbly leg. He sat on it, opened his knees wide enough so that there wasn't room for the two of us. "Why don't you take a seat?"

"I'll stand," I said.

"Any word from your mother?" he asked.

"She's in Reno and she's in love," I said.

"Is that so?" he asked. "Boy, no one saw her turning out like this."

"How did you see her turning out?"

"Well, once she met Vern, she was a real good girl. She was on the best path she could be, considering." He looked at me. "Considering her earlier troubles. All the boys she went around with. No self-respect at all."

"Maybe they should have just respected her," I said.

He looked confused by my comment. "I see part of my job as

keeping you off the same track as her. And I received the strangest call last night that someone saw you around that lady's phone house. Now why would they say a thing like that?"

I drew a sharp breath in. I forced myself to smile but I felt my cheeks burn. Denay must have said something, or was it someone else? I wasn't careful enough. I should have stopped going probably, just knowing what the church was capable of, but I was part of that house now. It was more my home than Cherry's.

"Maybe you could try to find my mother and bring her back and fix all this mess. Focus on that."

"Your teachers say they haven't seen you once all year. They actually assumed you had moved like so many. But that's okay, I'm not really of the mind that girls need such a broad education myself. But girls do need to keep busy. And this husband of yours is distracting you," he said. "I'd like to think he's a God-fearing man starting his path, but then, here he is out at all hours hanging around that Tent City, cruisin' for a bruisin'."

I tried the smoldering stare the women used in my romances. I looked him deep in the eyes. It always seemed to end conversations for the women characters, was a sort of hypnosis over whoever fell under their gaze. But Geary was not hypnotized. He said, "You on drugs?"

"What do you know about Vern before he came back to Peaches?" I asked.

"I don't like your tone," he said. "I know just what the good pastor's told me and I don't need any more."

"What if he's not who he says he is?" I said. "What will you do?" I reached out and touched his badge, hot under the sun. "What will you do if you find out that all these babies aren't God-given after all?"

"Say it straight," he said, standing.

"Maybe all these babies are coming from regular old sex."

He stepped off the porch. "Women sure have a hard time being obedient, don't they?" He stared up at the blinding sky as if looking for an answer. He got in his old patrol car and rolled away.

Chapter 18

I sat in the passenger seat as Florin parked us in front of an abandoned lone blue barn I'd passed a million times. It used to belong to the Sander family—dairy people—before they left town after the first bad drought, saying they didn't like Vern and his ways. I'd never thought of them again, other than to pray for their deliverance, and certainly never realized the barn was now inhabited for a very different cause. FARM OF SPIRITUAL BIRTHING AND UTERUS CELEBRATION was written on a little wooden sign over the door.

"Well, now this is happening," Florin said.

"Appears to be," I said.

She opened the door for me. I tried to imagine she was my partner, the father of the baby perhaps. This was just a normal appointment. *Ask your doctor about cord clamping. Ask your doctor about vernix practices. What happens to the placenta? Bring a cooler for transportation if you wish to eat it.* My magazines had whole checklists you could cut out and bring with you, but I had forgotten them all.

Inside were Hazel's doulas and several other women I had never seen, lit up from somewhere unearthly, their cheeks sun-flushed. They wore T-shirts that said things like *The Clitoral Truth* and *Feminist Killjoy* tucked into wide-leg canvas pants, and they smiled with their heads cocked to the side, lips pressed in feminine knowledge.

Hazel hugged me and led us to a back room. She patted my belly. "That baby in there wants to be a person in the world, I can tell."

In the room there was a poster advertising a womb continuum class and little twiggy flowers in mason jars on every windowsill, a double bed with a pure white duvet. Everything smelled of peppermint and baked bread. She poured cucumber water from a pitcher into a glass and I downed it in a loud, shameless gulp. The water was crisp and cold. The more I drank, the more I wanted. I thought of how my mother used to drink alcohol as if it were water, no hesitation, no savoring. Just pure need.

"More," I said, and she gave me more. She took a cloth and wiped dirt from my face.

"Pregnant women need a ton of water," she said. "I hope you've been watering that little baby in there."

I pictured myself pouring soda on a seed in the ground and expecting a garden. Useless. Perhaps the strange popping I'd been feeling was just the baby signaling for more water, begging for it, and there was not enough.

"You can wash here before you leave, too, if you want. Only if you want. No judgment."

"There's this weird feeling in my stomach," I said quietly. "I mean, it could just be gas. It probably is. But what if it's not, what if I'm doing this all wrong?"

"Pop pop pop," she said. She tapped on the drum of me, enthusiasm unthwarted. "Like that?" I nodded. "That's your babe kicking. It's saying, 'Here I am, Mom! Pay attention to me!'"

"It's moving in there?" I said. This possibility felt obvious to me suddenly. Of course it was moving. Hadn't the mama magazines mentioned this would happen? Yet I had felt certain these very normal things wouldn't happen for me. I had dreaded deep down that this baby would never move, that I would not be a good-enough host. But here it was moving despite everything. Goose bumps sprang up on my arms and legs. I wasn't in control of anything about the person inside me, a relief and a terror.

"Babies are known to masturbate in the womb, if you can believe it. They lick the wall of the womb, they suck their thumbs. It's incredible. Oh, you poor thing. Did you think something was wrong? Just kicks!"

Poor thing. I smiled at her, but I hated those words. I wanted her to see me as a glowing mama in a new bodycon dress showing off my bump, smiling dear husband on my arm. Nursery almost complete. I wanted to put my feet up in my new rocking chair that I would nurse in, and think of baby names, think of nothing but the swell of my feet. But instead, *Poor thing.*

"Is she gonna be too small to push this thing out?" Florin asked, looking at my crotch.

"A woman from Fresno had her babe in here a few days ago," a doula cut in. Her hair was pinned to the sides of her head in little bushes over her ears. "Eleven pounds, vaginally." She looked dreamily at the ceiling, toward some unknown doula heaven of elastic vaginas, still in awe. "We made her placenta pills. It was a gorgeous placenta."

"That's a big-ass baby," Florin said.

"They're all coming in from the city now that unmedicated birth is in style again," Hazel said. "She did amazing. Her mantra was 'I'm going to get enooooorrrmmous.' She kept saying that while pushing, 'I'm getting enorrrrrmous, I'm getting enorrrrrrrmous.' Never seen dilation like that. He came right out."

"What if I can't do it?"

"Nope," Hazel said. "Don't entertain that thought. Don't give it an ounce of power. Your thoughts create reality."

If my thoughts created reality I wouldn't be in this situation now, I thought.

I lay down on the bed and she took my blood pressure. "Good," she said. Then she pulled out a wand-looking thing.

"Time to hear the heartbeat," she said.

The heartbeat. This was another way I could fail. The baby could have a heartbeat but not the right kind. Perhaps it could have no heartbeat. I had just felt the popping minutes ago but now I didn't, so maybe in the last thirty seconds it had decided to stop. No no no. "I don't want to," I said.

"Come on," Florin said. "This is the fun part."

I sat up, my own heart skipping too fast. I wanted out of there.

"That's okay, Lacey May," Hazel said, putting her hand on my shoulder. "We should probably put together a birth plan for you. I want you to think about your ideal birth. Just meditate on it."

"I'll do what you want me to do." I got off the bed. Anything to leave.

"Take a walk, listen to your body, to your baby."

"Listen to the baby?"

"Of course," she said. "Your baby has all sorts of things she wants you to know."

"I mean," I said. "I just didn't know I was supposed to." It annoyed me a little bit, to be told to listen to something that was not going to speak outright, just like I was always told to listen to God, to decode divine messaging from dust-filled air.

We walked back to the car. Florin started the engine and scanned the radio. We sat for a minute.

"My mom loves that shit," she said. "All the oils and body positivity. I don't know. I'd want a real doctor, but that's me."

I thought of Hazel at the yoni magic meeting. How she had looked at all of us. She believed in us fully. I had never met someone like her and it seemed I could find the ends of my pain if she was there to hold my hand.

"I like it," I said. "You can tell she knows things."

"I hope so," Florin said.

"Wait," I said. I opened the door again. Got out of the car. My body took me back into the farmhouse, back into the room where Hazel was making notes on a chart. She looked up. "Forget something?"

I lay across the bed and pulled up my dress. I closed my eyes and said it. "You should know the father is not my husband but my cousin, mother's sister's son. Related."

She smiled. "Does it feel good to say it to another person?"

It did feel good, to say it so clearly. "Yes."

"Hon," she said. "You'd be surprised how many people make it with their cousins, and those babies turn out a-okay. It's not unheard of is all I'm saying. Some parts of the world it's pretty normal." She wanted me to believe nothing could faze her but I saw a red blush flower around her hairline.

She turned the Doppler on. It sounded like radio static. "Now, whether you wanted that to happen to you is another story. I'm here to talk about that too if you want."

She moved the wand around my small dome smeared with cold jelly. I craned my neck to watch and felt I was out of my body looking at someone else. The faintest brown line spread down from my navel. My skin looked tight and pulled. My thighs were larger, meatier, than ever before. It seemed to me I was turning into a series of lumps. I didn't understand how I was only going to get much,

much larger from here. It seemed impossible. I liked it, though. I looked nothing like the girl that had lain on the shed floor.

"It takes time to find the heart sometimes," she said. She looked up at the ceiling and let her hands guide her. Her eyebrows twitched and the softness of her tunic rubbed my skin.

She worked a minute longer. The walls were closing in. Here it was, my punishment. I braced. I saw my pink unformed baby floating in the boiling toxic waters of me, too hot to hold.

But then a quick two-step, a sharp gallop.

Hazel smiled like she'd expected this sound. To her, this very routine sound. "Strong."

It did sound strong. It sounded like rain.

ON THE WAY back Florin and I laughed like friends, and our sweat shone in the sun and the wind mussed our hair and I felt almost normal for a moment, so normal that it seemed right and sure that I should have a mother of my own and not imagine that Daisy was my mother, and so I asked Florin if she and Daisy could drive me to Reno to get my mother so we could all be women together in a car just like this on our way on our way, and she said not to get my hopes up but they were already up up up.

AT HOME THAT evening Cherry was at the stove humming, thwacking her cane around to the beat of an old country crooner crackling through her small radio. Steam rose from a pot. She was heating dark soda to make a syrupy glaze to drizzle over her apricot scones. She liked to make about two dozen scones at one time and eat them all through the night. In the morning there would be no scones left and neither of us would say a word when she made comments about how I'd gone and fattened myself with them.

The kitchen was the biggest area of the house, with a huge pink tiled island. On it, a dirty glass vase full to the brim with raisins from years ago, gray and mummified now. Another one full of misshapen moldy oranges that had turned green then white then become a kind of dust. I remembered just years before, the white wicker fruit basket full of peaches, figs, pears, plums, oranges, tangerines. Not anymore. I snatched a hot soda scone with candied apricots, hard as pebbles, and ate it in two bites. I put another in my back pocket.

I stared at the wall above the sink, where a framed picture of a man wearing a purple shirt falling to his knees hung. Behind him stood Jesus, weary and dirt-smudged with oval holes in his hands. He looked at the fallen man with loving sadness. He was trying to help him stand but his face was forlorn. It struck me that I could not imagine Vern standing behind any of us, holding us up.

"Did I ever tell you about when your mother won Miss Peaches Supreme?" Cherry said.

"One thousand times."

"She came out dressed as a raisin for the talent portion."

"Twirling a baton," I said.

"People figured you couldn't make sexy out of a raisin but she proved them wrong. I always thought you would grow up right like her with those long bones. When you were little you wouldn't stop drinking sweet milk drink from your bottle at bedtime. I told your momma, her teeth's gonna rot out her head, and they did! You ended up silver babies 'cross the front. Shame. Made everyone think you were some kind of white trash. Boy, you are getting thick around the middle. That baby is showing itself."

An image of Lyle on top of me flashed through my mind, and left. I got hot, then cold.

"Come 'ere," she said. I could smell her as I got close. Body odor, jelly, and baby powder. "Help me get at this hair," she said, pulling me into the bathroom. "It's a trickster. You've got to get to the root." She handed me the tweezers and shone a flashlight on her face. "See it?"

It was there poking out of her makeup. She wore a new matte orange bronzer I had noticed on her bathroom counter. Haitian Vacation. I clamped the hair and then pulled and pulled and finally it came out, wound corkscrew tight, a white stump root. "Here's the offender," I said. She opened a tiny velour jewelry box where she stored them and I dropped it in.

"It's always the same spot," she said. "Just wait until you get old. God a-mighty, hairs out the chin."

"By the time I'm old there will be some miracle cream that won't allow that to happen."

"You real sure this baby should be that rat boy's?" Cherry said. "Seen all these girlies around church touched by the light, highly prized. Thought, why can't my Lacey May be one of them? If you're running away from God's plan I feel that's a right shame. It's on my heart to tell you so."

"It's Stringy's," I said.

"Vern didn't even seem to care I'd brought a regular infidel into the Body. Thought he was going to have some reward for me. Something to say, at least. But he ain't been saying much of nothing lately. It don't give me a good feeling. My own daddy used to simmer simmer simmer. Us kids would think everything was fine, going on about our business. One time I dropped my mama's mixing bowl and it shattered all over the place, but my daddy just smiled. Helped me clean it. Then weeks later I got the beating of a lifetime. Guess what for?"

The mixing bowl, I knew.

"The mixing bowl!" She threw her hands up. "Not right if you ask me. If I'm going to be punished I like it served hot."

"You think Vern's like your daddy?" I asked.

"I didn't before, but lately. I don't know. I can't say who anyone is."

"You don't like his plan for the babies, do you? Not really. You know it's wrong."

She twitched, looked up at God, who was always watching. "Go call for Goldie, will you? I forgot today."

"I don't know why you still call for that cat. You know she's dead, don't you?"

"Mouth of trash! Go call for that pussycat." Cherry waved the bull penis cane over her head, threatening me, then withdrawing it as if I wasn't worth the cane treatment. She looked at it with love. "Made from real bull organs. If Grampa had been alive to see it he would have been impressed."

"If Grampa was alive you wouldn't need a cane," I said. "Wouldn't need to call for Goldie either. Grampa was alive you would have never joined up with the church in the first place."

"Devil speaking through you, girl."

I leaned out the door and called, "Goldie, Goldie, Goldie." I waited a few seconds. "Here she comes, Cherry!"

Cherry bolted up from her seat, dropping the cane. She ran just fine across the room, crowded the door frame, and stared into the blankness of the front yard. Wiley Stam's lifted truck passed by slowly like a patrol. "I don't see nothing," she said. She shielded her eyes from the sun. "Goldie? Goldie?"

She turned to me. "You're right and sure?" she said, but I was smiling in my anger.

"Oh, tricking an old woman like this. For shame, Lacey May. Get an old Cherry her cane."

"You only joined the church because you were scared," I said. "Now look what you've done to my mother. To me. If it wasn't for you we wouldn't be in this mess."

I threw the bull penis cane at her feet.

"Next time you're feeling low," she said, "I'll make sure to tell you I see your mama coming up the drive. I'll remind you how you laid there and let that Lyle do just what he did to you, how you never said no. I ain't stupid. I have eyes. You believed then, Lacey May. What happened?"

How could I explain to her that I thought I was following Vern's vision. I didn't know about the babies. Now everything was different.

Cherry twisted her lips in a sly half smile. Smug. Knowing. It was the face she got when she was freshly baptized. When someone in the congregation cited the wrong verse, and she could pipe up with the right answer, waving her hand, a proud schoolgirl. "He'll pull you back or cast you out, Lacey May. If you think you can ride the line between believing and not, you've got it wrong. One side's gonna getcha whether you like it or not."

I wanted to slap her for many reasons, but mainly because I knew she was right.

Chapter 19

"It's a hot-steam Friday night, babe," Stringy said to me, drenching himself in an awful cologne in the bathroom. "You coming out with me or what? And no drinking this time, you little lush."

"I drank one time," I said. My stomach rolled, remembering the rum from Tent City. Shame coiled in me. *I'm sorry, baby.*

"And look how you ended up." He pointed to my belly. He thought that was the night I got pregnant. Poor boy, math wasn't his strong suit.

I got dressed up to go, mother's linen, almost too tight on me now. We got in his truck, some punk band playing way turned up. "They're doing a news segment on me soon," he said. "They want to see how the magic of my lawns happens. I'm about to get famous. You'll have to stay out of the spotlight, of course." He grabbed my chin. He was full of something. "You listening to me?"

I pushed his hand off. "No one cares about your lawns."

As we neared the turnoff, he pulled over. He pointed to the front of his pants. "What's a wife for anyhow?"

"I don't see the point in doing that," I said to him.

"You haven't ever done it, have you?"

"Only ever been with you."

"Here, I'll do you first," he said. He unbuckled my seat belt and pulled my legs toward him with a rough strength, an energy drink can full of spit and chew jabbing my lower back in the center console. He peered at me from between my knees. "You'll like it." My stomach was all wrong in this position, heavy on me. He didn't know that pregnant women shouldn't lie on their backs. I imagined my veins collapsing under the weight of the baby. I tried to turn over, but he held my hips.

I could just wait through this like I'd waited through everything with Lyle. I could separate from my body and stream out the window and take a walk through the fields. I could try to remember that night when I'd felt an affection toward Stringy, when my cells were pulsing with hope. But the baby kicked and rolled. I felt light-headed. Then his rough old hand was on my thigh as he lowered himself toward me and I put my foot on his neck and pushed.

"What the hell?" he said. "You fucking kicked me, you little shit."

"I don't want it," I said.

"Get out, then," he said. "Walk home and think about what you did."

He talked to me like a bad dog. He came so natural to it, and I wondered how many other girlfriends he'd talked to like this. He leaned over me and pushed the door open. I got out and looked up at him. "This is the way you are," I said. "You'll never be another way."

I WALKED ALONG the canal back toward the small lights of town. It was quieter than quiet, my feet crunching the sticks on the ground the only noise. I felt a low ache in my stomach. *Twenty-five weeks*, I recited, *the size of a cauliflower, her wrinkled skin beginning to smooth. Your baby is enjoying a new sense of equilibrium, the knowledge of which way is up and which way is down.* I hoped the baby had no knowledge of which way was flat on my back in a dirty lawn painter's truck.

The pain deepened in my groin and I sat in the dirt. I was still two miles from Cherry's.

I called her on the cell phone and she answered on the first ring. "Fine," she said in a huff. "I'll send an angel."

PERD'S VALLEY PEST truck pulled over next to me.

Cherry's angel: Lyle, tan and healthy, thriving really, apart from his eyes, which had taken on a glazed wonder like he was in a trance. He sat behind the wheel, biting down on a toothpick. "Get in," he said. "Got Cherry in a state of worry."

"She's not worried."

He grunted. "How you found yourself out here, that's the real question," he said.

"Stringy parties at Tent City. I changed my mind, decided not to go."

"First wise decision you've made in a long time." His shoulders softened. "You hoping for a reconversion? It's not too late, you know."

I opened the door and hefted my way inside. Here we were, a family. The thought stung but I held it. What if he wasn't my cousin, what if we were in love, what if I'd wanted all of this? What would the ride feel like then? I could barely imagine. "Go to Grampa's grave," I said. "I've been missing him."

Grampa Jackie's grave, the small stone marked with a flag where Cherry wanted him buried in the middle of our family field, of the orchards he loved so dear. My mother thought it was sick to bury him there. He had killed himself on account of those orchards. The depression that leaked its way from the soil into his living body when nothing came from the vines, when the prosperity he'd known was gone. But there he was. Lyle and I had made it a habit as children to walk out there, sit near the grave and remember Grampa, try to decide who he had loved the most. And Lyle knew. Grampa loved me the most, something so obvious I barely had to hint at it. I wanted to go there then. To be alone with Lyle, and let him really see me next to Grampa, remember that before everything, we had been another way.

We pulled to the side of the field. "You know," I said, "you can just be you right now. Vern isn't anywhere near."

"Just a few minutes," he said. "Can't be out here all night."

The moon was a sliver and the stars wild. I reached forward and grabbed the back of Lyle's shirt to guide me as we stumbled through the patchy scratch of stump and stick, the greenless vines. We disappeared into the fortress of field like passing through a curtain.

Lyle stopped suddenly and I walked into him, our bodies pressed for a moment. I smelled the back of his neck and felt a sharp remembering. I sat next to the faded flag that marked the spot. In the small moonlight we wiped the dirt off the grave.

"The baby's the size of a cauliflower."

He lay down on his back.

"You hear me?" I said.

"I'm not a perfect person," he said. "But Pearl thinks I am now. And Vern thinks I'm the next big thing. Next pastor after him."

"What if there was a god who wanted us to ask questions," I said. I lay down next to him. We didn't touch. I knew that this way of being with him would never happen just this way, ever again.

"The Birthing Day is going to be bigger and more powerful than anything Peaches has ever seen," he said. "I don't know why you can't just offer that baby up to the church like all the other girls. It's the easiest way. This is about saving Peaches. This is the

ultimate unification. Vern said no one knows the meaning of community anymore. That we're going to redefine that totally. Isn't
that exciting to you?"

"He could have asked, 'Hey, girls, do you want to be a part of
this divine plan and get pregnant by a family member and then just
hand that baby over?' He never asked. Neither did you."

He sat up. "Hey. Don't say that. Don't make me out to be some
kind of bad guy. You and me both know Vern's orders are the ultimate order. If God sat right here in front of you and said eat your
own foot, you'd do it. Vern said girls are too emotional and that less
information is easier. You'd make something out of it that wasn't
even real and here you are doing just that, proving him right."

"If God asked me to eat my own foot I'd hope I'd realize he was
no God."

"If you won't comply, it might be better for both of us if there
just wasn't a baby at all," Lyle said, standing.

"Little past that," I said.

He picked up something heavy. "Maybe not." He held a rock
the size of a grapefruit over me. "Something could happen. An
accident."

"Stop messing around," I said, sitting up, turning my belly away
from him.

"It would be no more shameful than what you're doing, denying
where that baby came from," he said. His hands quivered and his
face screwed up. He dropped the rock to the ground next to me.
"Taffy's didn't take. That's on me. But you were shot. Now here you
are denying it in front of everyone."

Taffy. I wanted to tackle Lyle to the ground and beat him senseless. I felt protective over her like a little sister. I could just see her
under him, eyes so hopeful, grateful probably. It made me sick.

Lyle groaned, he was in full freak-out. "I wish you didn't exist," he said.

But my body did exist and was only growing bigger. I would only keep existing more and more, and then when the baby came she too would exist, angering men and boys all on her own. When did this end? I wondered. "Well, I do."

"You can't have this both ways. You can't be playing for the infidels and thinking you can stay in the fold. You have church property in you now, but as soon as that baby's out he'll do away with you and no one will go looking."

"You think no one will care?"

"Did anyone care when your mother disappeared?"

I knew the answer.

I left him there in the fields, walked back to Cherry's, deadbolted the door behind me. I imagined the rock crushing me and I lay there holding the paper with my mother's address on it. I imagined twenty different ways Florin might be asking Daisy to take me there.

Chapter 20

Florin typed the Turquoise Cowboy's address on Alibi Drive into her computer and it pulled up not a home but a place. A little square photo at the bottom of the map showing a squat beige building with blacked-out windows with PONY CLUB on the outside in faded green lettering.

"Your mom's a stripper," she said.

"What would you do if your mom left you like this?" I said.

"Hate her forever," Florin answered. "Never speak to her again."

"But you know that's not true."

She bit her nail. Looked at the screen. "Sometimes I don't know why we care about them at all after the things they do to us. There must be something to this mother-daughter thing. Some kind of binding spell."

"They don't deserve us," I said, trying it out. It was something my mother liked to say about Cherry to her boyfriends, that Cherry didn't deserve a good daughter. I never told her I saw it the other way around most the time—that Cherry didn't deserve a bad daughter. "Good daughters like us."

"But if Daisy up and left, I'd be the same as you. It would eat me alive."

"Please talk to her," I said.

She disappeared up the stairs to her mother's room and was

gone a long while. I fingered the stationery on Florin's desk, *Ain't nothing finer than a call with a Diviner* . . . the pens in a cup with satin roses taped to them, and tore each flower off in a fit of nerves. It panicked me to think that since my mother had left, she had already missed nine of my lives. We would never be the same as we were that day in front of the church in the photograph, even if she came back tonight, even if she appeared before me from thin air. She had already missed so much.

Daisy came down the staircase in white silk pajamas, her hair pulled up in a bun with chopsticks. She wore a clear plastic mask over her face. "My compression mask," she said. "Don't be alarmed."

I pulled skin from my cuticles.

Daisy pressed her lips together. "You really want to go stare down ugliness?" she said to me. "You really can't let well enough alone?"

"Nothing about this is well enough," I said.

She took a deep breath. "I don't know if I can," she said finally. She gestured to the door. I realized Florin was looking at her mother with an expression I'd never seen. Then I realized what it was: hope. She wanted this as much as I did.

I WAITED ALL day at the red house for fear that if I left, Daisy would flat out say no and my plan would slip away. I took a few calls and when I wasn't on the phone I sat next to Florin and we looked at Internet pictures of Reno, casinos and lights, strip malls and event centers. Desert plain everlasting, hilled mountains cactus-spotted with straggled trees.

She went to the weather page and both of our mouths fell open.

"You have any warm clothes?" she said, pointing at the snow-flake on the screen. *February, cold and possible snow showers.* "Been in this hellhole so long I forgot it's winter."

"I've never seen snow in my life," I said.

"They're gonna do a documentary or something on you one day, cult girl. What next, you've never seen the ocean either?"

I looked down.

"Oh my god."

WE WENT INTO the attic and filled a duffel bag with old clothes and sweaters of Daisy's, a puffy winter coat. "She used to love skiing," Florin explained, putting ear warmers over her dark hair. We dressed up in the clothes, bags and bags of beautiful wool sweaters, soft cashmeres. Long cardigans that dusted the ground.

"Look at these," Florin said, holding up a strange pair of jeans with a high elastic panel at the top. I recognized them immediately from my magazines. She tossed them at me and I put them on. The band stretched over my stomach and cradled it. They were the best invention I'd ever encountered.

"Maternity wear," I said. "The real thing."

"You can have them. No one's getting pregnant around here."

It was dark out the windows by the time we went back to the entryway and sat at Florin's desk. She messaged a boy she liked and a girl she liked and giggled softly to herself. I felt miles from her when she messaged her friends on the computer. Those were her real friends. I had just happened to her.

Daisy finally emerged from the stairs dressed completely in black leather. She stared at the door with determination. I thought of the time I saw a gymnast at the end of the vault runway on Cherry's TV over the summer, her face steely with intent. That was Daisy now, her gaze narrowed, her step a force. We followed her out without a word, afraid to break the spell. We got in the car and she clicked her seat belt. She put on lipstick in the rearview mirror with a shaky hand. Then she blazed down Old Canal Road, her hands a strangle on the wheel. I sat in the back and Florin sat eyes closed next to her mother. I wondered if she was praying.

We neared the turnoff for the on-ramp where Wiley Stam was stationed with his shotgun, the orange glow of the tip of his cigarette in the dark. He threw it to the ground as we approached.

I lay down on the floor of the back seat.

"What's this character doing out here like the goddamn Wild West?"

"Mom, slow down," Florin said.

"These pigs," Daisy said. "Think they own this town. Well, they don't." She bore toward Wiley, who stood pointing the gun at the car. Florin screamed and ducked and Wiley threw himself out of the way. We sailed under a banner that read: EXIT PEACHES AND ENTER HELL.

"Ride on, motherfuckers!" Daisy whooped out her window into the night.

"You almost killed him," Florin said, breathless.

"Well, hon," Daisy replied, "I believe that's what men like him would call *asking for it.*"

Chapter 21

The road stretched out ahead. I was glad for the dark of Highway 99. I didn't have to see Peaches slip from view, didn't have to see what was beyond the highway, to the side of it. I didn't want to know everything. I thought about how faith worked. I wondered, looking up at the endless black of starry sky, if God was someone I hadn't begun to know, but could one day. If God was nothing like Vern. If God was something separate, something not religious at all. And while I imagined the car being swallowed into layers of other realms ending of course in hell, I let it go. While waves of fear tried to consume me, to tell me I couldn't withstand this, I found myself smooth as stone. I was only a body moving through space. I let it go I let it go.

Daisy decided that to keep herself in forward motion we would have to listen to her affirmations CD on repeat the entire way. My legs are safe, they are on my body. My arms are safe, they are attached and able. My head is a mountain, unmovable, unshakable through any season. Just when it would almost lull me into sleep, the voice would get excited. No snow can defeat me! No wind, rain, or ice! Unshakable I am! It went on and on until I wondered if the voice would drive us all mad, cause Daisy to steer off the road and into a ditch to end it. That's when I remembered one of my mother's boyfriends, Boss, a name I was sure he had self-founded, but he claimed his mother chose it. He was one of the nicer ones, wasn't curious about me, but was obsessed with my mother. He wrote her long letters in tiny crooked script, total mania. She would smoke a million cigarettes while she read them, exasperated by his love. It wasn't ideal though, because my mother didn't love him the right way. I heard her tell Cherry that she wanted to be attracted to him, but just couldn't figure out how. Close your eyes, Cherry had instructed halfheartedly, but my mother said she didn't have that kind of imagination. When she finally ended it with him, really ended it, he drove off the very highway we were on, the 99, into a ditch, and died, which is how I suppose I knew such a thing could happen.

He killed himself over me, my mother pondered aloud for weeks. Over *me*. Almost like it made his love finally real. Almost as if he was the love of her life.

WE STOPPED HOURS later in Citrus Heights near the Sunrise Mall where the air was suddenly winter crisp. We piled on the sweaters and coats. I wriggled into the maternity jeans. The cold was nothing I could remember. It was about one in the morning. Daisy didn't move.

"Go in and pee, girls," she said.

"What about you?" said Florin, looking at her mother.

"I'll stay here. I don't have to go."

"Mom," she said.

"Go."

In the mini-mart Florin bought huge bottles of water and I drank two in what felt like a single gulp, expensive water in a fine blue bottle with a snowcapped mountain on the label. I drank the water, I drank the water. I stood in a strange town I'd never been to and nothing happened.

The man working, old in a fleece sweatshirt, sort of smiled at us, looked at my belly. He handed us hot dogs and said, "Free for you." I ate mine in three bites and felt energy rush back into my body, the dull headache that had lingered for so long it had become a normal state of being, gone. How lucky I was to be here.

We asked for another and brought it to Daisy, who ate it delicately like she could hardly be bothered with hunger. Her scars agonized under the bright light of the parking lot, but she was still beautiful, and I thought, What pain. Life was pain and this was mine. Was it more or less than anyone else's?

"I don't want your hopes to be way up here," Daisy said to me, tapping the roof of the car. "Because who knows what your mother's gonna want to do."

Daisy rolled down her window and poured yellow liquid onto the street from an old paper cup. She'd peed in the car. We didn't say anything about it.

"I'm her daughter," I said. "That has to mean something."

Daisy turned the key in the ignition and soon we were back into the between space of the highway, where life was paused. I had never been on a road trip and I liked this feeling of floating.

"You know," she said, turning down the affirmations CD. "You might not believe in past lives, but you and your mother have been traveling together for a long time."

"Here we go," Florin said. "She's been dying to tell you this."

I leaned forward in my seat.

"Once I met you I saw it all come together." Daisy tapped her forehead. "In your other lives, though, you've been sisters mainly, and you've even been her mother."

"Maybe," I said, not sure if I believed her but wanting to hear more anyhow.

"I only tell you because I don't want you to put so much pressure on this one life. Your mother's on a journey all her own. If this one doesn't work out, all I'm saying is that maybe the next one will."

"So I have to wait for the next lifetime to have a normal mom? Seems like a long wait."

"It means," Florin said. "Don't get super sad and desperate over your mom, 'cause your mom's batshit crazy and you can't fix batshit."

"Florin, manifest destiny," Daisy said, as simply as if she was asking her to put on her seat belt. "No one needs your low vibes." It seemed leaving the red house had invigorated Daisy into some new age version of a traveling preacher, enthusiastic and struck blind by potential miracles. Her usual sardonic tone had been replaced by this wellspring of hopeful talk and powers moving beyond awareness.

I sat back in my seat. Closed my eyes. "No snow can defeat me! No wind, rain, or ice! Unshakable I am!"

"She needs to hear it," I heard Florin whisper.

"No one needs to hear it," Daisy snapped at her.

I took myself away then, to swim in my unknown ocean, the water cool and biting with salt.

IN THE DARK of a night that still wouldn't show signs of morning for hours, we crossed into Reno and I rolled my window down to breathe my mother's air and the chill choked me. There was a dust of white powder on the ground. Snow, my mind told me. I wanted to touch it. We stopped in front of a McDonald's.

"You have to eat, Mom," Florin said. She held Daisy's hand. "There's no one in there. This is a good first practice. No one will hurt you."

I saw then that this trip was not so much about me for them as it was about Daisy finally changing course—leaving the house, then potentially leaving the life in Peaches that Florin so hated. I harbored a small dream that after collecting my mother we would just keep driving east. No more California, no more of this place called Nevada. Somewhere else entirely that none of my mother's boyfriends had ruined yet, and we would live together and change our names. We could become new this way. I would never ask my mother about this past life of Peaches again.

Daisy took a deep breath. "I'll go in the bathroom first, and come out when I'm ready."

I had never been to a McDonald's, let alone a 24-hour one. In the bathroom, I wiped myself clean with damp paper towels and I watched them in front of the mirror fixing each other, smoothing hair and cooing over Daisy's dissipating fear. "It's just McDonald's," Florin kept saying, like she was rehearsing the punch line of an inside joke, as Daisy tried to recite her affirmations but kept breaking out into nervous giggles halfway through. They didn't notice me walk out. It would never be simple for me, watching a mother and daughter together. I suspected these days that I wore the jealousy like a brand.

WE SAT IN the red plastic booth and ate oval hash browns so fast my tongue burned. Daisy produced two dollars from her cleavage and we bought three more cheeseburgers and ate those. It was the best thing I'd ever tasted. The extreme salt, the warm condiments, the sting of the chemical ketchup. Daisy sat shrunken down in the booth, eyes darting from side to side, paranoid. A toddler near the play area was shrieking at a young flustered mother who wore huge sweats and hoop earrings big as her face, for *just the bun just the bun* as her mother wiped bread on a napkin, unable to undo the ketchup of course, and the girl wailed on. I wanted to say, *Knock it off. At least your mother is here wiping bread for you. My mother never did.* If my mother had wiped ketchup from bread for me, if she had shushed me the way this mother was doing now, with a kindness that did not seem deserved by this child, I didn't remember it.

"What's the plan?" I asked Daisy.

"Thought you'd have one," Daisy said, pointing a fry at me.

"I guess we just show up," I said.

I looked at the go-phone and saw fourteen missed calls from Stringy. A text message that said *Where r u? We need 2 talk.* I turned the phone off and forgot him. We slept in the car for a while and when I woke a new country was delivered before me. But so far from the window, Reno didn't look much different than Peaches. The parking lot was asphalt, clunker and low-rider cars mixed with lifted trucks with big wheels. Beyond the lot the land was the land, desert and dry. The highways and the trucks rolling past, the same.

"Could you live here?" Daisy said. She was already set to work applying thick pancake makeup in the mirror of a small compact. "What do you think, little baby? Born in Reno, Nevada?"

"She can do better than this," Florin said.

I looked around, and wondered how a place made and remade you. "I don't know," I said. "Maybe I'll like the beach more."

DAISY DROVE DOWN what seemed like a main street until we made it to another parking lot. We were in front of a building with a moving sign coming out the top of it, a neon girl riding a bucking horse, and the horse's butt and hind legs went up and down, up and down, and the girl's body shifted and her cowgirl hat fell off then returned to her head. PONY CLUB. The window bore the words

Live Girls. Fantasy! The saddest man in the world sat slumped against the side of the building, teeth knocked out or in, I couldn't tell, and his hands lay dead and open next to him on the concrete like he hoped someone would fill them.

There was a sign that said 18 AND OLDER on the side of the building but with Daisy I felt confident to go in. It was dim and there was a long bar in the corner with a stout older woman behind the counter, hair piled on top of her head, breasts stuck out, and her shirt said *Ride 'Em!* She eyed us and decided we were no threat to her day and went back to tapping long nails on her sparkly phone. On the stage across the room a chubby younger girl swayed her hips while two middle-aged men in trucker hats sat with their elbows on the stage fanning themselves with one-dollar bills, never placing them on the stage for her to collect. They didn't turn when we walked in. No one in the place cared what anyone else was doing, not the dancer, who was barely dancing, her boobs sort of bobbing around to no one beat in particular, and the men could have been asleep as far as I could see, and might have actually been. The girl's eyes were far off to nowhere, and I wondered if this was how my mother danced, just like this, dead in the eyes, for it seemed certain now that she danced on a stage, this one in fact. The girl looked at us and sort of showed her teeth in a smile but her eyes didn't change. It looked like she was wearing braces.

When she got off the stage no one clapped and no one came to replace her, but a poppy song was turned up louder and made the depression of the air even heavier.

The girl walked past us, a puffy coat thrown over her shoulders, boobs free, and went outside. Daisy and Florin went to the bar to talk to the woman, Daisy clutching her daughter's arm. I followed the girl into the cold.

"Let me guess," the girl said, "you're really eighteen and some-one told you the pregnant thing was a big hit." She talked funny, lips twitching over teeth, her words garbled and spit-soaked. She shielded her mouth with her hand, sensing my stare. "And I ain't connecting you to my guy so you can sell twat either. He don't need no other girls right now."

"Do you know Louise?" I said.

"Who knows who I know."

I came closer to her. "I'm her daughter."

She looked at my stomach. "You got it bad." She spoke without her hand covering her mouth and I saw then that her jaw was wired shut. She ground her teeth together and sucked her spit back. She was maybe a little older than me. She had two belly piercings. Her legs were in bruises.

"What happened?" I asked, touching my own jaw.

"You ever had a man make you tie his shoes and you don't do a good nuff job and he kicks you just right?"

I didn't know what to say. It seemed she wanted me to know that in the pissing match of suffering, she was winning. "I think my mother works here. Or for Rick's Angels. This is the address they gave me."

"Little Lou. I seent her. I seent her but she don't talk to none of us much. She scribbles in a notebook, copying down lines from TV and shit. Then she tries to make us listen to her remember them. Comes and goes like some white trash princess."

"Can you tell me where she lives?"

She laughed and slapped her knee. "She was always on about how she was some beauty queen. Well, they're all beauty queens when they get here, ain't they? Not me. I know what's what. I al-ways have. My momma didn't spare me nothing."

I wanted to ask her questions. Where was her mother now? What did she mean she always had? There was something irretrievable about her. Something I felt sorry for but didn't trust. Had my mother ever looked at this girl and thought of me? Had she imagined how I filled my motherless hours?

Instead I said, "Is she coming in later?"

She flicked her cigarette and scratched up her shirt where I saw a smattering of small red fleabites. "If a woman wants someone to find her she'll tell you how. Oldest truth there is."

Florin and Daisy breezed out and Daisy took stock of the girl and held her head up higher. "Come on, Lacey." We got in the car and she drove away, the tires squealing, and I watched the girl until I could barely see her and she watched us back, smiling kindly sort of, like I was a friend leaving her behind. Finally her hand went up in a wave.

"I used to feel bad for people, too," Daisy said. She put a piece of paper on the dash and handed Florin her phone. "Look up that address, hon."

"You got it?" I said.

"You could kill a man in front of that bartender woman and she wouldn't blink. 'Course she gave it to me."

WE DROVE PAST casino after casino, and then smaller bars and clubs, and then those ran out and gave way to apartments, gray and grayer, the same two-decker stout buildings with small windows, abandoned plastic toys on concrete walkways, people shuffling around, heads down, and then a cement one-story low and long with numbers stenciled on the side. Nature nowhere. Not a single tree, or blade of grass, not even patches of dirt and deadness. Just concrete on concrete, the sky above the same color, the old dirty snow in patches. I knew this was where my mother was, in this in-between.

I felt heavy in the car seat. All the times I had imagined coming to her, it wasn't like this. It wasn't the stillness of a cold gray afternoon, the air flat. How would I have wanted it? I guess I wanted a night sky blazing jewels across it, the cityscape romantic, the Turquoise Cowboy somehow romantic. I wanted to find her happier than I could imagine, and then I wanted to find my place within her happiness.

Florin checked the address again. "There," she said. "Number four-forty-four."

I closed my eyes and I was back: my mother holding my hand, walking home from church after that first big rain. As if by magic, snowy mountains had sprung up all around us in the far-off distance. I had never seen them before. *What are those?* I had asked her. She laughed. *The rain cleaned the air! Vern brought the mountains back!* The plain felt lush and moist, the air crisp and mountains so perfect they looked drawn into the sky. We twirled and laughed. *Who knows why the sky is blue,* she sang, *who knows how I could love you this much?* I hadn't made that up. That had been real, the way she had looked at me that day. The time she went to one of my teachers and raised her voice about a boy who had been making fun of me, calling me names. When I'd sprained my ankle outside the ice cream shop and she'd carried me to the car, whispering prayers. When I'd been baptized the first time and she put flowers in my hair. *Everything is good now,* she'd promised. She would have wiped the ketchup off my bread. It just had to be the right day, the right mood, and she could pull it together and that was why I loved her this much.

"Well," Daisy said. She popped the glove compartment and took out a small handgun. "You never know."

I had never seen a gun so small. It looked like a toy. "Do we need that?" I asked. "What if it goes off?"

"Ask a woman with half a face again if you need a gun around a mind-loose man."

I took a deep breath. I was light-headed and nauseated, the McDonald's coming back to me. When I didn't move, Daisy turned back and patted my knee. "Whatever happens I want you to know I think you're brave as they come."

"I'm not brave," I said.

"Braver than I was at your age."

"You said you would have gone after your mom and dragged her back by the hair if she had left you."

"I say a lot of things."

Florin stood outside the car and waited as I slowly got out, hitched the maternity jeans up over my belly. My mother would see me and know. She would see me and want to come home. There could be nothing to distract her from me. "I have to go in alone," I said to Florin, who nodded, like she had always known this to be true.

I BARELY KNOCKED on the door before it opened and a tall someone's arms pulled me inside and locked us in. It was the Turquoise Cowboy, yes, but I didn't recognize him exactly. He looked older and slimmer than before. There were wires and antennas swooping down from the ceiling, crisscrossing over a small aisle kitchen. The whole place smelled like the musk of a skunk. *Ganga King* was written in marker above a computer like a banner.

"Now whichin' are you?" he asked, sticking his bottom lip out and jutting his chin at me. The place was dark, but there was a green plant under some kind of fluorescent light in the corner, glowing. He wore thick-cut glasses, and his eyes seemed to roll around behind them, looking every way but at me. "You're either late or early. I ain't got no auditions right now."

I looked at the pearled buttons on his shirt, how only one was fastened right over his paunch belly and the rest gaped open to reveal a hairy chest with a small gold shark's tooth necklace swimming in it. "It's me, darling," I whispered.

He centered his narrow face with mine and bent closer. He was completely toothless, I realized. "Well, I'll be. All the way from Cali-forn-i-ay. I didn't think you was coming, darling. Guess you were nervous to tell me you was already knocked up. What, your trigger-happy daddy do that to you? I seen worse."

I looked down and before I could answer he cut in and said, "It's fine. That kind of thing does well. Something for everybody. 'Course you can't be having no baby here. I can't be up half the night. But you can stay and work till the thing's borned."

He plucked teeth from a murky glass and popped them in his mouth over the kitchen sink. I had thought him charming in my mind, or somehow good-looking, something I wasn't remembering from the shadow man who had taken her away. But I could not find the redeeming thing. His head was peanut shell in shape, he wore no cowboy hat now, and there was a joke of stripy black hair on top of the bulb. My mother had kissed this man, I considered. She had done everything with this man, no doubt. I didn't have the words or sense to understand how. My mother had left me for this man.

He gestured to the wires surrounding an old-looking computer. "I have quite the following tuning in to my live broadcasts." Each word was slow and boxed alone, long pauses between. "People like girls live. I call it improv. Strip 'em naked and throw them in front of a camera. You'd be surprised what happens. But you ladies aren't the only stars. I like to share my stories from my bar-bouncer days.

Once met a woman named Sally Fryer after she was abandoned by her no-good boyfriend in the parking lot and she lived with me six months. I got things to say. I mean, 'course I promote what I need to promote, I ain't stupid. Don't worry, we'll get you famous real soon. Now, your face has some kind of sour thing to it, you ain't real angel pretty like I thought but it's okay, we can train you. What you looking around for like a lost pup?" he said, stepping in closer. "The future is now."

He was a crazy person. We were not in the same mindplace. Something seemed to be emanating from him, an electric current of evil, or the lack of God, maybe, which was evil after all. It felt like each of my nerve endings was screaming *run*. I looked behind me at the door. It stood tall and heavy, locked in a complicated system of dead bolts and sliders.

"I can make a real movie out of you," he said. "I've got plenty of gals that can be real good in it, too. Maybe we can do a whole doctor's check-up thing. Boy, people still go whackjob for a nurse's outfit. Don't ask me why. Hospitals always got me soft, personally. Spent seven years in the silly house droolin' on a deck of cards while they spooned me applesauce, but I been on the right meds for years, thank you, pharmaceuticals!" He bowed to no one. "Thank you, mary-juana!" He bowed again. "In any case, I'm gonna make you a star."

He brushed the hair from my face and I felt a nausea roll up in me, tasted acid on my tongue. This was the bad energy that Daisy always talked about. I felt it. Evil, bad energy. Whatever. He had it. When my mother had stood here like me did she realize her mistake? Or had she realized it in the car ride up, perhaps when he'd driven her over the Peaches county line and the breeze had blown his cowboy hat back and she saw him at last. I must have some of my daddy in me after all, I knew then, because unlike my mother, my intuition button was lit up and working.

I followed him down the dark hall, turning back to the front door every step as if to mark my place. *Brave, brave*, I chanted in my mind. I heard the murmur of a television playing. My mother might be somewhere watching TV. I felt her close.

He opened a door to a small bedroom and inside it was painted completely red. The walls bled down to a maroon rug and the large bed was slanted to one side, covered in red satin and stained in dark blooms. The window was foiled. My idea of hell melted and changed. Hell was this room.

He patted the bed with a childish glee. "Nice, huh?" He took a white cowboy hat from a stand of costumes and his face was swallowed by it, the high forehead of sun-spotted skin gone. "I told you you had to be sixteen. You don't look sixteen to me. But childbirth'll age you right up. Soon you'll look all dragged through the mud like every other Bessie out there who goes and pushes a bowling ball out of herself."

I wished Hazel was here to slap him for me. "Who else is here?" I asked.

He looked at me some more, at my body, and I was freezing cold suddenly. I didn't want Artichoke to have this memory in her cells.

"I'm a good man," he said, shoulders softening. His thumbs hooked into his pants pockets and he changed personalities, became timid. "Didja see that dog outside? I walk that thing every single night, midnight sharp, I take it out for my speed walk to get my exercise and let it pee and I care for it. And I love my girls as much as that dog."

I hadn't remembered seeing any dog on my way in.

"Maybe you can introduce me to the girls and I'll feel better," I said.

"You girls like to stick together, don't you? I don't care as long as it don't affect your work. And you'll have a lot of work ahead of you, but I'll let you meet 'em, sure. I'm a nice guy. All the girls are kept in here. Now some's ain't performers. Some's retired and Rowena's just my sister. Think of her as your talent manager."

"Where do the girls come from?" I said. I imagined twenty or thirty women behind the door in an orphanage situation sleeping in twin beds, wearing matching nightdresses.

"Once they get here they can't remember." He let out a growl of a laugh.

He unlocked the door at the back of the hall from the outside and threw it open. A small wash of sunlight came in under metal blinds, and the glow of the television shifted from dark to light. A rowdy talk show was playing where one woman was gripping another woman by the hair, screaming to show her the paternity test. My eyes focused on the room and at first I saw only a small child-sized woman in a high chair, beating her tray with a wooden spoon. She was elfin and seemed on the cusp of old age, grayish hair twisting out of loose pigtails. When Rick flipped the light on she went wild with the spoon. "It's Lacey May! It's Lacey May!"

He looked at me and confusion spread over him. "You all running something against me?" he asked.

"Oh, relax," said a woman with large low breasts left loose in a bejeweled halter top. *Juicy*, it said across the front. I thought maybe this was her name. She spoke in a deep rasp from a beanbag chair in the corner. "We've seen her picture a hundred times." I didn't know my mother had taken a picture of me with her. I felt a small comfort in the fact that she did.

Rick pushed me into the room and I fell hard to my knees. My stomach almost hit the floor. "Seen her? What do you mean seen her?" he barked.

"That's Lou's daughter," the Juicy woman said.

But I didn't hear the Turquoise Cowboy anymore because I saw her then, in too-big black carpenter's pants and a ratty oversized T-shirt with a Tweety Bird across the front. She sat in a lawn chair, a cigarette simmering between her fingers. She squinted across the room at me. Her hair was lank with grease and her skin broken out, her cheeks ruddy, covered in a shade of blush that wasn't made for her. Her frame was tiny, skeletal like I'd never seen, and the light in her face was out.

"What are you wearing?" I marveled. I walked to her, and kneeled by the lawn chair. My mother, who would never have been caught dead in an ensemble like this, who even at her most hungover managed to get a dress on.

Her hand went straight to my chopped hair. She looked at it sadly. "This is a terrible look on you."

"I know," I said. "The worst."

"Of course Lou gets visitors," the Juicy woman said, narrating her own misery. She lit a cigarette and scratched her head with long pointed nails, moving a crisp nest of hair around.

I hadn't factored an audience into my fantasy of begging. I gathered my strength and tried to focus only on my mother. "I've got a car out there and Daisy's here and everything."

But she looked at Rick instead of me.

"Mom," I said. I took her hands and pressed them to my stomach. "Lyle did this, Mom. This is what's happened since you've left. You left me and this is what happened."

"Now stop it," Rick said. He stepped between us. "This is just what I was saying your family would try to do. Derail your chance at your dreams."

"You know you could have called first," the Juicy woman said. "I would have cleaned up Rowena." She pointed her cigarette toward the small woman in the high chair, who had quieted and narrowed her gaze at me.

But something else caught my eye. There against the wall was a woman lying across a cot so thin it could be an ironing board, her flat gray hair streaming down both sides nearly brushing the floor. The woman wasn't moving at all.

"Rick's first wife, Sally," my mother explained. "Fell down the stairs ten years ago. Certified quadriplegic."

I thought he said Sally had lived with him only six months. My head swam. "Is she dead?" I asked.

"Not yet," my mother said, and I thought I saw a flash of her old energy, which could sometimes be biting and awful, but always a little funny to me, especially when nothing was actually funny. She looked at me and smiled in this relaxed way, like nothing was out of the ordinary.

"No more feeding," Rowena said. "Not even a cracker, no, but I slip her some, I do, and I don't tell him, no I don't." Littered on the ground were boxes and boxes of Chicken in a Biskit crackers. He hadn't made that up.

"Women are all liars," Rick said. "You just stay in here until I figure this out." He slammed the door behind him and I heard a heavy lock shift into place.

"Mom, feed her," I said.

My mother rubbed her eyes. "Rick wants us to let her phase out. He said he'll still collect the social security on her."

"Rowena can see into the souls of people," Juicy went on, shoving

a chicken cracker into the deadish woman's mouth. "There." She
looked at me. "We ain't completely fucked up."

Rowena pointed to my stomach. "She been a bad little kitty,"
she said. "Oh, she, oh she bad. She been a bad little kitty."

"Sees into souls, my foot," my mother said. "I've seen the blessed
and she ain't it."

I remembered Daisy's past-life idea from the drive, how my
mother and I had traveled for a long time together, and this life was
a mere chapter in a much longer history. I thought of my mother
as a girl, what I'd seen in pictures. How happy she looked, her sunburned nose, the sort of wild freeness that seemed to jump off the
print—always just out of the frame like she was off to someplace
else. I imagined that girl by my side now, showing her this room
with these women. Saying, someday, this will be your life. I could
see the girl's face, the glimmer of terror, but then disbelief. How
she would never be able to imagine a life could come to this, especially not her own. The idea of this girlmother made it difficult for
me to accept that my mother was in this room, with this man, one
of these women. But at the same time, I knew this room to be the
most absolute truth I had ever seen. I knew I would never be able
to explain it to another person, and it would haunt me the rest of
my days.

"Regular Judas Priest expert she is," Juicy said, looking at my
mother. "Got all kinds of stories about church and speaking holy
rolls and glitter falling from the goddamn heavens. Your mother
here trying to tell me I'm going to hell and in the same breath telling me her pastor set her up into regular sex work."

"We're all going to hell," my mother said. She looked at me.
Shrugged as if to say, *Even you, Lacey May.* "Everything's a lie. I figured it out. I ain't dumb. Vern wanted me to be his other wife,

Lacey. You know, *be* with him. I could have told you that straight to your face and you wouldn't have believed me. I tried to tell Cherry and she sure didn't."

"You told Cherry?" I said. This was new. Cherry seemed completely unaware of how or why my mother had distanced, started drinking again. Had my mother been asking for her help all along? Trying hard to do the right thing? I wanted to beat the walls. I wanted to scream. I was so mad at Cherry, so mad at Vern. But being so mad doesn't do anything. I knew deep down that I would never be able to fully blame anyone else for any of this. My mother had made choices all along to lead us here. She had said yes when she should have said no. She had gotten in the car with the Turquoise Cowboy. She had lifted each drink to her very own mouth. Most of all, she had never, not once, asked me what I needed. Taken me into consideration. The cup of my anger would never empty no matter how many times I poured it all out. She was always refilling it.

My mother put out her cigarette. I hadn't seen her smoke in a long while, not since I was a little girl and she'd sit on the lap of Sapphire Earrings and cackle in his ear. "Cherry told me to do what the pastor said. She said, 'Ain't that life better than the alternative?' But I didn't feel it was right in my gut." She poked her concave stomach. The veins on her arms crossed one another and bulged. I couldn't bring myself to ask the next inevitable question: How was she able to leave me?

"Is she on drugs?" I asked Juicy, who seemed the most coherent of them all.

"My own mother was a bad alcoholic," Juicy said. "You know what happens to them at the end? Skin turns soft as a rotten plum.

Can poke your finger right through. They empty all out, piss and shit everywhere."

"Rick's been giving me pills to keep me awake and some to sleep," my mother said. "I'm still adjusting. The air's thinner at this high elevation. That's why I can barely breathe."

"Come home," I said. "There's a God you don't know. You can be forgiven. We can go on like this never happened and you can help me with the baby. We can work with Daisy together. Whatever you want."

"We're in hell right now," Rowena said, and then repeated the line again, chirping it over and over like a parrot. "Hell right now. Hell right now."

I tried to make my mother focus on me. The television was screaming and Rowena was so loud and my mother was lifeless. Finally I said something that surprised me. "Choose me," I said. My words cut over the noise.

My mother recoiled as if I'd pushed her. She closed her eyes.

"Your mother's just plumb crazy on her very own accord," Juicy said. "Talking about how some pastor got her all screwed up. I said, honey, ain't you ever hear of saying *no?*"

"I did say no," my mother said, suddenly clear. "Look where it got me. You know he used to call in to the phone lines and pretend to be other people just to talk to me? I could tell it was him."

"Mom," I said, "I believe you." I did. I believed her.

"All I wanted was a good life for you. A church life. Safe."

I felt myself turning to dust. I could not withstand this sadness. The thought that safety and a good life was all she wanted and how far away we had landed from that goal was too much. I let myself harden. I had to. She had known Vern had twisted ideas, had a bad feeling about what was to come. And she'd left me alone in the rough waters of it as if I knew how to swim.

My mother held my wrists and I could smell that she hadn't showered in a long time. "The girls at the Pony Club don't know about being famous," she said. "He said I'd meet major producers working there and I haven't met a one."

"Mom, please. Please come with me."

She glanced at the locked door. "I don't have my things ready."

"It doesn't matter, we have everything for you. We'll get new stuff. We'll go shopping. We can forget this."

She leaned into me and I wrapped my arms around her. She was so small against my fullness. The three of us together. Me, Artichoke, my mother. For a moment I closed my eyes and relaxed into it. It was what I'd wanted. She whimpered softly, like she didn't have the energy to cry, like an animal dying and letting go.

"You need to leave," she said finally. "I'll get him to let you go, and you can't come back."

"Please come," I said.

Then she leaned in. Whispered into my ear so no one else could hear. "Give me until tomorrow. Let me talk to him and calm him down. I'll get my stuff and I'll meet you."

"Where? When?"

"Outside the Pony Club. Ten. Like I'm just going to work."

"Okay, in the morning," I said. "Ten."

I watched my mother pull up the half-broken blinds. She looked out through the glass at cracked asphalt. "Lyle did that you?" she asked, reaching out to brush her fingers against my belly again. "That baby gonna bring the rain?"

"I married a man so Vern won't take it," I said.

Disgust fell across her face. "A man? What do you mean, a man?"

"Cherry married us in the front yard."

"How old?"

"I don't know really," I said. I let her simmer. I had to admit I liked that for once she got to be worried about me.

"I told you not to tell Vern about your blood," she said.

I kept waiting for my mother to make her offer. For her to tell me to stay with her, or figure out another place for us to go. Knowing everything now, she would have an answer. But the answer didn't come. "God, Mom, seriously?"

She looked again at the thick slab window, no openings, no latch. No screen, no air. I wanted her to break it for me. For her to save me and bloody her hand. "Whatever happens, you'll do better than me," she said.

The lock undid and Juicy sat quickly in her chair, trained her eyes to the television. I stared at the door as Rick walked in.

"Visitation hours is over," he said. He calmly walked up to Rowena and patted her head, looked at me. "Don't come back unless you're ready to work. Can't have my best girl distracted." He patted my mother's head. I sent her a message with my mind: *tomorrow at ten, tomorrow at ten.* I could tell she heard me because she blinked long and hard. "Don't give Vern that baby," she said.

Rick pulled me by the arm down the hall.

"Don't touch me," I yelled. I shook free.

He seemed startled by my voice and held up both hands. Then he spat on my shoes, the duck boots I'd found in Daisy's attic. I willed myself not to react. I had won. My mother was meeting me and leaving him. He spat again. I remembered my father spitting on my mother this way. Did they all have a club where they traded these ideas with one another? I imagined a low-down shitty man meeting, all of them sitting in a circle, scrawling into notepads. *If you spit on them it really shuts them up.*

Rick opened the door and I stepped out into real air. "Don't come back, you little slut," he said. The door slammed and the portal to their universe was gone.

Florin ran to me, holding the tiny gun out from her body wild and scared of it. "Where is she?"

"She can't come now." It sounded so stupid when I said it out loud in broad daylight. I told her the whole story.

WE STAYED AT a motel called the Genie's Wish a few blocks away. Daisy hadn't seemed sold on my plan to meet my mother in the morning, but she got the motel room anyhow and tried to be nice to me, ordering pizza and watching whatever I wanted to watch on the yellow TV. She and Florin slept in the same bed. I fixated on them whispering together in the cruel impenetrable chatter of mothers and daughters.

I couldn't sleep. I kept thinking about the pills my mother had been eating, the red room. I felt ashamed of who she was and her shame coursed in my blood until it felt like a shame of my own. How could I be better than her when I was from her? I got up and looked out the window at the chilled stillness of Reno. What town was keeping the rain from us? Why couldn't Peaches be good enough for just a day of rain?

Hours passed and the light of the rising sun appeared in the window and the world revealed itself to me. I would never have a mother, I finally knew. Yet somehow I would have to be one. This seemed absurd, impossible. I was tired already.

I decided then I'd tell Artichoke to be ugly. To make herself as

ugly as possible and not worry too much about beauty or what anyone thought of her. To be unpainted, to live in the breeze and stand
under waterfalls and not be worried over the height of mountains,
of quiet trails deep in the woods. To not be scared of roads slick
with rain, of valleys dry in drought. I'd tell her *no fear* and she'd
know it as the deepest truth and she would be everything I was not.
She would be wild and free. And I wouldn't worry because I alone
knew the secret. That through all of her ugliness, all her hiking and
running and jumping and falling and getting back up and saying no
and saying what she wanted, her scraped hands, her freckled skin,
her smart brain, she would of course be beautiful.

My mother didn't come. And when she didn't, Daisy was in-
furiated. "Did she know I was with you?" she kept asking. "If she
knows I'm with you and she doesn't even care, I swear. How dare
she make us wait out here like idiots."

We squealed out of the Pony Club parking lot and soon we were
back in front of Rick's. Daisy took the gun from the glove compartment. "I've had it," she said. There was no trace of the zen-energy
past-life-affirmation reciter now. Florin and I watched as Daisy got
out of the car and held the gun to the sky, smacked her hand against
Rick's door. The door opened and the gun went off.

I'd seen an animal be shot and gutted. I'd smelled the hot blood
and I'd heard saw against bone. But it was different to see a man
shot. Rick fell down in the doorway and clutched his leg and Daisy
simply stepped over him. I stopped before his body and stared. He
might spit on me if I were down like this. But I was better. "Excuse
me," I said as I stepped over him and into the apartment.

Inside Daisy waved the gun around, ordering my mother to
the car.

But my mother ran to Rick, held him, and screamed. Juicy took Rick's shoe off and wrapped the blooming redness on his calf in brown towels. They fluttered around him like nursemaids. Grampa Jackie had loved to tell the tale of his teenage years when his alcoholic uncle had shot him in the foot. It had always sounded so entertaining, adventurous even. This was nothing like that. No gunshot wound could be. I understood now Grampa Jackie had created a version of his own story he could live with.

"How could you do this?" my mother said over and over. I watched her grasp him, I watched her feel sad for him, and I hated her. This was our chance and she was squandering it. She had never planned to come meet me. I pulled her arm. I tugged at her like a little child.

"Look at your daughter," Daisy said. She pointed the gun at Rick again.

"Call nine-one-one," my mother said.

"Look at her," Daisy screamed. The gun fired and I thought Daisy had finished Rick off, or shot my mother. But then plaster rained down on us and we all quieted for a moment and shielded our eyes. The dust landed on our sweaty skin just like God glitter.

"Come with us right now," I said, "or this is it."

"Get out," my mother said to Daisy.

"Mom," I cried.

Daisy grabbed my hand. "This girl's too good for you," she said to my mother.

We walked outside. Daisy herded me to the car. The moment was so many things at once. It remains hard to recall. It frustrates me endlessly. Some days, it feels like the moment my mother made her final choice, and other days it feels like the moment I made mine.

Daisy steadied her breath, looked at her own two hands on the steering wheel. "We really should go," she said. "I mean, I just shot a man."

WE DROVE AND drove and peed in the same Citrus Heights gas station as before and I wanted to tell Daisy all she didn't know then. That the baby was Lyle's. That I'd followed along hoping it was the godly thing to do. But what difference would it make? She would never know who I really was. She would never understand the church and all it had meant for us, the places it had forced us into.

"What kind of mother does something like that?" she said heavily, almost to herself. I bowed my head as she drove. What kind of mother? I knew just what kind of mother. Before everything, when Sapphire Earrings gave me those beers and I would sleep sleep sleep, I wasn't always so asleep. He got lonely, he said, when my mother wasn't any good, and he needed a nice girl to rub his shoulders. He needed a nice girl and wasn't I it?

I felt my breath get fast. How I'd pressed it down for so long. How I imagined it would never surface again, would never need to in God's kingdom. When he bent me over his knee to spank me, or to wrench those earrings in, it was the things he'd say that were hardest to forget. *Your mother is one of them throwaway women. Worthless. Just like you.* He'd make me feel we were the lowest creatures on earth and then the next day there my mother would be, curled on his lap, smiling at me in a kind of bliss from across the room.

She left me all alone, caged, with her boyfriends. I'd forgiven her when I became a believer because that's what a believer did. I'd forgiven. But not now.

We pulled up in front of Cherry's and Daisy looked at me, dark under the eyes. Said, "I'm sorry all that happened, but it did and now here you are. Better make the best of it."

Chapter 22

I didn't make the best of it. I took my heart out of my chest and I watched old crows eat it on the fading yellow-green painted grass in front of Cherry's. When I went inside, Stringy was a madman at the kitchen table, papers strewn around him, falling onto the floor.

"Thought I wouldn't figure it out," he said. "Thought I wouldn't see all your other little church girls knocked up and put it together? That baby ain't mine."

"I saw my mother," I said.

He shoved the papers at me. "You and that crazy granny try to pin anything on me, think again. I'll call up the popo and tell them right now we've got America's most wanted pastor right here in Peaches, at it again. You didn't believe when I told you before. Now here's proof."

My eyes blurred over the writing and stuck to the photo instead, of a young man. The curls were gone, the robes gone. But his pointed chin was the same. His arched eyebrows and the cock of his head, the same.

"Don't leave me now," I said.

"This baby belong to that pastor? He line all you girlies up and have him a time?" Stringy shook his head in disgust. That's when I saw Cherry creeping up behind him. She raised up a glass jug full of pennies. She smashed it hard over his head. It broke, and the pennies flew everywhere. He lay on the floor, knocked out cold.

"What?" she said, looking at me. "I didn't like the way this rat boy was talking about my pastor," she said, standing over him. "Now help me."

We dragged him by the armpits into the craft room. I could feel his sweat on my hands.

"He's dead," I whispered.

"I've seen a dead man and that ain't it." She wedged a chair under the outside of the door.

"When he wakes up he's gonna be angry," I said.

"Rather have him angry under my nose than flying around spreading the worst of rumors." She lit a match and burned the printed news articles, the ones accusing Vern of all manner of wrongs, in the kitchen sink. "Nothing was proved in this anyway, even if it is our pastor. He showed it to me all proud. But all I read was that nothing was ever proved. Just like the infidels to frame a holy man."

"My mother wouldn't come back."

"Oh Lordy," Cherry said. "That's what you were up to." She pulled me into her and I let myself give in. I cried and cried and my tears dampened the front of her dress, and she let me. I felt the warmth of her hand on my back and I felt how foolish I'd been, thinking there were a million other ways to live.

"Just like God to clear the path for you even when you're hanging on to every weed. But he did. That Stringy ain't no use to you now. The good God got rid of that boy to show you the way."

I felt all pulled out. I'd tried everything. Maybe she was right. God had gone and cleared it all away.

"You've seen the other side, you've seen the darkest low of hell. Have you quenched your thirst for the world?"

I nodded.

"I'd say it's time to buckle down while you can still be forgiven."
Her hand slid around and patted my belly. Artichoke turned vio-
lently inside me. "'Bout time to come back where God loves you
the most."

So I did.

I ATTENDED THE Bible study girls' prayer meeting after the service. We were deep into preparation for the Birthing Day. We
sat in a circle sewing birthing gowns for the blessed day in April,
when the children within us would be ready to meet their earthly
destiny and the rain would come at last. I could not sew and I tried
to watch the others, who seemed to have absorbed some instruc-
tion from Derndra in the time I hadn't been there. She looked
at my clumsy attempt and said nothing. She wanted to watch me
struggle.

Derndra trimmed my hair again so that it matched everyone
else's. She brushed my cheeks with creamed blushes, glittery gels.
Lined my eyes in red. *White rabbit*, I heard my mother tease as Derndra fed me Hershey's chocolate and patted my head.

"Sharon's gone looney," Denay whispered to me after Derndra
had gone downstairs to fetch more chocolate.

"How do they figure we're all gonna give birth the same day?" I
whispered back.

She shrugged. "Divine miracle don't care about specifics."

"They're gonna herd us all up like cows and watch the blood
spill," Sharon said.

"Shut it," Taffy said, covering her ears. "I can't take your
negativity."

Sharon shot up and grabbed at Taffy's stomach, jerked it from side to side. She pushed up her dress and pulled off what looked like a wadded up pillow covered in silver tape.

"We all know you weren't blessed," Sharon said.

I looked to Denay, expecting a rush of anger, but she stayed calm and sewing. "If Taffy's not pregnant, her parents will be most displeased."

"Well, what are you going to do when the Birthing Day comes?" Sharon asked her. Knelt down close to Taffy's face. "Just kill yourself?"

Taffy hugged her knees in. "I wanted to give the church a baby," Taffy said. "Now what will become of me?"

"And you," Sharon said, turning to me. "You know the truth but here you are like the rest of us anyhow. Just admit it already," Sharon said, looking around the room. "There was no white light. We were all raped! Raped!"

We were silent. What was there to say?

We didn't want to be girls raped.

CABBAGE, COCONUT, PINEAPPLE, leek, Swiss chard, sadness. Artichoke became other-sized fruits and vegetables and I turned fifteen without realizing it.

Chapter 23

No one could hear Stringy's screams out in the country, where sound died on contact with the still air. It seemed to me he could break the door down if he wanted, but he hadn't. He knew Cherry would call the police if he did, and besides, she had supplied him with big dusty bottles of bourbon from Grampa Jackie's old stash to soothe him. But the longer Cherry kept him there, the harder it seemed to figure out what we should do with him. I stood behind Cherry as she peeked in to offer him a can of pork and beans. She shrieked and I saw Stringy passed out in the corner. It took me a moment to realize he had opened the crate of her animal babies and spread them all out on the floor. The room smelled of urine. He'd peed on them.

"Get me my cane," she said. Her voice was a growl like I'd never heard.

"What are you going to do?"

"I'm gonna beat this halfwit senseless."

"What would God do, Cherry?"

Stringy stirred in the corner. An eye flickered open. I pulled Cherry away from the door and shut it. Locked it.

"Punish," she said.

"He would love him," I replied.

She snorted. "Fine. When the church babies come and God

restores us, Vern'll have some idea for that snake. Some use for him, surely. Until then, he can just think of all his sins in there alone. That's one way to break people into believing. Give them a real reason to need a savior, am I right?"

"You can wash the animals," I said. "It will be okay."

She stared at me. "Look at you. Got broked down yourself and now your faith's tighter than ever."

HAZEL CALLED AND called and when I didn't answer and didn't text back she came for a surprise home visit. She tried to get through to me, to remind me of Daisy and Florin and how much they cared. Stringy yelled and she flinched each time she heard him. "Do you hear me?" he kept saying. "Do you hear me? Send in the bourbon!" I lay back on the couch and directed her hand to my stomach. Asked her to make sure the baby was okay. She pressed deep into my pelvis. "Head down, hallelujah." But her smile wavered. "It's time to get some outside help," she said, quiet.

"This is God's child," I said. And then she went away from me, spooked.

I HAD TAKEN to sleeping on the couch while Stringy was in the craft room. I let the hours fall away. I didn't want to read anymore. Everything in the romances was a lie. I didn't want to watch TV and even Cherry had cooled off from her soaps and her televangelists, shutting herself in a corner chair tapping her hand on her green Bible. Periodically she would get up to shove hard raisins under the door to our prisoner and he would grunt something incomprehensible.

The baby in me shifted and moved and I pressed my hand to it but I didn't talk much. Words came to mind but did not have the strength to come out. I tried to detach, to stay in the moment, to not imagine it being taken from me. The phone rang several times and we didn't answer it. I watched the light turn dusky. I dreamed of water.

Cherry poked me with the bull penis cane. "Sharon Stam's asking for you. It's her mother. She says you're the only one she'll see."

I WALKED BESIDE the canal, but not down in it, all the way to the Stams', a tiny farmhouse on what was once a nice stretch of vineyard down about a mile from Cherry's. The house was like a box divided in four, and Sharon and Laramie shared a room. It smelled like yeast inside, like Wiley's whiskey and spoiled cheese.

Sharon's mother had lost weight, and she appeared distorted, her wide face bobbing above a too-narrow body. "In there." She pointed to the room as if there were a rabid animal inside. I passed Laramie eating canned pigs' feet on saltines lying in front of the television.

"Wiley's had to lock up all his guns, that's how she's acting."

In the room Sharon lay on the floor looking up at her ceiling. Her stomach was a huge hill pinning her body down.

"Don't lie on your back," I said. "I read it can cut off blood supply."

"A fine way to go."

"I'm supposed to tell you everything's okay."

"I called nine-one-one again," she said. "They said, are you a child? They said, let me talk to your father. But then I realized that even if they came, I'd still be pregnant. This will always be my life."

"One day you'll be old enough to leave and you will," I said.

"What about you? You're just gonna hand over that baby to Vern? You're just gonna push it out of your body and hand it to him?"

"It's easier this way," I said.

"I don't want to think about hell anymore," she said, sleepy-sounding. "I'd rather just be there than think one more day about it."

"Let's stand next to each other on the Birthing Day, okay?" I said.

I lay down beside her. I thought of Stringy holding the articles. The tales of a polygamist pastor trying to evoke blessings for who-knew-what reason by having many wives. How that hadn't done anything remarkable for the world. How we were all still begging for rain just the same.

She took a deep breath. "Swear?"

"On my life."

I WALKED THE canal home, surrounded by blackness. I didn't want the moonlight on me. I didn't want any light. I never felt safer or more untouchable than when I was in the canal. I dragged my hand along the wall of it. I imagined it full of water. Maybe one day it would have water again.

Then there was something ahead, a footstep maybe, a stick cracking. A whisper. I stopped and pressed my back against the wall. I reached for the go-phone but stopped. If I used it to light my way, I'd only reveal myself. The feeling of a thousand eyes crept over my skin. I just had to climb out of here and into the dim light of the moon. I felt the wall for somewhere to place my foot, for an edge to grab, but it was smooth. If I carved something it would make noise. Calm down, I told myself. You're imagining things.

But then a voice from above. "Where you off to?"

"Who's there?" I said.

"Going somewhere important?" another voice said.

I was so slow, so pregnant. Two bodies jumped in and landed before me, forming a wall. The tang of sweat and baby powder, dirt and salt: boy. How Lyle smelled when he was over me. How the boys' club smelled with their newly grown-out long hair, the stripes of glitter they wore on their cheeks like war paint. Vern's soldiers. "We have on good word that you've been going to the red house outside of assignment."

"Let me pass," I said. I folded my arms around my belly. I didn't want to scare the baby so I tried to keep my breath normal, but my knees shook.

"This is a punishable offense," a voice said behind me. There were at least three of them, all breath and spit.

"I don't go there anymore," I said.

"We're gonna take you there and let you prove just how steadfast you are." It was Lyle speaking now. "You have some of Vern's work yet to do."

Hands urged me forward and I dug my heels into the ground. My flip-flops slid in the dust and then one snapped. They lifted me into the air. It seemed like they had multiplied in the dark. They carried me over their heads, my arms folded across my chest like a dead person. I kept still so they wouldn't drop me, hurt the baby.

They set me down finally. The lights were on in the red house, and I knew Daisy was settling in for evening calls amid the incense, the tobacco candles, the crushed velvet robes, the curtains of silk. Longing consumed me.

"They didn't do anything wrong," I said.

"They make men stumble with glee." Lyle stepped closer to the house, holding a red gas jug. If I screamed maybe they would hear me inside. He pressed a book of matches into my hand. "Burn it."

"You think God would burn a house down with people inside?" I asked.

The boys' club considered this a moment. Then some of them

nodded. "Yeah," Lyle said. "I think He would if it was for the right cause."

The door swung open and there was Daisy in a pale nightgown holding that little gun out. The boys' club piled over one another like puppies, scrambled for coverage, every boy for himself. Lyle stood still and stared at her. He didn't know what she could do with that thing.

Daisy's face was bare, hair back. She looked taller than I'd ever seen. "You little fuckers," she said. "It's not enough you come to harass me and my daughter, now you've dragged Lacey along. Well, shit."

"Shoot me," Lyle said. "I'll catch the bullet in my teeth."

"Little boys," she said. One of the boys broke away from the rest and made a run for it. "Just lost little hick boys. What will become of you? You need a nice lady to teach you a lesson about the world, I think."

"Ma'am," Laramie started. "It's not too late for you to be redeemed."

She came closer. Pointed the gun at Lyle. "For some reason, I like you least of all."

"I'm sorry," I said to her.

"Lacey, you get inside."

"She ain't going in there with you witches," Lyle said.

"Oh yes she is," Daisy said. I scrambled behind her and hovered in the doorway watching. "Why are you all so concerned with Lacey May anyhow? Don't you have better things to do? You all want rain so much maybe you should be getting an education so you can figure out how to treat the earth right. Do things different."

Lyle laughed. "That's the problem with you infidels. You all think you have control. You all think you're God."

Daisy considered this. "So you think me out here minding my own business has something to do with you and your land? You think if I was like you, converted and holy, that the rain would just start falling?"

Lyle tensed his shoulders and his hands opened and closed. When she said it like that, it sounded pretty stupid and I could tell he knew it.

"You wouldn't understand how it works," he said. "You wouldn't understand sin."

"Still time!" Laramie offered, hungry for a baptism. I could just imagine how badly he wanted to run to Vern, say he was the one to convert the phone whores.

"Well, I'm glad there's still time," she said, slow and simple like she was talking to an idiot. She walked backward a few steps, eyes trained on them. "Now get." She fired the gun into the sky. The shot sent them running in different directions, yelping into the night.

She looked at the gun in her hand, then at me. "I'm getting the hang of this."

"They were gonna burn your house down," I said.

"Ha," she said. "I sleep with one eye on the night."

She ushered me inside and lit some sage, waved it around to cleanse the badness those boys had rubbed off on me. I closed my eyes and sat on a velvet chair, exhausted. I loved Daisy, I loved her. I wanted to be hers always. But I understood that I would not be able to stop what was coming toward us. I could hear it approaching like a charge of horses.

THE NEXT DAY at Cherry's I slammed open the door to the craft room. Stringy was lying on the floor staring at a blank ceiling. I thought of my first days at Cherry's in the same room, how alone

I felt, how the wallpaper had kept me company. He looked like a sad dog starved and dirty. He slowly turned to me.

"Tell me everything that news article said. Tell me all about Vern in New Mexico."

"I'm right," he croaked. He looked at me kindly then. Almost like he felt sorry for me. I hated that. He should feel sorry for his own bad way, but I knew he saw my life as worse off. I could tell he wasn't lying. "I'm right."

He pulled himself up. He was a swaying reed. He paused and looked at me. I held very still. "I thought you were eighteen," he said, loud as he could. "Anyone says otherwise is a liar." He walked slowly past me and out the door. I let him go, a ghost on his way somewhere else.

Cherry came out of her bedroom waving her cane as the screen slammed behind him, shaking the house. "What's this?" she said.

"Let him," I said. "Could have gone anytime he wanted, but he stayed. Let's just forget him now. It's easier to just forget him."

"He's gonna spread lies about our dear pastor. He'll ruin everything."

"Cherry," I said. I held her shoulders. "What if the rain just happened to come when it did that day? What if it had nothing to do with Vern out in those fields?"

"I saw what I saw. If you'd have been there you'd never question."

"You just don't want to be sad that Grampa killed himself," I said. "You just don't want to believe that could have happened to you, but it did."

"Husband just dead in the field," she said, quietly. "Didn't want to follow him to hell. Can't blame a woman for that."

"Tell me you think it's wrong that Lyle's the daddy. Just tell me that."

She sat on the floor and whimpered. Gave me a fearful glare. "God take me now. Put an end to my suffering."

BY MORNING CHERRY'S tears were resolved. She was composed and focused on the phone and what someone was saying to her. She said nothing of Stringy, nothing of Lyle. She hung up and looked at me.

"Parents are saying God took her in the night, but gossip is running that she killed her own self. Ate her mother's headache pills."

She didn't have to say a name for me to know. "She didn't mean to die," I said. "She was trying . . ."

"I know what she was trying to do," Cherry said knowingly, almost with compassion.

I ran out to the porch and tried to catch my breath. The air choked me. There was nowhere to breathe. Cherry stood beside me and pointed to the sky. I looked up but my eyes lied to me. For there were hardly any clouds ever, and if there were, they were white and filmy, on their way to somewhere else. Sometimes jet trails ribboned over us and faded. But now there seemed to be a mass of clouds forming a stone-gray sky. Smoke, I thought at first, but there was no smell. Shade had collected and the dirt took on a violet hue.

"The sun is gone," Cherry said.

We walked slowly to the front yard. Artichoke squirmed inside me.

Geary's police car was pulled over on down the road. He leaned out his window, marveling up at the sky, craning his head back and forth in disbelief. "You seeing this, Cherry?" he called. "Whoo-hoooo!"

I held out my hands, palms up. I closed my eyes and waited for my skin to report first contact. If the rain came now what could it mean? It seemed like a freedom might unfold, something would change. Sharon, even, would not be dead. Somehow everything would be worth this rain. Here, we could say. This was why.

Please. I put my hand up to the sky, to God. *This is when you save us all.*

What does it feel like for a raindrop to land on skin? It's a feeling that while you are feeling it you do not think to remember.

What did it feel like for my mother to kiss my temple? For her arm to fall around me in her sleep. I had forgotten each sensation just after it happened, knowing, as if it were a fact, that there would always be another to come. How would it be to see Sharon one more time? Just one more chance to convince her of her life? But now I would never know. Her body would be returned to the earth, dust to dust, ashes to ashes.

The sun broke through again and the clouds rolled away west and west. Cherry put her hand on my shoulder to steady herself.

"Funny," she said, wiping her nose. "I got real scared it was gonna come down on us there. I imagined being carried right out into the water. That He was just gonna flood us all. Lord. Maybe it's best the sun is out forevermore."

"He promised to never flood the earth again," I said. "Why would you think He would?"

"I don't know, Lacey May. Maybe my faith ain't as great as I thought."

Who could know why I love you this much? I heard my mother say into the still aching air. But I wasn't hearing her quite right. I had forgotten that too.

Chapter 24

A week out from the Birthing Day and the sky had turned a permanent low blue, not the usual blaze, but an odd gathering of color I had never seen, and the crows flew in great swooping arcs over our house then perched in a line on the fence, watching. The flies stilled at last, their bodies in piles in the corners of every room, the grooves of every windowsill. Without their buzzing, a heavy silence settled. I moved from room to room, aimless. Cherry prayed for rain in front of the glow of her television. She oiled herself and finally asked me to shave off all her hair. No barriers, she proclaimed, between her and God. She sat on the toilet and I buzzed her scalp clean. Grampa Jackie always said she had the most beautiful hair.

"You'll be grateful to your old Cherry for never giving up on you," she said when I was finished.

I turned the tap on in the kitchen and not a single brown drop came out.

Even after Sharon died there were still moments, I'm ashamed to say, when I wanted to wake up new and see the ways Vern had always kept us in heart and mind. That he was one with God like he promised.

"We're crazy not to buy bottled water," I said. "We're going to die. I can't take deep breaths anymore."

"All the closer to heaven's water, then," she said. I drank more warm soda and felt my veins throb.

She smiled out the window. "Paradise on its way."

THAT AFTERNOON, DAISY'S car pulled into Cherry's driveway, Florin in the passenger seat, headphones on, black lipstick.

I ran to the car before Cherry could see them. Stood by Daisy's open window.

"Thought you might need someone to help you pick out a crib. Some baby clothes," Daisy said. She wore a beige catsuit, her white hair a-gleam over her breasts. Huge circular dark sunglasses covered her eyes and her lips were a matte maroon.

I looked back to the still house. Cherry would be kneeling, praying before her mice until sundown. I couldn't stop myself from getting in that car. It was such a human longing, missing someone. I curled on my side across the backseat, my stomach hanging over. "Drive."

Daisy had a happy giddiness to her, chatting about pacifiers and butt creams, and she passed right by the Goodwill drop-off, the Pac. She went on down Old Canal Road and toward the place she'd almost run over Wiley Stam and we'd all screamed. He was no longer guarding the border, not since Sharon had died. No one was there. But the sign still hung. We cruised slowly past and I sat up, buckled in. I wondered if she was kidnapping me, my dream come true.

We crossed into Fresno and she pulled up to a masking-tape-colored stucco house in a cluster of other masking-tape-colored houses. Hazel bounded out, a large bag on her shoulder. A wrapped item poking up from it like a present.

"Heard you've never seen the ocean," she said, scooting in next to me. "We couldn't let you get away with that."

WE DROVE THROUGH farmland on and on, and then through
rolling golden hills and pastures with water spraying over them
and small planes overhead dropping dust. We drank cool water
from bottles we bought easily from a quickie mart. It was as if the
drought wasn't in these places, but I knew better. These places were
worth saving—that was the underlying idea. MAKE CALIFORNIA
FREE AGAIN, a sign said. IS GROWING FOOD WASTING WATER?
said another.

"Put your hand out," Hazel said. I rolled down the window and
felt the cool edge to the air and the freeway sign turned to the 101
and soon we were taking an exit called Avila Beach, driving through
hilled and narrow wooded green trails, magnificent houses like I'd
never seen, with verandas and balconies, long drooping ivy falling from them, adobe villas and storybook cottages. We wound
our way through the forested area until suddenly the blue ocean
emerged beyond the trees and the road opened up into a town and
seagulls flew over us and kids walked sandy-footed on the side of
the road eating popsicles with towels draped over their backs. I felt
light-headed. Realized I'd been holding my breath for some time.

We parked and got out and Florin said before anything happened she needed a sandwich and we walked into a deli and someone made sandwiches in front of us and we took them to the sand.
The sand was hot under me, but the closer we got to the water, it
took on the texture of cool clay. I let my feet just feel that and we sat
and ate the most delicious sandwiches I'd ever tasted, seedy mustard with salami and olives, balsamic and pepper, and I didn't want
anyone to see the emotion on my face, for all the gratitude I felt for
them in that moment was bigger than anything I'd ever known.
What could I have hoped for in this life that wasn't before me?

The waves crashed on the shore and I'd like to say I thought kindly of my mother then, missed her, or wanted her to be there with me, and though for the rest of my life I would feel that way at different times, seeing a particularly arresting vista, or eating a heavenly crème brûlée, right then I felt only the sting of resentment, that all my life she had deprived me of this place, this absolute paradise just a few hours from our desert kickdown town.

"We thought we'd have a little baby shower for you here, hon," Daisy said. In the bright, special sun of Avila I couldn't see her scars anymore. She only gleamed. I opened the presents slowly, savoring each one, the sweet footed pajamas and the little yellow sun hat with SPF protection built in somehow and the small bottles of shampoo, "samples so you can try them out and pick a favorite," Florin said, and Hazel got me a muslin blanket with the moon phases on it and then they presented me with the beautiful gauze shift Hazel had worn the night I met her. "For after you have the baby. You'll want to feel nice," she said. I was silent. I almost couldn't handle it. I needed time to freeze so I could grow a heart big enough to accept the day.

I got up and walked the beach. I let the water kiss my feet. It was cold but cleansing and I gulped the pure air. I waded in and let the water cover my belly so Artichoke could feel the ocean. I would take her here, I decided. I would take her exactly here one day. She would know the roar of the waves and she'd build sand castles and be like the children walking careless through the town with sunburned cheeks, with their blind hope for life. As long as I stood in that water, I had it. I felt it. I knew that God was bigger than my own understanding, and the thought was not frightening, but a sudden comfort. If after all my believing years I still didn't understand God, then that meant there was life outside of my own, that there were still yet other things I didn't understand, but could come to know if I wanted. I could let the possibility of the world slowly unfurl before me. Any thought that I could give this baby away evaporated as if it had never existed. A new power ran through me, something of the earth. My tears fell into the salt bath. I felt right then that anything great could happen.

"I don't want to go back," I said.

Hazel smiled a sad smile. Florin sighed. We linked arms and trudged through the water for a long ways, then returned to our picnic.

"We wish you could just stay with us," Daisy said. "But I have to tell you, that old Geary came by and threatened to shut us down if we interfered with you, Lacey. I don't mean to scare you. But we can't take you in right now. He seemed real serious.

"Something will work out," she kept on, but I could hear the shake in her voice. She doubted each word as she said it.

"Once you're eighteen you can do what you want," Florin said. "It won't be that long."

It was funny to me, and so of the world, that eighteen meant anything at all. It signified for them a time when my life would become my own and I could shift into a new person entirely.

We approached the car and I wondered if Sharon had ever felt the grit of sand under her feet. If she'd ever seen a crab scuttle into frothy waters. Maybe if she could have come today she would have seen the vastness of the sea and known there was more in the world for her than just what it had shown her. Maybe if I had shared the red house with her, something would have shifted. I regretted that day in the canal when I didn't take her with me. I was selfish with my survival.

———

AS WE DROVE, I watched the landscape change back to what I knew and Peaches pulled us into it. Someone had spray-painted two words on the welcome sign: *Fuck it.*

I SAT ON the porch at Cherry's, the sea still in my nose. I wanted to soak in this moment, before I became someone else. I knew as soon as I went back inside everything would change. I'd pack a bag quietly. I'd take a single mouse to remember her by. I'd bring my favorite romance. I'd take the hearse. Where I would go I didn't yet know. Maybe back to the beach. Maybe back to Hazel's house for a few nights. She could help me have the baby. I'd just show up and she'd have to take me in, at least until then. After the baby was out I could travel on and on, never stopping in one place too long.

Inside, Cherry sat on her stool covered in God glitter. She didn't look at me. A dead chinchilla rested in her lap and she stroked the top of its head with one finger.

"He told me to keep a close watch on you," she said, "and I wasn't going to let him down. Not at this hour."

Vern emerged from the hallway, Derndra at his side. They sat at Cherry's kitchen table like it was something they'd done many times before. He liked to own whatever space he was in. He wore tattered jeans and an old shirt, the color fraying. His hair was pulled back in a ponytail, no curls bouncing at his shoulders. They looked tired like they'd just cleaned out a basement, dusty and on edge. He gestured for me to sit. I stood where I was, leaned up against the counter. A single fly buzzed and hit the window over and over trying to get out.

"Derndra knew you couldn't be trusted. Even when I told her of the grapes we ate together, how we'd understood, together. I said, 'No, my dear, Lacey May is special. She is chosen.' But my Derndra is wise. She said, 'That girl needs to be kept close.'"

Derndra looked at my belly with hunger, her bangs flat to her forehead.

I ran past them to the bathroom and pressed against the door. My belly heaved and I clutched my crotch with both hands. The pressure was immense. I looked at the tiny window. I'd never fit. Artichoke beat my walls. My breath caught. "Please God!" I screamed. Pee trickled down my leg.

Vern pushed the door open. He put his arms around my upper body, squeezing me tight.

"Please," I begged. "Just let me leave."

"Derndra said my mistake was banishing your mother. Never separate a mother and daughter, she said. She said that's why you've submitted to your female hysteria."

"Cherry, help!" I screamed, but she sat still. Cherry had replaced the chinchilla with a framed photograph of my mother wearing a gold dress and red lipstick, sash across her chest. *Miss Central Valley*. "Can't let her go the way of Sharon, no I can't," she said to the photo.

"Cherry!" I thrashed. A sharp pain stabbed deep within me. I willed the baby to be okay.

Cherry seemed to twitch in her seat now. I thought she was going to get up, fight for me maybe, hug me, but she didn't. A growl rose from my chest but the pain in my stomach struck again. Vern dragged my dead weight out the door and all the way to the car. He pushed me into the backseat, and I kicked at the windows.

"Careful with that girth," Vern said. "See how reckless you are. All the more reason to stay with us until the Birthing Day. We need you ripe and ready."

He started the car and I watched Cherry's house get smaller. A week, I thought. I had a week until the Birthing Day. A week with Vern. I thought of the baby shower presents, the soft cottons.

"Someone's gonna come looking for me," I said. "Daisy and Florin won't let me just disappear."

"No one will find you," he said. "Not with God's fence of power around us. The house is a pretty holy place," he mused.

Derndra spoke up now, her voice soft and sweet. "We're finding a peaceful approach just isn't working anymore on those witches," she said. "I see why witches used to be burned. There's just no other way."

"I'll do anything," I said, "just leave them alone."

"She says she'll do anything," Vern said. "Anything to defend sinners of the worst kind, the very women who spoiled the goodness of her mother, but not willing to do anything for her church. Practically encouraged Sharon to kill herself."

"You spoiled the goodness of my mother," I told him. "You killed Sharon."

"I was deep in prayer when Sharon died," Vern said. He stopped the car in the middle of the road. A truck moved slowly around us, the arm out the window waving. "Help!" I screamed to it, but the scream stayed in the car, windows rolled up. Not that it would have mattered anyway. The good pastor could do anything he wanted.

He turned back to me, looked in my eyes. Spoke softly. "I felt her heart and the baby's heart stop in my own heart, so please don't tell me I had any hand in one of our own being sucked down under."

Derndra cleared her throat. "Lean Cuisines tonight?" she asked him.

He turned back to her. Smiled. "Yes, dear."

ONCE AT VERN'S house, his soft voice left him. They dragged me into the basement like I wasn't a human at all, but a huge sack of flour. They were careful about the baby though, Derndra even cooed to it. *It's okay, baby, it's okay.* Fear covered my eyes and sent the

world back to my mind distorted. They set me down on the floor.
All I could see was red. I thought it was the red of the Turquoise
Cowboy's performance room, perhaps somehow I was to relive that
again, but after a few minutes, after my breath caught up with me,
I realized the lightbulbs were red and the walls brown. Heat and
dust hung in the air. Derndra turned a radio up. Vern's sermons
came rushing though the speaker. *Sometimes I wish God would give me
a Holy Ghost machine gun*, he cried. *I'd blow every sinner's head clear off!* I
remembered the sermon when he said that, probably a little over a
year ago. I'd thrown my arms up, fists in the air. Yes, I'd screamed.
How I wanted sinners to eat of their sin, to grovel at the feet of
Vern, and then join us.

"We'll leave you here to think," Vern said. He kissed my
forehead.

"Please."

"The wages of sin," he said, putting his hands up, looking around
the room. "Is death."

IN THE BASEMENT I didn't know what time it was. The red light
washed over my skin. It seemed specifically built, windowless. No
one would know what went on here, who was here. A single black
painted serpent wound up the wall, yellow eyes on watch. Artichoke
was still and I kept time waiting for her kicks. I'd feel one and relax back into nightmares of pushing out not a baby but bunches of
bloody muscats. I birthed a pack of Cherry's chinchillas, Sharon,
my mother. I screamed for the images to stop. I sweated, and fever
became me.

Derndra came in and put her hand on my forehead. She was
calm as she ever was.

"Water," I said.

"If you're good you can come up for dinner tonight," she said. "I'm not a cruel woman." She put her hand on my belly. "I won't deprive this sinless being."

"You don't really want to be trapped with him forever, do you? You know Sharon shouldn't have died. You know we were all raped. Don't you care?"

Her spine softened and I imagined her a girl. How had she ended up here? But I knew how. It was the same way I had. Her belief had accumulated like a tumbleweed and it became too hard to go back once she'd come so far, sacrificed so much. "I've been with Vern a long time. I've seen him through much adversity."

"What he's going to do on the Birthing Day, it's all illegal," I said, then added, pathetic even to my own ears, "Think how it would look to outsiders."

"Nothing Vern does is illegal in Peaches."

"You can testify the truth and do the right thing. Imagine if I was Trinity Prism. What would you do?"

I saw her lip twitch at the mention of her daughter's name. Perhaps it was the only nerve I'd be able to hit.

"This isn't what God wants," I said. I heard it come out of me sure, and I felt the truth beam. The black dots crowding my vision pulled back. I was dizzy, thirsty, but I knew for a fact that this had nothing to do with God. "There's a God out there who loves us, who doesn't ask for signs and wonders."

She glanced back to the door. "Okay, smarty, where does that leave me? Trinity Prism?"

"You can go wherever you like. God would pave another way for you."

The door creaked open at the top of the stairs. There Vern stood square-shouldered, a plasticky orange cape to his ankles. "Girl talk?"

Her openness vanished. She pressed her hands into her long skirt before walking back up the stairs, bowing to Vern as she passed. But a part of her had wavered, had come to my side, however momentarily. I saw it.

"Don't sour the pure heart of my wife," Vern said. "She's strong but the devil is wise."

"I know you loved my mother," I said.

"I love all my flock," he said.

"No. You loved her different. You loved her so much you couldn't bear to look at her anymore."

He pressed his fingers into his temples. Closed his eyes. He was in pain. He was feeling something. "Everyone is subject to suffering, Lacey May. Even me." He closed the door softly behind him.

All this time I hadn't been the only one missing her. He knew something of my grief. He felt his own perverted loss. But I didn't have time to feel bad for him. The loneliness of a monster can only become sentimental after it is dead.

HOURS PASSED AND Trinity Prism came to get me. She walked me up the stairs and to the table without a word. She wore a long white shift and a gold cross hung to her belly button.

"How wonderful!" Vern said brightly. "Our wayward daughter is here at the table with us. Lacey, I think your rest has done you well."

The room tilted and deep pains stabbed the underside of my belly. Derndra set a Lean Cuisine before each of us, Salisbury steak and mashers, only 260 calories! I needed so many more.

"Where'd these fancy feasts come from?" I asked. I thought of me and Cherry eating canned chicken livers with our hands, meanwhile our pastor was gobbling up fine frozen fare.

"Dear saving father," Vern began. "May our blessings be rich as we eat of your bounty. As we remember the fields as they once were, life full, sprouting and vast. Bring us back to your holy land evermore, and if you will not bring rain to us, then send us somewhere far away. Pave our path in the gold of your love."

"Where are we going?" I asked. I tried to seem uninterested, a casual observer, but my heart thumped.

"There may be another place for us. A place we can all live together in one godly family. We won't need rules there. Water will be a rich bounty. Without all the distraction of the world, imagine the work we will do."

Trinity Prism looked at her mother. She was wide-eyed, like she didn't know this part of the plan.

"Then I guess there's no need to burn down the red house," I said. "If we won't even be here anymore."

He raised his eyebrows. "Eat. You'll need your strength."

"Why didn't you tell my mother about this place?"

"Tell me, Lacey," he said. "Do you wonder if your mother ever wanted you at all? You blame me for what's happened, but could it be possible that I only revealed her true nature? That she didn't want to be a mother and when she saw her way out, she took it?"

I considered what he said. Maybe it was true. The possibilities lay before me, but something rang off about it. For nothing could take away who my mother and I had been when we had loved each other, when we'd driven the town, heads back screaming along to her favorite songs, the way she looked so melancholy and how she'd rested her chin on my head while we slow danced in the living room to "Tears in Heaven."

I thought of the time before our conversion when she went to a two-week rehab and I got to visit her there one afternoon and she'd run to me, picked me up, held me so tight I couldn't breathe. She hated it there but her breath was clear. She could see me again. She loved me as long as she could see me.

"God will always be more powerful than you," I said.

"There's not God apart from me, Lacey. Thinking there is is your main problem."

THROUGH THE NIGHT Vern paced the halls. Trinity Prism slept silently. I couldn't even hear her breathing. She lay in a twin bed with plain white sheets. I curled on the floor beside her bed on a carpet, my hips aching. The carpet smelled like nothing. It was like no one lived in this house. She had few belongings in her room, some Bibles and notepads, one stuffed bear with no eyes. I could see the dark outline of Vern's feet under the crack in the door. He stood there for long periods and then paced the hall again, tapping something heavy on the floor.

"What is he doing out there?" I whispered. I sat up and put a hand on Trinity Prism's sheet. "What that's noise?"

"Holy Ghost machine gun," she murmured. "He asked God for one and God provided. He spray-painted it gold."

"A real gun?"

"He said it showed up on the doorstep of the church, blessed day."

"What's he going to do with it?"

"Stop your warring thoughts," she said, awake. "You'd be lucky to be Godshot with that gun."

"I would be dead."

"I can't wait for my earthly visit to be over," she said. "My reward awaits in the next life."

"Does Vern come in here? Does he just pace all night?"

She turned toward me and I saw her glassy eyes in the moonlight. It was a full moon, I could see from the window.

"He does just what he's called to do."

WHEN I WOKE in the morning Trinity Prism's bed was crisply made. The sun filtered into the room and the heat I was so accustomed to pressed its way through the window. The closet door was open and in it hung two dresses and nothing else. The pain in my stomach had intensified. What were labor pains like? All the things I'd forgotten to ask Hazel.

Trinity ate mush at the table, leaning over her worn green Bible. Derndra prayed on her knees before a low-hung cross. She kissed it. Vern was gone.

I knelt next to her and put my face close to hers. "Will you still help me?" I whispered.

She pinched my side, a tender spot, and I pulled away in pain. Her eyes were cold.

"What's he going to do to the Diviners?" I said.

"Flames can dance a beautiful dance, did you know that? Have you ever seen a house on fire? It's spectacular."

I ran to the living room, searching for a phone. Where was a phone?

She held it, unplugged. "We know you're a tricky heart."

"You're lying to scare me."

She balled up her hands and let out an exasperated sigh. "You shouldn't have made nice with those women. Do you think I like to watch a girl suffer? I'm a good person. I follow the rules. You're doing this to yourself. You and your mother. You just couldn't do one thing right and now it's come to this. It's all gone too far, if you ask me, but it's not my fault and I won't be made to feel like it is." Her pale face had reddened and she looked different and uncontained. "I won't be lured off the path by you."

A nervous laugh escaped me. She had never shown this much expression before and it was exhilarating and terrifying. She came close like she was going to slap me. I braced and lowered my head, but then her arms were hugging me. I could hear her chest pound, I could hear the human of her.

THAT NIGHT I had a dream and in that dream I called my mother. She said, What can I do to hold your heart still?

I don't love you anymore, I told her. A lie.

What can I do? she said again.

Help me, I said. And then leave me alone.

Chapter 25

The morning of the Birthing Day the sky opened up cloudless and everlasting. They loaded me in the backseat of the car. I wore my white gown. The neck came up to my chin in an itchy lace collar. It covered my body to the floor, sleeves falling past my wrists. Under this gown I disappeared.

We rode in silence, Vern's fingers drumming the steering wheel. Trinity Prism sat next to me, pressed into her side of the car, hands praying under her chin. We drove out and out on Old Canal Road. The Holy Ghost machine gun was in the trunk. Every time we stopped I could hear it shift, feel the bump of it against the seat. We neared the turnoff for the Diviner house and the car slowed then stopped.

Out the window, in the dry lands, I saw the bones of dead animals sticking up from the ground like stakes and I allowed myself finally to understand I would not be alive for much longer. I had known it for some time but I'd buried it. I could not be a prisoner with them forever. I could not be bound and gagged living in their basement and I could not be trusted to be released back to Cherry. There was no place for young girls.

A calm shrouded me. I felt the sun burn my hand through the car window. How I'd miss that ruthless sun, how I'd long for one more day of dryness, grateful only for breath. Soon I would not know the pleasure of my own exhalation.

God, I thought, please take me in your arms. I know you aren't the God of Vern. I know you aren't the God of man. If you're there and you're a sinner's God like I've come to hope for, will you bless me one more time? Will you let my baby be taken far from here and into another bright life? Not here. Not here.

When we stopped I opened my eyes. Cars were parked every way through the field, the girls of blood in white gowns being led by their fathers toward an unseen belly of the expanse. Mothers trailed them tight-lipped and rigid. I strained to see where they were going. Vern pulled me from the car, gripped my arm. The gun was strapped to his back, huge and gold. He'd adorned it with rhinestones. His hair gleamed in the sun, glitter twinkling on his scalp. I reached up and touched a tight curl, pulled it, and it bounced back up. Tears streamed down my face. "You could just let me go," I heard myself say.

"No longer a bastard, Lacey," he said. "You've got fathers all around." He kissed my temple. We went deep into the field beyond the swarm of cars, following the line of the Body. Cherry walked past me arms outstretched toward what she must have envisioned as God, her head shaved bald and gleaming with jelly and bronzer. All I wanted was water before I died.

I looked up and before me like a blessing was the red house. I saw the tallness of it, the leaning structure. I thought I smelled Daisy's incense. But I blinked and it wasn't the red house. It was a skeleton frame. The red had turned to char. The walls had begun to fall away. I thought of the velvet chairs, ruined. The silk robes in tall ornate dressers. Daisy's matches on the back of the toilet and Florin's moon chart.

"No," I said. My legs went weak. I leaned into Vern and he stumbled and the gun swung around and hit me in the head. I dropped to my knees and gripped the earth, white dress ruined. I tasted smoke in the air.

"Tell me they weren't inside," I said.

"Whether they meet their devil now or in fifty years, does it really matter?" he said.

I looked up for someone to help me, but the crowd walked past, eyes ahead, carrying lawn chairs and bags of chips like they were going to watch a football game. Vern pulled me up and we joined. When we came to the clearing, the full-bellied girls like me were kneeling in a circle on a clean white tarp. A huge plastic gas station NASCAR soda cup was in the middle. Denay was stretching her body like an athlete preparing for a competition. Taffy smiled with her lopsided pillow belly. The rest stood around dumb and gawking, clueless. Sharon was supposed to be with me for this. If she was here, we would find a way out.

Vern stood in the middle of our circle and raised his arms at the Body. "We are here," he said. "We have made it to the offering."

This was when the girls of blood were to raise our arms up to God and sing. I moved with them, my own voice trailing out of me. *Hell is hot, don't drink the water.*

After we sang, Vern held up the NASCAR cup. "God's own birthing elixir," he said. I tried to remember my magazines, the books. Had they ever mentioned a drink that would bring on labor? Vern solemnly handed Denay the cup. She didn't hesitate for a moment. I almost admired her willingness. Her face quivered and she gagged as she drank. The Body cheered. I thought of how I'd once known her before all this, in her room when she'd pulled down her unders and showed me her pubic hair. When she'd asked me if I thought she had too much. Now she was a girl with no memory of me or herself. I caught sight of Sharon Stam's father biting into a chicken leg, her mother glancing down at her watchless wrist over and over like a tic.

The boys' club stood closest to us, their hair shaggy and long, curled and glittered for just this moment. Their robes gleamed. They were the men of honor today.

Denay passed me the cup. Inside the liquid was red. I had so wanted it to be water. The smell of whatever it was reminded me of my mother's breath after she drank, of grapes gone bad. Vern stepped near to me. I reached my hand away from him and turned the cup over. The red spread across the tarp and some of the girls shrieked.

But Vern smiled. "I guess you'll need my help."

Lyle rose up with an old glass jug and refilled the cup. The crowd closed in, formed a wall with linked arms. I sensed the Body begin to grow frustrated. "Make her drink it!" someone yelled.

Lyle held my jaw open and I tried to close my throat but eventually it opened. The sting of it went down my throat. It was not my mother's Cuba libre but it belonged to the same family. *Sometimes wine can relax a woman in early labor.* A midwife had said that in one of my books, I remembered. Vern was trying to loosen us up. But I knew no amount of wine would bring a baby. It would only make us sick. The boys helped the rest of the girls drink. I closed my eyes for a while.

I thought of the red house. I was sure they hadn't been spared. I was sure no one in the town of Peaches, California, had been spared anything.

My stomach retracted and released. It took me by surprise, this feeling I hadn't felt yet. It was almost like the cramps that had come before my blood. Why was this happening now? I wondered if I was imagining the sensation, creating the thing I was most afraid of. Actually going into labor now was not an option.

But my waters had not broken. I could still move and think and be present. *Still time*, I thought. I remembered what Hazel had said about sphincter law, how if a woman wasn't comfortable in her situation, the holes of her body would clench, prevent release. It was the body protecting the body within it. I thought to the books I'd read that showed labor, black-and-white pictures of women with their knees hitched up in the hands of mustached husbands, or squatting by riverbanks, or bent over a bouncy ball, openmouthed in purposeful force, with another woman behind squeezing hips. The smiles that spread across their faces as the heads of babies crowned impossibly from their open, diamond-shaped caverns. "Sarah later described her birth as painless," one caption read. "She felt pressure, but not pain."

A shot rang out and it jolted me alive. I lurched up onto my knees and watched as Vern danced in his gold robe, jubilant now, pointing the Holy Ghost machine gun to the sky, where he sent a rain of bullets. Where the bullets would fall was God's decision, is what Vern would say. We might never know.

Cherry spun in circles like an overgrown toddler. She was in the God zone now. The body chanted around us. Spirit song. Vern's voice. *God rain down on us, as we offer ourselves up to you! We are the wise, bringing hope to the land!*

There was one comfort and only one: We were women together in our suffering. I watched us all together on the tarp. Our short hair matted to our faces. Our bodies weighed down with our purpose. We seemed so weak like this, but then Denay surged up to a stand and screamed in pain and I thought then she seemed stronger than she ever had, her eyes full of rage toward something, perhaps just rage against her pain.

I vomited onto the tarp, the wine rich and unwelcome. The tarp was not pure anymore. Taffy had turned gray and was slumped like a tired doll. Her stuffed belly was down between her legs now and she sweated in streams. No one seemed to notice her. She kept murmuring, *Vern?* But everyone, even Vern seemed to be separated from us by an invisible wall. They hovered like a committee of vultures, but they did not touch our blessing.

HOURS OR MINUTES passed. Time was nothing. The sun moved slowly over us and then it began to set. Perhaps the rains were nigh. The clouds were eating blue, peeling back the sky. No one was pushing a baby out yet, but my stomach cramped over and over, my spine a dull throb. I closed my eyes and I saw Revelation's great white throne. I saw the book of life. I saw God's hand upon it. And then I saw clearly what I'd never wanted to again. My mother, our apartment. The time I'd told her about Sapphire Earrings, told her I didn't like being alone with him. She talked to him about it. They screamed and yelled. *You're no mother to that girl,* he had said. *At least I care.* He packed his things and didn't come back. I was overjoyed thinking a new life could begin, a better life, but she lay crumpled in our sheets. "Who do you want to live with?" she'd asked me.

"What do you mean?" I'd said. I curled my body next to her but she didn't reach out to me.

"When I'm gone," she said.

"Where are you going?"

I begged her. I wept. Still she was cold. I saw the empty pill bottle. I watched the sleep greet her.

"Go play outside," she had murmured. I touched her hand and she flinched.

I had run from her down to the canal. I thought of jumping in and letting the cool blue water take me. The undertow was a strong pull, I knew, though the surface was placid. Valley kids were raised never to go near the canal. Someone always did though, the lure of it too much. I sat on the edge, tempted my toes in the rush. I felt the forceful carry of it. I lowered myself down so both ankles were covered. I couldn't see anyone around. The water was cool but not cold. My hand slipped and then I was in. For a moment my breath caught, my body froze, and I went under. This is how it happens, I thought. This is how to drown. I heard the rush of the water, my own blood pumping in my ears. But then there was the sun above me. My face broke the top. I felt a hand grab my own, pull me up and out. The hot bake of the dirt was beneath me again. When I looked up I was alone. The sun dried me and I walked back to the apartment in a trance.

I had tried to prepare myself for what I would find. But she wasn't there. The Rabbit was still in the parking lot. Inside, furniture had been moved around in a rush. A streak of vomit by the bedside. I lay in the empty bed and waited. In the morning she returned beaten-looking and half gone. But alive. I let myself think she had not gone through with it because of me and I loved her more. That was only a month before Vern brought the rains and saved us and put light in her eyes and I let myself forget the whole thing. We never talked about it and soon I knew that hand that had pulled me out of the canal was God's.

A black sky became the world around the birthing tarp and things were silent for a time.

———

I WOKE TO Vern's voice. He screamed up into the star-born sky: "We throw our earthly deeds before you and humble ourselves, Father! Send relief! Send your children forth." He had begun to look tired and frazzled. No babies had arrived yet and the girls of blood were ill. I was so hungry I imagined myself eating a stick of butter in two bites. Water. Just water.

The Body was on their knees begging in tongues. Trinity Prism wore white lace and twirled a crisp white parasol in the darkness, nervous. Derndra was still as a statue with one arm raised in a godly salute. The Body bowed toward us in a wave. Another pain stabbed at me.

"It's not working," Wiley Stam said, slurring from the crowd. "These girlies ain't doing what they 'posed to."

Lyle came to me and brought the cup to my lips. "Please," I whispered, but he wouldn't look into my eyes.

"Feed her, child!" Pearl screamed from the crowd. Her face red, eyes bulging.

"One more chance, Lacey," Lyle said. "Do the right thing. Tell them the child was from my quiver and I'll spare you for now."

Somehow my shame was his pride. "Fine," I said.

"Church!" he cried. "Listen to the spirit speak!"

He pulled me up. "The baby is from his quiver," I said lowly. "Forgive me my lies."

The Body cheered and whooped. He tilted my head back again but made sure the cup wasn't leaned far enough for liquid to meet my lips. I pretended to drink. He walked away from me without letting on and the kindness felt like a light coming in under the door of a very dark room; not enough to see by, but something.

Denay drank a long thirsty gulp from the cup and bore down in a squat. Her eyes were flying. She didn't look like the women in the books. She hadn't entered the transition I'd read about, where a self-doubt would come over her and she would beg for life and then it would be time to bear down. She was pretending. Her eyes were only fear. "Try pushing, Lacey," she gasped. "Hold my hand. We can push together."

I crawled to her. "You're not in labor," I said. "I bet you're not even dilated."

"What's that mean?" she hissed.

Cherry yelled out of the crowd to Vern. "Do it like you did before! Just do it again. We've all been so loyal."

Vern ignored her and began to preach. He commanded God to act out his promises but God was silent. With each proclamation he fired the gun into the sky. Was he trying to shoot God? The Body stirred. I looked at their hungry eyes turning tired. Turning doubtful. Sharon Stam's mother was lying down, her arms wrapped around herself. How long could this go on? I felt myself lapse into daydream. I saw my mother parting the crowd on a Clydesdale horse. I imagined her handing out cups of ice water to everyone, tri-tip sandwiches from Mike's Meat Market. I lay on my back and closed my eyes. No such meat angel arrived. Denay struggled to push next to me and nothing came from her except piss.

Then movement, feet stepping toward Vern. I turned and saw him put the golden gun to his side. It was Derndra. She put her hand on his shoulder and whispered something in his ear. He craned his head over the crowd and looked to the distance. My eyes followed and there was a flash of red lights approaching.

"It's time," he said. "God has spoken to Derndra. He said he will not bless us until we are in the new place. In the new kingdom. Don't waste time mourning this place. Girls of blood, in the vans!

Everyone else get in your cars and follow. Take nothing with you. They can't do anything to us if we all band together."

Derndra grabbed my wrists and led me to a black van parked behind the red house. "You get the cops to come here?" I whispered to her.

Her mouth tightened. She wouldn't look at me. "Blasphemy," she said, snapping her fingers in my face. If she had told the cops, she was a brilliant actress against it. "Get with it. You're too heavy for me to lift."

She thrust me up into the van and I crawled to the back and pressed against its empty steel interior. Where had it come from? There was a rush of bodies entering behind me, the full-bellied being pushed up and in, gray-faced, white gowns messed and wet and filthy. Some were almost passed out. Denay pulled herself together, turned to me, and said clearly, "Don't ruin this for us."

"Fuck you," I said. It felt great.

The door closed. Sirens cut through the black space around me. I thought of Geary, how he was just one of the Body. How he would sooner die than betray the church, condemn us to the laws of the world. Then came a voice on a speakerphone. "Hands up. Where are the minors?"

"Officers, you're intruding on a perfectly legal religious ceremony," I heard Vern say, pyscho calm. "You can go home now. It is well."

"We'll need you to step over here and get in this car, sir."

"This is the Devil at his best!" Vern assured the Body. "Every holiness will be met with resistance. Have faith."

"We'll need that van opened up," the voice said.

"Is there water in jail?" Taffy said.

"Shut up!" Denay said. "You should be praying for our pastor right now." She lapsed into her spirit voice, humming and tapping against the walls. My stomach quaked again, this time with a sharp pain that radiated down my legs. I held my breath. I beat the door. "Please!" I cried. "Help! In here!"

Outside I heard a man say, "Put the weapon down. On the ground. Show us your hands. Down on the ground. Now!" Then a shot sounded. I couldn't tell if it had come from the Holy Ghost machine gun or from the police. Derndra screamed. The van door slid open and Taffy fell out onto her back.

"Oh, Jesus," the cop said. He helped her up and a long string of drool hung from her lip, her fake belly up under her breasts. "Call medical."

The cop guided us all out one by one. "They're all . . ." He trailed off and stared at our pregnant stomachs in horror. I stepped out of the van and it was then that I saw Vern lying on his back on the ground as if asleep. His chin was scruffy and unshaved. His cape had come off and he looked ordinary in jeans and a T-shirt. There was still color to his cheeks, still life in the way his arms spread away from his body, reaching out toward something mysterious. His mouth hung open and I thought I saw those silver fillings twinkle way in the back.

A crowd of police stood over him talking into walkies, one made notes on a clipboard. But no one was really looking at Vern. Not a one of them knew they had taken down our leader. He was of no importance in their world, I realized. They did not look at him and see God. One cop held the golden gun. "Where'd he get a thing like this? Never seen something like it in my life." Vern's dirty tennis shoes were pointed oddwise and helpless. I always thought there would be more serenity on the face of a man who was now meeting his maker in paradise, who was finally, by his steadfast belief, going to meld with God forever. But something was pinched about his eyes like he was willing them shut, bracing. I thought they did not look like the eyes of peace. There was only fear there. The baby moved hard into my bladder and I peed a little.

The night was ending, the sun was rising over the flatland. Most of the Body had run, but not everyone. There were some on their knees in prayer. Some stood motionless as statues in shock and I caught a flicker of movement in the distance. Past the red house ran a man. He was tall and thin, a flash of sand-colored hair. I knew that gait. It was Lyle alone. I looked around to find the rest of the boys' club but they were gone, too. I didn't have the energy in me then to wonder what life awaited them. What things they would have to put away deep into themselves. Inevitably, some would lie each night next to a future wife and that wife would have no idea what they had done, the things they had found themselves a part of. A chill whipped through the valley, the first cool breeze I'd felt here in so long.

"Is there a Lacey May Herd?" a dark-haired officer said, looking at the lot of us in white. We were sitting on the ground like a little class. "One of you girls named Lacey May?"

I raised my hand. Rolled myself over to all fours and slowly got up.

"Come on with us."

Another cop stepped in with a notebook and began writing down the names of the other pregnant girls.

"I'm named by my creator alone," Denay told him. She stared at Vern's body on the floor. She looked almost annoyed.

The cramping feeling continued. It burned and radiated through me. I held my breath and it subsided. All good. But then a crash between my legs, turning the dust into mud under my feet. "Can someone call my midwife?"

The cop glanced up from his pad. "I'm sure you've got a lot of feelings happening at once about all this, but that's why there's laws in place to make things simple. You can leave feelings behind and let the law do its work. We'll get that baby delivered just fine," the cop said.

"I want to give birth at the Farm of Spiritual Birthing and Uterus Celebration. I just need Hazel. She can help me have the baby."

"There's a lot of paperwork to be done before that can happen."

Paperwork. What could the paperwork possibly say, I wondered. The cops were like another species to me, large men in the same suits, their faces so sure of what they were saying, able to make big decisions with confidence, like killing Vern.

"How did you know to come?" I asked the cop. He guided me toward a white square ambulance. I felt the wet of my dress against my legs. The cramping intensified, my bag of water no longer there to cushion it. "Who told you?" I held my breath and tried to focus only on him.

He helped me onto the small bed inside, then stood back. The paramedics began moving around me, wrapping things around my arms, holding a monitor to my stomach. He drew a thick finger under lines on his report. He hummed as he read. Finally, he looked at me as the doors to the ambulance were closing.

"Says here it was your mother."

Chapter 26

Saint Agnes Hospital. The huge building, the clean laminate floors, the bright pink of the nurses' smocks, heaven. They walked around in an orderly way, in a way that spelled routine, safety. This was a place where they knew exactly what they were doing and they were doing it with rhythm and function.

I went on a strange autopilot, morphing into a new self. They helped me off the stretcher and unhooked my IV and led me to a wheelchair and I sat down without question. The IV had made me feel suddenly alive again and the law was making decisions now. The clean sparkle of the hospital a blessing. The phones ringing and the people answering them. My mother never took me to the doctor after we were saved. The church would just pray over my sore throat, my cough.

A woman with long black hair, skin dusted in freckles, and large clean front teeth appeared at my side and wheeled me down a long hall where crucifixes hung and sweet pictures of Jesus smiling, kneeling before a crowd of children, His love gleaming from his hands.

"I'm Pam. I'm a labor and delivery nurse. How are you feeling?"

"Fine," I said. I looked away from the Jesus pictures and swallowed my tears. Was this the God I'd been hoping existed? The kind face, the soft arms. He was nothing like Vern.

"No reason to hide your real feelings."

"It hurts," I said.

"Well, you're still talking to me, so that's a sign we're probably still pretty early in the process, which is good. We can go find your room and get you settled."

"I can walk," I said. "I'd rather . . ." But the cramping feeling deepened, stopped my mind. Pam put her warm hand on my back and told me to breathe through it. "Okay, push me."

On our walk she asked me questions about my prenatal care. Had I had an ultrasound? No. Did I know if I was dilated? No. Did I know if I was close to my due date? The Birthing Day was my due date. It went on like this, me answering everything wrong until she said, "Great. Well, it's good you're here. We have lots of room right now and you can use the Jacuzzi."

"Will the other girls come here?" I said. "There are more than just me."

"Let's worry about you. They're getting situated where there's room and it's probably likely that you're the only one in active labor. The rest are pregnant but it would be a real strange thing if you all were pushing babies out on the same day, wouldn't it?"

"He made us drink wine or something to make the babies come out."

"When did you last drink it?" she said. Her face retained a cool calm which I was thankful for.

"A while ago. Hours."

She asked if I'd vomited. Yes. If I'd resisted the drink. Yes, but was only partly successful. What did it taste like? My mother. Rotten grapes. Blood.

"I'm fifteen. The baby is mine and I'll raise her. Write that down. No one can take her."

"Well, you're right. It's your choice."

"It is?" I asked.

"Of course," she said.

Another contraction, tightening, flames down my thighs, wrapping around my back. I screamed long and loud in her ear but she didn't pull away.

We finally arrived at the maternity ward and she typed something into a keypad and the door opened. That door and its safeness filled me with joy. I didn't know I could love a place in this way. I wanted to melt into the walls.

Pam took me to a room and I remembered I didn't have any of the little socks or the baby balm or the moon phases blanket. It was all at Cherry's, my precious little things, the only things that made me a real mother.

There was a huge tub in the bathroom and long windows looking out on the town, palm trees in rows and little square houses, 7-Elevens and delis. The morning in Fresno was as still and hot as in Peaches and I could see the waves of heat rising off asphalt.

Pam helped me into the tub, guiding me so my IV didn't get wet. "Can I cut this off?" she said. My gown. I let her.

Then the water. The sweet water. Nothing had ever been so luxurious. The bubbles surrounded me and I laughed. It surprised me even, to be laughing, but this tub—if nothing else, I would always remember this tub and find joy. A contraction took me over and I let out a moan, long and deep.

"That's it," Pam said, massaging my shoulders. She wiped my back with a washcloth. It only occurred to me later that she was cleaning me. I was filthy and had been for a long time. "You're a strong one, I can tell."

We stayed like that, the contractions coming a little faster then, about three minutes apart, I was told. In moments between them, she told me stories. First of her daughter and how she was almost five. How no one thought she would amount to anything when she got pregnant but her daughter made her want to be better. She wanted to inspire her. And her daughter had just got the highest grade in her class on her math test. So it was working.

I turned and held Pam's forearms and braced. The pain was suddenly not like the pain before it. This new pain bucked from the deepest part of my insides, ragged and mean. I could feel that it would adhere to no law. I did not know why this design was so violent. Why each woman had to be ripped apart to bring forth another.

"I can't do this," I said.

"Let me tell you about Saint Agnes," she said and looked out the window, beyond. "This hospital is named after the patron saint of girls just like you. Girls who have been through it. Survivors. Saint Agnes was desired by so many men, and she wouldn't have them, so they turned her in as a follower of Christ. Her punishment was to be dragged naked through the streets to a brothel. But any man who tried to rape her was struck blind. She prayed and prayed and hair covered her body."

"What happened?" I asked.

"Well, in the end it's no surprise that they finally found a way to put her out. But she fought. And now she lives on as a protector of young girls like you, Lacey. Her bones are still somewhere, I think. I'm not too religious myself but I do like to pray in the chapel here."

"I didn't fight like Saint Agnes," I said as another contraction speared me, harder than the last. I bore into Pam's shoulder and she held me, her pink smock wet in a map of my screams. I saw my mother then, cradling the Turquoise Cowboy's head. I saw myself under Lyle. Under Stringy.

"Seems like you're fighting right now," she said.

I vomited onto the floor and it sprayed Pam's shoes. She cleaned it up with ease and another nurse came in and said it was time to check me.

They wrapped me in a warm towel and led me to the bed, a twin with soft white sheets, slightly pilled flannel that smelled of the cleanest detergent. The other nurse was older with whiskers above her lip and she was rougher than Pam but I could handle rough. I smiled. They had no idea who I was, I thought, and before I came here I didn't know either. But now I did.

I was one of Saint Agnes's girls.

Something sharp stabbed deep into my crotch and I let out a low growl. Each contraction had its own personality. First there was the fear of the pain, then there was no room for fear inside the storm of it. Inside was acceptance. Each wave felt like its own death.

"Five centimeters. Five to go. Baby's heart looks good, Lacey's heart looks good. I'll be back in a while."

"That's Bee," Pam said. "She doesn't mess around."

I GOT OFF the bed and on my hands and knees and began a kind of dance. Pam and I moved around the room, from bouncy ball to bed, to the floor and back. Finally I sat on the toilet and screamed through the contractions. They were on top of each other and I couldn't see, I could only sense that she was with me. And there was someone else. An angel maybe, God. Agnes. Floating around over my head, directing me. I imagined gold God glitter falling from the ceiling but then I wiped that vision away. God didn't need glitter to be God, to be with me, real as anything. I vomited again and made my way to the bed, where it seemed I would either live or die.

I heard myself asking for drugs. I didn't even know what that meant exactly but I wanted them. *It's too late for that . . .* someone answered. Of course it was. This was what Hazel warned about. The moment that would bring me to my knees and I would meet myself in that space. And there I was, alone, but not for long.

I PASSED INTO dreamful places. I saw my mother in her yellow bikini driving us to the pool. The sweat sparkling off her, the sun a constant blanket. She had been the one to call. She had tried to protect me. She turned the whole thing on its head and now everything was different. I thought about what I had always wanted more than anything and I knew then immediately in my haze like the surest thing. I wanted unconditional love from my mother, and I was not going to have that. But somehow I held unconditional love for her. Perhaps giving it away could be its own reward.

I went to outer space looking for Artichoke. I flew through galaxies past heaven, looked for her little foot to pull her to earth. *Where are you, baby girl?*

And then something happened. I opened my eyes and my leg was hitched over Pam's shoulder, and there were blinding lights and the outlines of many people crowded around the bed and I screamed high in my throat and it felt like knives.

"All right, Lacey," Bee said. "We found some meconium in your fluids. It's time to get this baby out. Focus with me now. I want you to push down deep."

"What's wrong?"

Pam said, "The baby pooped a little and so it's time to get her out now. It's okay, love, it's just time to get her out."

I had died, I felt certain then. The figures around me, angels. Of course. I'd been dead for a while.

Bee snapped her fingers in my face. "Get this girl a popsicle, for Pete's sake." A moment later a purple popsicle appeared in my mouth and the zing of it, the way the ice melted to water on my tongue, brought me back.

I pushed. My body did it for me, like Hazel said it could, like the books reported. I couldn't breathe anymore. I only screamed. Golden threads wrapped a cocoon around me and then broke. I backed away from my own body toward the wall. Screamed. I tried to leave myself like I'd done before with Lyle, but Artichoke commanded all of me. She pulled me into her life.

"Throat's gonna be sore tomorrow," Bee said.

"My throat?" I snapped. "You're worried about my throat?"

"Long and low, long and low," Pam said. "You're doing it."

"There's the head," Bee said. "Oh, lots of hair. Want a mirror?"

I reached down and touched. The soft peach of her, there she was. Her head was out of me now, in the betweenlife. I convulsed again and threw my head back and wailed and she was out in a gust and everything was slippery and fast. They laid her on my naked chest and she screamed along with me, a scratchy cat cry.

"All good," a man's voice said, and the figures cleared the room and Bee worked between my legs and Pam put a tiny pink-and-blue striped hat on her. The baby, a real baby, crying into me, bobbing her head around, now wearing a hat just like a person. No longer me, but her own.

"She's perfect, she's perfect," I repeated over and over. My voice shook, I could barely speak but words flew from me anyhow. "She's perfect."

Bee pushed the weight of herself onto my stomach. "Here comes the placenta." I barely felt anything come out, but there it was. She held it up and showed me, a thick slab of meat, red and blue-veined with roots like a tree. "Happy placenta." She flopped it into a basin and went back to work between my legs. "Just gonna sew you up a little here. Few small tears."

I felt a prick and sting, but I wasn't with them anymore. I was only with this baby as Pam helped guide her to my nipple and her little eyes were open, glassy dark blue worlds, and her face red and dry, not purple and covered in clotted cream like I'd seen in pictures.

Pam looked at her. "You did real good, mama."

Mama, like in the magazines.

Chapter 27

I was full of sharp energy, tending to the baby when she cried, putting her to my breasts, already red and chafed, one nipple ringed by a crust of blood. A shallow latch, they said. Each time I guided her toward me I braced with fear. The pain seemed to go beyond my breast and through my chest down deep into my core. But I told myself it didn't matter. I'd keep trying and trying. I wouldn't give up. If I couldn't breast-feed they would surely take her from me. They would know I didn't deserve her and that would be the reason. *She couldn't even nurse the baby.* So I kept trying and Pam helped each time, applying cool gel packs to my nipples and telling me to drink water, so much water, and they brought me a milkshake, strawberry. Had I ever tasted anything so beautiful? I had not.

The sky out the window faded blackish but it was still alight with artificial life. It was not the true dark of Peaches and it kept me awake. The nurses came in and out, checking and poking. I tried to will sleep, but none came, and then the next day arrived and the social worker came in unannounced as I held a sleeping Artichoke. I pulled her closer to me. I covered my bleeding chest. She sat near the bed and hardly looked at me at all. She was a small frizzy-haired woman in a rush.

"This shouldn't take too long," she said.

She summarized everything that had happened, telling me my own story. In her version my mother was an unfit alcoholic. A neglector, an abandoner. Stringy was a child rapist, a pedophile. Vern was a cult leader, a manipulator. Cherry was an accomplice to child rape and an unfit guardian. But the one thing she wasn't clear on, she told me, was the Lyle situation.

"He was following God's orders," I said. "Well, Vern's."

She smiled. "You gonna protect the guy who did this? I see it all the time. Honey, he's a minor. He won't get it too bad, if he gets anything at all. Don't you want to tell the truth?"

The truth. And so I told her the truth in every detail. I told her of the shed, of Vern and his endless tentacles spread throughout the church Body and of Sharon Stam and of Daisy and Reno and the Holy Ghost machine gun and of saving graces, of the ocean. Of Hazel and Daisy and Florin and how they didn't know all these truths about my real life, that they knew only snippets but never everything. That I had kept the truths deep inside me, wrapped in shame.

"So this Daisy has been a real safe haven for you, would you say?"

I nodded.

"And you want to keep this baby? It's okay if you don't. There's lots of options," she said.

"She's with me."

She wrote more and cocked her head to one side. "It's best to keep the child with the mother when we can. But you're a minor and can't be on your own. I'd like to keep you out of the system, considering what you've been through. We'll try this for a while and I'll keep checking back in and if we think it's not going well, other measures will have to be taken."

"Try what?"

"She said you'd discussed it. That you and the baby would stay with her. She said she's been a real steadfast for you, having you work at her fruit stand and everything. Good for a kid to work a little. After school, of course."

I smiled. Fruit stand. "Daisy Darnelle." This meant she was alive. This meant she had not been burned.

"Am I free to go?"

"Well, you'll have to give another statement about your situation and then, depending on what charges are pressed against this Stringy person and the rest, you'll have to deal with some of that, but for now, sure. You can breathe a little and know that you won't be dealing with any of them for a very long time."

"What about my mother?"

"Your mother isn't the worst I've ever heard of. You would not believe some of the stuff I have to see. But if you want the truth, you're better off without her." She looked at her chart. "I know it's emotional but you have to think about your future. And you can't take any prisoners. Leave them all behind. Right now. Believe me. You hold on to them, you'll end up the same. This baby doesn't deserve that."

"Is Vern really dead?" I asked.

"It's very clear when someone's really dead, I think. Once you see a dead person you understand that right away. It's not an easy look to achieve if you're still alive."

I shifted the weight of Artichoke in my arms. Who was this baby? Her little circle face, soft as a petal. So long inside me and finally here. My mind could hardly accept it.

"You're a classic resilient," she said. "My number one tip for you? Don't skimp on therapy. All the resilients think they don't need it, but let me tell you. Oh, let me tell you. You will."

She edged toward the door as Pam came in and told me it was time for another feeding.

"Oh, and she's cleared for these visitors now." She handed Pam a list. "They're all waiting out there. Basically don't let in anyone blood related to her. Seems safest that way."

Pam nodded. "You do have a few visitors anxious to see you. But baby first. Feed that little baby. Drink drink."

She squeezed my breast and yellowish milk oozed out. Finally, the baby latched on, eyes closed, and it didn't feel like my tit was being stabbed. It felt okay, not great, but doable. "I think I'm getting it," I said.

"That's better," she said. A rush of warmth became me.

A few minutes later Hazel burst through the door. "Oh my god," she said. "They wouldn't let me in here, but I was sending in so many energies. I kept telling them, I'm her MID. WIFE. So typical of a hospital. They can't stand us. I'm gonna get your placenta for pills, don't you worry. Even if I have to steal it."

She hugged me and plucked the sleeping baby from my arms, danced her around the room, cooing in a light voice. I worried for a moment I would never look so natural holding my own girl, no matter how hard I tried. I pushed the thought back. Remembered Saint Agnes.

Behind her, Daisy and Florin held a vase of sunflowers, tears running down Daisy's perfectly drawn-up face.

"The red house," I said. "It's gone."

Daisy nodded. She wore a cream birdcage veil, like a bride. She came close to me and whispered, "So is the church, but that's between us."

"You burned it?" I said.

She shrugged. "Town needed a fresh start anyhow."

Hazel handed back the baby. We all stared at her in my arms.

"Your mother would be proud of you," Daisy said.

I nodded, though I wasn't sure it was true. Would she? It was the nice thing to say. I left it alone.

Daisy asked for some private time with me, and Hazel led Florin out to the hall.

Daisy sat next to me, and told me what I'd need to know. She talked about the bassinet sleeper she'd been researching for the baby, and the room I could have in her new place. She wanted to relocate to Oregon, a wet and green place where Florin would be going to school, and she didn't want me to worry over anything, and she'd love to work toward adopting me if it was all right, she kept saying that, if it's all right with you, if it's all right with you, and my eyes filled with tears and I remembered what the rushed woman just now had said, she had said to think about my future, to do the right thing. To take this blessing. To think about this baby and what was best, and I nodded along, imagining our new life in the trees where water would fall endlessly from a heaving sky, far away from the deadlands, from the scent of my mother rising from my pillow.

And for a moment, I was free.

Chapter 28

S ometimes now I pass by churches. I park my car in the back rows
of lots and watch the bodies file in. I don't follow. It doesn't
mean God is nothing to me now. It means I'll spend the rest of
my life trying to figure out belief, and if the good I know of God is
true, there is time enough.

BEFORE WE LEFT, Daisy took me to the small hospital room where
they had placed Cherry. She told me she was claiming mental disor-
der so she could stay out of that hell-house jail. I sat with her while
she complained and bemoaned her life and I waited for her to ask
about the baby or me or say something, anything about sorryness or
Lyle. What do you think became of him? I asked her. And Cherry
threw up her hands. "They won't even bring me my animals! Can
you believe that?"

I got up to leave and Cherry snatched at my arm, pinching the
back of it. She pulled me close and the bristles of her shaved head
scratched against my cheek. I thought of asking her if she had called
my mother and told her about the Birthing Day, if it was her who
had saved me in her own way. But I didn't. I realized looking at her
that I didn't want to know. I wanted to go on living my life believing it was my mother alone.

"Never forget who you are," Cherry said. As if any of us ever can.

———

WHAT SPREADS OUT past Peaches? For so long I was liable to think nothing at all. Nothing could be past there, for it was the world. Now I watch my daughter playing under the shade of Oregon Douglas firs on the land Daisy bought, land where we run a Christmas tree farm in the dark unforgiving winters, leaving the Diviners in the past, and my daughter and I ring up customers and she hands them candy canes.

The seasons run through us, my Peach and me. She tackles our husky dog on the lawn, sprays water from the hose. We drink iced tea, cool lemonade, warm turmeric tea. I find purpose in drinking the things I am supposed to drink. I can do that. I can go to co-op grocers and buy whatever I want, look up health benefits on my screen, search what other good mothers buy for themselves and their children: kefir water, pressed ginger juice with cayenne, organic watermelon already cut into perfect spears, elderberry syrup to ward off colds. My Peach will never see me nurse a beer, she does not worry that I might slip away. I can accept I may never writhe and fall in a fit of spirit speak, that I will never be covered in gold glitter from thin air, and I take all of this to mean I am well blessed.

Lately, I don't have many secrets, though there is one. One I come back to on these long stretches of days, after I'm home from work at the diner and I sit on the rocker on the porch and read my romances. I pause and look at the sky and I crave. I crave the way it felt to grow another, the strangeness of the expanse. My human heart misses the weight of my belly the most on these damp summer days when the trees stretch long into the sky and I can see nothing around. I wish for the far-spread flatness of the valley. The blankness of brown for miles and that muted blue of a smog-filled sky. I look to the fog of the rain and try my best to remember the deep heat stretching from my heels to my hair. I try to remember Grampa Jackie in his fields and I try, but cannot for the life of me, remember the burst of a sun-warmed California grape against the roof of my mouth.

I tell Lyle in dreams, because there's no other way: I named her Peach Agnes. One for the past, one for the future.

"When you gonna tell me who my daddy is?" Peach asks about once a year. I look into her eyes. I say nothing. I'll let her feel her own way. The truth does not always set us free.

AND MY MOTHER?

I call her once a year on Peach's birthday. She is still with the Turquoise Cowboy. I can hear him barking at her in the background sometimes, but we don't talk about that. We talk of Cherry's scones, of my mother's past beauty, her pageants and organza gowns, of Grampa Jackie's orchards. We talk of how when I was seven years old she held my hand on Old Canal Road waiting to cross the street and the sky opened above us and let down a beautiful rain. The way she arched her neck to it as if she had never been more grateful for life, for the earth, and where we stood on it in just that moment. How lucky we were to be together, the rain stilling us. When the talk starts to turn sad, we say goodbye. It is not nothing.

I don't tell her I'll always crave her embrace. I'll always wish she was with me, hand through my hair at night, voice vibrating through the same rooms. But I'm old enough to know it was never really her I wanted. It was the eternal mother. The mother I had dreamed up. The mother I was never meant to have. The mother, instead, I was meant to be.

Acknowledgments

Thank you to Samantha Shea who rooted for Lacey May from the very, very start. My endless gratitude to you—for every read, for every conversation, for every ounce of your belief in me.

To the best team in the world at Catapult: Jonathan Lee, sharp, encouraging, and funny as hell; your edits have made me a better writer, and have made *Godshot* a much better book. To Andy Hunter for reading my work and championing it. To Megan Fishmann, thank you for your enthusiasm, your tireless work getting this book into readers' hands, and, above all, your friendship. To Nicole Caputo for seeing my work so clearly and creating the golden cover of my dreams. To Katie Boland, Jenn Abel Kovitz, Elizabeth Ireland, Alicia Kroell, Wah-Ming Chang, and Jordan Koluch: my deepest gratitude for the time you spent on this book. And to everyone else, you are the most dedicated and kind and intelligent group I could have ever wished for.

Thank you to everyone at Georges Borchardt, and thank you also to Kristina Moore at Anonymous Content for your intelligence and vigor, the way you envision this story, and your gold sweater.

A very special thank you to the Rona Jaffe Foundation for your generous support and your support of women writers, and to the MacDowell Colony, who hosted me as I wrote the fledgling first draft of this book and offered me a lifelong writing community.

My deepest thanks and appreciation to the Portland State University MFA program, and to my teachers and mentors who helped light the path: Leni Zumas for the experiments, to Charles D'Ambrosio for telling me that first workshop to "wake mom up," and to Tom Bissell for always making me feel understood and well served. Special thanks also to Rachel Kushner at the Tin House Writers' Workshop; Todd James Pierce, Kevin Clark, and Teresa Allen at Cal Poly; and to Pat Walsh, Navdeep Dhillon, and Diane Honda for the early encouragement and vital book recommendations.

To the writers I have met along the way who became the dearest friends, who inspire me daily, who supported this book by reading early drafts and offering endless encouragement, you all are the greatest gift to come from this pursuit—my soul twin, T Kira Madden, you see me. To Anna Weatherford, for being there at 3 a.m.; Lauren Hilger, for the poems; Annabel Graham, for the astrology; Sarah Marshall, for the western vampires. Kimberly King Parsons, Leah Dietrich, Patrick McGinty, Teddy Wayne, Sophia Shalmiyev, Laura Lampton Scott, Kristen Arnett, and Lindsay Hunter—I'm so lucky to read your work and know you.

To Genevieve Hudson especially, wife and confidante, I'll meet you at the 24-hour Church of Elvis, any day, any time. Thank you for being my family, for having the same spiraling conversations again and again, for the long walks, for teaching me those years ago about grocery stores. I'm so glad we both showed up here.

To the F4: Carly, Katie, and Jaime, for the lifetime of magic and sisterhood. Let's never stop reuniting. To Amber, for your lovely friendship, and to Helen, my oldest friend, thank you for being there.

A big thank you to New Seasons on Woodstock for offering space to write and endless kindness, especially Lynn.

A heartfelt thank you to anyone who spent time reading this book, and to independent booksellers for all you do.

And finally, this book would not have been written without the inspiration of my family:

To my father, Flip Bieker: When the going gets tough, the tough get going. Thank you for your enduring belief in me, thank you for the stories. Thank you to Mary Glim, my mother, the first artist I ever knew, for the many lives we've already traveled together and the ones yet to come. I love you both so much.

To my grandfather, thank you for the raisins, for allowing me to see California through your eyes. To Putz, what did we do in life to be lucky enough to have each other? I am forever grateful for you. To my sister, Wendi. We're in it together, thank God. To Geraldine, thank you for teaching us to ride on. To Rachel, for the book mail. To my aunts, for loving books and sharing that love with me. To the dear family, friends, and teachers too many to name, who have nurtured my children so I could write, especially Honey, your time, love, and skill is immeasurably appreciated.

Most of all, this book is for my brightest rebel wolf-girl, Harper "Roo" Jewel, you are the queen of my world. I'm in awe of you every day. To Finn Ocean, your sweet spirit has opened up new places in my heart. You've both made me the luckiest woman. To Brenon, you punk: you set the show up, you take the show down. Thank you for always listening to me read, for the laughs, for showing our children what an equal partnership looks like. It's always sunny when I'm with you. I love you and I'm grateful for it all. When we were teenagers I told you I'd write a book. See.

And to the little girl in the Lakes: this one's for you.

CHELSEA BIEKER is from California's Central Valley. She is the recipient of a Rona Jaffe Foundation Writers' Award, and her fiction and essays have been published in *Granta*, *McSweeney's*, *Catapult* magazine, *Electric Literature*, and *Joyland*, among other publications. She has been awarded a MacDowell Colony fellowship and holds an MFA in creative writing from Portland State University. *Godshot* is her first novel.